'Another overlooked woman has be[...] between the lines of history, this one [...] is a bestselling novelist for good reason. Her narrative rollicks along in page-turning style, and convict-era Sydney comes to life in all its squalor and savagery and tumultuous promise.' —*Sydney Morning Herald* on *The Talented Mrs Greenway*

'Tea Cooper has delivered once again! … yet another engaging and masterfully crafted story. Not only does [it] provide a truly engaging story about the early days of colonial Sydney but she melds fact and fiction to present yet another strong female character from history.' —*Great Reads and Tea Leaves* on *The Talented Mrs Greenway*

'The immersive latest from Cooper interweaves two historical narratives linked by butterflies and family bonds … Cooper melds fictional lives, scientific history, and social issues into a compassionate story. This will please fans of historicals with smart women protagonists.' —*Publishers Weekly* on *The Butterfly Collector*

'Fans of Natasha Lester and Kate Morton will absolutely devour *The Fossil Hunter*. It is the kind of story you can easily get swept up in. Readers interested in Australian history, museums, and the fascinating world of fossils will be especially delighted with Cooper's stunning new historical novel.' —*Better Reading*

'Cooper fills the page with strong and intriguing female characters. There is a soupçon of romance but the real focus is on these trail-blazing women. Highly recommended.' —*Booklist* on *The Fossil Hunter*

'Elegant … Cooper's confident prose and deep empathy for her characters will keep readers hooked as she unspools her intrigue-filled mystery. Historical fans will want to dig this one up.' —*Publishers Weekly* on *The Fossil Hunter*

'Cooper is an accomplished storyteller, employing the dual-timeline device to foster tension and suspense about the fate of Anthea and the girls. The result is an absorbing tale with a strong mystery element and feminist bent, with special appeal for those interested in the history of dinosaur hunters.' —Historical Novel Society (US) on *The Fossil Hunter*

'Cooper again indulges her love of museums and historical relics to produce a fascinating tale.' —*The Australian* on *The Fossil Hunter*

'Tea Cooper's meticulous prose and deft phrasing delight the reader.' —Historical Novel Society (US) on *The Cartographer's Secret*

'Cooper gets to the heart of a family's old wounds, puzzles, and obsessions, while providing a luscious historical rendering of the landscape. This layered family saga will keep readers turning the pages.' —*Publishers Weekly* on *The Cartographer's Secret*

'Weaving together historical facts with fabulous fiction, Tea delivers a richly imagined world. Her research is impeccable and the era vividly drawn ... [she] excels at writing complex, strong female characters. Evie and Lettie, and their dual timelines and tales, are completely mesmerising. I devoured this novel over the weekend and haven't stopped thinking about it since. *The Cartographer's Secret* is an excellent Australian historical.' —*Better Reading*

'... a mesmerising historical mystery.' —*Herald Sun* on *The Cartographer's Secret*

'Refreshing and unique, *The Woman in the Green Dress* sweeps you across the wild lands of Australia in a thrilling whirl of mystery, romance, and danger. This magical tale weaves together two storylines with a heart-pounding finish that is drop-dead gorgeous.' —J'nell Ciesielski, author of *The Socialite*

'Readers of Kate Morton and Beatriz Williams will be dazzled. *The Woman in the Green Dress* spins readers into an evocative world of mystery and romance in this deeply researched book ... One of the most intelligent, visceral and vibrant historical reads I have had the privilege of visiting in an age.' —Rachel McMillan, author of *The London Restoration*

'... boasts strong female protagonists, an infectious fascination with the past, and the narrative skill to weave multiple timelines into a satisfying whole ... easy to devour.' —*Sydney Morning Herald* on *The Woman in the Green Dress*

'... weaves a seductive narrative of secrets, memories, lost love and mystery ... a freshly drawn bittersweet saga that draws nuggets of "truth" with timeless magic and might-have-beens.' —*North & South Magazine* (NZ) on *The Woman in the Green Dress*

'Cooper weaves historical fact and creative fiction through the two periods with success. The plot ... contains Cooper's signature mix of colonial and indigenous social history, scientific discovery, mystery and a hint of romance.' —Historical Novel Society on *The Woman in the Green Dress*

'Two women fight to reveal the truth about a scientific discovery in this crackling novel ... The author keeps readers guessing as she connects the two plot strands, each of which abounds with exciting scenes, including a chase on a windswept moor that evokes *The Hound of the Baskervilles*. This is one not to miss.' —*Publishers Weekly* (starred review) on *The Naturalist's Daughter*

'Cooper is a welcome inclusion to the rising ranks of female-centred historical Australian novels.' —*Herald Sun* on *The Naturalist's Daughter*

Tea Cooper is an established Australian author of historical fiction. In a past life she was a teacher, a journalist and a farmer. These days she haunts museums and indulges her passion for storytelling. She is the internationally bestselling author of several novels, including *The Talented Mrs Greenway, The Butterfly Collector, The Naturalist's Daughter*, the *USA Today*–bestselling *The Woman in the Green Dress, The Girl in the Painting* and *The Cartographer's Secret*, winner of the prestigious Daphne du Maurier Award.

www.teacooperauthor.com

Also by Tea Cooper

The Horse Thief
The Cedar Cutter
The Currency Lass
The Naturalist's Daughter
The Woman in the Green Dress
The Girl in the Painting
The Cartographer's Secret
The Fossil Hunter
The Butterfly Collector
The Talented Mrs Greenway

(Available in ebook)
Matilda's Freedom
Lily's Leap
Forgotten Fragrance
The House on Boundary Street

The GOLDEN THREAD

TEA COOPER

THE GOLDEN THREAD
© 2024 by Tea Cooper
ISBN 9781038906540

First published on Gadigal Country in Australia in 2024
by HQ Fiction
an imprint of HQBooks (ABN 47 001 180 918), a subsidiary of HarperCollins Publishers
Australia Pty Limited (ABN 36 009 913 517).

A catalogue record for this book is available from the National Library of Australia
www.librariesaustralia.nla.gov.au

Printed and bound in Australia by McPherson's Printing Group

Vale Chief Engineer
Denis Francis Brown
18 October 1956–2 June 2024

Prologue

The moon rose, elongating the shadows and casting a glimmering path over the serene waters of Sydney Harbour as the night enveloped the castellated towers and turrets of Government House. The never-ending cacophony of the colony's politics paused, curtains drawn, lamps extinguished, doors shut tight against the riffraff.

Confident the bustling household had settled, she turned from the window and retrieved the leather pouch of gold nuggets from beneath her narrow trundle bed, then tucked the small pieces of washed calico into the pocket of her apron along with her mother's silver needle case and a skein of silk embroidery thread.

Holding the candlestick steady, she crept into the cloying darkness of the eaves above the servants' quarters, the air heavy with the heat of the day and the scent of forgotten memories.

Step by careful step, lips clamped tight, she edged up the narrow ladder, determined to fulfil the promise she had made.

Some would think her foolish, but her word was her bond and no matter what thoughts plagued her in the darkest, loneliest moments of the night she couldn't doubt him.

Standing on tiptoe, she ran her fingers along the lintel, pulled down the key, slipped it into the lock and eased open the door. Amongst the detritus of past governors and their families, she found the trunk, the engraved name adorned with a frieze of breadfruit leaves just as she remembered, as bold as the man who had owned it—William Bligh. The name gleamed in the candlelight. Her nimble fingers traced its contours, trembling with anticipation as she pried open the timeworn brass hasp to reveal a treasure-trove of forgotten garments each with their own story, their own memories, silken whispers of the past—stories her mother had told of Governor Bligh's daughter, Mary, of her fiery nature and her love of clothes. And amongst them, the yellow silk dress, its vibrant hue barely dulled by the passage of time.

She sank down, yards of golden damask cradled in her lap, and marvelled at the intricate embossed patterns, seeing her mother's hands smoothing the material as she recounted the stories of the past, of the fledgling colony, the group of disparate men and women thrown upon an unknown land.

What better place to secure her own promise of the future?

By the light of the carefully concealed candle she bent to her task. With meticulous care, she unpicked the voluminous hem of the dress, eyes straining in the dim light, and attached the tiny little pockets she had made from an old calico apron to the underside of the hem, sandwiched between the layers of lining, at regularly spaced intervals.

The hours ticked by, the skirt hot and heavy in her lap, the atmosphere suffocating, as she cleaned and polished each nugget before carefully securing it in its resting place. And then finally, the long and arduous task of reattaching the hem.

Baste, stitch, polish, re-enforce, secure.

Tiny, tiny stitches anchoring the treasures in their hiding place.

Night after night, the eaves of the servants' quarters stood sole witness to her strained eyes and needle-pricked fingertips. A silent, lonely task, and each day when the horizon lightened she would return the dress to its hiding place and make her way back down the rickety ladder to her narrow bed to snatch a few minutes' sleep before rising to the beck and call of all, finding solace in the knowledge that the treasure was safe, until he returned to claim it.

1

Wednesday, 1 May, 1889
Maitland, Hunter Valley, NSW

Connie ran her finger along the sideboard, eyeing the six silver cloches sitting in a neat row atop the Spode oak leaf-patterned platters. No need to lift and inspect the offerings; they never varied—hadn't for as long as she'd been tall enough to make her own choice. Devilled kidneys, scrambled eggs, some sort of stewed tomato, fresh in summer, bottled in winter, sausages, delivered daily by Mr Boneham personally, along with the bacon, and last, but not least, boiled eggs because that was all her grandmother, Nell, ever ate for breakfast.

A totally ridiculous amount of food for a family of three women but tradition held the Montague household tighter than a whalebone corset.

A gentle breeze blew through the open window, lifting the muslin curtains and bringing the scent of slashed grass and the musky odour of the river. It didn't, however, mask the smell of bacon, sausages, and slightly charred toast. Dora, their poor, hard done by maid-of-all-work, could never get it quite right. 'Good morning, Mother.'

Faith emitted a small grunt and continued to sip her cup of coffee and crumble the single piece of dry toast on her plate.

Deciding it was not a day for boiled eggs, Connie settled on two sausages and some tomatoes then helped herself to a piece of toast from the rack on the table. 'What are your plans today?' she asked.

Faith didn't bother to lift her head from the form guide in the *Maitland Mercury*. 'We're racing at Rutherford tomorrow.'

Again. Faith's life revolved around horses, the ones the Montagues bred and the ones they raced, and had for as long as Connie could remember. Connie rather hoped something out of the ordinary might happen. She dreamt of out of the ordinary— not of the handsome young men ready to sweep her off her feet that Nell had in mind, but something truly different. She hadn't quite decided what *different* would entail but it certainly wouldn't be the usual round of events that punctuated the days at Horseshoe Bend, in this house of women. 'The lecture at the School of Arts last night was fascinating. Mr David spoke about …'

Faith's lips formed a moue of disapproval. It was quite acceptable for Faith to meet with her friends and indulge her passion for the racetrack and, if the smell on her breath when she arrived home was anything to go by, more than a glass or two of one of the wines produced on their doorstep, but such indulgences were not for the likes of an almost-twenty year old. It seemed one had to be married, or better still widowed, before free choice came into the equation.

Maitland's clocks could be set by the household's routines, Connie's life most especially. Breakfast on the dot of eight o'clock, a little bit of exercise, in the form of a walk along the riverbank or a round of the garden with Nell, a social call or a meeting of the Benevolent Society, back home for a light luncheon, then an afternoon reading, painting, or a trip to the School of Arts to change her books. Sometimes she longed for her school days. Not that they had been particularly exciting, though they had improved once she attended Maitland Girls High School, but Nell's far-reaching hand had continued to dictate her every move … never allowed to walk home alone. *It just isn't done.* Collected like a recalcitrant toddler from the school gates by Mrs Orchard, the cook. The pedigree of any friend she made vetted and pored over before contact beyond the school gates was permitted. Almost as though Nell feared someone might question her lineage.

Faith peered over the top of the newspaper. 'Did Nell know you were out unaccompanied after dark?'

'Mary-Ann and Elsbeth's aunt accompanied us to the lecture.'

'Their aunt? Their unmarried aunt? The one with the interest in all things unnatural?' She winced. 'Fossils and bones and underground waters. I'm sure they're expecting the Loch Ness Monster to swim upriver.' She turned back to her paper. 'Where is Nell?'

'I don't know.' Connie pushed aside her plate and rose. 'I'll go and check her room, shall I?'

'Sit down. She'll be here before long. I expect she's taking a turn down by the river or around the garden. She likes her morning constitutional.'

But never until after a boiled egg and two slices of toast, crusts removed, liberally spread with marmalade made under strict supervision from the Seville oranges grown in the kitchen garden, followed by a cup of coffee, made with beans she had regularly delivered from the Coffee Palace at the Haymarket in Sydney. Nell was a creature of habit. She claimed breakfast was a luxury that shouldn't be forgone. It was an opportunity to scan the newspapers, discuss the day's plans and ensure nothing untoward or unexpected occurred.

And besides, they had a meeting with Miss Quinn to organise the new accommodation for the women and children who were due to arrive from Newcastle and decide on the venue for the Hospital Ball.

Connie pushed the pile of soggy tomatoes around her plate for a few more moments, finished her coffee and collected her crockery.

'How many times do I have to tell you? No need to clear up after yourself—that's Dora's job. Plans for today?'

'Grandmother and I have a meeting with Miss Quinn. We'll be home for luncheon.'

Faith rolled her eyes. 'I won't be here. I've arranged to meet with the committee to discuss the flowers.'

And indulge in a quick trip to the racetrack to check tomorrow's competition, chat to the trainers and the jockeys. Connie offered a dutiful smile. 'I'll see you this afternoon, then.' She closed the door behind her and made her way outside.

After an unfruitful circuit of the kitchen garden, a walk around the rose beds and a quick stroll down the path to the river, Connie returned to the kitchen.

'Have you seen Grandmother?'

Mrs Orchard flapped her flour-covered hands in her face and shooed her out. 'I'm not Mrs Montague's keeper—never have been and wouldn't want to be. She's well able to take care of herself. It's young Mrs M I'd be keeping an eye on if you want my opinion. All those ladies' luncheons.' She gave a snort. 'And they say a man and his money are soon parted—as usual, they forgot the women. Be off with you; you don't want to keep Miss Quinn waiting.'

Mrs Orchard was quite right, Nell was more than capable of looking after herself, and she should know. Everyone who sought shelter at the house, from the laundry maid (and they'd been through a few of those thanks to Faith's exacting standards) to Mrs Orchard, who'd been with them since Grandfather had employed her straight off the ship, turned to Nell in moments of trouble.

Connie trudged up the stairs to collect her hat and gloves. Nell's bedroom door stood ajar, the bed neatly made, and as always, a pile of the cream writing paper she preferred placed with almost mathematical precision on the small desk at the window. Connie sank down on the satin counterpane and gazed at the desk. Something was missing. She searched the smooth timber. No sign of Nell's fountain pen that usually lay on top of the sheets of writing paper but nothing else amiss, except no Nell. Something must have come up; no doubt she'd find out when they met at the Quinns' house in Church Street.

Cheered by her rather bold new straw boater with its vibrant cornflower blue ribbon, Connie set off along High Street. She always enjoyed their meetings with Miss Quinn; she was such a pillar of Maitland society but beneath her very proper exterior lurked a heart of gold. She was the leading light behind the free legal aid available to deserted women to pursue cases of maintenance against the fathers of their children, and myriad other charitable causes. The Quinns had arrived in Maitland not long after Nell and Montague and they had been friends for many years.

Connie took the path at a bound and knocked on the door. A very pert young maid opened it.

'Good morning, Miss Montague. Is Mrs Montague not with you today?' The young girl, Trudy, if she remembered rightly, short for Gertrude apparently, offered a cheerful smile.

Connie's stomach fluttered. Question answered, but no point in alarming anyone just yet. 'Mrs Montague had an errand or two to attend to. Is Miss Quinn available?'

'Yes, she's upstairs in the morning room. You know the way.'

'Indeed, I do.' Connie ascended the cedar staircase, her mind spiralling. If Nell wasn't here, then where was she? If she'd come to grief they would have been notified; she was hardly unknown around town. Quite the opposite. They had lived at The Bend ever since Nell and Montague had brought Connie from the property to live permanently in their town house backing onto the Hunter River.

She knocked on the open door. Miss Quinn looked up from a pile of papers covered in her immaculate copperplate script. 'Ah! There you are, my dear. Come in, come in. Is Mrs Montague with you? The other ladies are tied up at the hospital so we're on our own today.'

'No, she had an errand or two to attend to. She'll be along shortly.' Connie parroted the words she'd used earlier. Quite what she'd say if Nell didn't appear was another matter. She'd have to make some excuse and leave early, and then what? Go in search possibly.

The hands on the carriage clock ticked their way laboriously past the hour. Connie wiped her palms down her skirt to dry off the dampness and quell the nervous twitch in her leg, then craned her neck to look out of the window. Not that it did her any good; a few clouds floated benignly against the bright autumn sky and the spire of the church glistened in the sunlight but unless she stuck her nose against the pane of glass, she hadn't any hope of seeing the street below.

'"Maitland Hospital Ladies Auxiliary request assistance for our forthcoming fete. Please contact our Secretary, Miss Elizabeth Quinn, to assist in this matter." Do you agree, Constance?'

Connie jumped and turned from the window. 'Yes, yes. Certainly. An excellent idea.'

Miss Quinn's eyebrows rose, and the corner of her mouth

twitched in what may have been the beginning of a smile. 'Can I help with anything?'

Probably not, but a second opinion wouldn't come amiss, and Miss Quinn might be able to shed some light on the matter. After all, she was much closer in age to Nell. Connie licked her lips; it seemed something of a betrayal to say too much. 'I'm a little concerned Grandmother hasn't arrived yet. I …'

'I expect she's been delayed.' Miss Quinn peered at the small timepiece clipped to her blouse. 'She's only an hour later than expected.'

'Grandmother is never late.' Connie clasped her trembling hands.

'You're quite right. Her tardiness is most unusual. Do you know anything of these errands?'

Connie shook her head. 'She wasn't at breakfast. I haven't seen her this morning.'

'Ah. Not at breakfast; no wonder you're concerned and quite rightly so. Why don't we pack up these ledgers and take a stroll along High Street and see if she's been delayed?'

'I don't want to raise the alarm unnecessarily. She might have some private business to attend to.' Although for the life of her Connie couldn't imagine what. Nell's life was an open book.

They set off, peering this way and that into shop windows and around corners. Connie stuck her head into the Booksellers and Stationers, but the shop was empty, Mr Paskin's Musical Instrument Warehouse appeared to be closed, which was unusual, but she doubted Nell would go in there; she freely admitted to being tone deaf.

By the time they drew to a halt outside the synagogue, hot and flustered, they were none the wiser. No one had seen Nell, not at the School of Arts, the post office, the bank, nor any of the other shops up and down the length of the high street.

'I must admit, Constance, I thought you were overreacting; after all, three score years and a few more does not preclude the ability to manage one's life. Have you absolutely no idea where Mrs Montague might be?'

'No. None at all. She was aware of our meeting today. Mother didn't know where she was.' In truth, if she cast her mind back Connie couldn't remember the last time she'd seen Nell. They hadn't eaten together last night because Connie had spent the evening listening to Mr David's lecture. She hadn't thought to disturb Nell when she returned home. 'There was nothing obviously awry in her bedroom this morning, although to be honest I didn't feel I should pry.'

'Quite right. Quite right. However, it might be time for a little prying before too long. I have one more suggestion.'

No, absolutely not. Connie inhaled deeply. 'I'm not going to report her missing.'

'Oh, my dear, I wouldn't dream of suggesting it and besides I doubt Sergeant Black would pay any heed. It's not even twenty-four hours yet. I was going to suggest you call in at the train station and have a word with Mr Marsh.'

'But Grandmother wouldn't have gone anywhere without mentioning it. She hasn't left Maitland since Pa's accident.'

'I see your point. If you don't mind, I'll mention it to Mr Quinn. He's often better at these kinds of things than I am. I can vouch for his confidentiality.'

Miss Quinn's brother owned the auctioneers in Maitland and had a finger on the pulse. There was even talk of him standing for parliament one day. 'Thank you. That would be most helpful. I'll go home and check she hasn't returned; I don't want to encourage any unnecessary gossip.'

'And please, keep me informed.'

'I will. Thank you so very much for your help.' Connie raised her hand in farewell and took off. She'd feel like an absolute fool if she walked in the door and found Nell sitting in her favourite chair on the back verandah admiring the view over the river but better that than any alternative. She couldn't remember a time when Nell hadn't been there. Her behaviour was so out of character.

Connie fell through the gate and darted around to the back of the house. Nell would be in her chair on the verandah, of course she would. She skidded to a halt.

The rattan chair stood in solitary splendour, its white linen cushions plumped, pristine and vacant.

2

'Dora! Dora? Where are you?' Connie pushed open the scullery door.

Red-faced and bedraggled, Dora lifted the dolly stick and peered through the clouds of rising steam. 'That you, Miss Constance?'

'Can you leave that for a moment? Come outside. I need to talk to you.' More than needed to, had to. Dora would have been the first up and always took Nell her morning cup of hot water and lemon juice in her favourite rose-patterned cup. Quite why she hadn't thought to ask her about Nell's whereabouts before she'd left for the meeting with Miss Quinn, she'd no idea. Too discombobulated and convinced Nell would be waiting for her at the Quinns' house. Talk about taking people, life, for granted. And now she'd wasted a good few hours.

'I've got laundry to catch up on, you know. I ain't got time for gossip; too much to do with just the two of us.' Dora wiped her hands down her pinny and stood arms akimbo, glaring.

Connie grimaced. Ever since Pa's accident, when Faith had moved into town, poor Mrs Orchard and Dora were run off their feet. They really did need more help but apparently a household of three women had no need for any more than a cook, a maid-of-all-work and young Cracker, who spent more time down by the river fishing than he did keeping the woodshed full and the garden under control.

'Did you take Grandmother her lemon this morning?'

'I did.'

'How did she seem?'

Dora wiped her hand across her forehead and shook the droplets of sweat onto the flagstones, then frowned.

The question wasn't that difficult. 'Dora?'

She scuffed her feet. 'Not real sure, Miss.'

The cold stone that had settled in Connie's stomach halfway down High Street, roiled. Had something untoward happened to Nell? 'Why not?'

'She weren't there, Miss. Bed was all made and room tidy but she weren't there so I brought it back down and started breakfast. I've got a full day, you know. What with this laundry and—'

'Where was she? Did she go out for a walk?'

'Dunno, Miss. Was just thankful she'd made her bed and there were nowt for me to see to.'

'So, the last time you saw her was last night, before Mother and I got home.'

Dora hung her head, nodded. 'She took a sandwich in her room, said she didn't want dinner. Can I get on now? Mrs Orchard has got a shopping list as long as her arm and Cracker shot through soon as he got the fire going in the scullery. Took off down to the river.'

'Yes, thank you, Dora. If you see Grandmother, can you let me know.'

Connie made her way through the garden and out of the back gate that led to the riverbank. She spotted Cracker perched on the end of the jetty. Cupping her hands around her mouth she hollered, 'Cooee.'

His head snapped up and he leapt to his feet. As soon as she beckoned he pulled his fishing line out of the water and ran towards her.

'Have you seen Mrs Montague this morning?'

'No. Why?'

'She wasn't at breakfast. I thought perhaps she'd taken a walk down the tow path.'

'Nah, not s'morning. Not that I saw, and I've been down here since I got the fire going for Dora.'

'Right. I want you to go and check the path, in both directions, and make sure she hasn't had an accident. Come straight back and tell me, or Mrs Orchard, even if you don't find her. Got that?'

'Got it. Check the tow path and come straight back. I don't reckon she's there; I would have seen her.'

'Just do it.' Connie turned on her heel and made her way back to the house and up the stairs. Why, oh, why, hadn't she thought to ask Dora earlier? Almost one o'clock and no one had seen Nell since yesterday evening.

The last time she'd seen Nell she was at her writing desk in her bedroom and when Connie had stuck her head around the door to mention the lecture again Nell had simply grunted and told her to enjoy herself and that she'd be having an early night. Without waiting for any second thoughts, or for Faith to reappear, she'd grabbed her hat and scooted off to meet Mary-Ann and Elsbeth. Fascinated by the descriptions of underground seas, the time had slipped away and when she'd arrived home the house was unnaturally quiet. She'd eaten the supper Mrs Orchard had left her under the tea towel on the kitchen table and taken her book to bed.

She clearly remembered Nell saying she needed an early night but hadn't given another thought to it. Nell hadn't looked sick;

her usual self, maybe a little preoccupied but nothing out of the ordinary.

The hollow sound of her feet on the timber risers echoed through the silent house. She pushed open the door to Nell's bedroom for the second time that day. Just as it had looked before she'd left for the meeting with Miss Quinn. She ran her eyes around the room and then stopped. To hell with privacy—this was no longer a joke. Nell would understand, and something felt different. Simply the stillness? Nothing out of place. The Chevalier mirror tilted just so, her silver-backed hairbrush neatly placed on the dressing table, the small crystal bowl where she kept her hair pins, along with the daguerreotype of Nell and Montague at the opening of the first racetrack not long after they'd arrived in Maitland. They looked so young, so very, very, young. Nell with her hat at a rakish angle perched atop her uncontrollable curls, a far cry from the neat silver chignon of today. Her arm threaded through Montague's, their bodies close, so close. She picked up the frame and tilted it to the light. Closer than close, pressed against each other as though nothing could come between them. And behind them the hustle and bustle of the jam-packed crowd, the vibrant atmosphere charged with anticipation.

Connie inhaled. Lily-of-the-valley scented the air as it always did but the blue opaline glass bottle with its filigree stopper which usually held pride of place ... where was it? She sank into the chair and peered behind the mirror, opened the top drawer, ran her hand over the collection of gloves, handkerchiefs and scarves. Not there.

The chair scraped across the floor, and she flung across the room, prised open the clothes press and sighed as another waft of lily-of-the-valley assaulted her nostrils. She ran her hands over the dresses and coats and ... nothing appeared to be different. The piles of muted silks, the greys, lilacs and dusty pinks Nell had worn since she'd finally come out of mourning, all impeccably fashioned by Mrs Beattie, the dressmaker—none of this catalogue nonsense for Eleanor Montague. Connie took a backward step. Everything very much as always … but no.

Beneath the neatly arranged rows of coats and dresses was an empty space. She dropped to her knees. What was missing? She hadn't opened Nell's clothes press for years and years, not since she was a child when after a particularly virulent spat with Faith who'd come to visit, she'd crawled into the dark, welcoming space and curled up, her head resting against the old carpet bag where Nell kept her treasures …

That was it—the carpet bag!

She rocked back on her heels. Nell had gone somewhere, and chosen not to tell, but where? And how? More to the point, why? And she'd left sometime yesterday evening after everyone was in bed or first thing this morning before anyone was about.

On the upside it was fair to assume that if Nell had packed a bag, however small, she'd deliberately left and hadn't come to grief down by the river.

She closed the door behind her and made her way downstairs. No point in trying to find Faith—she'd still be at her ladies' luncheon—and Nell wouldn't appreciate the whole of Maitland being alerted, which most definitely ruled out Sergeant Black. What were the alternatives? Miss Quinn's suggestion of the station seemed like the only sensible idea.

'Mr Marsh, excuse me.' Connie stuck her nose up against the ticket window and rapped twice. After an interminable wait the stationmaster lifted his head and smoothed down his bushy sideburns.

'Office isn't open yet. Next train doesn't arrive for another hour. Take a seat on the platform or in the waiting room.' He pulled down his green visor and turned his back.

'I don't want to buy a ticket.' At least not yet. Not unless she discovered Nell had. 'I wondered if you saw Mrs Montague this morning.'

'Why would I do that?'

Connie trapped the sigh in her throat and smiled sweetly. 'I wondered if she'd bought a ticket for the early train.'

He heaved himself out of the chair. 'First train didn't leave until eight forty-five s'morning.'

Nell must have been long gone by then. Breakfast was always served at eight sharp and if she'd waited for the train, he would have noticed her.

'And to be honest, I can't remember. The platform was packed. Everyone heading off to Newcastle. Big day in the history of the railway today.'

'Big day? Why?'

'Don't you read the *Mercury*? Hawkesbury Rail Bridge officially opened. Invitation only. No tickets sold. All right for some. Have to have a direct line to God I reckon to get one of them. Not a thought given to us poor buggers who slave away every day.'

'I'm sorry. I don't understand.'

Mr Marsh blew out his cheeks. 'Told you, Hawkesbury Rail Bridge opened. Means you can take a direct train from Newcastle to Sydney. Least you will be able to after today. Newcastle train only went as far as the new bridge to meet up with the two trainloads of big nobs coming from Sydney for the hijinks. Some party, speeches, ribbon cutting and champagne.' He sniffed as though thoroughly miffed he hadn't received an invitation. 'Then back the way they came.'

'And it was invitation only?'

'Told you that. The 406693 spent the night here. Got up a good head of steam and picked up the Maitland invitation holders; like I said, left at eight forty-five.' He gave an indignant groan and rummaged in the drawer of his desk and pulled out a well-thumbed piece of paper. 'We checked the invitations as they boarded.' He ran a stubby finger down the list. 'Mrs Montague's name's not here so she can't have had an invitation.'

Connie had no idea whether she did or not, but she couldn't imagine Nell not telling her, not inviting her along. 'Thanks for your time. If you happen to see her, could you tell her I need to speak to her, please.'

'That I can do. Now, do you want a ticket for today?'

'No. No, thank you.' Connie straightened up and made her way back onto the platform. A sixty-five-year-old woman couldn't disappear into thin air, not in a place like Maitland and not if she was as well known as Nell. The picture of Nell lying in a ditch somewhere or floating face up in the river refused to budge, simply wouldn't leave her, but why would she take her carpet bag with her and what in heaven's name had made her decide to leave without telling anyone where she was going? There was only one thing for it—the police station, gossip be damned.

'I'm sorry, Miss Montague, but there's very little we can do. We don't consider a person missing—not until they've been gone for at least a week. I'll mention it to Constables Button and Bonnet and ask them to keep their eyes open but to be perfectly honest there's no reason why a grown woman like Mrs Montague shouldn't take herself off without telling the whole world.'

Connie bit back the scream building in her throat. 'But she's a creature of habit. She's never gone anywhere without telling me before.'

The sergeant's eyebrows rose up his domed forehead and he shook his head. 'How long did you say she's been missing?' The clock behind his head ticked its way past the hour.

'Twelve hours, maybe more. We're not sure when she left the house. She didn't come down to breakfast this morning.'

He leant across the counter and patted her hand. Connie snatched it back. 'Maybe she's got a surprise planned, a secret. Got a birthday coming up? A celebration? Cheer up, love. I'm sure everything will turn out for the best.'

Heavens above. She plastered a smile on her face. 'Thank you, Sergeant. Please let me know if you hear anything. Carrington Street, Horseshoe Bend.'

'Yes, Miss Montague, we know where to find you.'

But sadly, not where to find Nell.

Connie trundled down High Street again. She didn't want to broadcast Nell's unexplained departure to the whole of Maitland. The tittle-tattlers would, sure as eggs were eggs, come up with some ghastly story.

When she finally reached home she found Faith, hat tucked under her arm, hair awry, rummaging through her reticule, eyes flashing with increasing frustration, about to pay the cab. Maybe Faith could throw some light on the subject now she was home.

'Mother ...'

'Ah, Connie, there you are. I'm sixpence short. I don't suppose you have any coin in your purse. It'll save going upstairs to my bureau.'

Connie delved into the pocket of her skirt and brought out a handful of coins and handed them over.

'I've decided those pockets are not such a bad idea. I might ask the dressmaker to stitch some in my winter coat.'

Well, that was a change of heart. Faith had kicked up hell's delight when she'd specifically asked the dressmaker to include them in her new skirt. Apart from anything else it saved having to carry a soppy little drawstring reticule wherever she went. 'Shall I call for some tea? You must be thirsty, and I have to talk to you.'

'I am but I'm also tired. I'll take tea in my room and have a few moments' rest. We can talk later.'

'I'm sorry but it won't wait.' Connie stepped in front of Faith, blocking her way to the front door. 'It's important. I'm afraid something might have happened to Grandmother.'

Faith rolled her eyes. 'Now what?'

'Come inside and sit down. I'll get Dora to bring some tea.'

'And so, you see, I really am rather concerned. I wondered if there was anything you could think of that might have happened, any reason Nell might leave with an overnight bag and not tell anyone where she was going. It's so unlike her.'

Faith poured a second cup of tea and sipped it, lost in thought. 'She has seemed a little out of sorts recently.'

Connie's pulse picked up a beat. 'How so?' She hadn't noticed anything untoward. 'Do you think she's sick?'

'You have to remember she isn't getting any younger.'

What rubbish. Nell was as spritely as ever; she'd ruled the dance floor at her sixty-fifth birthday party only a few months ago.

'Mumbling to herself, bad tempered and dwelling in the past. That might be the best way to describe it.'

'Talking about Grandfather?' Nell often did that. She loved to tell stories about their early years in the Hunter, the excitement of seeing the area grow, until Maitland Town's population was second in size to Sydney—the settlers, the businesses, the buildings, and then when the railway had linked Maitland, Morpeth and Newcastle bringing an influx of new people.

Faith rose. 'I shouldn't worry too much. I'm sure she'll walk in through the door soon and wonder what all the fuss is about. I really must go and have a lie-down.'

Connie slumped back in the chair. No one else seemed the slightest bit concerned about Nell but Connie knew something wasn't right.

3

Thursday, 2 May, 1889

Connie tossed and turned, rearranged her pillows, forced herself to remain calm while she counted backward from one thousand, but nothing worked. It was almost dawn when she finally sank into a deep sleep, her mind made up.

Only moments later, or so it seemed, Dora stood beside her, tray in hand. 'Your mother wanted to know why you didn't come down for breakfast, so I said I'd bring you a cuppa.'

Rubbing the sleep from her eyes, yesterday came back in a torrent of confusion. 'I must have overslept. What time is it?'

'Well past nine. Drink this and get dressed. I've saved you some breakfast. It's in the kitchen. Young Mrs Montague told me to tell you she'd gone to the dressmaker, something about a new winter coat, and then she's out again for luncheon at the races.' Dora sniffed and gave her head a shake. 'Shame she doesn't spend a bit more time worrying about what's happening under her nose than gallivanting around with them fillies.'

Connie had no intention of being drawn into a discussion

about her mother's activities. Both Mrs Orchard and Dora had taken against Faith the moment she had moved from Coloma, the Montagues' country property, into town after Pa's accident. The peaceful state of affairs that had existed since she and her grandparents had moved into town so she could attend school had disappeared overnight. 'Is Grandmother home?'

'Nope. No sight of her. Bed hasn't been slept in. I checked. And Cracker didn't find her down by the river. Leastways we know she hasn't come to grief down there.'

The moment the door clicked shut Connie shot out of bed. Nell wasn't in Maitland, of that she was certain. Even if she'd gone out to the property, she wouldn't have spent the night; hadn't since she and Grandfather moved into town. She wouldn't have taken the steamer; she avoided them like the plague because she suffered from seasickness. She must have taken the train. Whatever Mr Marsh said, he must have missed Nell.

She pulled her blue walking suit out of the clothes press along with a spare blouse, some underthings, a nightgown and her periwinkle shawl. Quite suitable for a trip wherever it may take her and with a spare blouse and the shawl it would do for the evening at a push. The evening. Heavens above. It couldn't take that long to find Nell.

Once dressed, she stuffed her clothes into her bag, took a final look around the room. She reached for the doorhandle and stopped.

Money! She'd need more than the handful of coins she kept in her pocket if she had to take the train, even more if her search led her to Sydney and she needed accommodation. What was the name of that lovely hotel she and Nell had stayed in when they last visited Sydney?

Tossing her bag onto the bed, she rummaged through the drawer of her small writing table, pulled out a collection of old letters, writing paper, broken pencils, and notebooks. She'd received a weekly allowance from Nell since she'd turned eighteen, meant to be spent on hair ribbons, chocolates and other fripperies, but she rarely touched it. The Montagues had accounts with all the local shops and nine times out of ten she'd find her pockets empty.

Reaching to the back of the drawer, she pulled out the large manila envelope that held the oversized card Nell had presented her with at her last birthday and tipped out her collection of gold sovereigns and half sovereigns—quite enough to finance a train trip and a night or two away if it came to that. She tucked them into her money purse, pushed it well down into her pocket, and put her loose change in her other pocket before trotting down the stairs and into the kitchen.

'Sit yourself down.' Mrs Orchard wiped her hands on her white pinny and pulled out the chair. 'I've made you some scrambled eggs and there's a couple of slices of ham and some tomatoes. The plate Dora left looked like a dog's breakfast. From the glint in your eye, you have a plan afoot and you need something decent in your stomach. You can tell me while you're eating.'

Connie tucked into her breakfast. She hadn't got a firm plan, but she had several ideas. What she needed was confirmation that Nell had taken the train. Invitation only, or not, and for all she knew Nell could have managed to acquire an invitation but if so, why hadn't she returned home last night? 'I think Nell's in Newcastle.'

'Why would she be in Newcastle?'

Connie lifted her shoulders. 'I don't know. Maybe she's got business there.'

'Who with? Messrs Brown take care of all the family's affairs as well you know, and I doubt they ever set foot in Newcastle.'

Mrs Orchard patted down her unruly hair, then pushed a cup of tea across the table, the fingers of her left hand drumming on the table. 'Ohhhh!'

'Ohhh what?'

'She could've gone to see the Mumfords.'

'She would have told me.' There was a time when she and Nell had visited Newcastle quite regularly. Mrs Mumford was the vice president of the Newcastle Relief Society and organised domestic service for impoverished girls, a cause close to Nell's heart and supported by the Maitland Benevolent Society, but like everything else the visits had come to a halt in the last two years.

'If she's in Newcastle that's where she'll be.'

'If she's even in Newcastle.'

'She can't be in Sydney. There was no train yesterday because of the Hawkesbury Bridge shindig.'

'Unless she got the train from Newcastle this morning having spent the night with the Mumfords.' And then all the noise of the lorikeets faded, and she remembered Faith's comment. 'Do you think Nell's been out of sorts, preoccupied?'

Mrs Orchard let out a great belly laugh. 'No, no more than usual. Who said that?'

'Mother.' Connie held back the rest of her words. Faith was not, despite the fact her name might suggest otherwise, the best with the truth. She thrived on gossip and there were plenty of people in Maitland who shared her passion, particularly those who frequented the racecourse.

'I won't respond to that; the look on your face tells me our thoughts are on the same track. You know your grandmother better than anyone, and there's no love lost between her and young Mrs Montague. Why would she say something like that?'

Connie lifted her shoulders. 'She said Grandmother was dwelling in the past.'

'Not that I've noticed particularly. She often talks about your grandfather.'

'I'm going to go to Newcastle. If I'm not home by six please tell Mother where I've gone. Until then just say I'm out looking around town.'

Mrs Orchard blew out her cheeks. 'You let me know the minute you find Mrs Montague. I don't want two of you gone missing.'

Connie pushed her plate aside and picked up her bag. 'I'm not missing; you'll know where I am.' Without waiting for a reply, Connie hurried out of the kitchen door and headed towards the station.

An autumnal chill hung in the air, and she pulled up her collar as she walked towards the station, glancing every now and again over her shoulder, an odd feeling making her scalp tingle—the sound of a footfall too close behind and the glimpse of shifting shadows in the doorways. The scent of something different in the air, unwashed, sweaty like the river at low tide, confirmed her suspicion. Someone was dogging her footsteps. She turned right instead of left at the corner of High Street and slipped between a barrow filled with vegetables outside the grocers then pressed against the wall near a doorway and dropped her bag at her feet, put her hands on her hips in her best impression of Dora in a tizzy and shouted, 'Come out and show yourself.'

A woman pushing a pram gave her a quizzical glance and scurried past, hotly followed by two more she vaguely recognised from church who pursed their lips and crossed the street. So much for Christian kindness. It was a good job she wasn't in real strife. The thought made her stomach lurch—but Nell might be and everyone had looked the other way. She didn't have time for this rubbish.

'Hey, Miss.'

She spun on her heel and came face to face with a scruffy-looking, gangly young chap with trousers that ended just below his knees and a cloth cap pulled down to meet a filthy scarf which hid the remainder of his face. The river-at-low-tide reek made her nose wrinkle. She reached into her pocket, pulled out a few coins and held them out. The boy stayed put, just shuffled his feet.

'Well? Do you want them or don't you?'

'P'haps. Are you Miss Montague?'

She narrowed her eyes. 'I am.'

'Mr Marsh said I'd got to find you and tell you.'

'Mr Marsh, the stationmaster?'

He nodded.

'Tell me what?'

'You got to promise first. Mr Marsh said I could say that.'

'I can't promise if I don't know what you're talking about.'

The boy gave a long-suffering groan. 'He lets me kip in the waiting room s'long as I'm gone before he starts work. I saw the old lady on the station yesterday morning.'

The air whooshed out of Connie's lungs, and she reached out. The boy moved faster than a cut snake and disappeared around the corner. 'Come back. I won't hurt you.' She stepped around the corner and found him crouched in a doorway, his arms wrapped around his scrawny shoulders. 'I promise I won't tell anyone about the waiting room if you tell me about Mrs Montague.' She held out a handful of pennies and farthings. 'You can have these, all of them, when you tell me.'

His eyes widened and his mouth opened and closed, then he spluttered, 'She was there on the station when I left the waiting room at first light. I didn't know who she was, but Mr Marsh asked me if I'd seen an old lady hanging about.'

'What did she look like?'

'Told you, an old lady. She had a bag, a bit like yours.'

Connie looked down at her feet. Her bag had gone.

The boy pulled it out from behind his back. 'Here.' He kicked it towards her and shrank further back into the doorway.

'And anything else? What was she wearing?'

'A hat and a coat.'

Connie's throat tightened. 'What colour coat?'

'Sort of dirty pinkish colour, like faded roses and the hat the same.'

It was Nell. 'Here.'

His hand snaked out and the coins vanished.

'Did you see where she went?'

He grunted.

'Well?'

'She left the platform and crossed the tracks.'

'What?'

'Went across the tracks, towards the siding.' He looked at her as though she was a half-wit; it made her want to scream. Why would Nell leave the platform? 'And then where did she go?'

'Dunno. I went the other way.' He stood up and absurdly brushed off his jacket. 'Thanks for the dough, Miss. Don't forget you promised.' He flew up the laneway, the words thrown over his shoulder, and vanished.

Connie reclaimed her bag. First stop, the station. Thanks to the boy she now knew Nell had been there, but anything could have happened in the last twenty-four hours. The question was what was Nell doing crossing the tracks? Why hadn't she waited on the platform for the train?

Connie found Mr Marsh in the ticket office. 'Thank you for sending the boy to find me.'

'I'd appreciate it if you could keep young Jonas's sleeping arrangements under your hat. It'll put my job on the line if word gets out.'

'Jonas's secret is safe. It's kind of you to offer him shelter.' The station waiting room might not be the best, but it was a darn sight better than sleeping under the Belmore Bridge in all weather. 'I don't know what we would have done if no one had seen her. At least we know she was at the station.'

'No guarantees she got a train or that she's in Newcastle, and it's been a while since she last travelled. Not since your father passed.' The stationmaster bit his lips, then hurriedly crossed himself. She shook her head. Such a dreadful accident. It had seemed so odd not to hear his booming voice. Not to see Nell's face light up when he called in, walked through the door. It was as though Nell's existence revolved around the men in her life, first her husband Montague and then their son. What she didn't understand was where Faith fitted in.

There was no love lost between the two of them; Nell even refused to refer to her as her daughter-in-law. She knew Nell saw Faith as a gold-digger, but she had given Nell a granddaughter. Faith and Nell were very different, but Nell usually embraced all types of people. She never put on airs or graces when she spoke to Mr Boneham, the butcher, or asked Dora for a spot more tea. And Nell loved Connie. Perhaps that was why she had insisted Faith left the property and moved into town to live with them after Pa's horrible accident.

'I will have that ticket, Mr Marsh. Mrs Montague has friends in Newcastle. The next train will be along soon, won't it?'

''Nother fifteen minutes. Go take a seat in the waiting room. Jonas won't bother you; he's gone for the day.'

4

With a lot of snorting, whistleblowing and billowing smoke the train chugged out of Maitland Station. Connie settled into the corner of the first-class carriage, next to the window, her small bag underneath the seat. She had forty minutes to plan her next move.

There was something delightfully liberating about leaving on the spur of the moment. No argument with Faith, just the message left with Mrs Orchard and a promise to let her know the moment she found Nell.

If she found Nell. It might be a bit of a wild-goose chase but it was the best she could do. And doing something was far better than sitting twiddling her thumbs. She'd go directly to the Mumfords. Mrs Mumford and Nell had been friends for years and they exchanged letters regularly; not as often lately, although she'd noticed a Christmas greeting card on the mantlepiece last year.

Before long the train crossed the river and entered the port of Newcastle. The town built on coal and the sweat of convict labourers had come a long way since the early days, or so Nell had told Connie the first time she'd taken her there. Connie found it difficult to imagine the 'coaly city', as Nell liked to call it, in

the early days. The most shambolic part of the town ran along
the wharves and the railway line but once they left the station
behind there were all sorts of wonders to discover. Nobbys Head
and the breakwater formed a protective arm around the town
and sheltered scores of ships from all corners of the world waiting
for their cargo. Hunter Street, the main thoroughfare, was lined
with churches, schools and the Town Hall, all well laid out and
paved—illuminated at night by gas lighting too.

As Connie stepped from the train and surveyed the bustling
station the enormity of the situation hit her like the contents
of one of the coal loaders dangling precariously out over the
water. Squaring her shoulders, she walked out of the station. She
couldn't for the life of her remember the exact location of the
Mumfords' house, but she knew they lived up on the hill, in the
parsonage—a cab driver would be bound to know.

Raising her hand, she flagged down the first cab to pass. 'I'm
looking for the Reverend Mumford. I'm not sure of the exact
address—somewhere up on the hill.' She waved her hand in the
general direction.

The cabbie looked her up and down. Thank heavens she'd had
the foresight to wear her new suit. It seemed she passed muster
because he leapt down and opened the door for her. 'I know where
you want to go. Corner of Church and Newcomen. Shouldn't
take long. It's a bit busy around here but once we get away from
the station, we'll be good.'

With that he clambered back aboard and took off at a smacking
pace towards the hillside where a collection of large, well-built
houses perched in a dress circle overlooking the hullabaloo of the
port.

'There you go, Miss. That there's the parsonage.' He gestured
to the solidly built two-storey brick house. A nervous flutter
tangled Connie's insides as she walked through the gate and up

the path to the shiny black painted door. She raised the knocker and brought it down with a clang loud enough to raise the dead. The corner of her lip lifted—probably not the best analogy for a parsonage; she was going to have to watch her manners, and hope that Mrs Mumford was home and remembered her.

A sallow-faced girl dressed in an ill-fitting black frock and apron answered the door.

'I'd like to speak to Mrs Mumford if she's available. My name's Constance Montague.'

The girl looked her over, her eyes coming to rest on the bag at her feet. 'Wait here.' She pulled the door to but didn't close it completely.

Connie gazed up and down the street at the elegant houses, a far cry from the area around the wharves and railway station. A wild-goose chase indeed … Why would Nell leave Maitland without telling anyone? Maybe Mrs Mumford could shed some light on the situation.

'My dear, how delightful to see you.'

Connie whipped around and smiled at Mrs Mumford. 'I'm sorry to arrive unannounced but I was wondering if you could help me.'

'It would be my pleasure. Come inside and have some refreshments and tell me how your grandmother is. It's so long since we've seen you both.'

Connie's heart sank. Nell obviously hadn't visited. Mrs Mumford ushered her into the room at the front of the house, every flat surface covered in framed pictures of an assortment of people, and every chair covered in a selection of crocheted antimacassars. The faint smell of last night's fire hung in the air.

Mrs Mumford reached up and pressed a button adjacent to the fireplace and a bell rang in the distance. 'Now, how can I help?' She sat down facing Connie, leaning forward, chin tilted.

There was no easy way to say it, no point in beating around the bush. 'I'm trying to find my grandmother. She disappeared early yesterday morning. She was last seen at the station in Maitland.'

'Oh, my dear!' Mrs Mumford's eyes rounded, and her hand covered her mouth. 'And you have no idea where she might be? Obviously not, otherwise you wouldn't be here.'

The door opened and an oversized tray appeared followed by the girl who'd answered the front door.

'Just put it here, Tilly. Thank you; you may go. I'll pour.' Mrs Mumford fiddled with the tray, all the while chewing the side of her mouth as though she couldn't quite make up her mind where to begin.

Her silence irritated Connie; she hadn't time to waste. 'It's all a little complicated because yesterday was the opening of the Hawkesbury Rail Bridge and as far as I know Grandmother didn't have an invitation for the train trip.'

'Yes, I see that makes it a little difficult. You say she was seen at the station?'

Connie nodded. 'But not getting onto the train.'

Mrs Mumford's frown deepened. 'Go on.'

'I've reported her missing to the police, but they say they can't do anything—'

'Until she's been missing for a week. They can be thoroughly insufferable at times. What makes you think she's in Newcastle?'

'I thought perhaps she had spent last night with you.'

Mrs Mumford gave a doleful shake of her head. 'She didn't I'm afraid. We would have welcomed her with open arms as I'm sure you know. Do you think she might have gone on to Sydney?'

'I don't know.' This was going to be difficult, but it really was the only gossamer thin thread she had to hang onto. 'It was something my mother said.'

Mrs Mumford's eyebrow raised. Was she aware of Nell's somewhat strained relationship with Faith?

Connie swallowed. 'She said Grandmother had been dwelling in the past.'

Mrs Mumford put down her teacup. 'I see. Do you think your mother could be labouring under a misapprehension?'

Unlikely. Beneath Faith's frivolous exterior there beat a heart as hard as tempered steel and she rarely said anything that didn't contain at least a grain of truth, though she was quite capable of pounding that grain to a pulp. 'Possibly, but unlikely. She's very perceptive.'

'Is there nothing you can think of that might have caused Mrs Montague to leave Maitland unexpectedly?'

Connie shook her head.

Mrs Mumford gave a long slow sigh. 'I'm not one to stick my nose into other people's business but perhaps you should know Mrs Montague was in service, in Sydney many years ago. I always believed it was the reason she was so supportive of our efforts to find employment for the girls from the school. It's not something she likes to talk about, although I have no idea why she should be ashamed. She worked as a lady's maid at Government House. But it was over forty years ago, before she married. I can't imagine ...'

Connie couldn't sit still a moment longer. She jumped to her feet and started pacing the floor. 'Is there someone in Sydney she might have wanted to visit?'

'The only name I remember her mentioning is a Mrs Alexander; I believe she was the housekeeper at Government House, when your grandmother was dismissed.'

'Dismissed? Whatever for?' Connie couldn't imagine Nell doing anything that would warrant such action. Leaving her position perhaps to marry but dismissed sounded as though she had committed some dreadful offence. 'I'm going to take the train down to Sydney and see if I can find this Mrs Alexander. If she works, or worked, at Government House I'm sure someone would know.' It was the only clue she had.

'Why don't you spend the night here and we'll talk to the Reverend. He has such a sensible head on his shoulders and, if you don't mind me saying, you look as though you could do with a decent night's sleep.'

There was no point in prolonging the agony. Another night tossing and turning, painting dreadful pictures of Nell in some terrible situation would only make matters worse.

'You're very kind, thank you. But I will return to the station and see if there is a train to Sydney.'

'I can answer that question. There is a new daily express, one, and only one; it leaves in about half an hour. It'll save you about two and a half hours on the old journey. You should be in Sydney by four o'clock which will give you plenty of time to find somewhere to stay. Now let me pour you another cup and eat some of that cake. And please make use of the amenities; you know the way. I'll be back in a moment.'

Not having eaten since breakfast, Connie made short work of the fruitcake and the second cup of tea and dashed to the water closet while she had the opportunity. As disappointed as she was not to find Nell here, the prospect of a train trip to Sydney and across the new bridge filled her with a sense of independence, bravery even. Once she knew nothing dreadful had happened to Nell, she would look back on this as her greatest adventure.

The chaos of Newcastle wharves and station hadn't improved in the time she'd been at the parsonage. A constant procession of loaders and quaymen streamed like ants across every available spot but the fruitcake and tea, and Mrs Mumford's sympathetic ear, had gone a long way to buoy Connie's spirits and with a first-class ticket tucked tightly in her pocket she found her seat opposite a beak-nosed woman clutching a large leather portmanteau.

The engine belched and billowed, emitted a high-pitched whistle, and clouds of steam filled the air. Finally as it started to pull slowly away from the station the door flew open, and a young man threw himself into the compartment. 'I do beg your pardon.' He struggled upright. 'Almost missed it.'

Connie picked up her bag from the vacant seat and put it on her lap. Without asking permission, the young man grasped it and threw it up onto the luggage rack before sinking down with a sigh. 'Thank you, thank you very much. This is all rather exciting, isn't it?' he said with a grin.

She nodded. If Nell had been with her, she was sure she would be less than impressed with the young man's familiarity but there was something about his wide smile and chocolate brown eyes that cheered her no end, and in the spirit of her newfound independence she blurted out, 'I'm going to Sydney.'

'One of the first passengers to travel to Sydney across the mighty Hawkesbury Rail Bridge.'

'The opening was yesterday. Wasn't that the first?'

'Yes and no. The trains met at the southern end of the bridge and the passengers disembarked. Then they all went for a trip downriver in the *General Gordon* before being ferried out to the pontoon in the middle of the river where Sir Henry Parkes, the premier, made a speech. The Sydney people returned to their train and the Newcastle people returned to theirs.' He waggled his head from side to side, pantomiming the toing-and-froing. 'This is the first express to make the journey all the way from Brisbane to Adelaide using the new bridge. How do you feel about that?'

Horrified. If that was the case, then how on earth could Nell have got to Sydney? Even if she had somehow wangled her way onto the train from Maitland and then Newcastle, she wouldn't have had a seat on the Sydney train. She dropped her head into her hands and moaned, long and low.

'Are you well?'

Through her fingers she could see the young man peering at her, his eyes full of concern. 'Yes. I'm fine thank you. I suddenly felt a little dizzy.'

'A touch of railway sickness.' He gave a great booming laugh. 'I hope it's not as debilitating as seasickness. Let me lower the window a fraction. You might find the fresh air helps.' He towered over her and cracked open the window a few inches. A great billow of mucky black soot and stinking steam flooded the carriage. He slammed the window shut again. 'Not such a good idea.'

The beak-nosed woman sitting opposite shook her head in despair.

'I'm perfectly all right, thank you.'

'Very good, then maybe you could give me some help.' He delved into his inside pocket and brought out a notebook. 'I've been up in the Hunter chasing leads and thought I'd make use of the trip and write an article about the bridge, get it published here and, if I'm lucky, in America too. I'd like an opinion. I'm sure you're aware of the fact that the contract for the bridge was given to the Union Bridge Company of New York?'

No, she wasn't. And was that a slight accent she could hear in his voice? 'Are you from America?'

'Nope. Born and bred on Australia's fair shores, lived all my life in Sydney, but my father hails from New York. Perhaps his accent has rubbed off on me. I feel a bit of a patriotic connection with this bridge since the Americans had a hand in the design— the largest bridge project in colonial Australia, completed in just two years. Mind you, they were paid fair and square; the tender price was three hundred and sixty-seven thousand dollars. It's the first time American style pin-jointed steel trusses have been used in this country.' He beamed at her, pride written all over his face.

Pin-jointed steel trusses. 'How marvellous.' She couldn't dampen his enthusiasm by asking what that meant.

'Tickets please. Tickets.' A voice echoed down the carriage.

'Oh dear.' He raked his thick hair back from his face with his fingers.

'I'm sorry?'

'I don't actually have a first-class ticket. This could be a little tricky. Better if I scoot off. Lovely to meet you, Miss … Miss …'

'Montague.' Connie held out her hand.

He shot her a quizzical look but was up and gone through the door before anything more could be said.

'Cheeky young monkey.' The woman sitting facing her scowled. 'I presume he's no friend of yours. You want to take care, especially in Sydney. It's a dangerous place for a young woman alone, a town full of pubs, oyster saloons and chophouses. You shouldn't encourage men like that. An American!' She peered down her overlong nose and sniffed.

Obnoxious woman. 'He said he was born in Australia.'

'Makes no difference where he was born. I've got a good mind to report him.'

Just at that moment the ticket collector opened the compartment door. 'Tickets please.'

The woman produced hers with a patronising flourish. 'I think you ought to know … there's a young man travelling in first class without an appropriate ticket.'

Connie shot to her feet with a shriek. 'Oh no. Oh dearie, dearie me.' Letting out a strangled cry, she pointed at a random spot above her bag nestling in the luggage rack. 'There's a spider.'

The woman leapt to her feet with an ear-piercing scream, grabbed her bag and forced her way past the ticket collector and disappeared down the carriage.

After a lot of banging and crashing, the ticket collector pushed his cap back from his head. 'Can't seem to see no spider up there, Miss.'

'Oh dear, perhaps I imagined it.' Connie sank back into her seat, flapping her hand in front of her face, trying very hard to mask her grin and hoping against hope that the young man was firmly ensconced in the second-class carriage where he belonged. She pulled her ticket from her pocket and handed it over with her most charming smile.

There was nothing for it; she'd simply have to sit back and enjoy the trip. The clanking and creaking of the wheels against the tracks, and the rhythmic chugging of the engine, combined with the sound of metal against metal, created a soothing symphony and lulled her into a sense of optimism.

Once she got to Sydney she'd try and find this Mrs Alexander and discover one way or the other if Mrs Mumford's comments about Nell's past held a kernel of truth, and Nell had somehow made it to Sydney searching for someone from her past. The whole idea filled her with a sense of anticipation and curiosity—a Nell she knew nothing about, a Nell she wanted to meet.

The train ran down the coast along the shimmering waters of Lake Macquarie and drifted through the small township of Woy Woy and into a tremendously long, dark tunnel. Through the window the dank, seeping walls seemed to press in, and she fancied she could hear the voices of the men who'd dug through the rocky hillside. Before her maudlin thoughts had truly caught hold the train blew its whistle and they were catapulted into sunshine once more. Along narrow ledges precariously balanced in the rock face where blue-green water sparkled, finally they'd reached the Hawkesbury River and ahead the new bridge, which more than lived up to expectations with its broad lines of delicate tracery accentuated by the dappled olive green of the surrounding hills. As they approached the bridge, the tone of the wheels changed. Two huge buttresses and six oblong piers sunk into the river supported the mammoth span—amazing to think it had taken only two years to complete.

The last time she and Nell had travelled to Sydney they'd had to disembark from the train and clamber onto the *General Gordon*, the paddle steamer that took passengers and their luggage across the Hawkesbury River. It took forever but made the trip to Sydney something of an adventure for a young girl and a nightmare for Nell who was always concerned Connie would slip under the handrail and end up swept down the mighty river and out to sea. But all in all, the bridge was long overdue. Trains ran from Adelaide and Melbourne to Sydney and Newcastle to Brisbane—just the missing link across the Hawkesbury River. Not anymore. Next stop Sydney.

The landscape gradually transitioned from rural vistas to the urban sprawl of the city as the train wormed its way through the sprawling suburbs and finally announced its arrival at the Sydney rail terminal with a triumphant whistle.

5

With a wheeze of steam, the iron monster ground to a halt and before Connie reached her feet the guards threw open the doors and the platform erupted into a seething mass of people all talking at the tops of their voices about the wonders of modern science and the genius of men.

She'd spent snippets of the time since they'd crossed the river replaying her conversation with Faith. Nell was as sharp as a tack, nothing like the picture Faith had painted of an old woman dwelling in the past. If anything, it was Faith who'd been preoccupied. Besides, Nell knew Sydney like the back of her hand. They'd had several visits over the years to the Botanic Gardens, the Art Gallery and the Museum, stayed in a lovely hotel and indulged in strawberry ices in the Domain.

Once the platform cleared a little, Connie stepped down, hotly followed by the woman with the long nose who continued to tut and complain about everything. With no idea in which direction she needed to go, Connie simply followed the trail of people through the ticket barrier and out into a large hall. She stood for a moment drawing on her memories. It had been more than two years since their last trip to Sydney. The shaft of sunlight pouring in through the open doors at the end of the hall seemed familiar, so she headed that way. She needed directions to Government House. It was only four o'clock; she had several hours to spare before she had to worry about a place to stay for the night. She'd go to the … the Berkeley in Bent Street! The name of the hotel popped into her mind. She could clearly visualise the wizened little manager, a Mister … Mister … Sladdin. That was it.

'Miss Montague. Miss Montague, hold up.'

Spinning around, she almost crashed into the young man from the train.

'I'm so glad I caught you. I wanted to thank you for your good humour. The spider was a stroke of genius.' His laugh echoed in the rapidly emptying hall.

'How did you know about that?'

'I was watching through the connecting door, waiting to rescue you if necessary. I didn't want my actions to cause you any trouble. Thank you. Is there some way I can repay you? A cup of tea?'

As much as she'd love a cup of tea, she had to get to Government House. Had to find out how to … 'I'm afraid I don't have time for a cup of tea, but could you give me some directions? I need to get to Government House, and I have absolutely no idea whether I can walk or if I need a cab, or where to get a cab for that matter.'

'Easily fixed. It'll take you less than half an hour on foot. I'm afraid I can't escort you as I have an appointment within the hour.'

'I can manage quite well. If you can just give me directions; I am vaguely familiar with Sydney, but I haven't been here in recent years.'

'Come with me.' He took her arm and led her outside. 'See that street over there? That's Elizabeth Street. Straight down there, until you reach Hyde Park.'

'Oh yes, I remember Hyde Park.'

'Then across the park onto Macquarie Street and follow your nose. You'll pass the cathedral and then you'll see the barracks, Parliament House, the Library, and the Government Stables. You can't miss them.'

'I remember. The big white castle.'

She did remember the castle. She and Nell had stood in awe, imagined it had been picked up and transported brick by brick from some medieval castle in England.

'Government House is just a hop, skip and a jump from there. Head for the trees and you'll see the gatehouse and carriageway on the right.'

How very strange. If Government House was just around the corner, why had Nell never mentioned it? Was she so ashamed of the past? Maybe the public weren't allowed through the gates. There was only one way to find out. 'Thank you, thank you very much. Mr ... I'm sorry, I've just realised I don't know your name.'

'Very remiss of me. It's Robert; most people call me Bob, Bob Ballantyne.'

She took the hand he held out and smiled up at him.

'I very much hope our paths cross again soon. Good luck.' With a wave of his hand, he loped off across the courtyard.

She stood for a moment feeling a tad bereft, then set off along Elizabeth Street.

Bob Ballantyne's directions proved faultless and within about half an hour she stood shading her eyes and looking up at the impressive castle, blinding against the bright autumn sky. Quite a building for stables, more like a palace really. She squinted down the road to the trees. Government House would have to be special to compete.

Hefting her bag into her left hand, she stretched her shoulders, strode down the hill and covered the last few hundred yards almost at a run until she came to a small green gatehouse.

The door was firmly closed and the little window to one side shut tight. 'Hello!' She knocked on the door, not once but twice, then walked around the small building. It appeared deserted. With a final glance over her shoulder she lifted her chin, marched up the carriageway and came to a grinding halt.

A grand and imposing architectural masterpiece rested in a commanding position overlooking the harbour, oozing authority and power. It might have fallen straight from the pages of a novel; Mr Rochester would have been quite at home. She clapped her hand over her mouth, half expecting to see Jane Eyre tripping across the perfectly manicured lawns surrounding the building. Her eyes drifted to the upper windows, searching for the mad woman, Bertha, and shuddered. Such nonsense. She couldn't give up now. Not after she'd come all this way.

Steeling herself, she stomped up the steps of the large portico to a set of impressive, windowed cedar doors and raised her hand, searching for a doorknocker or bell, when suddenly the door swung open. There stood a terrifying chap in breeches that might have been the height of fashion about a hundred years ago but looked simply foolish, topped off by a scarlet coat, an intimidating scowl and the bushiest eyebrows she'd ever seen.

'I'm looking for a Mrs Alexander. I believe she works here. Or did.'

He peered down his formidable nose. 'I don't recall anyone by that name.'

Insufferable man. 'Could you go and check, please. Someone in the servants' quarters might remember her name.'

'I can assure you, Miss, there is no one of that name here, nor to the best of my knowledge, has there ever been.' With a slightly apologetic grimace he added, 'I am not at liberty to divulge private information.' The door closed with a determined clunk.

Biting back a string of words that would have impressed Cracker, Connie remained under the portico, looking left and right. Now what? The place was as silent as the grave, but he hadn't told her to leave the grounds.

She ducked around the corner of the building where a long verandah shaded by the branches of a massive Morton Bay fig overlooked an expansive view of the harbour. A formal garden spread before her, its four paths meeting at a fountain shooting a plume of water high into the sky. She stood still and let the tranquillity quell her frustration. So many dead ends. Why, oh, why hadn't Nell told her what she was doing, where she was going? She might not even be in Sydney. She could still be in Maitland. She might have arrived home and was sitting on the back verandah overlooking her rose garden sipping tea.

'Oi!'

Connie sighed and slowly turned around, expecting to see the bushy-eyebrowed, breeches-wearing, arrogant ...

'You can't go sneaking past the gatehouse. Who gave you permission to enter the grounds?'

She smiled sweetly at the rotund, uniformed man—the gatekeeper she guessed. 'Oh, I'm so sorry. There was no one at the gatehouse; I did knock and wait for several moments.'

The top of the man's ears turned carnation red, and he mumbled something about calls of nature. Dreading further information, Connie walked back towards the gatehouse. Maybe this man might have heard of Mrs Alexander or know of someone who did; better still, he might take her to the servants' quarters. She continued down the carriageway until she reached the gatehouse and dropped her bag to her feet and stood, head bowed and hands clasped in front of her, a picture of demure contrition—she hoped.

'So, what is it you want?' He adjusted the buttons on his coat and pulled it straight.

'I'm looking for a Mrs Alexander.'

The gatekeeper scratched his stubble. 'Don't know any Mrs Alexander and I know everyone; they have to check with me before they pass the gatehouse.' He glared at her.

'Could you tell me where the servants' quarters are? Maybe somebody knows her.' If Mrs Mumford was correct and Mrs Alexander was the housekeeper at Government House surely someone might remember her.

'I can't leave my post and take you visiting.' He glanced back up the road. 'The servants' quarters are up there, in the same building as the stables. Walk up the hill and tell the bloke on the gate that Horace sent you.'

'Thank you, thank you very much.'

'Off you go, and don't forget your bag.' He gave it a little tap with his shiny toecap.

She bent and picked it up, lifted her hand in farewell and trudged back up the hill to the palace for horses.

The sun was beginning to sink behind the buildings and a chill breeze blew in across the water. Connie crossed her fingers and prayed someone could give her some information.

A little breathless when she reached the top of the hill, she stopped and straightened her hat before approaching the gate. An oldish chap sat just inside the gate on a stool, a newspaper resting on his lap. He tipped his head to one side and squinted up at her.

'Excuse me. Horace, the gatekeeper at Government House, sent me up here. I'm looking for a Mrs Alexander, or anyone who might know where I could find her.'

'Well, that's a shiver from the past. What would you be wanting with Mrs Alexander?'

Connie's heart started to thud in her chest. She licked her dry lips. 'She was a friend of my grandmother's.' No lie in that, well none that she knew about, only it did sound rather as though there'd been a death. She didn't want to go into any more details, not until the old man had said a bit more.

'You and your grandmother won't find her here.'

Why couldn't the man speak more than one sentence at a time? 'Do you know where I can find her?' she repeated, trying very hard to keep the tone of impatience that had crept into her voice under control.

'That I do.'

The horrible thought that he might be going to direct her to some cemetery flitted through her mind. She'd rather presumed Mrs Alexander would be a similar age to Nell, but she could be older, much older, and Nell couldn't be described as a spring chicken, which brought to mind Nell darting around the garden chasing the chickens and geese back into their pen with Cracker. Sixty-five wasn't that old. The man sitting on his stool in front of her had to be much older if his creased face was anything to go by. 'Can you tell me where I can find Mrs Alexander?' Please, please get a move on.

'Last I heard, and mind you I don't know this is gospel, she's down Parramatta way.'

'Parramatta?' The word shrieked out across the courtyard. A groom hanging onto the reins of a large stallion started, causing the horse to snort and dance.

'That's what I said. Parra-mat-ta.'

Mrs Alexander couldn't be in Parramatta. She had to be in Sydney. As far as Connie knew Nell had never set foot in Parramatta, but then she stilled. There wasn't an awful lot she did know about Nell's life before she moved to Maitland—after that, plenty, but the time before was a great empty void. 'I don't suppose you know where in Parramatta.'

The old man scratched at his jowls again. 'Government House.'

Oh dear. Government House was just down the road, not in Parramatta. Everyone knew that.

'Old Government House, that is. They've turned it into a guesthouse.'

'I didn't know there was another Government House. Is it easy to find?'

He gave a snort. 'Not real difficult. On the hill overlooking the town. Now, if that's all ...' He turned back to his newspaper.

'Just one more thing, if you wouldn't mind. How do I get to Parramatta?'

'Road, river, rail. Take your pick. Rail's quickest these days. I can remember when it took ...'

No, no, no. She didn't want to be rude, but he couldn't start reminiscing now. 'Thank you so much for your help.' She bent down, picked up her bag and flew back along Macquarie Street, dodging and weaving her way through the crowd, all on their way home if the fading light was anything to go by.

6

Parramatta, NSW

Connie flung herself into the railway carriage and stood looking this way and that for an empty seat. She'd forgotten to specify a first-class ticket, but it was too late. Here she was, stuffed like a pickled cucumber in a preserving jar, in the second-class carriage amid all the strange smells—tobacco, beer, some horribly strong, sickly sweet perfume wafting off the woman standing next to her, never mind the horribly pungent odour of unwashed bodies.

By the time the guard called 'Parramatta Park' and the train stuttered to a halt, her head swam with confusion. She'd have to ask how to get to Old Government House. She emphasised the word *old* in her mind; it seemed everyone got confused if she said Government House and tried to direct her to the Gothic folly overlooking Sydney Harbour. If nothing else she'd discovered how little she knew of the history of Sydney. She'd learnt more at school about London and people like Christopher Wren and Sir Robert Peel and everyone's favourite—the mighty Queen Victoria.

She stepped down from the train and waited for the first rush of people to leave the station and then walked across to the ticket office and rapped on the window. The man behind the glass lifted his visor and blinked at her, then waved her away, mouthing the word 'Closed'. She rapped again and after a lot of headshaking, he finally cracked open the window.

'Can you tell me how to get to Old Government House, please?'

He shook his head. 'Just follow your nose.' He flicked his thumb at a set of glass doors. 'Down Church Street, past the Police Barracks and left into George.' The window slammed shut.

'Right. Thank you.' She glared at the glass pane, picked up her bag, which seemed to be getting heavier every time she lifted it, and trudged through the doors and into the twilight, her nose pointing in what she hoped was the right direction.

Dodging the incessant stream of people presumably heading home after a day's work, some quite smartly dressed, others obviously labourers or shop assistants, a butcher with a carcass slung over one burly shoulder and a man pushing a two-wheeled cart stacked with firewood, she forged ahead. As the stationmaster had said, the Police Barracks appeared on her right and she dodged across the road and into George Street.

Connie staggered to a halt. Sprawling lawns and majestic trees framed a park-like expanse and sweeping gravel carriageway. The imposing two-storey, whitewashed house glowed amber in the setting sun. She stood for a moment admiring the handsome symmetrical building with its entrance framed by towering columns, dignified and more formal than any of the buildings in Maitland. She pressed her hand against her stomach to ease the nervous fluttering.

Staring at the upstairs windows, a flicker of movement caught her attention—a woman in a pale high-waisted gown drifted across the room. In the blink of an eye she vanished, faded into the darkness.

Shaking away the image, she mounted the steps, sadly in need of a decent sweep, and studied the view through the blurry windows flanking the front door; a sepia glass image foxed with age, damp and dust revealed a wide hallway with lofty ceilings.

For an instant she wished she'd stayed in Sydney. She'd be ensconced in a nice comfortable room at the Berkley, not standing like a waif wondering what to do next, and truth be told, nothing, nothing at all indicated that Nell would be here—Mrs Alexander possibly.

Connie pressed her nose against the windows and peered in. A black and white chequered floor stretched to a further doorway and in the dim distance an impressive flight of cedar stairs wound its way upwards.

She took a couple of steps back, searching for a bell or knocker and there, tucked to one side of the door, embedded in the sandstone façade, she found a circular doorbell. The faintest sound echoed in the distance when she pressed it and after a few moments a young girl with flyaway chestnut hair haphazardly pinned beneath a crooked cap and sporting a harried expression tip-tapped her way across the tiled floor. She stopped, straightened her somewhat grubby apron, and opened the door. 'Yes?' She tossed her head, obviously thinking better of her terse enquiry. 'How may I help you?' She offered a shy gap-toothed smile of apology.

The murmur of voices drifted in the comforting air and cooking smells wafted up the hallway. Connie licked her dry lips—what she wouldn't give for a cup of tea. It had been a long, long day. 'I'm looking for …' Something made her pause. If she said 'Mrs Alexander' and she was in the wrong place the conversation could be closed off in a moment. She cleared her throat. 'I wondered if you had a room for the night. I've just arrived from Sydney and the stationmaster suggested I came here as you were closest to the station.'

The girl's eyebrows twitched, and Connie batted down the flush rising to her cheeks. 'We don't take overnight guests. You need to find something in Church or George Street back that way.' She threw her a quizzical glance. 'This is a guesthouse— long-term visitors only.'

What had she got to lose? 'Is Mrs Alexander available?'

The front door creaked a little wider and the girl pointed to a ladderback chair against the wall. 'Wait here,' she said, before disappearing back the way she had come.

Connie sank down thankfully and tucked her bag beside her feet.

The girl's response to her request to see Mrs Alexander indicated she was in the right place but what of Nell? Try as she may, she couldn't imagine Nell walking this hallway, straightening her pinny and answering the door, or worse, hunched on her hands and knees scrubbing the floor. Mrs Mumford must be wrong— her formidable grandmother was never in service.

Across the hall a wide door stood open revealing a large dining room table flanked by eight chairs and laid ready for a meal— dinner, judging by the array of silver cutlery. Her stomach gave an appreciative rumble. A large sideboard stood against the far wall, a series of chafing dishes awaiting their offerings, and above a large oil painting of a supercilious-looking uniformed gentleman on a white charger rivalling in size the enormous marble fireplace. And the furnishings, though well used and out of fashion, retained a comfortable elegance with their faded damasks and well-worn velvets but nothing to indicate Nell's presence. She twisted in her chair, tipped her head, and studied the matching, firmly closed door on her side of the hallway. She fancied she could hear the murmur of conversation, a deep voice, then two higher pitched and something that sounded remarkably like a flirtatious giggle. She leant closer, almost toppled as the drawing room door flew open and an imposing woman in a dark gunmetal grey silk costume that harked back to an earlier time, with her hair centre parted and pulled tight into a bun at the nape of her neck stepped into the hallway. The woman's only ornament, a series of keys dangling from an impressive gold chatelaine around her waist, clanked with every step.

Connie shot to her feet. 'Mrs Alexander?'

The woman smiled—a terrifying stretch of her thin lips. 'How may I help you?'

7

Nell peered into the hallway, blinked rapidly and shook her head. Her eyes couldn't be deceiving her. They weren't. Connie was standing next to Mrs Alexander. What in heaven's name? She couldn't be here, she simply couldn't. 'That'll be all, thank you,' Nell snapped at the poor little maid who had just set down her pre-dinner sherry. She barged through the door into the hallway, grasped Connie's hand, and pulled her into a hug. 'What are you doing here?' she whispered in her ear.

Connie pulled back, and two bright pink spots illuminated her cheeks, and she gave a shaky laugh. 'I was worried, so worried. I thought something had happened to you.'

'You can't stay here. You must leave.'

'I'm not leaving. If you're here then so am I.' Connie straightened her back, bit her bottom lip, her lovely dark blue eyes sparkling. 'It's a guesthouse; they must have a room for me.'

This simply wouldn't do. Nell couldn't allow Connie to announce herself as Constance Montague, her granddaughter.

There was too much at stake. With a great deal of subterfuge, she had managed to control the situation. The slightest hint of anything untoward and the past would all come rushing back. She would not have Connie's reputation, her future, her very life, heaven forbid, blighted.

Making a snap decision, Nell turned to face Mrs Alexander and blurted out, 'I'd like to introduce my companion, Miss Constance. She'll be spending a few days with me.'

Connie's open mouth betrayed her surprise then she raised one quizzical eyebrow, forced a smile and said nothing.

Nell squeezed Connie's arm in thanks. 'I am so very pleased to see you managed to get here. Mrs Alexander, I wonder if we might be able to find a room for Constance.'

Dear god, please don't let the child say anything to contradict her. Connie pulled her hand free, took off her hat and pushed back her tangle of chestnut curls.

'Let me see what can be organised.' Mrs Alexander led the way into the drawing room, where Mr Whitfield, Miss Pettigrew and Miss Milling sat, looks of blatant curiosity etched on their faces. 'Tea, or a small sherry perhaps?' she enquired.

'That would be lovely. I'm sure you're parched after your journey, aren't you, Constance? Why don't you sit down?'

Before Connie had a chance to sit down, Mr Whitfield, the older gentleman Nell had met on her arrival, lumbered to his feet and made a beeline for Connie. 'How delightful to meet you, my dear. Percy Whitfield.'

Connie offered a faint smile and he grasped her hand and brought it to his lips, the twisted ends of his handlebar moustache grazing her skin. Both she and Connie shuddered and their eyes met as Connie retrieved her hand.

'You made no mention of such a delightful companion, Mrs Montague.' Nor of anything close to her heart when she'd spun him the yarn about her recently deceased husband and strained circumstances.

Some more introductions were in order and then once Mrs Alexander showed Connie to her room she could explain—not everything, but enough to convince Connie to maintain the charade. 'Mrs Alexander, would you like to introduce your guests, or shall I?'

'Why don't you, Mrs Montague, and I shall go and see about a room for Miss Constance.' She rang the bell pull, smoothed her skirt, and waited for the maid to reappear.

Nell cleared her throat and moved to the window where Mr Whitfield now stood, his hands resting on the back of Miss Pettigrew's bathchair. 'Constance, this is Miss Pettigrew, another guest of the establishment.'

Connie strolled across the room, tucking her hand safely in one of the disreputable pockets she insisted on having in her skirts. 'Miss Pettigrew.' She offered the slightest dip of her knee then bent and held out her hand. 'How nice to meet you.'

Miss Pettigrew raised her cupped hand to her ear. 'Speak up, child.'

'Nice to meet you, Miss Pettigrew, my name is—'

Nell caught the glint in Connie's eye just in time. 'Miss Constance, my companion,' she interrupted.

The corner of Connie's lip tweaked into a smile, and at her nod of acquiescence Nell continued. 'And over here we have Miss Milling. She works in town for Mademoiselle Gautier, the dressmaker.'

Miss Milling pushed aside her embroidery and jumped to her feet. 'It will be so delightful to have someone younger ...' Her words petered out and a flush rose to her cheeks. 'Pleased to meet you.' She subsided back onto the sofa with a mumbled apology.

'What did the girl say?' Miss Pettigrew's voice boomed out. 'She insists on mumbling. Miss Milling, it's time I went to my room to prepare for dinner.'

Miss Milling gave an apologetic grin, bundled up her embroidery and stuffed it into her tapestry bag then pushed Miss Pettigrew's chair out into the hallway as a large clatter and bang of the front door heralded the arrival of someone else. 'Taylor! We've got new guests. Go and say hello!' Miss Milling's voice echoed and in strode a tall, statuesque young woman Nell hadn't met before. She pulled off what looked remarkably like a man's bowler hat and released a tumble of corn-coloured curls. 'Hello! I'm Taylor Fotherby.'

8

Connie raised her eyebrows and grinned. Whatever Nell was up to would at least include an interesting array of characters. Miss Fotherby's no-nonsense close-fitting waistcoat and shirt and tie made Connie regret her vivid cornflower blue skirt and jacket. It seemed so … well, so feminine, frilly and flouncy and most definitely not suited to her current mission. 'Hello, Miss Fotherby. This is Mrs Montague and I'm her …' She paused for a moment. She needed to get to the bottom of Nell's subterfuge before she dropped a bombshell. '… companion, Constance,' she finished, and earned herself a relieved nod from Nell.

'Is there any tea?' Miss Fotherby ran her hand over the silver teapot and grimaced. 'I'll go and ask for some hot water. I'm spitting feathers. I've been stuck in the courthouse all afternoon.' She threw her hat onto the sofa and bounded out of the room, almost knocking Mrs Alexander over in the doorway.

Mrs Alexander clutched at the doorjamb, rolled her eyes, and recovered her balance. 'These young things. Mrs Montague, if you and Miss Constance would like to accompany me upstairs. The room is prepared. It's not large but I'm sure it will suffice. Miss Fotherby and Miss Milling manage with similar accommodation, and it has a connecting door to your room which I'm sure will be convenient. Follow me.' She swept from the room.

At last, she might have the opportunity to get Nell on her own and find out exactly what she was doing here. It may well have once been the home of governors but the peeling wallpaper, worn carpets and frayed upholstery spoke of an interesting history. She picked up her bag.

The wide, ornate cedar staircase led from the back of the hall past a grandfather clock and up to the first floor.

When they reached the top of the stairs Mrs Alexander worked her fingers through the large collection of objects dangling from her chatelaine and slipped an ornate key into the lock. The door opened to reveal a four-poster bed in the centre of the room, flanked by two large windows. 'Mrs Montague has Mrs Macquarie's room,' Mrs Alexander announced with a touch of pride. Nell certainly wasn't slumming it although the odd patch of mildew marked the corners of the room, and the late afternoon sun highlighted the faded patches on the curtains. Two cane-backed chairs stood either side of a small fireplace and against the opposite wall on a narrow table Nell had arranged a pile of papers, her journal, and her fountain pen—Montague's last gift to her. She should have known the moment she noticed it missing from the desk in Nell's bedroom that she wouldn't be returning home anytime soon.

'Your room is through here, Miss Constance.' Mrs Alexander opened an interconnecting door to reveal a much smaller room which must have once served as a dressing room. It held a very peculiar single bed with a bowed canopy, a bedside table, and an upright chair.

'I thought maybe Constance might prefer the larger room next door.' Nell raised her hand and gestured to the opposite wall.

'Oh no.' Mrs Alexander shook her head. 'That room is never occupied.' Her eyes flitted this way and that. 'I keep it for unexpected visitors,' she added.

Connie's mind darted back to the shadowy figure she'd seen at the window when she'd arrived. 'This is quite adequate.' She threw her bag onto the bed and plonked down to check the mattress, more than willing to forgo a larger room if it kept her close to Nell. There was something about the whole atmosphere and Nell's almost subservient attitude to Mrs Alexander that made the hairs on her arms prickle—a sure sign something was amiss.

'I'll leave you to settle in. We serve breakfast, an evening meal, and a light luncheon on request. Mrs Montague will show you the amenities.' Mrs Alexander opened a door opposite the bed and stepped out into the corridor.

Connie turned and studied Nell. She didn't look in any way different. Her tailored dress impeccable as always, her white hair neatly coiffed in her trademark chignon, her bearing upright; all that seemed to be missing was her usual sense of confidence. What Connie had to do now—right now, before her courage slipped—was to find out exactly what Nell was doing here with a disparate group of strangers.

'Why don't you unpack? I'll be downstairs when you've finished.' Nell made for the door.

Oh no. 'Before you go, Nell, I'd like to have a word—several words really. What's going on? We were so worried about you. You didn't tell anyone where you were going.'

'We?'

'To be honest, Faith wasn't terribly concerned but Miss Quinn was, and when I tried to report you missing to Sergeant Black, he said he couldn't do anything about it until more time had passed because you were an adult and—'

Nell's sudden laugh silenced Connie. 'Come next door, out of this cupboard. I never imagined I'd sleep in Mrs Macquarie's bed.' Nell stuck her head around the door leading to the corridor and shut it firmly and shot the bolt then led the way into the larger room and sat down in one of the cane-backed chairs. 'I'm sorry if I worried you but I really needed to get away.' She turned her gaze to the window. 'When you get to my age you realise that time is slipping by and all those people you once counted as friends might not be around for much longer. It's years since I've seen Mrs Alexander. She was the housekeeper at Government House in Sydney. That's how she managed to secure the lease on the guesthouse here.'

Connie took a deep breath. This was the most ludicrous explanation. She had to get to the truth. 'When you were in service?'

Nell visibly jumped. 'How do you know that?' Nell pressed her lips tight, frowned and gave a decisive nod. 'You spoke to Mrs Mumford.'

'Did you work for Mrs Alexander?' Was that why Nell seemed less self-assured than usual?

Nell nodded. 'At Government House in Sydney. Lady O'Connell arranged the job for me after her husband died and she returned to England.'

'Lady O'Connell?' Mrs Mumford hadn't mentioned a Lady O'Connell. It seemed there was rather more to Nell's past life than anyone imagined.

'It's a very long story. Please trust me for now. We'll have plenty of time to talk about it later.'

'But what about the other people here? That Whitfield man seemed very attentive.'

'I've never met him before, nor any of the others. Please, no more questions for the time being. I'll explain everything later.'

Which didn't go any way to *explaining* why Nell had introduced her as her companion and not her granddaughter. And then a horrible thought struck. 'Are you ashamed of me?'

'Ashamed of you!' Nell leant forward and reached for her hand. 'How could I ever be ashamed of you?'

Much to Connie's horror tears welled in her eyes. 'Why did you say I was your companion not your granddaughter? Why didn't you tell me where you were going? I would have come with you. You only had to ask.'

'Oh, sweetheart. It's nothing like that.' Nell's gaze slid back to the window. 'I just wanted to talk to someone about the past and thought you'd find it all terribly tedious. There's no one in Maitland that remembers the girl I once was. I miss your grandfather so very much.'

Connie reached for Nell's hand and ran the tips of her fingers over her worn wedding ring, a plain band, without gemstones, engravings or other embellishments, which for forty years had rested against her skin.

'Montague had it made especially for me, from the first nugget he found. I've told you that before, haven't I?' A blush stained Nell's cheeks and she withdrew her hand. 'Enough of this.' She stood up and smoothed down her skirt and smiled. 'Why don't you stay the night and take the train back tomorrow morning?'

Connie shot to her feet. 'I'm not going home, not without you. Besides, it would look foolish if your companion only stayed overnight. I won't get in the way. I won't interfere but I'm not going home. I'm going to send Faith a telegram and tell her—'

'I don't want you to tell her anything,' Nell snapped. 'Not where I am and certainly not why I am here.'

'You're being unreasonable. She'll be concerned. And by now half of Maitland will be wondering where you are. You know what Miss Quinn is like, never mind Sergeant Black or Mr Marsh.'

Nell dropped her head into her hands. 'Is there anyone you didn't tell?'

'I was worried. Seriously worried. I had Cracker searching the riverbank. I thought you might have fallen …'

'Cracker as well.' Nell let out a series of tuts and wandered across the room, her hand coming to rest on an ornate cabinet, the doors decorated with inlaid tree of life motifs. A smaller timber box sat atop the cabinet and Nell's fingers traced the ivory pattern on the lid—some Indian goddess, legs crossed, and her many arms held high.

After a few moments of uncomfortable silence Nell turned back. 'I think you better send that telegram first thing tomorrow morning. Tell Faith you've found me and I'm with friends in Parramatta and we'll be back in about a week.'

Connie smiled. *We. Back in about a week.* That was more like it.

'But you're going to have to amuse yourself. Miss Milling and Miss Fotherby will be able to show you around. You might be able to pick Miss Fotherby's not insignificant brain about chasing up those men who abscond and leave their wives and children destitute. I believe she works for Ramsbottom & Son, the solicitors in O'Connell Street. And perhaps discuss the Benevolent Society's work in assisting deserted women and their children. I'm sure Miss Quinn would appreciate any suggestions.'

Connie had no intention of going anywhere until Nell had filled in a few more blanks. Why had Nell never told her of her earlier life? More to the point, why had she never asked? A situation she intended to remedy. She slipped her arm through Nell's.

'How did you get here?'

Nell lifted her shoulders in an inconsequential shrug. 'By train.'

'You haven't taken a train since Pa's accident.' Connie swallowed the lump in her throat. Two years on, the tragedy still haunted her. When the train had pulled into the station at Rutherford and the door to the loose box was opened the strapper had discovered that the rope securing the stallion had broken and the panicked horse had trampled Pa to death. She shook the memory of the appalling incident aside. 'Besides, you couldn't have caught the train.'

Nell paled at her bland statement and sank slowly back into the chair. 'Why ever not?'

'Because only one train ran yesterday, and it only went as far as the Hawkesbury River.'

Colour tinged Nell's cheeks. 'And then I took the punt across the river and picked up the Sydney train.'

'Nell, please. Don't lie to me. It was the opening of the Hawkesbury Rail Bridge, special ticketed seats by invitation only, and Mr Marsh said your name was not on the list.'

'I'm not lying ...' She covered her face with her hands and spoke through her fingers. 'Glossing over a few details,' she admitted in a whisper.

Connie took Nell's cold hand. 'What happened?'

'I set off for the station early hoping to catch the milk train to Newcastle. I took the shortcut to the station from the end of Victoria Street and walked along the tracks. The place was deserted, and I got cold feet. I decided to leave. I crossed the tracks. There was an engine building up steam. The driver yelled at me, told me to get out of the way. He explained it was the bridge opening and invitation only, and the train would be leaving after eight o'clock. We got talking and he invited me aboard.'

'Into the engine! Heavens above, Nell, anything could have happened to you.'

'Something did happen.'

Connie's stomach sank, and she cast a surreptitious glance over Nell's person. She couldn't see anything untoward; the same gentle waft of lily-of-the-valley, neatly dressed hair, no scratches on her hands or broken fingernails.

'We had the most interesting conversation about the power of steam, and I ate the most delicious breakfast.'

'Breakfast?'

'Bacon and eggs and toast. All cooked on the shovel once they'd got the firebox stoked. And by then my fears had subsided but there were no seats available on the train, so I travelled with the engine driver and the fireman. But you mustn't tell anyone—I was sworn to secrecy. It's against the law to carry passengers in the engine and they'd lose their jobs.'

Connie coughed into her hand, hoping to mask her gurgle of laughter. Nothing as sinister as an attack, more like a garden party on a steam engine. Trust Nell. 'And when you got to Newcastle?'

'I stayed in the engine while the additional carriages were attached and when we got to Hawkesbury everyone got off the train and we took a tour of the river. We were served the most delicious oysters, then taken to a pontoon with a canvas awning, a huge floating marquee filled with rows and rows of tables; there had to be at least seven hundred people. So much fanfare. Official guests from around the world. The governor, Lord Carrington, declared the bridge open and the premier, Sir Henry Parkes, made a terribly boring speech, proposed a toast to a united Australia and said the bridge was a symbol of federation because it linked Charleville in Queensland to Coward Springs in South Australia. One for the record books, he said, before declaring the bridge open. When it was over, I simply blended in with the people from the Sydney train, found a seat, and arrived in Sydney around seven in the evening and got the train here this morning. Mr Sladdin at the Berkeley found me a room for the night.'

'Oh, Nell. Why didn't you let us know you were in Sydney? We were so worried.'

'I didn't want those men to lose their jobs; they have five children between them!'

9

Nell had known that the Hawkesbury Bridge would be opening, the newspapers had been full of it, but when the ghastly letter had arrived she couldn't think straight and it had slipped her mind. She'd thought at first the letter was for Faith—not a lot of difference between Mrs E Montague and Mrs F Montague; just the dash of a pen. She'd blamed her eyesight, and vanity. She did hate her beastly pince-nez; they made her look years older. It wasn't until Mrs Orchard handed her the envelope that she'd realised her mistake and when she'd opened the letter it had sent her into such a spin. It had taken only a moment for her to realise the implications—she would have to pander to his request and meet with him alone. She couldn't catch a breath and she'd felt so physically sick she'd had to run from the room, and blamed poor Mrs Orchard for the unpleasant stench of her morning egg. She really must apologise when all this was finally sorted out. However, it wasn't until the meeting with Edwards she truly understood the damage he could do.

The mere thought that Faith might have opened the letter and not told her made her blood run cold and once she'd decided to take matters into her own hands, the solution had come to her like a flash out of the blue—a message from the heavens, from Montague himself. Their name had to be protected at all costs and so did Connie; she had her whole life ahead of her.

'Nell!'

'Wool-gathering, I'm sorry. What did you say?'

'The next morning you came directly here, made your way to Parramatta?'

'Not exactly. I went to Government House in Sydney looking for Mrs Alexander. The nice young maid who opened the door told me she was here, so I caught another train. I arrived about eleven this morning. Now it really is time we went downstairs; we don't want to miss the evening meal.'

'I think Mr Whitfield will be pleased to see you. He looked most disgruntled when Mrs Alexander dragged you away.'

'Don't be so ridiculous. We were simply chatting before you arrived. He told me Mrs Alexander has had the lease for about five years. The guesthouse came fully furnished. A bit run-down because it hasn't been used as a vice-regal residence for over thirty years; FitzRoy was the last governor to live here. I think it still has a certain air about it though. Come along.'

Nell slipped her arm through Connie's as they made their way down the stairs. It really was delightful to have Connie's company, though she was going to have to make sure she didn't slip up. Connie always managed to get under her guard.

The clatter of china and silverware drifted into the hallway interspersed by a few giggles. 'That's May and June, the two maids, filling the chaffing dishes and putting the finishing touches to the table.' Nell led the way across the hallway and pointed up at the picture above the fireplace. 'Mad King George no less. Oh, if only these walls could talk what tales they'd have to tell. Breakfast is served here between seven-thirty and nine

and the evening meal at seven sharp. No latecomers so take that
as a warning and if we require a light luncheon, we have to leave
a note over there on the sideboard. Mrs Alexander is a stickler for
routine, and I don't want to upset her.'

'Ah. What a wonderful find. Not one but two lovely ladies.'
The odious Mr Whitfield's deep, husky voice sounded from the
doorway.

Connie groaned aloud, sending a shiver of dread across Nell's
skin, but she lifted her eyes and gave him a smile. It was vitally
important not to antagonise anyone; there was too much at
stake.

'Let me show you to your seats.' Mr Whitfield inserted himself
between the two of them, hooked his cane over his arm, and
guided them to the table. 'Come along, ladies.' His mottled face
broke into a sycophantic smile.

Nell cringed at the waft of pomade and the whiff of camphor;
she'd noticed it earlier when they were in the drawing room. His
clothes smelt as though they had been put away for the summer
and only recently retrieved from storage. His grip on her arm
intensified and rather than cause a disturbance she allowed him
to lead her to the table.

'Why don't you sit here, Mr Whitfield?' Nell patted the seat
between her and Mrs Alexander.

'Nell,' Connie hissed. 'What are you doing?'

'Do not question my actions,' she muttered under her breath.

Another man Nell hadn't met before appeared in the doorway
and, with a nod to Mrs Alexander sitting at the head of the table
in front of a large roasted duck, stood behind the seat opposite
her. 'Mrs Montague, I presume.' He sketched a small bow.

She detected a slight accent, French unless she was mistaken.
'Yes, and you must be Mr Humbert.' Nell smiled at the man, in
his late thirties, early forties, close in age to Faith's friends but

a good foot shorter than any man she'd ever met before, with cropped dark hair and even darker eyes. 'Won't you sit down?'

'Thank you. You have been introduced to the other guests? Madame Pettigrew, M'selle Milling and M'selle Fotherby,' he said as they entered and took their seats.

'We met earlier. This is my companion, Miss Constance. She arrived on a later train.'

Connie's dark blue eyes flashed and the corner of her mouth quirked as she repressed a smile. 'Good evening, Mr Humbert.'

Mr Whitfield inhaled then cleared his throat and rose, looking around the table in what appeared to be an attempt to ensure he had everyone's attention. 'Mrs Alexander, let me carve. It is not a job for a lady.' Without waiting for her reply he drew the serving plate towards him then brandished the carving knife rather as though he was about to engage in a duel.

Mr Humbert leant forward and spoke in an undertone to her. 'Mr Whitfield is not one to hide in the shadows. He is a recent addition to this fine establishment. He arrived only a week or so ago. I however have been in residence on and off for some time. I run a small business trading in haberdashery and other notions that appeal to the ladies. Mrs Alexander is kind enough to keep a room for my use when I return to Parramatta. Something of a luxury after days on the road.'

While Nell helped herself to some vegetables to accompany the rather dry-looking slices of duck breast, she ran through the guests in her mind. Miss Pettigrew, who according to Mr Whitfield had been in residence from the very beginning, although apparently she was rapidly becoming more feeble and now required assistance with personal matters. Young Miss Milling had stepped up and Miss Pettigrew covered a portion of her rent in exchange for her services but only after she had finished at the dressmaker's shop. Miss Fotherby, Taylor, such a masculine name and such masculine attire. Not that she was unattractive, but her choice of clothes was most odd. Nell was all in favour of practicality but the stark black and white in a girl so young didn't bear thinking about, although thankfully she hadn't succumbed to a pair of men's britches.

The thought of Connie sporting such a costume made her wince—a tie and waistcoat, and that ludicrous bowler hat, and whoever heard of a girl working in a solicitor's office? Messrs Brown would never stand for such a thing in Maitland.

With herself and Connie that made seven, eleven if she included Mrs Alexander, the two maids, and the cook—Mrs Trotter she'd heard someone call her. She presumed it was her name and not some nonsense one of the girls had invented.

Dinner progressed, largely dominated by Miss Milling who had a particular interest in the Parramatta Players, the local amateur dramatic group who performed at the Victoria Theatre, and Mr Whitfield who appeared to have encyclopaedic knowledge of all things theatrical. Mind you, Connie didn't let the side down either, singing the praises of Maitland's establishment—coincidentally also known as the Victoria Theatre.

By the time dessert was served, a runny lemon syllabub, Connie was visibly wilting after her long day and Nell could think of nothing better than some peace and quiet, which hopefully would provide her with the opportunity to decide how she would deal with her granddaughter's unexpected arrival.

'Coffee and tea will be served in the drawing room.' Mrs Alexander placed her napkin on the table, signalling the end of the meal.

'Thank you for a delightful dinner, Mrs Alexander. Constance and I will forgo the offer of a nightcap. We've both travelled a significant distance in the last days and are very much looking forward to turning in for the night.'

Mr Whitfield groaned to his feet and helped her from her seat. Connie moved a little faster and managed to save herself from the unsavoury combination of camphor and pomade.

'Goodnight, everyone,' she trilled as she slipped her arm through Connie's and they made their way upstairs.

Nell woke with a start; a bright shaft of moonlight played on the palampore eiderdown. She struggled upright, momentarily disorientated until her gaze came to rest on the gilt mantle clock where a small statue of the Roman goddess Diana highlighted the midnight hour.

A silence hung over the house. She sat up and swung her legs to the ground but resisted the temptation to go and check on Connie. She was going to have to let Faith know that Connie was safe. And then she remembered—the telegram. Connie had said she'd go into town in the morning and deal with the matter. Somehow, she doubted the news would overly concern Faith. Such a difficult girl. She'd known from the moment Fred had brought Faith to the property that it wouldn't be an easy path.

He'd bounded down from the buggy, his lovely smile lighting his face, his eyes sparkling, picked her up and swirled her around, her feet skimming the grass and the scent of the roses making her dizzy. 'Fred, put me down this instant. What will everyone say?'

'They will say your son is the luckiest man in New South Wales.'

'Have you and your father been at the racetrack again?'

'Yes, we have, but our success has nothing to do with luck. It's knowledge and breeding that builds winners.'

'I thought we'd agreed there'd be no more gambling, not until—'

'There's someone I want you to meet.'

Nell grabbed onto his sleeve, hoping the ground would settle. She'd been dreading the day but had always known it would come. Fred Montague was seen as a catch throughout the Hunter. With the Montagues' not insignificant success on the racecourse and their fine stud on the banks of the river it was hardly surprising.

'Come, Mother.' Fred tugged at her hand like a young boy spotting a particularly delicious iced confection.

It was only when she'd taken a closer look at the buggy, a buggy containing a highly decorated bonnet, the brim turned up to reveal a cluster of blonde ringlets, an upturned nose and pouting lips tilted in an ingratiating smile, that her heart sank.

Not that Nell objected to Fred's various dalliances—she wouldn't want it any other way—it was just that his roving eye often landed in the most inopportune places. There had been the seamstress, a couple of actresses, the daughter of the disreputable Lord Someone-or-other and—horrifyingly—the young dancer he'd brought home from Sydney, who claimed to be related to Lola Montez. Fortunately that hadn't lasted long. Fred was like his father: he liked a risk better than most men, more especially when it paid off. Unfortunately, unlike his father, he didn't know when to call it quits.

'I'd like to introduce you to Faith Taunton. Her family breeds horses outside Melbourne so we've plenty in common.' He stretched out his hand and Miss Taunton stepped from the buggy with a cat-like elegance, her chin lifting as she eyed the house.

'Faith dearest, this is my mother, Mrs Eleanor Montague, but everyone calls her Nell. I've invited Faith for tea. Do you think Cook can rustle up something if I ask nicely? The garden's lovely at this time of the year.' And with that Fred had loped off to the stables and left Nell and Faith to acquaint themselves.

Faith had a pretty little laugh and the bluest eyes, and an apparent love for the excitement of the racetrack. In that matter she and Fred were ideally suited. Fred was besotted and Faith had him well and truly ensnared. The wedding followed shortly thereafter.

Quite how the two of them had managed to produce such a well-grounded daughter she had absolutely no idea. Connie had truly disproved the old adage that fruit never fell far from the tree—thank goodness.

10

Friday, 3 May, 1889

There wasn't a sound from Nell's room the next morning so bearing in mind the advice that Mrs Alexander was a stickler for punctuality Connie made her way to the dining room on the dot of seven-thirty for breakfast. She had every intention of presenting herself at the Telegraph Office the moment it opened before Nell could have second thoughts about her informing Faith of their whereabouts and that they would be spending a week taking in the sights. If she worded the telegram carefully, she wouldn't upset Nell.

She had enjoyed the previous evening which had passed in a flurry of chatter and, much to Connie's surprise, delight. Miss Milling and Miss Fotherby proved to be highly amusing company and before dessert was served, they were calling each other by their first names and had discovered they had plenty in common, not least an interest in the theatre.

By the time she'd settled into her surprisingly comfortable bed in the room next door to Nell, she'd come to the conclusion that the whole escapade had been an excellent idea. She had few friends of her own age in Maitland and Maisie and Taylor offered a tantalising possibility of filling that aching void.

She found the two girls in the dining room and they greeted her with wide smiles. 'We're always the first at breakfast. Apart from the fact the eggs are better eaten the moment they're cooked, we working girls haven't got time for a lie-in. What are your plans for the day?' Taylor wiped a piece of toasted bread around her plate, mopping up the last of the egg yolk.

'I have to send a telegram to my mother, to tell her I've arrived safely.' No lie in that. 'Then I thought I'd take a walk around the park. Mrs Montague won't need me until later in the morning.' The role of companion wouldn't be difficult to fulfil because it was pretty much what she did at home, as long as she remembered the Mrs Montague bit.

Maisie pushed her plate aside. 'I can show you the way to the Telegraph Office; it's not far from the salon. Taylor goes in the other direction. Then you can walk down Church Street along the river and cut back through the park. It really is delightful at this time of the year. There are a few interesting things to see. There's a monument to Governor FitzRoy's wife; she was killed in a carriage accident years ago, such a heartrending story. The governor was driving, and the horses bolted. The carriage tipped and threw his wife, Lady Mary, and his lieutenant headlong into one of the oak trees along the avenue Mrs Macquarie had planted. Lady Mary died instantly, and the lieutenant only minutes later. The governor was heartbroken. Her funeral was one of the biggest Parramatta had ever seen. Then the house was closed up. He was the last governor to use Parramatta as a country residence.'

Maisie continued without pausing for breath. 'The monument was only unveiled last year. It was an amazing day—a street procession, a sports carnival and children's picnic then fireworks. I love fireworks.'

It sounded as though Paramatta was quite the social hive.

'And there's the bathhouse and the observatory. The path along the river is lovely in the morning. Take a couple of slices of toast and you can feed the ducks.' She pushed the toast rack across the table. 'I usually wrap them in a napkin, then drop it back in the scullery. Mrs A won't notice it's missing; she rarely appears at breakfast. I'll be leaving in about fifteen minutes, after I've checked on Miss Pettigrew; she's taking breakfast in her room this morning. Will that suit?'

Connie nodded and sliced the top off her boiled egg. 'I'll meet you out the front, thank you.'

'And I'm off too.' Taylor straightened her trim waistcoat and picked up her hat from the chair next to the window. 'I'm expected at the office by eight. We'll catch up this evening.' With a wave she strode off.

Connie met Maisie out the front of the house and together they made their way to the large and very ostentatious Telegraph Office in Church Street.

'This is where I leave you. When you've sent the telegram just follow your nose, and you'll see a bridge; cross the river and walk along the path. I can't be late for work. See you this evening.' With a wave Maisie turned back towards George Street.

Connie stood for a moment gathering her thoughts then entered the Telegraph Office, picked up a pencil and filled in the form:

Nell Parramatta visiting friends. Returning in week. Constance

There! She'd kept it within ten words. She handed the form and the two shillings over at the counter and within moments was, once again, back outside.

The river slid beneath the willow trees following its ancient route to the sea. Parramatta was a busy, bustling town but after Sydney it seemed calmer, more like Maitland, making Connie quite at home. She drew in a lungful of fresh air and followed the path as Maisie had suggested, through the park, basking in a sense of accomplishment now she'd let Faith know Nell was safe and sound. A week, Nell had said. She wouldn't mind if it stretched a little longer; it had been an age since she'd set foot beyond Maitland and she would very much like to get to know Maisie and Taylor a little better.

She found the pyramid obelisk surrounded by a small wall and iron railing. The inscription on the marble panel told the sorry tale of Lady Mary's demise and brought goosebumps to her skin. Another accident involving horses. Despite Faith and Pa's love of horseracing, the snorting puffing beasts put the fear of god into her, and after Pa's horrible accident she stayed well clear of the racecourse and the horse stud. Not that Faith had ever suggested she might like to go with her, which was probably just as well because Nell had said time and time again she didn't think the racecourse a suitable place for young ladies.

The crushed sandstone path meandered along, partly in sun, partly in shade, a delightful spot. She could imagine families picnicking on the grass, children racing around playing hide-and-seek in the willow trees but so early in the morning she met no one except a group of ducks swimming in ever-decreasing circles searching for breakfast.

She pulled the napkin from her pocket, crumbled the toast and scattered it across the water then slowly made her way cutting across the wide-open space back towards the guesthouse. The building reminded her of an old lady, elegant, well dressed and stylish but in dire need of brightening. She hadn't truly appreciated its elegance when she'd arrived last night. Far too worried about finding Nell. She gave a laugh. She should have known better. In that respect Faith was quite correct—Nell knew how to look after herself. Something she'd learnt in her younger years, no doubt. Her curiosity deepened; if nothing else she was determined to learn more about Nell's earlier life. She picked up her pace and took the steps two at a time into the hallway.

Breakfast hadn't been cleared so she slipped the napkin onto the dining room table and stuck her head around the drawing room door. No one there either. The perfect opportunity to explore, and if she was discovered somewhere she shouldn't be she could always claim she'd lost her way while searching for Nell.

At the base of the stairs the building divided: to the right a discreet sign proclaimed Private. Mrs Alexander's rooms most likely. Ignoring the sign, she tiptoed along the hallway and peered around the half-opened door.

Mrs Alexander sat at a small desk, head bent studying what looked to be a large book. She took a step closer, making the floorboard creak.

Mrs Alexander lifted her head, a look of surprise on her face.

'I'm just having a look around, trying to get my bearings.' Connie stepped over the threshold and into the room, then came to a sudden stop. She was forgetting herself. Mrs Montague's companion wouldn't be so familiar. 'I beg your pardon. I walked into town ... for a look around, and then came back through the park.'

Mrs Alexander snapped the leather-bound book closed and placed her palm flat down on the cover. Heat sprang to Connie's face. She wasn't welcome. She cleared her throat. 'I'll go to the kitchen and find myself a glass of water. Can I get you anything?'

'Perhaps you'd take the tray to the kitchen.' Mrs Alexander gestured to a breakfast tray on the right-hand side of the door.

Definitely the hired help. She was going to have to come to terms with this companion role. Unable to resist, Connie threw a quick bob, picked up the tray and backed from the room. If nothing else, it gave her the perfect excuse to explore the servants' quarters.

Her heels clicked on the timber floor as she made her way back, past the front door and staircase, down the matching hallway towards the sounds of banging and clattering coming from what she could only guess was the kitchen. A row of curled metal springs supporting small bells hung high on the wall above a timber dresser. Without a doubt, she'd reached the servants' quarters and for a moment she hesitated, remembering Mrs Orchard's stalwart protection of her domain. No, no need. She gave a wry smile. If she was Mrs Montague's companion, somewhere between guest and servant, she had every right to be there. All in all, it was rather liberating.

The kitchen door stood wide open, and a ferocious heat belted out from the range. 'Mrs Alexander asked me to bring her breakfast tray down. Where would you like it?'

The hustle and bustle slowed, and three faces turned as one. 'Thought you were one of the guests.' The stocky red-faced woman she took to be the cook, judging by her large white apron and floury hands, cocked her head to one side.

'I'm Mrs Montague's companion.'

'Ah! Betwixt and between. I'm Mrs Trotter, the cook. You can take that through to the scullery.' She hitched her thumb over her shoulder at the young girl who had opened the front door when she'd first arrived. 'June'll take care of the tray, then you better sit yourself down. We're about to have elevenses—a bit early but we've been at it since sparrows.'

June took the tray without a word and Connie returned to the kitchen. In the middle of the scrubbed table on a metal rack sat a row of steaming scones, a series of jars containing what looked very much like an assortment of jams and a large bowl of creamy yellow butter. Her stomach gave a rumble.

'We don't serve a midday meal, unless by arrangement. The guests generally sort themselves out—except for poor old Miss Pettigrew—but if you and Mrs Montague would like luncheon then stick your head in around midday and pick it up. Help yourself.' Mrs Trotter pushed a knife and plate towards her. 'So heard tell your Mrs Montague once worked for Mrs Alexander in Sydney. Looks like she did all right for herself.'

Connie broke off a large piece of the warm scone and waited, more to give herself time to think than anything else. She was going to have to be very careful, and what was Nell's favourite adage? When in doubt stick as close to the truth as possible. 'I knew she was in service as a young girl, but I wasn't aware of the fact that she worked with Mrs Alexander.'

'With or for? Not sure. Mrs Alexander worked for more than one of the governors, you know. That's how she got the lease on this place. They wouldn't give it to no one. Some of the furnishings and fittings date back to the Macquaries, before even. That room she's got your Mrs Montague in used to be Mrs Macquarie's bed chamber. You have a good look at the bits and pieces in there; got to be worth a bob or two.'

Connie chewed diligently, lapping up every word Mrs Trotter uttered, her curiosity spiralling out of control. Nell hadn't told her the whole truth, of that she was certain. She wasn't looking up old friends; she was up to something else—but what? She pushed back her chair and picked up her plate and cup and saucer. 'Thanks very much; the scones were delicious. I was hungry after my walk.'

'Did the ducks enjoy the toast?' June piped up, her cheeks pinking at her audacity.

Connie laughed. 'Yes, they did. Very much. I better get moving; Mrs Montague might need me.'

'How about one good turn deserves another?' Mrs Trotter tipped her head to one side. 'I've got a sandwich here for Miss Pettigrew's midday meal. It'll save my legs. Poor old dear is feeling a bit peaky this morning. She doesn't have much company until Maisie gets back from work and takes her into the drawing room. Tray is over there on the dresser. She's in the room on this side of the stairs. You'll have to knock loudly. Deaf as an old fence post she is.' She stood up and clapped her hands together sharply. 'Come on, May and June, the dining room needs clearing. We've got work to do otherwise there'll be no dinner for anyone tonight.'

Connie made her way along the hallway, and squinted down the colonnade at Mrs Alexander's sitting room. The door was firmly closed. She knocked on Miss Pettigrew's door.

'Miss Pettigrew,' she called before knocking again. Receiving no response, she eased the door open and stuck her head in. 'Miss Pettigrew, I've brought your luncheon.'

The woman sat with her back to the door staring out of the window to a small courtyard, apparently lost in contemplation.

Terrified she'd startle her, Connie cleared her throat. Miss Pettigrew swung her chair around with more vigour than expected and gazed at her perplexed. 'Do you know where he is?'

'I'm sorry, it's Constance, Mrs Montague's companion; we met last evening. I've brought your luncheon.'

A look of confusion flickered across Miss Pettigrew's face. 'Have you seen my brother?'

'I beg your pardon.'

'My brother. Obadiah.'

Connie reached back to the previous evening. There had been no mention of Miss Pettigrew's brother. 'Your brother?'

'He was here.' She gestured to the wide windowsill. 'Right here. He's gone.'

Connie glanced across at the window where a small easel stood. Empty.

Miss Pettigrew sketched a small square with her hands and stifled a sob. 'His portrait. It's gone.'

Connie deposited the tray on the table in front of the window and began to remove the plate of sandwiches all the while gazing surreptitiously around the room in search of a portrait. 'I'm sorry, I don't know where it is.'

'It's all I have to remember him by.' She dabbed at the end of her nose with an embroidered handkerchief. 'It was painted just weeks before he was taken. Beautiful tousled hair and a lovely smile. So true to life—except for the floppy pale blue bow the artist insisted on tying around his neck. My darling boy thought it made him look like a girl.'

'Would you like me to ask May or June if they saw it when they were cleaning?'

'Thank you, that would be most kind and I shall speak to Mrs Alexander. Nothing has ever gone missing before.' She frowned and gazed around the room once more, then shook her head slowly from side to side.

'Is there anything else I can do for you?'

'I can manage. Off you go.' Miss Pettigrew tipped her chin to the door.

A thank you would have been nice but Connie wasn't about to draw attention to herself. Betwixt and between—it described her position well and reminded her of Nell. She truly had to find out how she ended up in service and more to the point how she met Montague. Somehow it had never occurred to her to wonder before. He must have changed her life.

11

Nell pulled the cane chair to the window and sat staring out at the play of sunlight on the carefully tended grass. An older man was raking up the cuttings while a young boy trailed behind him filling a wheelbarrow. If she squinted into the sun, she could see herself standing with her flower basket. Being at Parramatta after so long had brought the past flooding back—how the time had flown.

The cry of a laughing jackass serenading the rising sun broke the silence. Nell inhaled the damp dew laced with the potent fragrances of eucalyptus, lemon myrtle and tea tree, basking in the light dappling through the trees.

The days spent at Parramatta filled her with a sense of freedom and joy, the space and slower pace away from Sydney's chaos and commotion. Not that her life was particularly difficult. She'd been more than lucky when Lord O'Connell had returned to Australia to take his place as a member of the upper house of parliament. Lady O'Connell had, of course, accompanied him. She'd hunted her down and offered her a position as lady's maid. Who would have thought that little Nell Rivers would be rubbing shoulders with the closest Australia had to royalty? It was a shame Mam wasn't here to see it; but for her, Nell would still be working in the hospital kitchens. Mam had set the ball rolling when she'd turned up with her needle and thread to work at Government House for the governor's daughter all those years ago.

Nell hitched her basket further up her arm, searching for the deep purple cluster of the boronia bushes. Whenever she visited Government House in Parramatta with Lady O'Connell she willingly took on the task of keeping the vases fresh. The governor's wife, Lady Gipps, liked her cut flowers, especially the native blooms.

'Hey! Koo-hoo-hoo-hoo-ha-ha-ha-hey-hey-hoo-hoo-hoo!'

Shading her eyes, she looked up; the jackass peered down from his perch on a dead branch, opened his beak and let rip again.

'Koo-hoo-hoo-hoo-ha-ha-ha.'

A greeting, an alarm, or the simple pleasure of the morning? Difficult to tell.

Shrugging, Nell hoicked up her skirt, tucked it into her waistband, ducked below the jackass's perch and darted deeper into the bush where a fresh, musky pine-like scent hung in a delicate cloud. Tiny native bees hummed, darting this way and that, drunk on the aroma of the dusty pollen of a flowering boronia bush.

Basket full to overflowing with the waxy, purple bell-shaped flowers, she returned to the carriageway, collecting small branches of red-tipped, grey-green eucalyptus leaves along the way and a wonderful posy of furry, white flannel flowers.

'Hey!'

The call brought her to a halt. No answering cry from the jackass, instead a movement between the trees. A tall, rangy fellow with his hat tilted and his fingers jammed in the pockets of his waistcoat stepped into the clearing.

Grasping the flower basket tight, she glared at the intruder. 'This is the governor's private domain. Public ain't allowed in here.'

A hint of a smile crossed his face, and he took a measured step closer before removing his hat. 'I need to speak to the governor. It's a private matter.' He spun his hat on his finger.

'Then present yourself to the front door and ask. Don't like your chances but …'

'Is there not anything you can do for me?'

'Like what?'

Then he truly smiled; one of those all-encompassing beams full of warmth and joy lit his entire face. Such a handsome face with its strong jawline and piercing blue-black eyes shimmering with mischief.

'Introduce me. I saw the governor walking over there.' He flicked his thumb towards the stables, eyes never leaving her face. 'So, there's no point in me going up to the house. If we could just take a wander that way …'

Her heart gave a resounding thump. She took a deep breath, straightened her shoulders, and stared at his outstretched hand. 'He has nothing to do with me. I'm just staff, Lady O'Connell's maid.'

'Come on. Where's your courage? He won't be turning down a pretty young lass like you.'

She narrowed her eyes, stared into his open face. 'Why do you want to talk to the governor?'

A strange intensity lit his eyes. 'I've found something I think might interest him.' He slipped his fingers into the pocket of his waistcoat and brought out a bright, shiny golden rock, all smooth like an overgrown grape. 'Can you keep a secret?'

'What is it?'

'I'm not certain, but I'd wager it's gold.'

'Gold?' Her heart pitter-pattered. 'Where did you get it?'

He slipped the rock back in his pocket, and brushed back the lock of dark hair falling across his forehead. 'I'm not free to say just yet. Now, where do you reckon we'll find Governor Gipps?'

She couldn't resist. 'He'll be with the horses. He rides every morning.'

'So you did know where he'd be. Will you introduce me?' He held out his hand.

For moment she hesitated, his gesture over familiar, then threw caution aside and placed her hand in his. His warm grasp tightened.

She stopped in her tracks, inhaled the masculine mix of leather and saddle soap and pulled her hand free. As tempted as she was, she couldn't, just couldn't. She bent to her basket and rearranged the flannel flowers, trying to hide the flush burning her cheeks. 'I can't.' She cleared her throat. 'I don't know your name.'

'We can fix that quick as a flash.' He took a couple of steps back, bowed low. 'Grainger Montague, at your service. Everyone calls me Montague, just Montague. And who might you be?'

She couldn't control her own smile; the very sound of his voice, with just the hint of the Irish in it, made her skin tingle. Dropping her very best curtsy, she murmured, 'Eleanor Rivers, but everyone calls me Nell. Very pleased to meet you, Mr Montague.'

He winked. 'The pleasure's all mine, Nell. Now can we go find the governor?'

What harm would it do?

As luck would have it, at that very moment Governor Gipps rounded the corner of the stables. 'Hello there, Nell. Picking flowers for Lady Gipps again I see.'

She dropped another curtsy. 'Good morning, sir. This is Mr Montague. He'd like a word if you've got a moment.'

'Only a moment, or I'll be in trouble for spending more time with the horses than the ladies. What can I do for you, Mr Montague?'

Not wanting to pry, Nell wandered off back down the carriageway to collect some of the gum blossoms she'd noticed on her way out of the house though she kept half an eye on Mr Montague and the governor. Their conversation made her skin prickle. There was lots of headshaking and arm-waving when Montague showed the golden rock to the governor, then there was more arm-waving and headshaking and the governor strode off leaving Montague kicking his feet in the dust, looking all forlorn. She couldn't stand it. He'd been so excited only a moment or two ago. Her heart went out to him.

Throwing a quick glance around to make sure no one was searching for her, she ran back along the carriageway to Montague. Before she had a chance to utter a word he launched into a tirade. 'The man's a fool. He told me he already knew about the gold, said some reverend had found some out that way and he'd tell me the same as he told him. I should keep my mouth shut, that we'd all have our throats cut if word got out and the convicts took off hunting for gold.' He pushed his hair back from his face with an irritated flick and rammed his hat back on, all the bounce gone out of him.

His misery clutched at her heart. His eyes, bleak, stared at her. 'Forget what I said. Not worth the worry.'

She dropped her basket and stepped closer, wanting only to ease his pain.

As though he could read her thoughts he offered a lopsided grin. 'I can look after myself.' He reached for her hand.

Their palms touched and a breathlessness seized her, making her knees almost buckle. His grip tightened and a lingering glow spread through her and lodged deep in her belly, and without thinking, she closed the space between them.

He gazed deep into her eyes then tilted her chin and dropped the gentlest of kisses on her lips. The birds ceased their chatter, time stood still and the world faded into insignificance.

'Oh, Nell, you're a darling, you truly are.' His lips, tender, warm and gentle, moved against hers sending a rush of emotions that she didn't understand and couldn't prevent flooding through her.

Unsteady, she stepped back from his embrace, stared deep into his blue-black eyes.

'Stay safe, Nell. Times'll change, mark my words, then I'll be back to make you mine.' And with another of his radiant smiles, as bright as the noonday sun, he let his arms fall and turned towards the town.

Montague didn't look back, not once, although she stood rooted to the spot with a smile playing on her lips until he disappeared through the trees. A sense of relief overtook her because if he had she would have chased after him. As mystifying as the encounter was, she believed him; she knew he would return.

And there in the shade beyond the trees if she half closed her eyes, she fancied she spotted Montague. Hat rammed down hard, fingers in the pockets of the waistcoat he liked to wear, even then. Nothing like the impressive silk ones Mr Scissors, the Maitland tailor, created for him though. She sighed. How she missed him. Just that one, first glance, a hint of a smile and she was lost …

So long ago. A lifetime in fact.

Then quite suddenly she was crying. Silently. Tears tracking down her cheeks and her shoulders quivering.

'Nell! Whatever is it?' Fingertips brushed the nape of her neck. Not Montague's workworn touch, though she could smell him still—that mixture of clean fresh air, hay and horses.

'Here, take my handkerchief. Why are you crying?'

Nell drew a deep breath and composed herself, took the proffered handkerchief and mopped her cheeks while Connie's worried face slipped into focus. Exhausted, she slumped back in the chair. 'I must have dropped off.' Not the truth but how to explain that being here, speaking with Mrs Alexander, had broken down the walls she'd built around the past, and taken her back in time?

'Has something happened?'

'No, no. Just musing on the past. What have you been up to? I missed you at breakfast.'

'I walked into town with Maisie, Miss Milling. Then I called into the Telegraph Office and sent Faith a telegram before walking back through the park.'

'Saying what?' she scowled. Oh! Far too harsh. The thought of Faith always raised her hackles.

'That we were staying in Parramatta for a few days, and all was well.'

Nell exhaled. 'I could do with a drink of water, better still a cup of tea.' Also a few moments to gather her scattered thoughts.

'I'm sure the kitchen won't mind if I go and get a tray. I took Miss Pettigrew some sandwiches earlier. The poor dear is quite upset. She's misplaced a small portrait of her brother, painted just before he died. I feel for her. She must be lonely; she spends most of the day in her room, waiting for Maisie to return from work. Why don't you come downstairs with me? We could sit out the front and ask her to join us; the sun is lovely.' Connie held out her hands.

After a moment Nell took them, thankful for the tangible touch of the present. All the memories had left her feeling quite disorientated.

They made their way slowly down the stairs and outside. Connie plumped cushions and fussed and fiddled and settled her in one of the wicker chairs in a patch of sun, but before she had time to go to the kitchen two high-pitched voices involved in a rapid-fire conversation punctuated by shouts of laughter drifted through the air.

'That sounds like Maisie and Taylor.' Exactly what she needed to take her mind off her mournful thoughts. Nell couldn't remember the last time she'd cried.

The two girls bounded around the corner then slowed. 'Good afternoon,' they chorused in unison. 'I hope we didn't disturb you.'

'No, not at all. Constance was just going to see if she could organise some tea. Why don't you join us?'

'I'd love to, but I must go and see to Miss Pettigrew. Would you mind if I brought her out here?' Maisie tipped her head to one side.

'Miss Pettigrew was a little upset when I took her lunch. She might like some company. She's misplaced a portrait.'

'Oh dear! Not the one of her brother. She is so very forgetful; I expect she's tucked it away somewhere.' Maisie strode across the lawn and disappeared through the front door.

'Tea for five then; I'll see what I can do.' Connie followed Maisie into the house.

'And maybe some biscuits or cake even,' Taylor called after her.

Nell patted the chair next to her. 'So, Taylor, we're left with the task of keeping each other company.'

The girl offered the widest smile and thankfully removed her ghastly bowler hat. Why in heaven's name she would want to cover such a delightful head of hair was beyond comprehension. 'Work is finished for the day?'

'Thankfully my services are not required this afternoon, so I am a free agent. I met Maisie as I was coming past the theatre.' Taylor pulled down her waistcoat and stuck her hand into her skirt; more than likely she had one of those new-fangled pockets Connie favoured. She couldn't bring herself to consider it, although she'd noticed Mrs Alexander still sported the same chatelaine she'd always worn—presumably the collection of keys had changed. 'The theatre?'

'Oh yes. Maisie and I are great fans. She does some of the costumes for the amateur group—the Parramatta Players; they make use of the Victoria Theatre when there's a lull. Maisie likes to think of herself as a sort of unofficial wardrobe mistress. And look!' Taylor held up some tickets. '*Still Waters Run Deep.* These are for the opening, this evening. Do you enjoy the theatre, Mrs Montague?'

'It's been many years since I've seen anything on the stage.' Fred's dalliance with the actress had rather put her off. 'We do have an amateur dramatic group in Maitland; Constance likes to attend. Now tell me about your job—you work for the solicitors. An unusual occupation for a young girl.'

'Not that unusual. I'm following in mother and father's footsteps. They've recently retired to our property outside Bathurst and sold the business to Messrs Ramsbottom & Son. You could say I was part of the deal. I've worked there since I left school. I'd very much like to study law at Sydney University but there doesn't seem to be much of a chance. Women have been admitted into medicine now and some other subjects, but it'll be a while until the bastions of the judicial system crumble.' She gave a dry laugh. 'In the meantime, I'm keeping my hand in and I'm unofficially studying my articles of clerkship while I manage the client correspondence, law briefs, type contracts and documents and do some drafting and conveyancing.'

Which possibly accounted for her masculine attire, but no shirt, tie and waistcoat would hide those curves.

'I do hope they open the profession to women in the near future. I don't want to be stuck behind a typewriter for the rest of my life.'

'All very commendable but ... I'm sure when you marry ...'

'Oh, I have no intention of marrying. I like my independence far too much to shackle myself to any man.'

Good grief. Hopefully her ideas wouldn't rub off on Connie. 'Constance and I are very committed to our Benevolent Society, helping deserted wives and their children find a roof ... Here she is now. She might have some questions for you. Could you bring that table closer, and I'll pour.'

By the time Taylor reorganised the furniture and Connie the tea tray, Maisie had returned, bumping Miss Pettigrew's chair across the uneven grass. 'So lovely to make the most of the warm afternoon. It'll be turning chilly soon.' Maisie adjusted the chair, sat down next to Miss Pettigrew, and pulled open her tapestry bag. It seemed the girl never kept her hands still. After much delving, poking and prodding she sighed, so loudly even Miss Pettigrew heard.

'Is something the matter, dear?'

'It's very odd, but no, I'm not sure. I can manage without it,' she mumbled.

Miss Pettigrew's teacup rattled in the saucer. 'Speak up, dear, I can't hear you.'

'I don't seem to be able to find my thimble. It doesn't matter. I probably left it upstairs in my room.' She placed a piece of material in her lap then took a cup of tea from the table. 'I have to have this finished for opening night, tonight—it's a waistcoat for

Mr Kingsley.' A hint of colour pinked her cheeks as she smoothed the brilliant chintz. 'He's playing Captain Hawksley. He's ever so good. Positively thrilling and so witty. We're terribly lucky he offered to perform. He's quite famous, travels all over the country.'

'Ah, Taylor told me you had tickets for the theatre.' The force of her brilliant idea almost rocked Nell from her chair. 'I wonder if you'd consider letting Constance use the third ticket. I'd be more than happy to cover the cost.'

Maisie threw Taylor a glance, which received a nod in reply. 'We'd be delighted. And there's no cost. I was given the tickets because of my help with the costumes.'

Nell masked a self-congratulatory grin. Someone had mentioned last evening that Mr Whitfield and Mr Humbert would be out tonight so with the three girls off at the theatre she'd have ample opportunity to wheedle some information out of Mrs Alexander.

'Thank you so much for the invitation but I'm not sure Mrs Montague can manage without me.' Connie's jaw clamped tight. Nothing to do with managing, more to do with having her life organised for her. She could be such a cantankerous child, always had been if she thought she was being dictated to.

'We'd love you to come, Connie.' Maisie broke the somewhat terse silence. 'Mr Kingsley is perfect for the role. His brooding good looks …'

Taylor cleared her throat and widened her brilliant green eyes, making it clear to everyone, but Maisie, that her secret passion was out.

'You deserve some fun, Constance. A bit of time off. I can't monopolise you every hour of the day. I won't hear another word about it.' Nell brushed her hands together. 'That's settled then. What time does the performance start?'

'Seven o'clock. I better get a move on with this.' Maisie picked up the waistcoat. 'We'll need to be there a few minutes early so I can deliver it to Mr Kingsley.' She bent her head to her sewing.

'More tea, anyone? And maybe some cake. If the performance starts at seven, you'll miss dinner,' Nell chirped, trying very hard to keep the crow of delight out of her voice.

12

Connie buttoned her coat against the chill in the air while she waited for Taylor and Maisie to appear. She'd last seen them manhandling Miss Pettigrew and her chair into the drawing room. It was fortunate the woman had a ground-floor room because the stairs would be impossible.

Quite why she'd kicked up such a fuss about Nell organising her evening for her she wasn't sure. She simply had to get to the bottom of this absurd companion charade; nevertheless, an evening with some people of her own age promised to be a wonderful tonic. Even at home, in Maitland, she seemed to spend more time with people two and three times her age except for the odd visit to the School of Arts or the theatre with Mary-Anne and Elsbeth and the poor women and children she helped, but that couldn't be described as fun. It was worthwhile and she derived an enormous amount of pleasure knowing she'd gone some small way to helping but sometimes she longed for a true friendship with someone her own age.

With a flurry of chatter, Taylor and Maisie arrived. Maisie looked nothing like the little seamstress who used Madame Gautier's back door, more as though she'd stepped from a window display, with her plumed and beribboned hat which would undoubtedly incur the wrath of the poor unfortunate person seated behind her. Connie brushed down her skirt, feeling very much like the dowdy country cousin, although Taylor's only concession to the evening was to change her white lawn workday blouse for one of black and white stripes and a rather dapper hat perched atop her corn-coloured curls.

'I mustn't be late; I promised Mr Kingsley he'd have his waistcoat well before the curtain went up.' Maisie set off at a smart clip. 'It should only take us about twenty minutes. The moon's rising and we'll be walking towards the busy end of George Street. They've been promising gas lights in the streets and the park for donkey's years, but nothing's come of it.'

Thankful for her sturdy shoes, Connie scurried after the two girls. When they finally crossed Church Street Maisie led them through a warren of back alleys—Nell would have a conniption if she told her. 'Another few minutes and we'll be there. Come on.'

The theatre lights blazed and a surprising number of people milled around on the footpath, even spilt into the road. A huge poster proclaimed the title of the play, *Still Waters Run Deep*, and sported a rather dashing figure in a dark tailored frockcoat, well-fitted trousers, long polished boots and black top hat standing in front of a beautiful young woman in a low-cut ruffled evening dress. 'That's Orlando Kingsley. He's playing Captain Hawksley.' Maisie pointed to the poster, one hand to her breast clutching the waistcoat she had to deliver. 'He doesn't usually work with amateur dramatic groups. Here are your tickets. I'll go around to the stage door, deliver this and meet you in there.'

'And hopefully get to flutter her eyelashes at our dashing lead actor, who must have come down in the world if he's performing with an amateur dramatic society,' Taylor added with a smile at Maisie's retreating back. 'I've already heard all about his physical charms and brooding nature. Come on, let's go and find our seats.'

They eased their way through the crowded foyer and into the auditorium. Far more impressive than Connie had imagined. The flickering gas lights and the smell of ladies' perfume and something Taylor assured her was greasepaint added to the sense of excitement. Their seats in the front row seemed very impressive until Connie sat down and realised she'd have to lift her chin almost to the ornate plaster ceiling if she was going to see any more than the actors' feet.

'Have you been to many plays?' Connie asked Taylor once they'd settled.

'We came to one a couple of months ago, but I've been enormously busy at work so there hasn't really been the opportunity. Maisie's the authority; she helps with the costumes and seems to know anyone who is anyone. I expect it's because of her job. Madame Gautier is apparently the most favoured dressmaker in town, and you know how women can gossip when they get together.'

Connie didn't reply. She didn't really know; this whole excursion made her feel more and more like a poor relation. Mrs Beattie always came to the house in Maitland to take her measurements and for fittings. She glanced around at the audience filing into their seats and the plush red velvet curtains with a sense of trepidation until Maisie slipped into the seat next to her. 'Did Mr Kingsley like his waistcoat?'

Maisie shrugged; her mouth turned down at the corners. 'I didn't see him. The bossy old floozie in charge backstage snatched it from my hand and chased me out.' A grin broke out on her pretty face. 'But you'll never guess who I did bump into.'

'No idea.'

'Mr Whitfield, dressed up to the nines in a flamboyant waistcoat that would rival Mr Kingsley's, escorting the leading lady to her dressing room. Wily old fool. No wonder he was out for dinner tonight.'

The lights dimmed and a wave of applause rocked the theatre as the plush velvet curtains drew back to reveal a drawing room, various doors leading who knew where, and along the back of the stage a glass wall with French doors meant to represent a conservatory judging by the number of potted plants and ferns, and beyond a garden—a painted backdrop but realistic nonetheless. The Parramatta Players had gone to a lot of trouble for their famous visiting actor—streaks ahead of the plays she'd seen in Maitland.

One by one the five actors made their way on stage and took their positions, some lounging in easy chairs collected around the fireplace, another at the small writing table and a couple just standing chatting.

Connie lurched and uttered a muffled squawk as Taylor's elbow dug into her ribs. 'It's just like the guesthouse, all this banal conversation and toing-and-froing. Do you think there'll be any action? Where's the delectable Captain Hawksley?'

'Be quiet!' Maisie hissed. 'He'll be on any moment.'

And true to Maisie's word the much-admired Orlando Kingsley stepped onto the stage dressed in the most appalling pair of tweed trousers and a very drab waistcoat, nothing like the glamorous affair Maisie had spent so much time on—a sort of buff-coloured nothingness. A woman accompanied him, her nose buried in a single red rose and her eyelashes fluttering like weathervanes as she shot coy glances at her companion. Maisie gave an audible sigh.

'Why isn't he wearing the waistcoat you made?' Connie whispered.

'Ssssh! He will, later, in the third act. Just be quiet; you'll upset everyone.'

Connie subsided into her seat and gradually, very gradually, sank into the play. The world around her disappeared and nothing was real but for the dastardly Captain Hawksley and his obscene blackmail demands. Secrets and hidden truths, dual identities and deceptions that rippled with a sense of foreboding and tension, as the play unfolded before her.

13

Nell ran a comb through her hair. In the long distant past, it skimmed her waistline, a mass of dark, almost black waves, her pride and joy. Montague used to wrap it around his hands, draw her into his lap and cover her face with kisses.

She snorted at her reflection; no chance of that happening these days. Montague lived only in her memories, and now, nine years later, he wouldn't recognise the figure she presented. She wrangled her white locks into a chignon, shoved a disordered hank behind her ear then stabbed a series of pins into the knot to hold everything in place. At least her hair had remained thick, and her scalp didn't peep through. Vanity might well be a sin, but she couldn't bear to wear a wig.

With the three girls out at the theatre, Mr Humbert and Mr Whitfield elsewhere and Miss Pettigrew requiring an early night it was the perfect opportunity to have a chat with Mrs Alexander. It had been all smiles and false bonhomie this morning when they'd passed on the stairs but if she was going to solve her dilemma, she had to ask some pertinent questions. Questions better answered away from flapping ears and prying eyes.

She almost skipped down the stairs in her eagerness, took a quick glance up at the grandfather clock—hands just a moment before seven—and knocked on Mrs Alexander's door.

'Come.'

Nell pushed open the door. Mrs Alexander sat on the sofa, a large scrapbook in her lap and a slightly disgruntled expression on her face. A look that took Nell right back. In the past Mrs Alexander had terrified her. Ten years her senior and light years ahead of her in status. The maid-of-all-work and the housekeeper. Was there a wider chasm below stairs?

Nell plastered a smile on her face and pushed back her shoulders. 'I take it dinner isn't being served in the dining room tonight.' Nell tried for an imperious tone.

Mrs Alexander closed her scrapbook with a snap and stood. 'I've given Mrs Trotter and the girls the evening off. You'll find soup and scones in the kitchen. I'm sure you haven't forgotten how to serve yourself.'

'Thank you.' The last thing Nell wanted to do was to eat in her room. She couldn't let the moment slip through her fingers. 'Would you like me to bring you something?'

A flurry of emotions flitted across Mrs Alexander's face and then the fight leached out of her and she sat back down on the sofa. 'Thank you. A little soup.'

'Back in the twitch of a lamb's tail.' Nell bustled off before the laugh she'd manage to trap in her throat exploded. Unknowingly she'd reverted not only to the sort of language she'd used back in the days before Maitland, but she'd felt a surge of long-forgotten youthful anticipation.

She made her way down the corridor to the servants' quarters. The flames from the kitchen fire flickered, throwing quite enough light to see the two trays laid on the kitchen table and a pot on the damped-down stove. She lifted the lid and inhaled the clear chicken soup, a scattering of finely chopped vegetables floating enticingly on the surface. With long-forgotten skill, Nell ladled the soup into two bowls and draped the linen napkins over the top to keep them warm then rearranged everything onto one tray, hitched the corner of her skirt into her waistband to ensure she didn't catch her toes and she pranced, yes, pranced, back down the corridor with a grin from ear to ear. If only Montague could see her.

With any luck Mrs Alexander would feel obliged to invite her to join her. Her door remained ajar, so she nudged it open with her hip and made her way inside. In her absence Mrs Alexander had drawn up two chairs and cleared a pile of books from the narrow table that rested against the wall. This was going to be much easier than she'd expected.

'I thought you might like to eat here, with me.' Mrs Alexander stretched out her hand and indicated to the table.

'Thank you. The tray was prepared and the soup smells delicious.' Nell unpacked the bowls, moved a pair of silver candlesticks aside, and set the small table.

'Please, sit down and accept my apologies for asking you to arrange our supper. It is no longer my place. I expect you have servants of your own these days, and of course your companion ...' Her eyebrows rose just a fraction and she let the silence hover for a moment.

Refusing to be drawn into a conversation about Connie, Nell offered a benign smile.

'I've been very much looking forward to an opportunity for us to have a quiet chat. We have so much to catch up on. Forty years gone in a flash. There are few people who remember those days.'

Nell clasped her hands tightly in her lap, unable to believe her good fortune.

'But first let's eat. I can guarantee you Mrs Trotter's chicken soup will banish any ills of the body or the mind.'

Nell picked up the soup spoon and ladled a small amount into her mouth. To the best of her knowledge she had no ailments of the body; the mind was another matter. Hers had been in turmoil since she'd opened that abominable letter, but she had no intention of mentioning it to Mrs Alexander or anyone for that matter. The problem was hers, and hers alone; nevertheless this woman sitting next to her could well hold the key. The question was how to approach the topic and carry off the plan without besmirching the Montague name, or worse see the repercussions taint Connie's future.

They ate in what seemed on the surface to be a companionable silence and when they'd finished the soup and cleaned the last crumbs from the plates Mrs Alexander stood. 'Why don't you go and sit in front of the fire? I don't usually light it this early in the year but there is quite a chill in the air tonight and I fancied the comfort.' She shooed Nell away and stacked the plates onto the tray before joining her on the sofa.

'Now what brings you to my little guesthouse, Nell? You don't mind if I call you Nell, do you? I find it difficult to think of you in any other light.'

Nell inclined her head in agreement. Anything to ease her path. 'As I told Constance when she asked the same question, I found I had reached a time in my life where it was important to look up old friends. None of us are getting any younger and since I lost both my husband and my son, I've felt opportunities slipping through my fingers like quicksilver.'

Mrs Alexander's face fell. 'Your husband and your son? I am so very sorry. I cannot believe … I remember Montague as such a vibrant young man on that day you left.'

Nell smothered a snort and formed a frail smile. 'Indeed, he was.' A little too vibrant on occasion but the love of her life, nonetheless. More than friends, more than lovers, as essential to each other as light or air, neither complete without the presence of the other. 'We lost him to a very unpleasant case of pneumonia brought on by a dose of influenza.' Something she would never come to terms with. Younger than she was now. Sixty-two was simply too young for a man like Montague to die. If only she hadn't brought the wretched chill home from the hospital. She'd suffered no more than what passed as an unpleasant cold, but it had gone straight to Montague's chest, never as strong as it should have been after his time in California.

'I'm so sorry. And your son?'

'Two years ago. A riding accident.' No need to explain the ins and outs or the repercussions. 'However, I have Constance, and ...' Nell bit her tongue. She must control herself. Perhaps it would be easier to admit to Connie's heritage.

Mrs Alexander shot her a sideways glance and added, 'A delightful young girl.'

A change of subject might steer the conversation in a more acceptable direction. 'As are Taylor and Maisie. It must be wonderful to have a house full of young people.'

'Hardly *full* of young people. There are stories I could tell but currently we have a delightful mix of guests.'

Nell lifted her head and offered a companionable glance as the conversation veered in the direction she'd hoped. 'How did you manage to secure such a responsible position?'

'Contacts. Nothing more than contacts. Being in the right place at the right time. After you left, I stayed on at the new Government House.'

Nell clamped her lips tight and smiled. Left wasn't the word she would have chosen. Bundled out under a cloud was more in keeping with the facts but obviously Mrs Alexander had no intention of discussing the incident.

'After Lady FitzRoy's tragic accident, the house here was boarded up. It wasn't for another ten years or so that the government decided to lease out the property to a man by the name of Andrew Blake and then when the lease came up again Governor Denison suggested that I might like to take over here and run a guesthouse. My days in Sydney were nearing an end. The entertaining was becoming more than I could manage. No one really knew what to do with all the furniture and knick-knacks the various governors and their wives had left behind, so we brought them down here. It's become something of a repository for the past.' She gestured to a row of shelves lining the wall on either side of the fireplace—leather-bound books, silver trinkets and a pair of miniatures, the Macquaries unless she was mistaken. 'They needed someone who could be trusted.' Mrs Alexander lifted her chin and gave an egotistical smile. 'And here I am. The very person for the job. I see it as both a responsibility and a blessing.'

Nell could hardly control her response. *A repository for the past!* Exactly what she wanted to hear. A repository that included a trunk once belonging to Governor Bligh she hoped. 'There are some wonderful pieces in the house. Glorious paintings and the silverware and dinner service, not to mention that beautiful whimsical jewellery box in my room ...'

'Ah, a gift from Macquarie to his beloved wife. I can't imagine how she could have left it behind. I just wish that I could encourage the government to invest some money in the upkeep of the house. I'm sure you have noticed the odd patch of damp and much of the wallpaper is faded and fragile.'

'I would very much enjoy a tour; so much must have changed since I visited with Lady O'Connell. If you could spare the time.' Nell lay down her trump card, fingers crossed beneath the folds of her skirt.

'I'm sure it could be arranged. Let me go over my commitments for the next few days and let you know.'

'I have so enjoyed our little chat. Goodnight.' Nell gritted her teeth and tried to rein in the bounce in her step as she made her way back to her room. So, Mrs Alexander had come straight from Government House to Parramatta, and she was responsible for the possessions past governors had left behind. Her gamble had paid off and she knew exactly what she was looking for. She could remember it as though it was yesterday.

She'd landed the job of clearing out all the old trunks that had been brought from the original Government House in Sydney before it was demolished. It was Lady O'Connell's suggestion that she might be the one for the job. Governor and Lady Gipps had moved lock, stock and barrel into the new building down near the harbour, a veritable palace with its gargoyles and turrets, like something out of a fairytale—it even had water closets. Such luxury after the windy, white ant–ridden building that had served all the governors since Arthur Phillip.

She hadn't been over excited about the idea of the old trunks— rats and mice would undoubtedly have nested in them; they managed to squeeze their way in everywhere—but she'd asked a couple of the men who tended Governor Gipps's two camels that grazed in the Domain and in exchange for a few bottles of ale talked them into bringing the trunks downstairs. Somehow rodents seemed much less intimidating in bright daylight.

She'd emptied every trunk and spread the contents out all over the main dining room. Much to her amazement they contained mostly clothes—Lady O'Connell's clothes; clothes that her own mother, Alice, had helped make. No, not so much make but alter when she'd worked as a seamstress. It wasn't until she'd pulled out a flimsy dress, a silvery sheer blue confection, and a pair of matching pantaloons she'd remembered the story Mam had told about the ruckus Lady O'Connell—Mary, daughter of Governor Bligh, as she had been then—caused.

Mam had rubbed her hands together with glee and they'd settled down at the table in the little house down near the warehouses. 'She came with her da to the colony as first lady because his wife, her mam, was too busy with the other children. Mrs Bligh was set on Mary making her da proud so she'd be shipping clothes and fashion papers to her. In return Mary would send her all sorts of curious odds and ends, interesting shells and plants and such. That was all before her da landed himself in a load of trouble with Mr Macarthur and the other toffs.' Mam shook her head. 'Mary was deadset on getting all eyes on her, making a name for herself. Maybe if she'd worn one of the other grand dresses her mam sent instead of the see-through piece with the pantaloons, Governor Bligh might've held onto his job ...'

And there she was sorting and packing, packing and sorting, wondering what Lady O'Connell would do with the clothes or if they'd just moulder away in another attic when a deep voice had called her name, and the flesh on her arms danced.

She hadn't heard hide nor hair of him for two long years, almost given up hope, truth be told, and there he stood, right in front of her, in the middle of the dining room at Government House. He had such a look in his eyes her stomach had turned itself inside out, just as it had the first time they'd met in Parramatta when he'd had that argument with Governor Gipps.

She didn't blink, didn't turn away, just stood spellbound, the heat inside her building. Before she could utter a sound Montague pulled her into his arms. His lips touched hers and a momentary panic swarmed through her as her lips parted and she closed her eyes, leaning into his kiss. She didn't want him to stop, ever. The scent of him made her mind spin until there was nothing but his warm lips and the wonderful sensation of being in his arms, close to him. He took a single step back and smiled down at her.

'What?' Her breath came in shallow gasps.

'You.' Then his arms tightened around her again and his lips traced a path down her neck. 'You are beautiful.' His voice reverberated deep inside her. 'I've got something to tell you, and something to ask.' The serious note in his voice made her skin prickle.

'I'm off to California. There's gold to be had, legal gold, and I'll be learnin' all about the mining of it.'

Her heart plunged and she sank onto the nearest chair, her hand raised to her chest to soothe her erratic heartbeat. It wasn't as though they had any kind of real understanding; she'd always known that. It wasn't as though she hadn't looked at another man since she'd first met Montague but none of them made her heart beat faster and her blood tingle. She'd even consulted the fortune teller who'd come to town one Christmas: she'd said a handsome man with laughing eyes would arrive from over the seas and said that patience was the only path. She'd always thought she might be right. Going away again wasn't what she wanted to hear.

His gaze roamed her face as though waiting for her to respond. What did he want her to say? That she didn't want him to go, that she'd miss him more than the very air she breathed?

He'd looked nervous for a second. 'Will you still be waiting for me?' And with that he'd reached into his pocket and then offered his open palm. The light scattered this way and that, reflecting off the beaten gold like tiny sunbeams.

'Yes,' she'd said, just 'yes' despite her fears, because she'd always known it would be, just not when or how. He'd slipped the ring into the palm of her hand, closed her fingers around it and pulled her into another kiss. It was then she'd known she'd wait forever if it took that long because there'd never be anyone else.

'There's something more, Nell,' he'd whispered, his breath warm against her cheek. 'A token to prove I'm a man of my word.' He handed her a worn leather pouch. She'd pulled at the drawstring, but he'd stopped her hand. 'It's gold, same as the ring. Some of the gold I found while I was out Bathurst way—the stuff the governor didn't want talked about. It's a down payment on the future. Keep it safe, and when I'm back, we'll build our dreams. Can we manage that?' As if she would have said no.

14

'All is not gold that glitters.'

The play on Shakespeare's words brought the show to a close, the curtains drew together, the actors and actresses frozen in their final stance and the audience erupted.

The skin on the palms of Connie's hands stung. She couldn't remember ever clapping so hard. Finally, the curtains reopened to reveal the cast, hands joined, faces beaming as they took their bow and acknowledged the applause.

After the third encore Maisie slumped back in her seat and the lights came up to reveal the tears on her cheeks and a smile of beatific proportions on her flushed face. 'Oh, that man is wonderful,' she whispered, 'just wonderful.'

Mr Orlando Kingsley had certainly performed his role with a great deal of flair, but Connie wasn't certain Maisie's ardour was quite merited; stage makeup and the right clothes could change anyone. The amused grin on Taylor's face mirrored her own thoughts. She massaged her neck and shoulders. Three acts with her head tipped to the stage had played havoc with her muscles.

Maisie suffered no such limitations and leapt up. 'Come along.

Hurry up. We need to get around to the stage door. The backstage floozie-manager promised an introduction to Mr Kingsley. I want to ask for his autograph. I have my new album ready.' She tapped her tapestry sewing bag.

They stepped out into the aisle but since their seats were in the very front row, a crowd of people swarmed in front of them heading for the exit. Maisie stopped in her tracks. 'There is another way out. Follow me.'

If they left the queue, they'd lose their place, and it might take even longer. Before Connie had a chance to respond, Maisie had spun around, ducking and weaving back through the line of people behind them towards the stage.

'Come on.' Taylor grabbed Connie's arm. 'We'll never find our way backstage without Maisie.'

By the time they'd reached the curtain Maisie had clambered up from the orchestra pit, ducked underneath the heavy velvet drapes and disappeared.

Darkness and the overwhelming smell of greasepaint and camphor enveloped Connie and Taylor as the curtain fell behind them.

'Over here. This way.' Maisie's disembodied voice floated across the stage.

'How can she possibly know the way?' Connie hung tightly onto Taylor's arm while her eyes slowly adjusted to the gloom.

'She's been here a lot—delivering costumes, taking measurements. Quick, we mustn't lose track of her.' Taylor dragged Connie towards the frail beam of light in the wings. The hum of voices grew but no sign of Maisie amongst the crush of actors and actresses hovering around the dressing rooms in varying states of excitement.

'We've lost her. Best thing we can do is get out through the stage door and wait there. We don't want to miss her. She might head back to the guesthouse thinking we've already left. She shouldn't walk home alone in the dark.'

'Maybe she's tracked down the elusive Mr Kingsley and is, as we speak, sipping champagne in his dressing room.' Taylor dug Connie in the ribs. 'Don't worry, Maisie knows how to look after herself. No one grows up in an orphanage without learning a few self-preservation skills.'

'An orphanage? I didn't know. How ...'

'Not my story to tell. You can ask her some other time. It's no secret. Come on, I think the door is over there. Lots of people are heading in that direction.'

In a matter of minutes Taylor and Connie stood in a rather smelly alleyway, stamping their feet against the cold and scanning everybody who stepped through the stage door.

'Look!' Connie hissed into Taylor's ear. 'There's Mr Whitfield; Maisie said she saw him.' She darted to the door and came to a halt in front of Mr Whitfield and a woman wearing a scarlet coat and a garish hat that resembled a dead pheasant. 'Mr Whitfield.' Her voice snatched in her throat. 'Good evening.'

Mr Whitfield raised his topper with a flourish and then tucked the woman's hand into the crook of his arm. 'Good evening, ladies.'

'I wondered if you had seen Miss Milling. We lost her in the crowd and—'

'I can't help you. Come along.' He as good as dragged the pheasant-hatted woman around the corner.

'Well, pardon me. You better not toady up to my grandmother again, not if I have my say.'

'What was that about your grandmother?'

Connie stared up into Taylor's grinning face and slapped her hand across her mouth.

'Your secret is safe with me. I didn't imagine for a moment you were Mrs Montague's companion, but I must admit I'm curious to know why she's telling everyone you are.'

'Look, there she is.' Connie scooted back to the stage door and threw her arms around Maisie, thrilled to have found her but also to be saved from a conversation she really didn't want to have. She'd talk to Nell in the morning and demand that they tell the truth about the companion rubbish, or else insist on a very, very good reason why not.

'There you are. Did you get Mr Kingsley's autograph?' Taylor slid her arm through Maisie's and pulled her close. Tethered might have been nearer to the truth. 'Tell us on the way home. It's late and we can't risk walking through the back streets; we're going to have to go the long way.'

'So, your autograph?' Connie asked. 'What did he write? Something romantic?'

'Nothing. I didn't even get to see him. That odious backstage madam was standing guard outside his door and then when someone called her, I thought I'd got it made. I knocked on the door, slipped inside and ...'

'And?' Taylor and Connie shrieked in unison.

'And he wasn't there. The room was empty. I don't understand. Why bother guarding the door when there's no one inside?' Maisie kicked at a stone and slouched her shoulders. 'It's left a very nasty taste in my mouth.'

Taylor's eyes danced and Connie snuffled a hoot of laughter behind a make-believe cough.

They linked arms. 'Never mind. I'm sure you'll have another chance to get Mr Kingsley's autograph. The play doesn't end until Monday.'

'Oh, that's a good idea. Would you come with me? We'll never get tickets for the last night, but we could wait outside.'

'Of course we will. Won't we, Taylor?'

'We will.'

15

All in all, Nell was more than satisfied with the evening she'd spent with Mrs Alexander. And she intended to achieve the tour of the house promised last night.

She sat down at the small desk by the window and pulled out her notebook to make a plan of the house. How she wished she could let Connie in on her secret, but the less Connie knew the better. Connie was the daughter she'd never had ... it was just like her and Mam, the two of them against the world in those long years after the O'Connells left for Ceylon. It was vital that she was in no way involved. Who knew what might happen once they returned to Maitland?

It didn't take more than a few moments to sketch a quick floorplan of the house, partly from memory, but it did make her realise that there were sections which she had no idea about. A little spot of breakfast and then a walk in the grounds, which would disguise her interest in the building. The number of windows on both the upper floor and lower floors would ensure she missed nothing and the outbuildings—they could well be important. Back in the day she'd slept in the outbuilding, in a dormitory with the other serving girls, but it seemed that the building had fallen into disrepair.

Sadly, when she arrived in the dining room Mr Whitfield was there, the newspaper spread on the table and a half-drunk cup of tea in front of him. She rather hoped this late in the morning he would have gone for the day, and she could have taken a closer look around the room. Gone? Gone where? What did he do with himself all day? Mr Humbert came and went at all hours but that was understandable given his business. Mr Whitfield, however, seemed to disappear after breakfast and hadn't been at dinner since the first night she'd arrived. And where was Connie? Perhaps she was with Taylor and Maisie. Did they work on a Saturday? She had absolutely no idea. Poor old Miss Pettigrew would be back in her room for the day. She'd call in for a chat later—the perfect excuse to check out another part of the house.

'Good morning, Mr Whitfield,' she trilled. 'Another beautiful autumn day, is it not?'

Whitfield half raised himself from his seat and grunted a greeting before returning to his paper, none of his flamboyant behaviour of the first evening evident. She helped herself to some toast and tea—no marmalade on offer, unfortunately—before sitting down at the far end of the table, her eyes roaming the paintings on the wall and a rather overblown bronze statue of the Duke of Wellington. The fine sideboard sported two large three-pronged silver candelabrums and the ostentatious fireplace and mantle dominated the room. She pulled out her pince-nez—unless she was very much mistaken, it was only painted to resemble marble. Not the real thing.

By the time she was onto her second cup of tea Whitfield had excused himself and there was still no sign of Connie. Either she'd breakfasted early, or she was making up for her late night. She hadn't heard the girls return from the theatre, but it had to have been well after ten o'clock because she'd lain awake for at least an hour after she'd left Mrs Alexander.

Resisting the temptation to clear the remnants of her breakfast—it simply wouldn't be right to do Mrs Trotter or her girls out of a job—she picked up her notebook, put on her hat and gloves and made her way outside. There was a definite autumnal chill, but the sky was the brightest blue, and the sun would soon warm the air.

She stepped down from the portico onto the gravel carriageway and walked backward across the grass until she could see the full extent of the building—remarkable to think that it had been standing longer than she had. Mind you, there had been some additions and alterations. The central part of the house, above the portico built by the colonial architect Francis Greenway, was totally symmetrical, incorporating the drawing and dining rooms, hallway, staircase, and the three downstairs bedrooms and above it another six bedrooms. She carefully counted the windows to ensure they matched—one extra window upstairs above the portico, Connie's room, and the front bedroom on the right which Mrs Alexander had insisted was kept for unexpected guests. Nell chewed the end of her pencil. Perhaps it was used for storage; it might need exploring.

Two single storey wings ran either side of the centre of the house, the southern colonnade containing Mrs Alexander's rooms and the northern the kitchen and servants' quarters.

She made her way around the side of the house, past the kitchen where the fallen leaves of the wisteria lay like a yellow carpet. Supposing, just supposing the trunks had been stored in the stables. It was as good a place as any. Ridiculous. She was chasing nothing but a wild goose around and around. Whatever had possessed her to imagine she could find Lady O'Connell's possessions in a house of this size. She couldn't ask just out of the blue. *By the way, Mrs Alexander, have you any idea where Governor Bligh's trunk ended up because there's something important I need to find. I left it behind the day you accused me of stealing* … She shook her head; that absolutely wasn't going to happen and besides she'd left it too late. If she was going to take that route then she should have asked the moment she arrived.

She retraced her steps, balanced her notebook on the sundial and marked all the windows then straightened up and turned towards the river. It really was the most excellent placement for a house, on the small rise overlooking the town.

'Nell! Nell! What are you doing out here? I've been looking everywhere for you. Mrs Alexander wants to talk to you.'

Nell twirled around, heart hitching at the picture Connie made running across the grass, one hand holding her straw boater in place, her wide generous mouth curved in a smile and her skirt and blouse a perfect match for the sky. Worthy of a painting. She was so precious, so very, very, precious. She tucked her notebook into her waistband, hopefully out of sight; she didn't want to have to explain her drawing. 'Good morning, sweetheart. I missed you at breakfast.'

'I'm sorry. I had some earlier with Taylor and Maisie, and then went upstairs to change and when I came down, I couldn't find you.'

'Did you enjoy your trip to the theatre?'

'I did. Maisie and Taylor are excellent company.'

'Now what's all this about Mrs Alexander?'

'She's looking everywhere for you. She can't find Mrs Macquarie's jewellery box. Apparently, it was in your room and now it's gone. I said I'd find you and we'd have a look for it. I thought maybe you had moved it for some reason or another.'

'No. I most certainly haven't.' Too worried she might drop it and damage it. Nell gave a sigh. The remainder of her walk would have to wait. 'Come along. Let's go and see what all the fuss is about. And you can tell me more about your trip to the theatre.'

'We had a wonderful time. The play was excellent, and the scenery and the costumes ... they were amazing. Maisie has a definite talent and the waistcoat she worked on for Mr Kingsley looked divine; he wore it during the third act. I thought I might ask her to make me an outfit—something like the costume Taylor wears. She looks so very up-to-the-minute.'

Nell's lips pinched together. Connie would be the laughing-stock of Maitland if she wore one of those drab skirts, matching waistcoats, and masculine shirt and tie. 'Taylor is a working girl. She spends her day in an office dealing with the public—most likely dubious public, if she works for a firm of solicitors. It's not the image you want to portray. You have some lovely clothes and if you're in need of any more I'm happy for you to talk to Maisie. Clothes are meant to enhance a woman's femininity not detract from it. Now come along and let's see about this jewellery box.' She took Connie's hand and slipped it into the crook of her arm and together they crossed the lawn and made their way into the house to find Mrs Alexander.

16

Connie had very much hoped she'd have the chance to talk to Nell about the ridiculous companion charade but now was not the time. A very changed Mrs Alexander stood, face ravaged and a crumpled handkerchief screwed in her hand in the middle of Nell's room turning this way and that, emitting a low moaning sound.

Nell crossed the floor in a couple of paces, patted the bed and eased Mrs Alexander down. 'How can we help?'

'What have you done with it?' Mrs Alexander shrugged Nell off, eyes flashing. 'It's impossible to trust you for a moment. It's always been the same. Your morals are …'

Nell reared back, her eyes blazing. 'You have no right to accuse me of taking the infamous box. I haven't touched it. When I went downstairs to breakfast it was on the chest over there.' She waved her hand in the direction of the cabinet. 'I locked the door before I left and you're the only other person I know who has a key.'

A nasty prickle worked its way up Connie's neck. She didn't have a key to Nell's room, but the door between their two rooms didn't lock. 'I'm sure there's been some mistake.'

'And what about the silver candlesticks from my sitting room?'

Mrs Alexander's steely gaze came to rest on Connie and to her horror her cheeks flushed. 'They were on the table last night, and this morning they have gone. This only began when the pair of you arrived.'

Connie opened her mouth to counteract Mrs Alexander's accusations, caught sight of Nell's raised eyebrows and swallowed her words.

'First Miss Pettigrew's portrait of her poor departed brother. How low is that? The only thing she has to remind her of him. And Maisie's silver thimble.' Mrs Alexander stabbed two fingers in the air. 'The first edition calfskin-bound copy of *Pride and Prejudice* is also missing from my shelves, the silver candlesticks and now this …' she gave a dramatic pause '… Mrs Macquarie's jewellery box. It's priceless.'

Connie doubted that very strongly. Pretty but not priceless; the inlaid ivory was cleverly constructed but far from a masterpiece. Nevertheless, it was strange that these objects had gone missing all of a sudden but what was even stranger was Mrs Alexander's remark about Nell. She would have counted Nell as one of the most trustworthy people she knew. Why would Mrs Alexander think differently? 'Why don't I have a good look around and see if I can find the box? Could one of the girls have moved it when they were cleaning—'

'I expect everything to be returned.' With that, Mrs Alexander flounced from the room.

Nell crumpled onto the bed. 'I haven't touched it. What would I want with it? She has no right to accuse me. The candlesticks were on the table when we had dinner last night and I haven't set foot in Miss Pettigrew's room.'

Connie was at a loss. 'Why don't you have a rest? I'll have a quick look around, then I'll ask in the kitchen, see what I can find out. I'm sure there's a simple explanation.'

She scanned the room for anything unusual. The girls had obviously cleaned because the water jug had been refilled and the bed made. She couldn't imagine they would risk their jobs stealing anything as obvious as the jewellery box, and then Maisie's lost thimble and Miss Pettigrew's portrait popped back into her mind. She tiptoed away from the bed and opened the cupboard doors and ran her hand beneath Nell's neatly folded clothes and found nothing. Nell's perfume bottle and her fountain pen lay on the top of the dressing table and when she eased the drawers open, she found them empty.

Trying to make sense of the puzzle, she slipped through the connecting door into her room. Her empty bag sat on the floor where she'd left it; her shawl and nightgown thrown on the chair yielded nothing. She ran her hand fruitlessly over the counterpane on the bed and then dropped onto her hands and knees and checked under the bed. Mrs Alexander was right about one thing—the jewellery box had gone. And then Connie stopped still. What had made Mrs Alexander come looking for it in the first place? Connie quietly closed the door to Nell's room and wandered downstairs in search of Miss Pettigrew. She'd been reading something when she'd taken her luncheon into her yesterday, but she hadn't paid much attention. Mrs Alexander claimed one of the books was missing from her shelves. Was it possible Miss Pettigrew had borrowed it?

Rather than simply barge into Miss Pettigrew's room she made her way into the kitchen. If she took Miss Pettigrew her luncheon tray, she'd have the perfect excuse to have a look for the book. She'd also be able to speak to Mrs Trotter and see if she could find out about the other missing items although she'd have to be very careful not to sound accusatory.

A mouth-watering smell assailed her as she walked into the kitchen. Pastry, and unless she was very much mistaken some sort of meat, sausages even. Mrs Trotter stood over a sizzling hot baking tray sliding tiny pillows of pastry onto a serving platter. 'You timed your arrival well. Followed your nose, did you?'

Connie laughed. 'The smell is absolutely delicious.'

'My speciality—sausage rolls. Don't make them for the guests. Mrs Alexander says they're common, but me and the girls are not above a bit of market food. What about you?'

'I don't think I've ever tried a sausage roll.' Connie licked her lips and tried not to look too enthusiastic. 'Mrs Montague is having a rest and I thought I could take Miss Pettigrew her tray or is it too early?'

'I'd say your timing is just about perfect. Why don't you sit down with us, have a snack then take the tray? It's a while off midday.' Mrs Trotter jerked her head towards one of the chairs.

Connie took a seat, as did June and May. What a perfect opportunity to ask a few questions. Carefully though. She had to be careful.

'Watch it, they're hot, and you'll want a bit of my tomato relish.' Mrs Trotter dropped two of the pastry rolls onto a plate and pushed it across the table. 'You pass the relish, June, and stop licking your lips. Yours is next. Mrs Alexander don't know what she's missing out on with her hoity-toity menus. Still, her loss. Said she didn't want nothing today.'

It didn't sound as though there was a lot of love lost between Mrs Trotter and Mrs Alexander. Connie swallowed a delicious morsel and scooped some more relish onto her plate. 'Mrs Alexander is a bit worried. Several things seem to have gone missing, amongst them the inlaid ivory jewellery box from Mrs Montague's room.'

Three faces, eyes wide, lifted to hers in unison and May and June clapped their hands over their mouths. They really were like bookends with their shy, gap-toothed smiles. Connie wasn't even sure who was June and who was May; they had to be sisters—twins even. 'We didn't take nothing,' one said. 'Didn't see the jewellery box,' the other added.

'Tut-tut. No one's accusing you. Mrs Alexander hasn't mentioned anything missing, and you know how she's always checking that inventory of hers.'

It was very strange Mrs Alexander hadn't spoken to Mrs Trotter. The first people she'd ask would be the two girls who did the cleaning. Connie took another mouthful of the sausage roll to stop herself from interrupting. She'd learnt that trick after hours of talking to the deserted women in Maitland. Often, they'd answer all her questions without her having to ask them, given time.

'Calm yourselves. I expect it's just been misplaced as Miss Constance said. Think hard. Was the jewellery box in Mrs Montague's room when you tidied up?' Mrs Trotter popped the final morsel of her sausage roll into her mouth.

The two girls lifted their shoulders in unison. 'Didn't notice,' they chorused. 'And we haven't dusted since day afore yesterday.'

'Very well. It's time to get on. You happy to take Miss Pettigrew's tray, Miss Constance?'

'More than happy.' In truth she'd walk barefoot over hot coals if it meant more sausage rolls. 'The sausage rolls were delicious.' Maybe she could get the recipe and take it back to Mrs Orchard. Say they were a delicacy that was all the rage in Parramatta, or some such thing.

Tray in hand, Connie made her way along the hallway towards Miss Pettigrew's room.

She balanced the tray carefully and knocked on the door. As before, she received no reply, so she knocked once more and nudged the door open with her hip. 'I've brought your luncheon, Miss Pettigrew,' she trilled, hoping she wouldn't take the poor woman by surprise and frighten her.

Miss Pettigrew snapped the book on her lap closed. 'How delightful.' She breathed in, eyes closed. 'Sausage rolls, my favourite.' The woman might be hard of hearing but there was nothing wrong with her sense of smell. 'Have you got the tomato relish?'

'I have indeed.' Connie placed the tray on the table. 'Would you like to sit here, or shall I bring the plate to you?'

'I'll come over there.' With a dexterity Connie hadn't given her credit for Miss Pettigrew rolled her chair to the table and passed the book on her lap to Connie. 'Put that over there, would you.'

Connie turned the spine, to confirm her suspicions … 'Oh, *Pride and Prejudice* by Jane Austen; it's one of my favourites. Are you enjoying it?'

Miss Pettigrew nodded and covered her mouth with her hand; obviously she had something to say. Connie waited patiently while she swallowed and patted her mouth with the napkin. 'I haven't been able to put it down. It's taken my mind off my missing picture. It was dear Maisie's suggestion that I might enjoy some Jane Austen. Mrs Alexander has a full set in her sitting room. I like to think that they were once read by royalty.' She gave a sharp little laugh. 'Or as close to royalty as I'll ever get.'

Connie picked up the book and turned it this way and that; it was just as Mrs Alexander had described it—bound in calfskin, the title picked out in gold script.

'Would you like me to read to you while you're eating?'

'That would be lovely. I've marked my page with a scrap of ribbon Mr Humbert gave me.'

Connie picked up the book and lost herself in the antics of the Bennett sisters. When she reached the end of the chapter she looked up.

Miss Pettigrew beamed her thanks. 'It's so lovely to have some unexpected company. Please give my compliments to Mrs Trotter;

the sausage rolls were truly delightful. I think I might have a little rest and prepare myself for afternoon tea.'

Connie picked up the tray and made her way back to the kitchen. Nothing made any sense at all. Why would Mrs Alexander say the book was missing when it patently wasn't unless ... had Maisie borrowed it on Miss Pettigrew's behalf and then somehow, along the line, forgotten to tell Mrs Alexander? It was possible but it didn't answer the question of the ivory box nor, come to think of it, the candlesticks, Miss Pettigrew's portrait or Maisie's thimble. Although a thimble wouldn't be difficult to misplace.

As she reached the servants' quarters she stopped and looked up at the row of bells. One of them bounced silently on its spring which meant it had to have been rung; the only problem was she couldn't tell which room it came from. She hadn't noticed any bell pulls upstairs, only in the drawing room and dining room, and presumably Mrs Alexander's quarters, and she'd noticed one in Miss Pettigrew's room. Shrugging her shoulders, she pushed open the door to the scullery and unpacked the tray.

'No need for you to be doing that.'

Lost in her reverie, Mrs Trotter's call made Connie jump. 'It's no trouble. Miss Pettigrew offered her compliments. She positively inhaled the sausage rolls.'

'I feel sorry for the poor old biddy. No family, no one to care for her in her old age. Mind you, I suppose it could be worse; at least she can afford a roof over her head and young Maisie does a wonderful job. Suits them both. Maisie wouldn't be able to live in a place like this without the money from Miss Pettigrew, and Miss Pettigrew couldn't live here without Maisie. I can't imagine Mrs Alexander offering a helping hand ...' She covered her mouth, currant eyes dancing. 'Mustn't speak ill of our steadfast leader. We'd all be out of work but for her. Like another cuppa? There's some sausage rolls left too.'

Connie nodded and sat down at the kitchen table. It was becoming a bit of a habit, one she rather enjoyed. Mrs Orchard didn't like anyone hanging around in her kitchen unless invited, said it put her off her stride, but Mrs Trotter seemed quite the opposite. 'How long have you worked here?'

Mrs Trotter grunted as she slurped her tea. 'I've been here ever since Mrs Alexander took over and it became a guesthouse. It was all plain sailing at first, and then there was that fire a couple of years back. Thought we were all done for.'

'Fire?'

'Bloody terrible it was. The roof on the old barracks went up. One of the labourers and his pipe I reckon, but they never truly worked out how it started. The wisteria caught. We were so sure the sparks would jump across to the roof to the attic. Weren't catching me or June and May sleeping there no more. That's when we moved in here. I took the old office as my room and May and June have the dry store pantry. Don't have need of as much space these days.' Mrs Trotter pushed back her chair. 'Can't be sitting around here all day I've got dinner to prepare. I've a mind to cook a curry. You like a curry?'

Connie lifted her shoulders. 'I've never eaten a curry.'

'I can guarantee you'll like this one. It's Macquarie's original recipe, brought it back from India. One of the few recipes Mrs Alexander doesn't keep secreted in that scrapbook of hers. What I wouldn't give … we found the curry recipe tucked in the desk drawer. Give us a tick and I'll show you.'

'I really must go and see Mrs Montague. She was having a rest but I've been gone a good hour.'

'She'll find her way around, don't you worry. Anyone who's been in service would …' Mrs Trotter tipped her head to one side like an enquiring sparrow.

Connie toyed with the remains of the pastry, licking her finger and dabbing the last flakes. It would seem like a betrayal to Nell to be drawn into another gossip session, though it might be interesting. 'Not that I'm aware of but I've only been with her for a year or two.' Isn't that what a companion would say? 'I believe she's lived most of her life in Maitland.'

'Her married life maybe. Before that I'm talking about. Heard tell her mam worked for Governor Bligh's daughter back in the day.'

Connie reined in her curiosity. Nell rarely mentioned her mother and as interesting as Mrs Trotter's comments were she'd rather ask Nell herself, not settle for scuttlebutt; besides, the woman was digging. 'Thanks for the tea, and the sausage rolls.' Connie pushed her chair under the table and wandered off down the hallway.

It wasn't until she got to the row of bells that she remembered one of them had been swinging when she'd gone into the kitchen. It sat as still and silent as the others now. Perhaps Mrs Alexander had called for her tray and May or June had delivered it.

As she turned, her toe caught in the lace of her shoe. Somewhere along the line it had come undone. She crouched to retie it and as she rose noticed the door on the opposite wall. Not a panelled door like all the others but a very plain door painted white, to blend with the walls. She reached for the handle and turned it, gave it a little rattle but to no avail; it was locked tight. It wasn't until she stepped back she noticed it was set on the top of a step, not at floor level. And then it became clear. It was the door to the attic.

17

Nell woke with a start and swung her legs over the edge of the bed. She'd wound herself into such a dither about the jewellery box. There had to be a simple explanation but when Mrs Alexander as good as accused her of taking it the past had flown back with blinding clarity. That horrible, horrible day when she'd sent her packing. If it hadn't been for Montague, she wouldn't have survived it …

The weather was glorious that day, still spring but warm enough; winter had packed up and the sun smiled down. The gardens at new Government House were a sight for sore eyes and she'd taken a bit of a break, sneaked down to the water's edge. The set of steps from the garden led to the little harbourside beach. She liked to go and paddle her feet and watch all the ships making their way in and out of the harbour, dreaming that maybe one day soon Montague would step ashore. Promises tended to wear a bit thin after not a word for so long but deep down she knew he'd be back, just like last time.

With her face tilted to the sun and her toes skimming the water, she didn't notice the little rowboat until it rounded the point.

Oars shipped, the boat bumped onto the sand and her breath stopped, just stopped. She rubbed her eyes, peering through the sun flares. He dragged the boat onto the sand, taller and stronger than she remembered.

He walked to her, swept off his hat and gazed into her face, eyes blazing with happiness. 'My Nell. You must've known I was on my way. Sitting there pretty as a picture.'

Serendipitous it was. Truly serendipitous. She'd heard the governor's wife use the word, sneaked into the library, and looked it up. So many events in her life were serendipitous. Her skin tingled and her palms grew damp.

'I'm back, Nell. Will you still be having me?' He'd smiled, and took her hand.

What a question! Heart hammering, she threw herself into his embrace, inhaled his familiar scent overlaid with a tinge of the ocean spray. It had seemed like a lifetime of waiting, praying he'd be true to his word. 'I thought you'd never come back.'

'My word is my promise, never doubt that, Nell.' He threaded his fingers through hers and settled her back on the nice flat rock she liked to sit on. 'Everything worked out just as I'd hoped. I met a fella in California who knew all there was to know about gold panning and found out we had the same idea—get in fast and get out quick. We pooled our resources, set ourselves up, found a bit here and there, even made enough to hire a few hands, and before too long we'd sunk a mine and made a fortune.' He brushed back his hair, revealing a hint of darkness, maybe despair, on his face. 'The goldfields are no place to be, filth and famine, hardship and heartache. A veritable hellhole befouled by misery, dirt and human waste. We hit our mark and agreed to part ways. And here I am.'

'How did you know where to find me?'

'Not too hard, my love.' He offered a crooked smile. 'Last time, you were working for Lady O'Connell. I did a bit of asking 'round, heard she'd gone home after her husband passed. They told me you'd got a job here; I didn't expect to find you sitting waiting for me though.'

She elbowed him in the ribs. Cheeky devil.

'I've a notion to make a move. Will you come with me?' He raised his eyebrows in question and pulled her closer, his thumb tracing the ring she'd worn around her neck every day since he'd left.

How could he be so unsure? Didn't he know what her answer would be? She opened her mouth to speak but his finger crossed her lips.

'Remember what Gipps said when I told him about the gold I found out west?'

She nodded. 'He told you a gold rush would start a riot. Well, it's started; there's ships arriving from all four corners every day and people leaving Sydney in droves.'

'I don't want any bit of it, Nell. I've had my fill. There are better ways to make a life, and a more comfortable one with the Californian gold behind us. I've a thought to buy a parcel of land and breed horses in the clean, fresh air. I've got my eye on a piece, three thousand acres, between Maitland Town and Morpeth, along the Hunter River.'

Three thousand acres. More than her mind could fathom. A parcel of land? The air swept out of her lungs. More like a small country.

'A man will always be in need of a horse, and there's money to be made on and off the racetrack. So, will you be coming with me?'

Leave Sydney? She'd never left Sydney before, not once in all her twenty-odd years. She shot a sideways glance at Montague, the rugged planes of his face, the fall of his dark hair, the swell of his lips and knew, had always known. 'I will.'

He leapt to his feet, picked her up and swirled her around and around, then brushed his lips against hers in the tenderest caress. 'Go and fetch your goods and chattels and bid your goodbyes. I've secured us passage on the steamer leaving tonight for Morpeth.'

'Put me down!' Her feet hit the sand, and she put her hands on her hips. 'And how, Mr Grainger Montague, did you know I'd say yes?'

'I didn't know, Nell. I hoped, hoped with all my heart.' His wide broad palm lay flat against his chest. 'Will they mind you leaving?'

That she didn't know. She couldn't imagine Mrs Alexander would be very pleased but there wasn't much she could do about it—and it wasn't as though she'd need a letter of introduction. 'I'll pack my bags—oh!' She swallowed, words refusing, for a moment, to form. Then she whispered, 'And get your gold.'

'Get it? Don't you have it?'

'After you left for California I kept it in the leather pouch under my mattress at Lady O'Connell's, but it burnt a hole in my conscience, terrified me. That someone would find it and accuse me of stealing. When I moved here I hid it in Governor Bligh's trunk, in the hem of one of Lady O'Connell's dresses. She hadn't room nor interest to take all her possessions, not after Lord O'Connell died. She said she'd maybe come back to Australia one day.'

'And where is this trunk?'

'In one of the storage rooms under the eaves in the servants' quarters. Come on.'

Hand in hand Nell and Montague ran across the grass and slipped through the kitchen garden and up the backstairs.

'The key's up here.' Standing on tiptoe Nell ran her fingers along the lintel, pulled down the key, slipped it into the lock and eased open the door.

Everything would have been just fine if it hadn't been for Mrs Alexander and her interfering nose but at that point neither of them were any the wiser. Nell rubbed at her jaw; just remembering was enough to make her teeth ache. This accusation about Mrs Macquarie's jewellery box wouldn't be happening if Mrs Alexander hadn't caught her and Montague.

The memory still made colour heat her cheeks. Mrs Alexander had swept in like an avenging angel and found the two of them ransacking Governor Bligh's trunk.

And that was the end of that. Theft was not to be tolerated, and no discussion entered into and so she'd got her marching orders, but she had Montague. With her nose in the air, she'd dropped the key into Mrs Alexander's open palm and they left— left Government House for good. Arms linked, she and Montague had walked down the carriageway, out into Macquarie Street their backs firmly turned on the past.

The only problem was the gold got left behind. There wasn't much they could do about it. Montague with his usual devil-may-care attitude had shrugged his shoulders, said they'd plenty, enough to last a lifetime and those nuggets from Bathurst wouldn't build a life, not the kind he dreamt of. And he'd been right.

If she could find the yellow dress and retrieve the gold she'd be able to get rid of the cloud blighting their existence, extricate them from this horrible mess, and life could go back to the way Montague intended, and they could concentrate on the future— Connie's future. Sometimes life played the strangest games.

She shook her hair and sat at the table. All this reminiscing wasn't going to help. She had to find Lady O'Connell's belongings.

Nell toyed with her notebook. After her tour around the outside of the house everything was beginning to fall into place. Plenty of spots to store an old forgotten trunk—the dilapidated barracks, even the room next door that Mrs Alexander had said was kept for unexpected guests, could store all sorts of treasures.

She pinned the last strand of hair into the chignon. She hadn't thought this through. More than that she needed some help. She'd have to take Connie into her confidence. Who else was there? She'd started out determined Connie would be kept out of the whole sordid business and her reputation and the family fortune would remain intact but now ... it didn't bear thinking about.

18

'Nell.' Connie pushed open the connecting door and found Nell sitting at the dressing table staring blankly into the mirror. 'The gong's just rung. Shall we go down?'

Nell was dressed in one of her lovely soft silk frocks, and the skirt and blouse she'd worn that morning lay on the end of the bed. She peered over Nell's immaculate hair into the mirror; their eyes met.

'Yes. I'm rather hoping Mrs Alexander will announce that there was a mistake, and the jewellery box has turned up. I don't like being accused of something I didn't do.'

'I'm sure Mrs Alexander doesn't mean what she said. Why would she?' Connie didn't like the hollow ring to her voice. She clearly remembered Mrs Alexander's reference to the past, to Nell's morals. Nell had the principles of a saint and if there was such bad blood between them whatever would have possessed Nell to come here. 'I expect she was worried and jumped to the easiest conclusion. Mrs Trotter told me that there is an inventory of all the furnishings, fittings and the like, part of the lease agreement, so it's understandable that she'd be concerned.'

'Whose side are you on?' Nell snapped.

Snapped! Nell never snapped.

'Right, I'm ready. I intend to put Mrs Alexander straight if she mentions it again.'

Their eyes met and Connie grinned. Much more like the Nell she knew and loved.

Everyone was seated at the table by the time they entered the dining room. The curtains were open although the setting sun had taken the glow from the day and a breeze chilled the air.

Mr Whitfield and Mr Humbert stood and helped them to the two vacant seats while Mrs Alexander barely acknowledged them. She sat at the head of the table presiding over a large tureen. The most amazing aroma of spices filled the room. Mrs Trotter's curry. Connie had forgotten all about it.

As soon as everyone was seated, Mrs Alexander lifted the lid of the tureen.

'Has something died?' Miss Pettigrew leant forward and peered at the rising steam.

'Mrs Trotter has a treat for us tonight. Dear Mr Whitfield ...' Mrs Alexander bestowed an ingratiating smile on the gentleman at the opposite end who had decided to grace them with his presence '... made an important discovery. We have recovered some of the misplaced ...' she emphasised the word almost as though it had come from someone else's mouth ... 'silverware. It would seem that one of the girls had taken it to the kitchen to be cleaned.'

'But ...' Connie pressed her lips tightly together. It wasn't her place to correct Mrs Alexander but she was certain May or June would have said something when she was in the kitchen. She shot a glance at May, standing to attention beside the sideboard, her face the colour of plum jam. Poor child having to take the blame. She had every intention of putting the matter straight but not until after dinner.

'And the copy of *Pride and Prejudice* is safely in Miss Pettigrew's possession, as a loan mind you.' Maisie flashed a smile at everyone.

'What was that?' Miss Pettigrew gave an agitated twitch.

'The book you're reading. You're taking good care of it.' Maisie patted the old lady's hand.

'Oh, indeed I am. Fitzwilliam Darcy is such a lovely man, but that Collins chap is a selfish, self-absorbed peacock. You can never trust a clergyman.'

Connie muffled a snort and Mrs Alexander's eyes bulged as she deftly changed the subject. 'Let me tell you about our dinner tonight. It's a recipe from my vast collection, passed down to me from Mrs Macquarie herself.'

Connie tried to do a few sums in her head. She wasn't quite sure how old Mrs Alexander was, but she doubted very strongly she'd have received the recipe firsthand. Far more likely that Mrs Trotter had found the recipe in a drawer as she said.

'A curry made in the Indian way. A little warm on the palate. It's the peppercorns and coriander seeds, which we grow in the vegetable garden these days but would originally have come from the Indian sub-continent.'

Connie waved her hand over her plate to make the steam waft towards her. It smelt simply delicious. A quick glance around the table told her she might well be in the minority.

Bowls of rice circulated the table and once everyone was served Mrs Alexander picked up her fork, a signal to begin. She didn't however take a mouthful; instead she gestured to May with a wave of her hand. May closed the windows and drew the curtains then lifted the silver candelabrum and set it in the centre of the table. Mrs Alexander twisted in her seat. 'The other candelabrum, May?'

With a look of confusion on her face, May bent to the sideboard, opened the door, and peered inside. 'I think I must have left it in the scullery when I was cleaning the silver. I'll go and …' The poor child slipped out through the door. Maisie shot Connie a look, eyebrows raised.

Silence reigned as the tasting began, forkful by forkful sniffed and ingested.

'Delicious,' Nell pronounced, much to Connie's amazement. 'I haven't eaten curry since I was a girl. Lady O'Connell used to enjoy a good curry. She always said she'd picked up the taste when she and her husband were in Ceylon. You'll remember, won't you, Mrs Alexander?'

Whatever Nell was up to, she certainly wasn't hiding her past.

Mrs Alexander cleared her throat and all eyes turned to her. 'It was my pleasure and privilege to serve a long list of governors. That is why I take such pride in the responsibility I have for their possessions.' She gave a curt nod of her head in Nell's direction.

'I still haven't found my thimble.' Maisie's plaintive tone echoed.

Connie had completely forgotten about Maisie's thimble.

'Then we should all help you find it,' Mr Humbert announced in a bright voice, smoothing back his dark hair. 'When I was young, Hunt the Thimble was quite a favourite game. What do you say?'

Maisie's cheeks flushed and Connie felt her surge of embarrassment, as if it was her own.

'A capital idea.' Nell smiled coyly at him. Whatever was she doing?

'Is there any possibility you've left your thimble at work?' Connie turned to Maisie in a frantic attempt to soothe the tense atmosphere.

'No. Absolutely not. I always put it back in my sewing pouch with my needles and threads and that goes into my tapestry bag. I always have it with me.'

Which was quite right—she always did. 'What about when we went to the theatre? You took the waistcoat to Mr Kingsley; did you take your thimble out then?'

'You know I didn't. I didn't even get to see Mr Kingsley, just that awful stage mistress.'

'That's quite enough, Miss Milling. I have no doubt your thimble will turn up, in the same way the missing book did.' Mrs Alexander successfully brought the conversation to a close and dinner progressed in a desultory fashion.

As soon as they had finished dessert Connie made her excuses and fled to her room. She peeled off her clothes and deposited them in a pile on the chair, slipped into her nightgown and jumped into bed, pulling the covers up under her chin. The entire evening had left her flustered and confused.

She covered her face with her hand, shielding her eyes from the intrusive moonbeam slicing through the window. In her haste to go to bed she'd forgotten to draw the curtains. She tossed back the bedcovers and swung her feet to the floor.

The brilliant moonlight edged a grey, mottled sky and cast cold shadows across the grass.

As she went to draw the curtains, a flicker of movement between the trees caught her attention and she pressed her forehead against the damp glass to correct the high angle.

She blew on the windowpane and scrubbed her hand across it to clear the condensation. A stark silhouette emerged, gliding across the lawn, arms clutching a large bag. The figure moved from the tree line towards the house, skirting the portico and hugging the wall, then disappeared around the corner of the building.

Her heart quickened and she drew a resolute breath, crept out into the hallway, and descended into the darkness, her grip slipping over the smooth worn cedar of the banister.

At the base of the stairs, she paused, straining for any sound. Nothing from the front door. The only other way into the house was through the kitchen courtyard, but surely it would be locked overnight.

She glanced up at the grandfather clock. In five minutes, it would strike the hour. Like a wraith she slipped past Miss Pettigrew's and Mr Whitfield's rooms and flattened herself against the recessed doorway of the drawing room.

Barefooted and cold-toed she waited, every tick of the clock vibrating through her. The chill in the air raised the hair on her forearms and as the chimes echoed, the door to the attic creaked open and the shadowy figure slipped up the stairs.

What to do? She couldn't follow; she might become trapped in the stairwell. She couldn't call for help and create a commotion; besides who would believe her? She cracked open the drawing room door and slid inside, just enough space to keep the attic door in sight, ears pricked for the sound of footsteps.

An eternity passed and then faint footfalls, one step at a time, almost as if avoiding any creaking risers. A click, perhaps a key, then the figure pivoted towards her. Shrouded in darkness it glided along the corridor.

Connie edged further into the drawing room and ducked behind the sofa. The grandfather clock boomed the hour. She couldn't risk being seen, no excuse to be roaming in the hallways wearing nothing but her nightgown. The footsteps sounded louder as the figure passed the drawing room. Going where? Up the stairs? Out of the front door? Into Mrs Alexander's quarters?

As the footfalls faded, she peeped around the corner. Silence. No sign of the dark-clad figure, no movement, only the outline of the grandfather clock. No click from the front door, no figure heading into the southern colonnade towards Mrs Alexander's quarters.

She scurried along the hallway and flattened herself alongside the grandfather clock, each beat of her heart thudding with the metronome of the clock's hands. Five past two. Just minutes from the time she'd first seen him slip up the attic stairs, mere moments.

The clock ticked its way through another five minutes. Her hands and feet were like ice, goosebumps covered her skin. Whatever had possessed her to leave her bedroom without a robe? She peered around the grandfather clock. No movement, no sound except the ticking of the clock. The figure had disappeared. Vanished.

Without a second thought she darted up the stairs, into her little room and threw herself under the blankets, arms wrapped tight around her body to calm her trembling.

Nothing made any sense. Who was skulking around the house at such a late hour? No one she recognised as a guest. And the man, and she was certain it was a man, dressed in trousers, boots and a dark jacket, clutching something to his chest, hadn't stayed long enough to search for anything. Only long enough to climb the attic stairs and return, and the way he'd stepped so carefully on the downward trip as though he knew every creaking floorboard. Thoughts whirled in her mind as her eyes grew heavier until the sky lightened to a pale grey-lilac colour heralding morning, and she sank into an uneasy sleep.

19

Sunday, 5 May, 1889

By the time Connie corralled her befuddled thoughts into some form of order, washed and dressed, Nell had left her room, presumably for breakfast. Who to tell about the strange night-time prowler remained a conundrum. It couldn't be Miss Pettigrew; she could barely get out of her room on her own never mind climb that steep flight of stairs. Mrs Alexander wouldn't need to sneak up into the attic, nor would Mrs Trotter, or May and June. Besides, she was firmly convinced it was a man—the confident way he moved, controlled and deliberate, but too slim for Mr Whitfield, too tall for Mr Humbert.

She had to tell someone, but not Nell, not in her present state. Maisie or Taylor was her only option—for her own peace of mind if nothing else.

Connie pushed open the dining room door. Mr Whitfield sat in his usual spot poring over the *Cumberland Mercury*. He placed his palms flat on the tabletop and half stood, gesturing to the chair next to him. 'Good morning, my dear, you're looking very fetching.'

Connie ignored him and slipped into the seat next to Nell who lifted her head and smiled before buttering her toast with her usual precision. No sign of Taylor, or Mr Humbert—perhaps they'd breakfasted early. Miss Pettigrew finished her cup of tea and dabbed at her lips while Maisie waited patiently to return her to her room.

As Maisie wheeled Miss Pettigrew from the table, Connie made a snap decision. 'Maisie, would you like to come for a walk with me? I'd love some company.'

Nell's head jerked and she raised her eyebrows in question.

'Sounds lovely.' Maisie smiled. 'I'll be about ten minutes. Why don't you have some breakfast and pocket some toast for the ducks?' With a flourish she swept Miss Pettigrew from the room.

Connie wandered over to the sideboard and lifted each of the cloches. Nothing interested her in the slightest, so she settled for a couple of slices of toast and tea and sat down again.

Nell studied her for a moment, spoon poised halfway to her mouth. 'You look tired.'

When in doubt stick as close to the truth as possible; it's always better than an outright lie. The mantra Nell had drummed into her years ago played in Connie's mind. 'I didn't sleep very well. I foolishly left the curtains open, and the moonlight woke me.' She dolloped a square of butter onto her plate and studiously spread it on the toast. 'I thought a walk would clear my head. What have you planned for the day?'

'I want to have another chat to Mrs Alexander. I've been trying to remember the names of some of the other staff at Government House. I thought I might try and track them down.' Nell turned over her empty eggshell and thwacked it with her spoon. 'No boats for witches!'

Just one of the stories Nell had told her as a child to encourage her to finish eating her egg. At least it cheered her. The story apparently came from Nell's mother, Alice—someone else she'd like to ask about. Breaking the bottom of the eggshell stopped witches using the shell as a boat. She reached out and squeezed Nell's hand. 'Must we keep up this companion pretence?' she murmured. 'Taylor has already called our bluff and I'm certain no one else believes it.'

'Too smart for her own good, that Taylor,' Nell huffed. 'It's not right for a girl to be gallivanting around dressed as a man.'

'She doesn't dress like a man; she just steers clear of frills and flounces. It's not like you, Nell. I thought you were all for women's rights.'

Nell turned to Mr Whitfield. 'Have you finished with the paper, Mr Whitfield?'

'Indeed I have.' He carefully smoothed and folded the paper and placed it alongside Nell's side plate then pushed back his chair. 'There's an article in there about the opening of the Hawkesbury Rail Bridge that might interest you.'

Nell pulled out her pince-nez and perched them on the end of her nose.

'Written by some chap who believes the Americans saved the day with their design and engineering.' He pulled his waistcoat down over his ample stomach, a garish red and gold pattern today, and turned to pick up his cane. 'Good day.'

Connie sighed with relief as he left the dining room. The man made her uncomfortable. She poured Nell another cup of tea. The paper would keep her amused while she and Maisie took a walk.

Connie dropped a conciliatory kiss on Nell's soft cheek. 'I'll be back in an hour or so.' She picked up a couple of slices of toast, wrapped them in a napkin and put them in her pocket. 'We should go for a walk in the park together. It's lovely. Maybe this afternoon?'

'We'll see. Off you go.'

Connie stood at the front door looking over the carefully trimmed grass to the trees—the trees where she'd first spotted the black-clad figure last night. She walked down the steps onto the carriageway and looked up at her bedroom window: right in the centre above the portico. It gave possibly the very best panoramic view from the house—no wonder she'd spotted the stranger.

Maisie hadn't appeared so she followed the path the intruder must have taken, around the side of the kitchen. She waved gaily to June as she stood at the scullery sink up to her elbows in suds, then ducked into the courtyard. The door into the servants' quarters was propped open.

'What're you doing skulking round here?'

Connie jumped and whipped around.

May stood, a wide grin on her face and a basket of washing tucked under one arm.

'I ... um ...' stay with the truth '... I'm waiting for Miss Milling. We're going for a walk.'

'She won't be around the back here. Not Miss Prim-and-Proper-Mind-Your-Manners. Be too worried about getting her silks and satins grubby.'

Connie swallowed down the words of defence that jumped to her lips—Maisie wasn't prim and proper, and she couldn't imagine her telling anyone to mind their manners—and offered a smile instead. 'I better go and see if she's around the front of the house. I don't want to keep her waiting. See you later.' Without giving May an opportunity to respond, Connie shot around the corner, lifted her skirts, and dashed back the way she'd come.

'I'm sorry,' she panted, as she staggered to a halt in front of Maisie. 'I got caught by May, hanging out the washing. Those poor girls have to work so very hard.'

'Neither of them would know a hard day's work if it slapped them in the face. Nothing better than a light-fingered baggage, that May. Come along, otherwise I'll be the one getting my face slapped.'

Obviously not a lot of love lost between Maisie and the two girls. 'Do you think they're responsible for the missing jewellery box?'

Maisie pulled her mouth down at the corners and shrugged. 'Or my thimble or Miss Pettigrew's portrait. Stands to reason, doesn't it; they've got the run of the house.' She slipped her arm through Connie's. 'Come along. I thought we'd walk through the town. I'll show you some of the shortcuts—that way you'll get to know where everything is. I've got to call in to the shop and sort out a few things. Madame Gautier won't mind. I've told her all about you.'

'That would be lovely and Nell ...'

'Got you! Taylor's right. You're not Mrs Montague's companion any more than I am. Come on, tell me.'

Connie licked her lips. 'Mrs Montague, Nell, is my grandmother.' There, it was done. She'd tell Nell as soon as she got back to the guesthouse.

'Ohh! Well, I'll be blowed. I knew you were a bit too familiar. Why are you hiding it?'

'To be honest I'm not really sure.' And she also wasn't sure how much she should tell Maisie. Nell was entitled to her privacy just the same as everyone else. 'I took Nell a bit by surprise when I turned up and she thought Mrs Alexander would be more likely to offer me a room if I was her companion.' What a load of rubbish. She wouldn't get away with that.

'I don't really see what difference it makes one way or the other. Far as I'm concerned, you're Connie and it's lovely to have a new friend. Right. Lickety-split—I don't want to waste the day.' Maisie picked up the pace, saving Connie from having to elaborate on her relationship with Nell.

They followed George Street and headed down towards the theatre, the footpaths quiet so early on a Sunday morning.

'It's not much further. Madame Gautier's original business was on the corner just up here.' She pointed to a small building tucked between a printing shop and a cobbler, the curtained windows keeping out prying eyes.

'Her original shop?'

'Yes. She's done very well for herself. She opened her first shop—Maison de Gautier—with an inheritance from an uncle. Not that she's any more French than I am but it draws the customers. That and the range of goods she stocks. She moved down here a bit, into bigger premises, a year or so ago.' Maisie ducked into Church Street and came to a halt outside a building proclaiming itself to be Gautier's Arcade. A mannequin stood in the window sporting a flamboyant feathered hat, rather like the one Maisie had worn to the theatre, an emerald skirt, and a tight three-quarter sleeved blouse.

'Not bad for a woman on her own, is it? Just shows you what you can do if you're determined. One day ...' Maisie delved into her bag and brought out a large brass key. 'Come in and have a look around.'

The shop's long shelf-lined interior carried a huge range of fabrics—bolt after bolt of muslin, silk, satin, taffeta, velvet, and other materials Connie couldn't name, and displays of plain and patterned waistcoats, much like the one Maisie had sewn for Mr Kingsley, dress shirts, work trousers and jackets, even a selection of readymade clothing.

A counter with measuring tapes and scissors ran across the back of the shop and underneath glass cabinets stocked with box after box of cottons and embroidery thread, ribbons, lace and enough tassels, silk flowers, hatpins and veils for the most discerning milliner.

'Impressive, isn't it?'

Connie exhaled, expelling a streak of jealousy. What she wouldn't give to own her own business; not a dressmakers or milliners—she had no idea where her passion lay—but to be in control of her own concern, at no one's beck and call. The prospect filled her with awe.

'Anything else you'd like to know about the town?' Maisie quirked an eyebrow. 'Sometimes I feel as though I know everyone.'

Which is exactly what Connie was hoping for, but she didn't want to get Maisie into trouble. 'I wondered if we could have a little chat. Something very strange happened last night ... have you got time?'

Maisie's eyes grew wide as she studied her face. 'Of course I've got time. Sunday's my day and Madame Gautier will be none the wiser. She never comes in on a Sunday.' She pulled out a stool. 'You sit here.' She patted the seat then propped herself on the other side of the bench.

Once they'd settled Connie pressed her hands together, plucked up her courage and turned sideways so she could see Maisie's face, so she'd know if she believed her or not.

'Come on then. I'm all ears.' Maisie tipped her head to one side. In her smart white blouse and dark skirt, she looked for all the world like an inquisitive wagtail.

Connie drew in a breath. 'I couldn't sleep last night, and I was standing at the window of my bedroom and saw this figure come out from the trees. He went around the back of the house into the kitchen courtyard. I raced downstairs and caught him going up the stairs to the attic.'

Maisie's jaw dropped. 'You did what? Why didn't you call someone? Anything could have happened!'

'Because I didn't think, I just acted. It was all very strange …' Connie recounted the remainder of her story, and even told her about the figure she had seen at the upstairs window when she'd arrived. '… and when he left the attic he vanished into thin air.'

Maisie's eyes bulged. 'Oh! My. So, it is true. You saw one of the ghosts. I've heard tell the place is haunted but Mrs Alexander practically bit my head off when I asked about it.'

The hairs on the back of Connie's neck prickled to attention. 'Ghost? No, this was only one flesh and blood person. I'm certain, absolutely certain.'

'Ask anyone around here and they'll tell the story. A tall man in dark clothing, I'll bet.'

Despite the warmth of the shop, a whisper of coolness traced the back of Connie's neck and made her shiver. She nodded.

'It's true then! The story says a man, a convict, working in the stables, fell in love with one of the guests staying at Government House. He broke into the house and fell down the stairs to his death. Years ago, it was. Oh my!' She clapped her hand over her mouth. 'You said you saw a woman at an upstairs window when you arrived. Which window?'

'Next to Nell's room, on the right of the portico. It could have been a shadow.'

'No, it wasn't. It was his lover. She was sleeping in the room above the dining room; that's why Mrs Alexander never rents it out.'

Connie dug her gloved fingernails into her palms. Maitland was full of ghost stories, especially with all the happenings at the gaol and the hospital, but she'd never really believed them, positive it was all hearsay, even though Mrs Orchard swore by some of them. But last night she'd seen the man with her own eyes. The woman she'd seen when she arrived she wasn't so sure about; she could easily have been mistaken. 'I really don't think

I saw a ghost. The man crept up the stairs into the attic.' She couldn't mask the waver in her voice.

'Let me tell you the whole story.' Maisie shifted on the stool, leant forward, and took Connie's hand. 'The man entered the house searching for his love, to beg her to run away with him, but someone caught him, grabbed him and he fell over the balustrade and down the main stairs. The servants got to him first and dragged him up into the attic, frightened they might be held responsible, but when he died, they had to fess up. They say he haunts the attic and the stairway, looking for his lost love. That's why Mrs Trotter and May and June sleep downstairs. And that his lover watches for him, summoning him by ringing the bell pull, waiting for him to come back to her.' Maisie raised her eyebrows. 'It fits. Perfectly. I knew it was true.'

A rash of goosebumps stippled Connie's skin. The bells! She'd seen them silently moving to and fro. 'No, I just don't believe it. Mrs Trotter said they closed the attic after a fire.'

'Tosh and nonsense. It wasn't a big fire, just the wisteria that shaded the verandah, all those dried leaves and dead branches.'

Connie shook her head. 'I don't believe in ghosts.' Who was she trying to convince? Herself or Maisie?

'Hmm, I'd keep it to yourself for the time being if I were you. We'll talk again this afternoon.'

Connie rose swiftly from her seat as the bell over the shop door rang and two well-dressed young women stepped inside.

Maisie grimaced. 'I can't send them away. Will you be all right walking back all on your own? I'll see you at the guesthouse later.'

Alone was exactly what Connie wanted. It would give her time to think; maybe she'd even write down what she'd seen. It always helped her to get things straight. 'I'll be perfectly fine. I'll walk down to the river and feed the ducks on the way back.' She patted the toast in her pocket.

Connie nodded to the chattering women and wandered out into the street and headed towards the river. Once she'd crossed the bridge, she found a bench seat and sat down, her eyes closed and her face tilted up.

How long she sat there she wasn't certain but when a cloud crossed the sun, she heaved herself upright and followed the path in search of the ducks, hoping the breeze would blow away her sense of discombobulation. She was certain the man she'd seen was flesh and blood, not a ghost.

The path skirted a bend in the river and beneath the overhanging willow trees she found the family of ducks paddling around in ever-decreasing circles. She pulled the napkin from her pocket and scattered the crumbled remains of the toast wide across the water, sending the ducks into a frenzy of squawking. Such a simple pleasure. She and Nell used to feed the black swans quite regularly on their morning walks but, like everything else since Pa's accident, life had become far too serious for frivolous swan feeding. Brushing the crumbs from her hands, she headed back over the bridge to Nell and the present.

The house basked like the old lady she was in the morning sun. There was no sign of Nell; the drawing room and dining room were empty. As she walked into the hall the grandfather clock struck the hour. Eleven o'clock. Where had the time gone?

The hollow feeling in her stomach had nothing to do with phantoms or apparitions and everything to do with the fact she hadn't eaten enough breakfast. Instead of going up to her room as she'd intended, she turned on her heel and walked down the colonnade to the kitchen, studiously avoiding glancing up at the servants' bells.

The smell of fresh baking wafted out of the kitchen. She stuck her head around the door and found Mrs Trotter, May and June perched at the kitchen table, lathering scones with cream and jam.

'Back from your walk?' May asked.

June tipped up her head and gave a gap-toothed grin. 'Did the ducks enjoy their breakfast?'

'Oh yes, they did.' She reached into her pocket and pulled out the napkin she'd wrapped the toast in. 'Where shall I put this?'

'Are you feeling all right, love? You look a bit pale. I expect you're hungry; toast ain't enough for anyone's breakfast.'

Mrs Trotter slid a plate across the table. 'Help yourself. May, get Miss Constance a warm cup of tea. She's all done in.'

Enveloped in the warmth of the kitchen and the caring attention, Connie settled and a sense of calm descended. So much so that she began to wonder if she hadn't dreamt last night's escapade. She must have been out of her mind to go chasing down the stairs wearing only a nightgown.

'That's better; the colour's coming back to your cheeks. Drink up your tea. Come on, girls, get to it. There's vegetables to peel for tonight.'

Connie finished her tea and picked up her plate and cup and saucer. The least she could do was tidy up after herself. The three of them must rarely catch their breath. 'How many servants were here in the old days?' The row of bells in the corridor must have rung nonstop.

'It's not like it was. Not that I remember too much. I was the kitchen maid when they closed the house after the carriage accident. Went elsewhere after that and worked my way up. I only came back when Mrs Alexander tracked me down. We had a big staff in the old days, butler, housekeeper, cook, and the lower servants—kitchen maid, scullery maid and the like. Course the governor's wife would bring her maid, and the governor his valet; not like today when we're run off our feet. Mind you, we're not catering to a vice-regal establishment so ...' She lifted her shoulders and spread her hands. 'I need to get on. Leave your plate and cup where it is. May can sort that out after she's peeled the potatoes.' Mrs Trotter pulled her recipe book towards her and started flicking aimlessly through the pages.

Connie found Nell in her room poring over her notebook and mumbling to herself. When she walked over to the little desk at the window, Nell snapped her notebook shut. 'Back from your walk?'

'Maisie showed me the shop where she works and when some customers arrived I wandered down to feed the ducks again. Remember when we used to feed the black swans on the river? It seems like years ago.'

Nell emitted some sort of humph-like sound and tapped her fingers on the cover of her notebook.

Connie pulled up a chair.

'Taylor and Maisie have both guessed that I'm not your companion.'

Nell quirked a smile. 'And did you inform them of our relationship?'

Connie wrinkled her nose. 'I couldn't brush it over and Maisie said she didn't care who I was; it was lovely to have a new friend. She's such a dear girl. I feel a little bit sorry for her. No family and being at Miss Pettigrew's beck and call, although Mrs Trotter seems to think the arrangement suits them both.'

'And what about Taylor?'

'She said my secret was safe but that she was curious to know why you'd said it. I'm curious too. Why do we have to keep up this silly charade?'

Nell gave a wan smile. 'I was so shocked to see you standing there, I didn't want you involved.'

'Involved in what?'

'Reputation is so important. I couldn't stand it if my actions jeopardised your chances of a good marriage.'

'Oh! For goodness' sake.' Connie flounced out of the chair. 'Don't be so old-fashioned. I know you're up to something and I will find out sooner or later.'

'Sweetheart, sit down. I really don't know where to start.'

'Let me know when you do and if you're prepared to take me into your confidence. I'll see you at dinner.' Connie stalked out of the room.

20

Connie waited at the bottom of the stairs as Nell made her way down, still annoyed with Nell's evasiveness. The hum of conversation wafted out into the hallway from the drawing room and she mentally ticked off the voices—Mr Humbert's lisping whisper, Miss Pettigrew's high-pitched titter, Taylor and Maisie's laughter. She was going to have to apologise to Nell; she hated it when they argued.

'Ladies.' Mrs Alexander stood just inside the doorway. 'Won't you join us for a sherry before dinner? Mr Humbert has all the latest news from London.'

'Delightful.' Nell offered the smile she reserved for the gatherings of the Hospital Committee, the one through gritted teeth.

'Come along. Mrs Montague, we have this seat reserved for you.' She led Nell to the chair by the window. A small table with two glasses stood next to the chair and Miss Pettigrew's chair was pulled up alongside. 'Mr Whitfield won't be joining us tonight. He has a prior engagement but I'm happy to say Mr Humbert is back from his travels. We must take care of him. We can't have the only man in the house regretting female company.'

Nell sat where Mrs Alexander indicated and accepted her glass of sherry. Maisie and Taylor moved along the sofa and patted the cushion, indicating that Connie should join them.

'Now, Mr Humbert, pray continue with your tale of Sydney Town. New shops you were telling us.'

Mr Humbert droned on, much talk of ribbons and bows, and when he produced what he called 'the latest from London' everyone leant forward to receive the printed sheets.

Maisie blew a lock of hair from her forehead. 'These aren't the latest,' she whispered. 'Look at the date.' She pointed to the print along the top of the sheet. 'It doesn't take six months for mail to arrive from England anymore, not for years, not since steamships. The new David Jones catalogue came last week and there's big changes afoot. Take the sleeves for example.' She plucked at Connie's dress. 'No more little puffs, much bigger, pleated into the armhole, tapering to the elbow and tight to the wrist—they're calling them leg-of-mutton sleeves. Not quite sure what we'll do for a jacket, but they'll think of something.' She raised her forefinger to her lips, eyes staring blankly at the wall. 'Cloaks! Cloaks will come back, mark my words.' She dropped Mr Humbert's paper into her lap. 'This is just rubbish.'

Connie leant towards her. 'You haven't said anything about the prowler, have you?'

Maisie shook her head and cupped her hand in front of her mouth. 'But I have an idea. I remember talking to Madame Gautier about the other world. She's very, very keen you know. She attends seances regular as clockwork.'

Connie's heart sank; Maisie couldn't have involved Madame Gautier. 'You haven't!'

'No, I haven't. I told you I wouldn't. I think we should see if either of our friends appear again tonight and if one of them does, go to a seance and see if we can call them up.'

'That's the most ridiculous idea!' The other conversations in the room halted and all eyes turned to Connie. She'd spoken far too loudly. 'Why would we want to go and see the play again?' she improvised.

Maisie grinned and picked up the conversation without batting an eye. 'Because I might be able to get tickets for the final performance.'

Connie gave a wry smile. 'Oh well, in that case, why not? When is the last night?'

'Tomorrow. Do you think I should ask if anyone else would like to go? Taylor?'

Taylor screwed up her nose. 'Let's wait and see.'

Maisie took little notice of Taylor's remark but her question provoked a discussion and later, when they were seated around the dining room table, towards the lack of skill amongst amateur dramatic societies which Maisie took as a personal affront to her costume skills. She was so incensed she left the table before dessert was served, leaving poor Miss Pettigrew in the unenviable position of having to ask someone to wheel her to her room.

'Let me help you, Miss Pettigrew. It would be my pleasure.' And the perfect opportunity to escape. Connie could barely keep her eyes open. An army of wraiths could descend on the place for all she cared. She intended to sleep the clock around.

The moment she reached her room she discarded her clothes, slipped into her nightgown and crawled beneath the blankets.

Only moments later, or so it seemed, she shot upright, a sudden disturbance jolting her awake.

'Sssh! It's me.'

The moonlight slanting through the gap in the curtains illuminated Maisie's face. 'What is it?' She blinked, once, twice. A large key dangled in front of her face.

'Want to go and see if the ghosts are wandering?' Maisie's proposition cut through the night's silence.

'Where did you get that?' Apprehension rippled across Connie's skin.

'I borrowed it. Keys are in the dresser. I thought you'd want to come. We'll go up the stairs; just a quick peek.'

'To the attic?' Why would she want to go up there? And in the middle of the night. 'Are you mad?'

'Inquisitive. Not mad. Put your jacket on over your gown. It's cold.'

'Let's do it in the morning. We won't be able to see a thing.'

Maisie pocketed the key and held up a lantern and a box of waxed matches. 'All prepared. Come on. We'll settle this once and for all. We can't go wandering up there in the middle of the day. Even if we managed to get past Mrs Alexander, Mrs Trotter would spring us, sure as eggs. I thought you'd want to come.' She shrugged her shoulders. 'If you're not coming, I'll go by myself.'

Connie rubbed the sleep from her eyes. She couldn't let Maisie go alone. If anything happened to her the responsibility would lie with her; she'd started the whole nonsense by telling Maisie in the first place. She raised one shoulder in a brief shrug and slipped her arms into her jacket. 'Right. We'll go but just up the stairs. A quick look around and then I'll expect an apology.'

'Or we'll prove the rumours.' Maisie cracked open the door and peered out into the hallway. 'Come on.' She slipped out into the darkness, looking for all the world like an apparition herself.

Connie tiptoed behind Maisie through the gloom, casting a quick look over her shoulder at the closed door next to Nell's room. The tick of the grandfather clock beat in time with their footsteps as they floated down the stairs, then faded as they passed Miss Pettigrew's and Mr Whitfield's rooms and the water closet.

Moving from patch to patch of frail light they made their way along the colonnade until they stood before the attic door.

'Take this, and these.' Maisie held out the lantern and matches. 'I'll need both hands to unlock the door.' She bent down and wriggled the key into the lock then looked over her shoulder and grinned. 'Got it.' A slight click acknowledged her success and the door swung silently open. 'Someone uses this door and often. It's quieter than the one to my room or Miss Pettigrew's.'

Connie wiped her clammy hands down her nightgown. Maisie was correct. This door was used, and frequently. No wonder she hadn't seen or heard the prowler enter or leave the attic. Had he simply helped himself to the key from the dresser as Maisie had? That would mean he wasn't a stranger, that he knew his way around. She stepped past Maisie and onto the first step, then the second step into a tunnel of dust and darkness.

'Don't light the lantern until I've closed the door.' Maisie's whispered words drifted up to her and the door clicked shut. Darkness descended, a dense, suffocating blanket of nothing but the musty scent of the past. 'Let's see if we can do without the lantern, just in case anyone takes a visit to the water closet.'

Connie blinked several times and waited for her eyes to adjust to the dim light, then reached for the rail attached to the right-hand wall and felt her way up onto the next step, then another, and another. Behind her, Maisie's gasps echoed in the confined space as they edged up the never-ending staircase.

It wasn't until her toe caught on the runner and she lurched forward that she realised she'd reached the top. 'Be careful.' Connie moved aside, making room for Maisie, and took several deep breaths and brought her palm to her chest, willing her racing heart to slow.

The veiled moonlight shining through the dormer window revealed the skeletal remnants of a forgotten era. Stacks of boxes and wooden crates, old trunks, a rolled carpet and bundles of discarded furnishings, curtains more than like, and a jumble of curios and irregular shapes stacked haphazardly and draped with sheets, the upturned legs of furniture peeping through like bleached bones.

She plonked the lantern and matchbox down on the trunk beneath the window and faced Maisie. 'What are we going to do now we're here?'

Suddenly the whole escapade seemed even more foolhardy than before. What did Maisie expect? That an apparition would appear from behind the furniture and introduce himself, or worse was even now preparing to spring out and terrify them with a spine-chilling shriek? 'What now?'

In the eerie stillness Connie heard, rather than saw, Maisie's head shake. 'I don't rightly know. It seemed like a good idea.'

'We're wasting our time. There's nothing here.'

'Sssh!' Maisie's hissed exclamation broke into her thoughts and her cold hand clamped Connie's arm. 'I can hear something.' She ducked down behind a large table and wormed her way beneath the dust sheet, dragging Connie with her.

Footsteps echoed. Long confident strides. A man, taking the steps two at a time. Every hair on Connie's body rose. Maisie's fingers dug into the skin on her arm. Then the sound of a snatched gasp and a slow exhalation.

Connie lifted the corner of the dust sheet. The silhouette of a tall, thin figure thrown against the mass of tumbled furniture moved slowly to the southern side of the room, towards the kitchen end of the house, then lifted the corner of one of the sheets and squatted down. He paused for a moment, at least five of her erratic heartbeats, then opened a small leather bag. Beside her Maisie's body vibrated with fear, or was it excitement? Horrified she'd leap from their hiding place, Connie leant on her leg, pinning her in place.

A rattle broke the silence, and a beam of silvery moonlight struck a multi-branched metal object. The figure studied it, ran a gloved hand up and down the length of it then removed a dust sheet and placed it atop the small cupboard next to a pair of matching candlesticks, a tiny cruet set and several bundles of cutlery, silver no doubt.

Maisie's muscles tensed and she pointed. Connie nodded; she'd recognised it too. One of the candelabrums that held centre stage on the dining table every evening, the one May hadn't been able to find. The gloved hand delved into the bag once more and pulled out another object. Moonlight reflected from the surface sending distorted images this way and that. Connie dug her elbow into Maisie's ribs. No doubt about it—the ivory box from Nell's room. He placed it next to the candelabrum. A succession of smaller pieces emerged—a silver matchbox, an enamelled pot, two handfuls of beads, earbobs and brooches, and finally a set of calfskin-bound books. He held one up and fanned the pages, then pulled a small painting from the bag and placed it alongside the other miniatures.

'That's Miss Pettigrew's portrait of her brother, and those are the other Jane Austen books from Mrs Alexander's room.' Maisie's enraged voice cut the silence and she leapt to her feet, incandescent with rage. 'She blamed me.'

The figure turned, jumped to a standing position. Tall and lithe, he loomed over Maisie.

Launching to her feet, Connie reached out, her fingers closing around the cold metal of one of the candlesticks. Without a second thought she raised it above her head.

The figure snatched at Maisie's arm and dragged her close. A fiery slash of fury coursed through Connie's body, and she brought the candlestick down with a resounding thwack. The man stumbled and crumpled at her feet.

A strange rushing sound filled her ears and she sank slowly to her knees. One staring eye glared accusingly at her and a thick river of blood wormed its way across the man's forehead. She reached out for his shoulders, the musky coppery scent tainting her nostrils, and tried to straighten his body, turn him over, but the weight of him was too much.

'He's dead.' Maisie's bland statement ricocheted in the small space.

'He's not. He can't be. I didn't hit him hard.' Connie reached out and brushed his hair aside. She could smell his sweat, and the tang of her own, mixed with fear and horror at what she'd done. 'We've got to get help.' She pushed Maisie's hands away and stumbled down the stairs, a tangle of arms and legs.

By the time she reached the bottom Maisie was right behind her. 'We can just lock the door. No one will know how he got there. You were right. Not a ghost, a real live intruder. Dead now.'

'He's not dead. He can't be. I'm going to get help. Get Nell, a doctor.' Connie pushed open the door at the bottom of the staircase and flew along the colonnade and up the stairs.

By the time she reached Nell's door Maisie was once more behind her. 'Wait! Just for a moment. I've locked the door to the attic, put the key back in the dresser under the window. No one will go up there. We've got time to think—think about the best thing to do.'

'No, we haven't. The longer we leave it the worse it will be.' Connie cradled her head in her hands. Whatever had possessed her. It had happened so quickly, without a second thought, and now the man lay on the floor, blood pouring from the gash on his forehead, that single eye peering accusingly at her while she stood over him staring with disbelief at the candlestick in her hand, his body at her feet.

She'd never hit anyone before in her life. The lesson had been drummed into her almost before she could walk. Pa's brawls at the racetrack were legendary and Nell had insisted she watch while the doctor patched him up and made her promise she'd never, never get into a fight with anyone, and most of all never hit anyone. And here she was, role reversed, worse than Pa— she'd killed a man.

She threw open the door and came face to face with Nell, her shawl covering her nightdress, hair plaited, and arms akimbo. It didn't bode well. 'Where have you been?'

'Oh, Nell.' Connie crumpled into her grandmother's arms seeking solace and a way out of the pandemonium she'd unwittingly unleashed.

'Come and sit down. And you, Maisie, you better come inside too and shut the door behind you.'

21

Nell sat on the bed, her arm tight around Connie's shoulders, as she'd done a thousand times before, and listened to the sorry tale. 'Whatever possessed you to go up there?'

'Ghost hunting.'

'Ghost hunting—whatever next. I didn't think you believed in all that nonsense. You'll be telling me next you've been attending Mrs Cartwright's seances in Morpeth.'

Connie bit deep into her lip. She hadn't intended to tell Nell about the prowler she'd seen but there was no other way to explain what she and Maisie were doing up in the attic. 'I saw someone skulking around the grounds last night. I went downstairs to see what he was up to.'

'You did what? Are you insane, child? Anything could have happened to you.'

Connie dropped her head into her hands.

'Right. That's enough of this wallowing.' Nell patted Connie on the shoulder and stood up. First things, first. How she wished Montague were here. He'd have the matter sorted in a moment, but he wasn't, and would never be again. At least Maisie had the foresight to lock the attic door and give them time to think. Already the first glimmers of predawn lit the horizon. Before long the servants would be about their business. She hadn't any time to waste.

She drew in a fortifying breath. 'You better show me the results of your foolish sojourn and then we'll decide what to do.'

'Decide what to do? We must call the police, a doctor at least.'

'Let's take one step at a time. We haven't got long before the rest of the house will be stirring. Maisie, take yourself back to your bed. Connie, come with me.'

'But I …' Maisie started.

Nell threw her most ferocious scowl and pointed to the door. 'Go.' At least with Maisie out of the way she'd be certain she was getting the whole truth. Not that she doubted Connie, but it would be easier to deal with the situation without any conflicting opinions.

Connie might, unwittingly, have answered the question she hadn't dared ask. When she'd described the contents of the attic, the furniture and then the old trunk under the window Nell almost failed to control herself.

'Come along.' She made for the staircase, making sure Maisie's bedroom door was closed tight.

Moments later they stood at the bottom of the attic stairs, the door unlocked. She herded Connie up the stairs in front of her. 'Can you remember where you left the lantern?'

'Under the window, on top of a trunk, but we'll have to step over …' Connie's voice wavered.

'Don't even think about crying. I won't have it.' Poor child. There'd be time for recriminations later. 'Keep moving.' They must be almost at the top. She gave Connie's back a prod and she tumbled forward into the attic and froze.

'He's not here.'

'What do you mean *not here*? I thought you told me you'd killed him.'

Connie turned in a full circle, her arms out, hands palm upwards. 'He was lying right here. At the top of the stairs. I had to step over his body …'

The hairs on Nell's arms stood to attention. One of two things. Either Connie had imagined the entire episode—but that couldn't be the case; Maisie backed up her story. Or … her heart picked up a beat or two … the man was somewhere in the attic. Hiding. Waiting to pounce. Her foot hit the candlestick and Nell bent to retrieve it.

'Get the lantern you said you brought up here.'

Connie picked it up from the trunk; the box of matches sat beside it just as she'd described.

'Come and light the lantern.' Nell dragged her gaze away from the trunk, raised the candlestick ready to strike.

The lantern flame flickered and grew, sending out a puddle of yellow light. Not a sound though. No movement other than Connie's terrified gasps. 'Hold it up high. Move around a little. If he's here it will draw him out.' Her words sounded braver than she felt but she'd managed bravery before, and this was for Connie. The seconds ticked by and the raised candlestick grew heavier until she had to ask again. 'Are you sure you weren't mistaken?'

'No, I am not mistaken.' No wobble in Connie's voice this time. 'I hit him high up on the side of his head. He fell down at the top of the stairs. There was blood trickling across his forehead and down into his sideburn.'

The light wavered as Connie carried the lantern across the room and crouched down. Nell followed two steps behind, candlestick ready.

'See here.' Connie wiped her finger across the floorboards, then raised it triumphantly. 'Blood! I didn't imagine it.'

'And when you touched him?'

'I tried to turn him over, but he was too heavy.'

'You didn't check to see if he was breathing?'

Connie shook her head. 'I pushed his hair back from his forehead; he didn't move.' Her voice quavered, the lantern in her hand making the shadows dance around her.

Nell shook her head. The child really had a much too sheltered upbringing and she had no one to blame but herself, all that mollycoddling, ensuring she never endured the seamier side of Fred and Faith's life.

No matter, this was far too good an opportunity to waste. 'Hold the lantern high and I'll make a final check.' She raised the nearest dust sheet—a small occasional table, alongside a matching pair of dining room chairs, one missing a leg and the material on the seat ripped—and then made for the trunk. She could see every detail in her mind's eye: camphor wood to protect against the moths, brass handles, and hasp.

'We must go. I have to go to the police.' Connie's words stopped Nell in her tracks. 'You'll do no such thing. I think we can safely say that the worst you can be accused of is assault. I'd hazard a guess that our interloper has made a quick getaway. There's nothing the police can do.'

'How could he? Maisie locked the door and put the key back into the drawer.'

Nell stilled. The child was right. It could mean only one thing. 'He must have had another key.'

'We have to go.' Connie tugged at her arm.

Nell shrugged her off. When would she have another opportunity to come up here? She was so close she could almost smell success. 'I won't be much longer. One final check.'

She squeezed her way between an old wardrobe and a moth-eaten rocking horse. Heart in her mouth she bent forward and ran her fingers over the engraving on the front of the trunk. The words *William Bligh* above the wreath of breadfruit leaves. No doubt it was what she was looking for. She bent to the lid, fumbled with the hasp, all to no avail. What had she expected? She could remember dumping a key in Mrs Alexander's outstretched hand as she and Montague left, but was it the key to the door or the trunk? Memory was such a fickle companion. 'Come over here and help me.'

Connie crouched down beside her and held the lantern close. No padlock, no sign of rust. Nell wiggled the hasp, but it remained stuck fast. 'You try; your fingers are more nimble and stronger than mine.' Nell took the lantern, heart racing and the pounding of blood loud in her ears. The dress had to be in there. Where else could it be ... and then she paused. More than forty years since she'd last seen it and who knew if Mrs Alexander or anyone else had tampered with the contents of the trunk after she and Montague left.

Connie grunted, rubbed her fingers together. 'It's stuck fast. I don't think we should be doing this. Why are we doing this?' She turned her face, her sweet dear face.

Because life as Connie knew it hung in the balance. Nell shook the thought away; she couldn't say that to Connie, not without the explanation that had to come with it.

'Have one more try.' She placed the lantern on the floor. 'Here, give me your hands.' Rubbing Connie's cold fingers between her palms Nell tried to instil her sense of urgency. 'Try again.'

Connie dug her fingernails under the hasp, flexed her muscles, then pulled her hand away and slammed her palm against the brass plate. 'It won't move.' As she spoke, she gave one last try and the hasp flipped up. 'Done it.'

'We have to hurry; the sun's almost up.' Nell doused the lantern, nudged Connie aside and lifted the lid.

A large calico bundle filled the top of the trunk—nothing she remembered. She pulled it out and dumped it on the floor. Underneath she found piles of neatly folded clothing, but no sign of the yellow silk dress.

'Nell, it's just old clothes. What are we doing?' Connie's voice held a plaintive note. 'We have to go.'

'One last chance,' Nell murmured as she fumbled with the drawstring of the calico bag, her fingers stiff and shaking. The gathered calico spread as she stretched the tie. Even in the half-light the silky fabric shone. 'This is it.' Nell clambered to her feet, the dress clasped tightly to her chest. Someone must have recognised the quality of the fabric and placed it for safekeeping in the calico bag. 'Close the trunk and bring the lantern. We don't want any accidents.'

'Nell …' Connie tugged at the bag '… you can't.'

She teetered back towards the stairs, but Connie's grasp was too strong. The yards of heavy yellow silk damask spilt like a waterfall at their feet. 'I'm not stealing it. I'm borrowing it.' She sank to her knees and scooped up the dress, dragging it across the floor and bundling it into her arms, her fingers fumbling for the hemline and closing, oh so very slowly, around the weight within. Whoever had placed the dress in the bag hadn't discovered its secret.

'Nell!'

'I'll explain when we get back to my room. Help me put it in the bag and we need to wipe up this blood. We haven't any time to waste.'

With the dress safely stuffed in the bag, Nell bent down, struggling to tear a strip from the hem of her nightdress. It would suffice to clean the worst of the blood. She scrubbed at the floor, then ran her hand across the floorboards. When it finally came away dry, she heaved the calico bag to her chest, staggering under the cumbersome mass of the bundled material.

'Give it to me.' Connie wrapped her arms around the bundle. 'You go down the stairs first. I'll follow.'

As loath as Nell was to let the dress out of her hands she nodded. Connie was far more stable on her feet and the last thing they wanted was for either of them to fall down the steep staircase and end up a broken mess.

'Nell.' Connie's urgent whisper filled the attic. 'What are we going to do about the things he was stashing in here? Mrs Macquarie's jewellery box, the candelabrum from the dining room ... all the other things.'

'We'll cross that bridge when the sun's up. Time to leave before the rest of the house wakes.' With a final glance over her shoulder, Nell made for the stairs, Connie right behind her clutching the bag tight.

Step by step they eased their way down until they reached the door. Faint noises of morning-stirrings drifted from the kitchen— May and June more than likely stoking the fire and filling the kettle. Nell raised her finger to her lips, ushered Connie through the door. 'You go. Straight to my room as quickly as you can. I'll lock the door and put the key back. I'll be right behind you.'

Once Connie disappeared up the stairs Nell turned the key then returned it to the drawer in the chest beneath the row of bells and tiptoed away, muffling her cry of pure pleasure.

22

Connie dumped the calico bag on the bed, sank down and dropped her head into her hands. She'd lost all sense of reality. Whatever had possessed her to raise the candlestick and bring it down on the man's head? Her entire life had spiralled out of control from the moment Nell had vanished from Maitland.

Nell slipped into the room, closed the door, and rested her back against the timber, a glazed expression throwing her features into stark relief. 'I knew I'd find it. All our problems are solved.' Myriad emotions flitted across Nell's face—a beatific smile, followed by a small frown and a determined puckering of her lips—then she dusted off her hands and released the drawstrings.

In the early morning light, the material shimmered, turning the bed into a pool of gold. The intricate pattern of the embossed silk blossomed into life. Connie stared at the pieces and gradually the jigsaw came together. Not random pieces of material but a dress, half-stitched, half-unpicked and so very, very beautiful. 'I think you better explain.'

Nell turned to her, a small piece of the silk held against her cheek, her eyes closed. 'It's a dress, a very special dress. The material was designed in London over one hundred years ago, in Spitalfields, by a woman called Anna Maria Garthwaite, the finest silk designer of her time, and woven into cloth only a few streets away from her home. It was bought by a man who had it made into a fine, fine wedding dress for his favourite daughter—Elizabeth Betham.' She sighed, her damp eyes fixed on some distant point beyond the horizon, sparkling in the morning light.

A frisson of fear traced Connie's skin and she rubbed at her arms, trying to bring some warmth to her body. Nell's voice reminded her of the tone she'd used when Connie was a child; she would sit clasping her hand, gaze fixed on some faraway image, telling her a bedtime story. Connie had absolutely no idea how to react. 'Come and sit down, here next to me,' she soothed, reaching for Nell's hand.

'I knew I would find it.' She sank onto the bed, the piece of the material clutched to her chest. A large tear welled and trickled down the smooth skin of her cheek.

When Faith had said Nell was living in the past, she hadn't imagined anything like this. 'Did you wear the dress?'

An inkling of a smile crossed her face. 'Mam dreamt I would wear it, but that was not to be.' She gave a little shake of her shoulders. 'She never knew Montague.'

Well, that at least Connie knew to be the truth. Nell's mother, her great-grandmother Alice, passed away when Nell was just fourteen. Afterwards, Nell met Montague, married him, and together they moved to Maitland. They purchased a property by the Hunter River, naming it Coloma after the river where Montague had first discovered Californian gold.

Then everything went quiet. Nell hadn't married at fourteen; she clearly remembered her saying she'd turned twenty-four only days before she'd married. It had never crossed her mind to question what had happened in the intervening years.

'Help me.'

Connie turned her attention back to Nell with a guilty start. 'What can I do?'

Nell's hands were compulsively threading a length of the material through her fingers. 'It's here. It's still here. My manicure set. Bring me my manicure set. It's in my bag under the window.' Connie found the small box and opened the lid; relieved that Nell had suddenly returned to the present, she held it out. Nell took the tiny curved scissors, flipped the silk over and started stabbing at the stitching holding the hem then huffed in frustration. 'I need my pince-nez; I can't see.'

'Give it to me; let me try. What do you want to do?'

'Unpick the stitching holding the hem.' Nell held out the swathe of material.

Surprised by the weight, Connie spread the skirt on her lap and ran her fingers along the hemline. 'There are weights sewn into it.' She knew all about them. Little metal buttons that were intended to weigh down the bottom of the gown and hold the fall of the skirt. She'd had to stand for hours while Mrs Beattie had pinned and fussed when her eighteenth birthday dress was fitted.

Nell reached for her hand. 'Very special weights.'

Curiosity aroused, Connie managed to slip the point of the nail scissors under the stitching, until a section of the hem loosened.

'Put your fingers inside. Can you feel anything?' Nell bounced on the bed, her impatience visible. 'Give it to me!'

Taking no notice of Nell's demand, Connie ran her fingers between the lining and the silk until she found a small, raised lump, a tiny pocket holding it firm. 'I've got it.'

'Gently. Unpick the stitching around the patch. Ease it out.' Nell's upturned palm butted against her arm.

'Be patient. We might have to cut the material.'

'No, we won't. Come on. Keep trying.'

If Nell would just sit still, move back a little, give her a bit more space it might be easier. She batted Nell's hand away and eased the warm irregular shaped stone out from the little pocket. 'I've got it.'

'Oh! It's just as I remember.' With a degree of reverence Nell plucked the nugget from Connie's fingers and closed her palm. 'Pure gold.'

'Gold? How do you know?'

'I put it there myself. We'll get the rest out later. It's almost morning. We need to rest.'

Rest? Connie could no more rest than fly to the moon and besides, there was the question of the stolen goods in the attic and the vanished intruder. 'Nell ...'

Nell's eyes sparkled, and she had her arms wrapped tightly around the bundle of yellow material again.

'Tell me about the gold. Why did you put it there? Where did it come from?' A thousand questions bubbled on Connie's lips.

'Montague gave it to me for safekeeping. I kept it under my mattress but I was frightened someone would accuse me of stealing so I had to hide it.'

'And you've waited all this time ...'

Nell thought for a moment then gave a determined nod. 'The gold belongs to the Montague family. Now what are we going to do about this intruder and the stolen goods in the attic?'

'I should go and get dressed and go straight down to the police station. And Mrs Alexander needs to know what we found in the attic. It solves the problem of where all the missing knick-knacks have got to.'

'I applaud your sentiments but think for a moment or two. How are you going to explain the fact that you and Maisie were up there in the first place, most especially the way the prowler has vanished into thin air?'

'The bloodstains.' Connie had almost forgotten about the bloodstains. 'Where's the cloth you used to wipe up the blood?'

Nell foraged through the pieces of silk damask until she found the lawn she'd torn from her nightdress. 'Stick it in my bag, out of sight.'

'People don't just vanish into thin air.' Connie tucked the bloodstained rag into Nell's bag. 'We're going to have to tell Mrs Alexander. She can't keep accusing everyone of stealing things.'

'Mmm.' Nell chewed on the corner of her nail, a sure sign her mind was elsewhere. 'There's something I need to explain to you first.'

The silence hung while Nell pleated the ripped skirt of her nightdress. Whatever did she mean? She couldn't be responsible for the stolen items, but she had been very familiar with the door to the attic and unlocked it without a moment's hesitation. Had known where to find the key. Had Maisie mentioned it? Had she? Connie couldn't recall.

A knock sounded on the door connecting Connie's and Nell's rooms. Nell stared at her in horror. 'Just one moment,' she trilled and the two of them bent and shovelled—no other word for it, shovelled—the beautiful silk under the bed and sat demurely hands in lap, side by side. 'Come,' Nell called.

When the door cracked open and Maisie's head appeared they exchanged a relieved glance.

'I couldn't wait a moment longer. Is he dead?'

Connie blinked rapidly trying to push beyond her thoughts of Nell, the missing trinkets, the dress, the gold nugget ... 'He's gone.'

'Gone?' Maisie's high-pitched shriek rattled the glass in the windows.

'Ssssh!' Nell and Connie hissed in unison. 'He wasn't there. We searched the attic and there was no sign of him.'

Maisie flopped down on the bed, her mouth gaping. 'So he isn't dead. Oh my.'

Why did Maisie have to keep stating the obvious? She bit back a sharp retort and paused for a moment before speaking. 'There was a bloodstain on the floorboards where he fell—a fresh bloodstain,' she added.

'What about the other things? Were they still there?'

'They were, and we left them. I'm going to tell Mrs Alexander what we found.'

'Oh, but you can't do that.' Maisie stared at her wide-eyed. 'She'll kick me out for snooping, sticking my nose in where it isn't wanted. I'll have nowhere to go, and how will poor Miss Pettigrew manage?'

Nell lay back against the pillow, eyes closed, motionless but for the beating of her pulse, barely visible in the hollow of her throat. 'I see your point. What are you suggesting?'

'She doesn't need to suggest anything. I have no intention of involving Maisie. I'll tell Mrs Alexander I went on my own—I did the first time so I'm sticking close to the truth.' Connie caught Nell's wry smile as her words came back to haunt her.

'Oh! Would you do that for me?' Maisie's voice wavered. 'No one's ever done anything like that for me before.'

'Right.' Nell stood up and dusted her hands together. A sure sign she had a plan of action. 'Off you go, Maisie. And start your day the way you mean to go on—everything as regular as clockwork.' As if in response, the grandfather clock boomed seven times. 'We've got work to do.'

'Oh yes, I will. Mum's the word.' Maisie covered her lips with her fingers and slipped out the way she'd come.

'That was a particularly lovely thing to do for Maisie. Are you sure it is what you want?'

Connie smiled. 'I like her. I like her spirit of independence and it makes no difference to what has happened if her name isn't mentioned. I'll go and get dressed and go directly down to breakfast, everything as clockwork as you said, then go and speak to Mrs Alexander and we'll take matters from there.'

A range of emotions flickered across Nell's face. 'I think it might be sensible if you postponed your meeting with Mrs Alexander until we have returned the dress.'

Connie narrowed her eyes. 'I don't understand. If the gold is yours, if you put it there, then why shouldn't we simply explain to Mrs Alexander?'

'Explain that I came here under false pretences? Explain how the gold came into my possession? If Mrs Alexander finds out about it, she won't believe me. She'll claim it for herself. Least said soonest mended is a very good axiom. We can't risk going up into the attic during the day so we wait until tonight, when everyone is asleep, put the dress back where it belongs and then in the morning you go and see Mrs Alexander.'

'You have to tell me what's going on, Nell. Why, after all this time, do you need the gold? Why are you being so mysterious? You're frightening me.'

A rather nasty harrumph sneaked its way past Nell's lips. 'You're right but now is not the moment. It's very important that we keep things on an even keel. Go and get dressed, have breakfast, and tell everyone that I have woken with a head cold and will be remaining in my room. Bring me a tray, tea and toast, once you have eaten; it will give us time.'

Nell's gaze pinned Connie to the spot and the words on her tongue dried. Nell would not be hurried; there was little point in arguing. She let her shoulders drop and walked to the door, the sound of Nell's yawn echoing in her ears.

23

Monday, 6 May, 1889

Connie buttoned her blouse and straightened her hair then made her way downstairs to the dining room, questions chasing each other around in her mind like moths batting against a closed window. She'd set off from Maitland in search of Nell because she'd known deep down in her bones that there was something very wrong but not in her wildest imaginings had she thought it revolved around gold. Gold! Why would Nell have need of gold? Something had to have happened in the days leading up to her departure from Maitland, but she couldn't for the life of her imagine what, and why, if the gold belonged to the Montagues, had she waited so long to retrieve it?

Maisie's stare bore into her back as she stood at the sideboard helping herself to some breakfast and a cup of tea. When she finally sat down Maisie's raised eyebrows questioned her. She had no answers. She'd told her that she would keep her name out of it. What Maisie didn't know was that she couldn't speak to Mrs Alexander until the dress was back in the attic. Surely her

180

first reaction would be to go up there and check Connie's story about the stolen items. What if she noticed the blood on the floor or worse still that the trunk had been opened? How long would it take to unpick the hem of the dress? Exactly how much gold had Nell stashed in there? Nell's eyesight simply wasn't up to the task; if only she could ask someone to help.

'What are your plans for the day?' Maisie's voice broke the silence. 'If you're going into town, I would enjoy the company or we could meet later for a walk?'

'I think I'll stay here. Mrs Montague is not feeling terribly well. She thinks she might have caught a chill.'

Miss Pettigrew tutted. 'Poor dear. The night air is not the best at this time of the year.'

Connie jumped and gazed at Miss Pettigrew, trying to ascertain if there was anything sinister meant by her words. After all, her room was on the ground floor. Had she heard, or worse, seen them sneaking past? She shook the thought away. It was ridiculous. The woman was scarcely capable of leaving her room without assistance and her hearing was atrocious.

'I do hope it's not contagious.' Miss Pettigrew patted Maisie's arm. 'Are you quite well, my dear?'

'I am, thank you, Miss Pettigrew, except that I will be running late for work. I must start a bit early because I've got a half-day. Have you finished your breakfast?'

'I suppose I have, although I wouldn't mind staying here a little longer, perhaps chatting to Miss Constance.'

Connie raised her head and met Maisie's questioning gaze. 'I'd be more than happy to take you back to your room, Miss Pettigrew, but first I must go to the kitchen and organise a tray for Mrs Montague. Would you like to look at the newspaper for a few moments?'

'Then that's settled. Off you go, Maisie. I'll expect you this afternoon.' Miss Pettigrew reached for the paper and dragged it towards her while Maisie and Connie pushed back their chairs and made for the door.

'Is Mrs Montague sick? She looked perfectly fine earlier,' Maisie murmured.

'She's simply tired.'

'And you're going to see Mrs Alexander this morning?'

That was a trifle difficult. 'No, not immediately. I need to think about what I'm going to say.'

Maisie laid a hand on her arm. 'You know I really can't thank you enough for keeping my name out of this. Is there some way I can repay you?'

And then the thought came to her. 'Possibly, but I have to speak to Nell first.' Why hadn't she thought of it before? With Maisie's sewing skills they could get the gold out of the dress in record time, and it would be fair exchange for Connie's promise not to involve Maisie when she fronted Mrs Alexander. But would Nell be prepared to share her secret? Oh! All this skulduggery was so very difficult. 'I'll see you when you get back from work.' Connie left Maisie at the bottom of the stairs and headed for the kitchen, her skin prickling as she walked past the attic door and took a quick glance at the chest of drawers under the window.

'Excuse me, Mrs Trotter, but I wondered if I could bother you for a tray. Mrs Montague is a little under the weather, but I think she should have a drink and something to eat.'

Mrs Trotter dusted her hands on her apron. 'Poor dear. I hope there's nothing nasty brewing.'

'So do I.' The words popped out of Connie's mouth with more vehemence than she anticipated. She too was tired, hardly surprising. 'Let me help.'

'No, I'll get June to see to it. You sit down here for a minute. You look a tad wan yourself.' She bundled off into the scullery and Connie rested her head back and closed her eyes, letting the warmth of the kitchen and the homely smell of freshly cooked bread soothe her.

'Here we are.'

Connie jumped as the tray plonked down on the table and June's smiling face filled her vision. 'A pot of tea. Some toast, butter and honey. I know Mrs Montague doesn't like too much for her breakfast, but she needs something inside her. Mrs Trotter says to let her know if you need anything else.'

'Thank you, that's perfect. I'll take it up to her right now.' Connie picked up the tray and made her way back along the corridor and as good as bumped into Mrs Trotter in the hallway outside the attic.

'Got what you need?' Mrs Trotter slammed the top drawer of the chest of drawers closed, the attic key dangling from her fingers.

Connie couldn't drag her eyes away. No doubt about it. The attic key; the long brass nameplate dangled. 'Yes, thank you,' she stuttered, and made for the stairs.

She nudged open the door to Nell's room and found her sitting in one of the cane-backed chairs, eyes closed and a gentle smile on her lips. Connie tiptoed across the room and placed the tray on the occasional table then slipped back out to rescue Miss Pettigrew.

Much to her surprise strains of laughter greeted her as she reached the hallway. She peered around the dining room door. Miss Pettigrew remained at the table, the open newspaper in front of her. Mr Humbert had appeared and was recounting some tale which had Miss Pettigrew in hoots. He leapt to his feet the moment he spotted her. 'Good morning, Miss Constance. And a very fine morning it is too. Aren't these autumn days a delight?'

'Mr Humbert was telling me about his latest excursion to Windsor and the interesting characters he met. Have you come to take me back to my room?'

'Yes, I have. I'm sorry I kept you waiting.'

'I have enjoyed myself enormously. Thank you, Mr Humbert. I hope to hear more of your stories.' She bestowed a glowing smile on Mr Humbert and for a moment Connie saw the woman she might once have been. Full of laughter and happiness. Life could be a cruel mistress.

'I still haven't found my portrait,' Miss Pettigrew said as Connie settled her in her room. 'I told Mrs Alexander it was missing. She said she'd make enquiries but nothing has eventuated.'

Connie batted down the flush rising to her cheeks. She couldn't tell Miss Pettigrew that her portrait was in the attic, certainly not until she'd spoken to Mrs Alexander. 'Why don't you read your book? It'll take your mind off it. I'll have a word with Mrs Alexander.' No lie in that.

'Would you, dear? That would be most kind. I miss Obadiah's company.' She opened her book where the ribbon marked her place and began to read, her lips forming the words.

Connie closed the door behind her and trudged back up the stairs to Nell. As much as she'd like to crawl under the blankets and go to sleep, they needed to sort out the dress and maybe, if she chose her words carefully, she could convince Nell that Maisie's help would be invaluable.

She cracked open the door between the two rooms. Nell remained in the cane-backed chair, her hands clasped in her lap, blindly staring out of the window, her breakfast untouched.

'Are you not hungry?'

She turned to her with a vacant gaze and Connie's stomach somersaulted.

'Nell?' Connie took the cold, alabaster white hand resting on the arm of the chair and smoothed it gently.

After an eternity Nell's lips moved, as though she was framing her words. No sound came out and then she snatched back her hand and sat turning her wedding ring, around and around, a habit as familiar to Connie as the ring itself, but somehow today it was different; then Nell opened the palm of her hand where the gold nugget sat. 'It's the same gold, you know.'

'The same?'

'Montague's gold.'

Nothing made sense. Connie had heard the story a thousand times, how Montague had left Australia for California and made his fortune, returned, and claimed Nell, fulfilling a promise he'd made years earlier. How could Montague's gold have ended up in the hem of a dress? Not just 'ended up'; Nell had already said she'd sewn it into the dress. 'From California?'

Nell shook her head, a frown creasing her brow. 'Not the Californian gold.'

Then what gold? Connie suppressed her frustration and cupped her hand around the warm teapot. 'Why don't you have a cup?' Without waiting for a response, she poured it out, added a slice of lemon as Nell preferred and handed it to her, hoping it would clear Nell's head. 'Come on. Drink up.'

Nell sipped the tea slowly and a touch of colour returned to her cheeks. 'There was gold before California. Montague found it in a river, near Hartley on the western edge of the Blue Mountains. That's how we met.'

'In the Blue Mountains?'

'No, silly girl. He brought the gold here to Parramatta to tell Governor Gipps what he'd found. That was the first time we met. I was visiting with Lady O'Connell; she liked me to travel with her as lady's maid. While I was picking flowers for the house I came across him wandering around the grounds. He asked me to introduce him to the governor.'

All well and good but it didn't explain why Nell decided to hide the gold in a yellow silk dress that had once belonged to a woman called Elizabeth Betham. 'Why didn't Montague keep the gold? Use it to set himself up.' That was what people did in those days when they discovered gold. The country was full of stories of the gold rush and fortunes made overnight. 'Why did he go to California?'

Nell's eyes suddenly lit up and she leant forward in the chair with a ferocious glare. 'Because he was honest. Too honest as it turns out. Governor Gipps told him to take the gold away, never speak of it, because they'd all have their throats cut if news got out.'

'Their throats cut?'

Nell waved her hand in the air, dismissing Connie's interruption. 'You seem to forget, in those days New South Wales was a penitentiary; even though transportation had ended there were thousands still working out their sentences. The governor and the ruling elite thought if the convicts struck it rich there'd be a rebellion and the status quo would be destroyed.'

'So, you hid the gold?'

Nell's mouth quirked in a smile. 'Not initially. Montague left it in my safekeeping while he went to California.' Nell twisted her wedding ring. 'He had this made for me before he left. He wouldn't take me with him, didn't know what he would find there. He said the ring and the nuggets were a down payment on the future. It worried me, no end, all that gold bundled under my mattress in the servants' quarters and a ring more suited to a lady than a lady's maid. I was terrified I'd be accused of theft and someone would find the gold nuggets, so I hung the ring on a piece of golden embroidery thread around my neck and stitched the nuggets into the hem of the yellow dress. Mam had always said it made all the difference in the world if a hem was weighted. In some strange way I hoped it would take the gold off my mind if it was hidden from sight. It took me hours, night after night by the light of a candle, tiny little pockets to hold it in place, just like Mam had taught me. It was long before I had a pair of pince-nez to make things easier. I knew the dress would never be worn. Mam had told me Lady O'Connell's mother wore it on her wedding day and she sent it to Australia so it could be remade into something suitable. Lady O'Connell hated it, said the colour made her look sallow and besides, she had a reputation to keep up—ever since she'd first arrived in the colony with her father, people had looked to her for the latest fashions.'

But it still didn't explain why Nell had decided she needed the gold now, after all this time. 'Why don't you drink your tea and eat your toast? I'm going to go and wash my face and change my clothes. I'll be back in a little while and you can tell me why you came in search of the gold.'

24

Nell stretched her hands above her head, positively invigorated by the turn of events. She'd found the trunk, and the dress and the gold. Everything would work out. Only she and Connie knew about the gold. All they had to do was unpick the rest of the hem, return the dress to the attic and go home.

She'd rather hoped she'd be able to stave off Connie's questions for a little longer. She owed her the truth but there was no good reason to subject her to the whole horrible, sordid tale until she knew the gold could be exchanged for sufficient money to deal with Edwards.

The only difficulty was she would have to rely on Connie to unpick the hem of the dress. Her own eyes simply weren't up to it, pince-nez or not. She'd done far too good a job, all those little pouches forming a neat pocket around each nugget. And the dress simply had to be returned before Connie told Mrs Alexander about the intruder and the contents of the attic. She'd hoped they'd be able to get away with it, simply make no mention, but there was always the possibility someone had seen or heard something, and she certainly didn't want Connie accused.

The sound of the interconnecting door opening brought her back to the present. Connie stood leaning against the doorjamb, her face pale and shadows beneath her eyes.

'Are you dreadfully tired?' Neither of them had had more than a couple of hours' sleep but there was no time to waste.

'Not dreadfully, but I wouldn't mind a nap later on, if you can manage.'

'To be honest I can't. I wish I hadn't been so diligent when I'd sewn the gold in the dress. All those tiny little patches are a nightmare to unpick, and we must have the dress back in the attic tonight.'

'Tired or not then, we better get started.' Connie dropped onto her hands and knees and pulled the bundle from under the bed. 'I did have a thought ... we could ask Maisie to help when she gets back; she's got a half-day today.'

'Maisie? Tell Maisie about the gold? No, we absolutely cannot. It's bad enough that she was with you in the attic. I don't want anyone else to know about it.'

'But ...'

'No buts. Here are my nail scissors. I don't suppose you brought yours with you. Two pairs would make things faster. I'm sure I can help a little.'

'No, I didn't bring my manicure set. I left in a bit of a panic. If we spread the dress out on the bed and you hold the hem tight, I think it might make it a little easier. The material is so slippery.'

Nell ran her fingers across the silk damask, the stylised foliage and flowers woven into the material bringing back so many memories—of Mam and the stories she told her, and of Lady O'Connell. She shook the thoughts away; now was not the time. As much as she'd love to have the dress it wasn't hers to keep, but the gold was.

'It might be a little easier to slip the point of the scissors under the threads.'

The top of Connie's head filled her vision, the irrepressible mess of curls; she couldn't count the hours she'd spent trying to tame them but what a godsend her granddaughter was. How she wished she'd taken Connie into her confidence from the beginning but how could she explain the terrible mess they were in? She just wanted to get the gold, go home, and pay the wretched fellow off. Just three more days until the fateful rendezvous.

'A bit tighter, Nell, while I snip the thread.' Connie slipped the point of the scissors under the tiny stitches, tugged each one free and dropped it onto the floor. They'd have to make sure they were all collected up.

'Got it! Put out your hand.' A second gold nugget dropped into her palm. 'Have you any idea how many there are?'

'I can't remember.' It had taken her weeks to sew them all in, snatched moments between jobs, nights hunched under the eaves working by candlelight. It seemed history might well be repeating itself.

'I'll put them in my pocket for safekeeping.'

Nell resisted the temptation to snatch the nugget away from Connie. How foolish. This was all for Connie and her disreputable pockets were finally proving their worth.

The time ticked by on Mrs Macquarie's clock and Connie's pockets began to fill but the nuggets just kept coming and coming.

Connie straightened her back and clambered to her feet. 'I've got to stop; I've got no feeling in my fingers. How many more do you think there are?'

'I told you, I can't remember.' Nell pulled the hemline between her fingers, counting each raised bump. 'At least another twenty I'd say.' More than enough to meet Edwards's demands unless the price of gold had fallen dramatically.

'At this rate we're not going to get it finished. Are you sure you don't want to ask Maisie for some help?' Connie glanced up at the clock. 'It's past midday; she'll be back before long.'

But could Maisie be trusted?

'I'm sure she won't say anything. She can't tell anyone without admitting she was in the attic with me. With her help we at least have a hope of getting it finished. You could give her a nugget as payment.'

'Buy her silence you mean?' It was bad enough intending to buy off the dreadful Jack Edwards. She seemed to be sinking further and further into the mire.

'Yes, that's what I mean. We need help. I can't do this on my own. And the longer I put off speaking to Mrs Alexander the more suspicious it'll become. Do you think she knows the yellow dress is there?'

'She might well know the dress is there, along with the other clothes belonging to Lady O'Connell—she's probably got a list of the contents of the trunk—but I am certain if she knew the gold was in the dress, she would have helped herself ages ago.' She'd be long gone. She was certain the gold would be worth more than it was when Montague gave it to her. In those days three pounds an ounce was the benchmark. The man in Sydney, Mr Golding, who'd exchanged Montague's Californian gold would know but she hadn't thought that far, hadn't expected to find it, truth be told, and she had Connie and her ghost to thank for that. And Maisie come to think of it. 'Perhaps we should have a word with Maisie.'

Connie's face broke into a gigantic smile. 'I'll go and see if she's back from work. I'm sure she'll be better at this than I am.' She bounded out of the room, her tiredness forgotten.

Nell ran her hand across the lustrous material; the iridescent brightness reflected the sunlight as it drifted between the shiny embellishment and the opaque background. She had thought herself composed but she suddenly couldn't catch her breath because of her choking tears.

She hadn't appreciated the beauty and the rich detail all those years ago. It was no wonder damask was chosen to decorate palaces and royal residences, for priestly robes and liturgical vestments. She turned over the sleeve to admire the lace and her heart stuttered.

Small blobs of blood splattered the sleeve. She picked hopelessly at the brown marks, spat on her fingers and rubbed, but to no avail. When she'd dropped the dress in the attic it must have landed in the pool of blood staining the floorboards.

Lost in her thoughts she jumped when the door opened and Connie appeared with a wide-eyed Maisie in tow. Obviously she had already told her about the dress because she had her tapestry sewing bag clutched under her arm and a rather sharp, nasty-looking implement in her hand.

'Maisie has just the thing. She says it will make our job so much easier. It's the latest thing, a seam ripper.'

That sounded a trifle dangerous. Nell couldn't bear the thought of the beautiful material being torn.

Maisie sat down on the bed next to Nell. 'Mr Humbert gave it to me. He said it was the latest gadget and he thought it might be helpful. It has this little fork here, and there's a sharp blade tucked in the joint. The point makes it easy to slip it under the stitches. It's much finer than your scissors.'

The dagger-like implement stabbed into the silk and Nell flinched. Not such a good idea. 'Don't damage the material.'

'Someone did a very thorough job. I promise I won't hurt the material.' Maisie reached out her hand and ran her palm over the yellow damask. 'It's beautiful. I'd love to wear something like this. It would be so deliciously soft against your skin and make the perfect wedding dress. Silk damask has always been the fashionable choice for brides who can afford it.' Colour stained her cheeks. 'May I?' She lifted the bodice of the dress, holding it from the shoulders. 'Golly gosh. From the style, the sloping shoulders, the pointed, fitted waist and the wide skirt, I'd say it's over a hundred years old, a hundred and fifty even.' She turned this way and that, picked up the skirt and laughed. 'Not very practical. Look at the size of it.' She spread out the material. 'The proportions are perfect—four times the width of the shoulders at the hem was the rule. Panniers would have been worn underneath it to hold out the skirt. You'd need to turn sideways to get through a door! See the back, the intricate stitching, every bit hand sewn, not like the new-fangled machines we use today. And it hangs so well because the hem is weighted. That's quite unusual.'

It seemed young Maisie did know her business. And her comments brought them very nicely to the task in hand. 'Which is why we need your help. We need to remove the weights in the hem.'

'But why?'

'Because they don't belong there,' Connie interrupted. She reached into her pocket and brought out a handful of nuggets.

Maisie's eyes bulged. 'Is that gold? Real gold?'

Nell nodded. 'Do you think you and your little unpicking tool can make the job easier?'

'I can try. I'm sure it can't be too difficult.' She turned the hem over. 'It's very strange the way the hem is sewn. These little pockets. I suppose the person who stitched it in didn't want to run the risk of any of the nuggets falling out.'

'No, *I* didn't.'

There was a long, fraught pause. A countless array of expressions flickered across Maisie's face—incredulity, awe, wonder. 'You sewed them in there?'

'That I did. Now shall we get a move on?' At this rate they'd be here for the next week. 'We need to get the dress back in the attic tonight.'

Maisie sat on the bed, the dress draped over her lap, and carefully inserted the point of her little gadget under the stitches until they were resting in the fork then with a quick flick of her wrist, she lifted the tool and the blade sliced through the thread.

'Oh, that is so much easier.' Connie threw an I-told-you-so look at Nell as Maisie plucked the threads of embroidery silk from the hem and picked out the gold nugget, closely examining it before handing it somewhat reluctantly to Connie.

'How do you know it's not fool's gold?' Maisie squinted at the next row of stitches.

'Because I do.' Nell's voice sounded sharper than she'd intended, and she regretted her impatience as Maisie moved to the next patch of stitching, released the nugget, and moved on.

One by one Maisie freed the remaining nuggets, Connie's pockets bulged, and the sun lost its brilliance.

'That's the last one.' Maisie handed it to Nell.

'That one is for you.' The look of astonishment on Maisie's face cheered Nell almost as much as the fact the task was complete.

'I couldn't, really I couldn't.'

'Yes, you can. It's a job well done. Thank you. Connie and I will wait until the house retires, and then make our way to the attic and replace the dress in the trunk. All this excitement is a bit much for an old lady like me.' Nell did feel quite exhausted, but she suspected it was a mixture of lack of sleep and nothing since breakfast topped off by a good dose of relief. 'We all need to make sure we are at dinner this evening and then once the house settles ...'

'Oh. I've forgotten poor old Miss Pettigrew. I must go and see to her. She'll be wanting to change and go into the drawing room for a chat before dinner.' Maisie reached the door then turned back. 'And thank you so much for this.' She held up the gold nugget. 'I didn't expect any payment. Are you sure?'

'We're sure,' Nell and Connie chorused. 'Keep it safe, and not a word.'

Once the door had closed Connie dragged the bag from under the bed then laid the dress out on the quilt. 'It's really such a shame that it has to be hidden away—the stories it could tell.' She lifted one of the sleeves and spread it over her hand. 'I can just imagine Elizabeth Betham's hand resting on her husband's sleeve, the lace draping down. Who did she marry? Do you know?'

Nell masked a smile, a test for Connie's history lessons. 'William Bligh, Admiral of the Blue.'

'The *Bounty* bastard?'

'Constance Montague, I shall scrub your mouth out with soap if you use words like that.'

'He was a horrible man. Oh! But is that how the dress came to be in Australia? Did his wife bring it with her when he was governor?'

A shame. Connie's history wasn't as good as Nell hoped. 'His wife didn't accompany him. His daughter, Mary, later Lady O'Connell, did.'

'The Lady O'Connell you worked for?'

'The very one. She returned to Australia with her second husband Lord O'Connell when he was appointed a member of the New South Wales Legislative Council and went in search of Mam but it was too late.' Nell swallowed the lump in her throat, pushing back the memory of the misery and hardship they'd endured. 'When she learnt Mam had died she offered me a position in their household.'

'So, Mrs Mumford was right when she said you'd been in service.'

'I thought she'd be more circumspect.' Nell gave a little shake of her head. Nothing she could do about it now and not very important in the scheme of things. 'Let's get ourselves changed for dinner, make polite conversation, and once everyone has turned in for the night, we'll put the yellow dress back where it belongs.'

'Nell …?'

Nell had no doubt she could guess what Connie was going to say and she had no intention of going into details about the reason she needed the gold.

25

By the time Nell and Connie had made themselves presentable and gone down for dinner everyone else was seated. 'Please excuse our tardiness; the time got away from us.'

Mrs Alexander gave what could only be described as a faux smile. 'Let me introduce our new guest.' She held out her hand, palm up, and gestured to a young man in a somewhat shambolic brown suit and matching hair who was struggling to his feet. 'Mr Robert Ballantyne, he will be staying with us for a few days.'

Connie gave a surprised squeak. 'Mr Ballantyne and I met on the train to Sydney.' Her cheeks pinked. 'Hello, again.' She sank into the nearest vacant seat.

'So, you have met Miss Constance.' Mrs Alexander waved her hand towards her. 'And this is Mrs Montague. I believe I've introduced everyone else.' Mrs Alexander peered down the table like a schoolmistress checking her pupils were all present and correctly attired.

The young man moved to hold out the last empty chair for Nell, his manners a vast improvement on his sense of dress. No one wore a worsted wool suit to dinner. 'Thank you.' Nell gazed around the room. No Mr Whitfield, no Mr Humbert either, everyone else present. 'And what brings you to Parramatta, Mr Ballantyne?' Nell looked pointedly at Connie. She had made no mention of the man, or any meeting on the train.

He dragged his gaze away from Connie's tell-tale pink face. 'I'm … um … I write articles for newspapers and periodicals, and I'm researching a story on the history of the various government houses in New South Wales. Mrs Alexander was kind enough to offer me the use of Mr Humbert's room while he is travelling.'

Nell's scalp prickled; the name sounded familiar. She leant back in her chair as May, or was it June, placed a bowl of beef consommé in front of her. Ballantyne—she'd heard it quite recently, not from Connie, who hadn't seen fit to tell her of her meeting on the train; she'd seen it written somewhere. Ah! A writer. 'Mr Ballantyne, I believe I may have read one of your pieces in the *Cumberland Mercury*. A report on the new Hawkesbury Rail Bridge?' She swallowed her sigh of relief and picked up her soup spoon.

He gave a charming smile. 'That's correct. I met Miss Montague on the train to Sydney a few days ago.'

And there it was. No point in attempting to hide their relationship now both Maisie and Taylor were already aware of her foolish pretence and she suspected Mrs Alexander had come to the same conclusion. 'My granddaughter and companion.' Now why hadn't she thought to say that before?

Miss Pettigrew held her hand to her ear and leant forward. 'What was that? Speak up.'

'Miss Constance is my granddaughter,' Nell boomed.

Miss Pettigrew frowned. 'Not your companion?'

Good grief. 'She fulfils both roles.'

Maisie and Taylor both covered their mouths, eyes dancing. She really needed a change of subject.

Miss Pettigrew provided it. 'It's very dark in here this evening. Could we light the other candelabrum?'

Connie's and Maisie's eyes bulged. They knew the other candelabrum was up in the attic along with all the other stolen bits and pieces, as did she. When she and Connie took the dress back, she'd bring it down and slip it into the sideboard. She couldn't bear the thought of May or June taking the blame.

'Unfortunately, no. It required some repairs. I'm sure there's sufficient light. Mrs Montague, do you require your pince-nez? I'm sure your companion-granddaughter could fetch them for you.'

Mrs Alexander's snide tone made Nell's fists clench. 'I can manage quite well. So, the candelabrum isn't missing? So much confusion; all these pieces here one minute and gone the next.'

'My portrait is still missing.' Miss Pettigrew's plaintive tone echoed.

Mrs Alexander puffed out her cheeks and lifted her eyes to the ceiling. 'As I told you, Miss Pettigrew, the staff have been alerted. May I suggest a thorough search of your room to ensure you haven't misplaced it.'

A weighty silence reigned while the girls collected the soup plates and replaced them with a rather insipid slice of meat covered in gravy and a dollop of mashed potatoes.

Nell turned to Maisie. 'Have you found your missing thimble?'

Maisie gave a mournful shake of her head. 'No, I haven't.'

'Are you sure you didn't leave it at the theatre when you were fitting Mr Kingsley's waistcoat?' Taylor asked.

Maisie simply sat with her head in her hands, a picture of abject misery.

'Why don't we go back to the theatre and see if it has turned up there after we've finished dinner?' Connie patted Maisie's hand.

'We can't. Tonight's the last night. I tried to get tickets but they'd sold out. And besides, the play started half an hour ago, at seven.'

'And it's dark. You can't roam around the streets at night.' Mrs Alexander looked askance.

'We walked to and from the theatre the other night and came to no harm. I'll come with you,' Connie offered.

'And so will I.' Taylor placed her knife and fork down on her plate and pushed back her chair. 'We can go around to the stage door and ask if anyone's found it. It's better it's done now before the show ends. Please excuse us.'

Nell gaped at Connie. Whatever was she thinking? She shot to her feet. 'Connie, a word before you go.' Taking her arm, she as good as dragged her into the hallway. 'You can't go into town,' she hissed. 'We've business to attend to.' Nell threw her most ferocious frown; it simply wouldn't do. 'What time will you be back? And why didn't you tell me about this Ballantyne chap?'

Connie shrugged. 'I didn't think Ballantyne was particularly important. We'll only be an hour or so. We'll put the dress back when I return.'

And with that Nell had to be satisfied. She wandered back into the dining room and sat down. 'These young things.' She shook her head. 'What's for dessert?'

'A peach trifle, I believe.'

Mr Ballantyne rubbed his hands together. 'Excellent. Trifles are a joy to behold—and ingest,' he added more as an afterthought.

Now seemed the ideal opportunity to bring up the jewellery box, particularly as the girls had given her the perfect opening. 'Maisie is very concerned about her thimble. I do hope they find it. Possibly just a simple case of misplacement, like Miss Pettigrew's portrait and perhaps the jewellery box.' She glanced down the table at Mrs Alexander and raised her eyebrows. 'Hopefully the candelabrum will be repaired before too long. It must be such a responsibility being the guardian of all these historical treasures.'

A faint flush tinged Mrs Alexander's cheeks. 'A responsibility and a privilege.'

Surprisingly it was Miss Pettigrew who saved Nell from having to manipulate the conversation any further. 'You said you had an inventory of all the furnishings and fittings unless I'm mistaken, with the history attached? I'm sure Mr Ballantyne would be interested. There are some fascinating pieces. Do tell.'

Mrs Alexander's nostrils pinched as she inhaled, saved by May's appearance with a large cutglass bowl of trifle. 'Thank you, May. You may go. I'll serve the trifle. We'll only be needing four bowls; the girls have gone into town. Maisie still hasn't found her silver thimble and thinks it may be at the theatre.'

'Yes, Ma'am.' May dumped down the four bowls she already had in her hand on the table, proving without a doubt there was little that happened in the house that the kitchen wasn't aware of. Which brought Nell up with a nasty jerk. Just how much did they know about the goings-on in the attic? Connie had mentioned the fire—surely there was no real reason for them to go up there.

Nell passed a bowl of trifle to Miss Pettigrew and settled the second at her place while Mrs Alexander fussed around making certain Mr Ballantyne had more than his fair share before picking up her spoon and signalling that they should commence.

Only the sound of silver hitting the glass dessert bowls and Ballantyne's moan of delight broke the stifling tension. Nell really didn't want to raise the topic again, but she very much hoped Mrs Alexander's sense of self-importance would save the day.

She didn't have to wait long.

With her bowl pushed to one side, Mrs Alexander rested back in the carver at the head of the table. 'Now where were we? The inventory—a complete and comprehensive list of all the artefacts in the building. From the largest piece of furniture to the smallest teaspoon, all catalogued and my personal responsibility. As I'm sure you know, for seven decades this house was the country residence to the first ten governors of New South Wales until Governor Denison handed it over to the care of the Parramatta Park Trust in 1855. And there isn't one of the early governors or their wives who hasn't left their mark.'

Mr Ballantyne placed his spoon in his bowl and looked longingly at the remains of the trifle. 'I'm sure you have some fascinating stories to recount. I would be very interested to hear them.'

Nell curbed a grin. She couldn't put her finger on the exact moment she had begun to suspect Mrs Alexander knew more about the vanishing and reappearing of bits and bobs but it was delightful to see the pompous woman trip herself up. 'I'm surprised the contents of the guesthouse haven't been removed to Government House in Sydney, or the museum; they are part of Australia's history. I heard Premier Parkes speak,' Nell said. Possibly not the best topic of conversation. She really didn't want to have to explain how or where she heard Premier Parkes talking but she couldn't back down now. 'He is very taken with the idea of federation—allowing all our colonies to govern in their own right as the Commonwealth of Australia, independent from the Mother Country.'

A hush fell. Mrs Alexander and Miss Pettigrew stared at her as though she had committed some dreadful faux pas. Mr Ballantyne simply smiled.

'Independence from Britain?' Miss Pettigrew's voice wavered. 'That would never do.'

'It most certainly would not.' Mrs Alexander's eyes flashed. 'You are undoubtedly mistaken. Why, everyone in Australia is wedded to our remarkable past. There is such a market for these reminders. These paintings ...' She waved her hand towards the massive oil painting hanging over the fireplace—George III after the Battle of Waterloo. 'We have a shared history that cannot be swept away. That painting alone would be snapped up by any number of people. The contents of this house are worth a small fortune.'

A small fortune Nell was now convinced Mrs Alexander had earmarked for her own benefit.

26

The moon hadn't risen, and a fine drizzle slicked the street. Connie pulled up her collar and sank her hands deep into her pockets, thankful for the warmth they provided until Taylor insisted they should link arms and, walking three abreast, make haste down the carriageway and into George Street.

In the distance the theatre lights blazed but the streets were deserted. 'The play's still underway. We'll go around the back, to the stage door.' Maisie led them down the alleyway at the side of the theatre. The damp miasma settled, emitting a reek Connie didn't want to contemplate. And she'd thought life was unexciting and longed for some adventure. What was it Mrs Orchard liked to say? Be careful what you wish for. In less than a week, she'd travelled over one hundred miles, found Nell, thankfully unharmed but buried deep in some, yet unresolved intrigue, discovered an intruder, possibly a thief, and unearthed a cache of gold that would thrill anyone. Life was looking up.

Maisie ground to a halt. 'Here we are. The doors will remain locked until the end of the performance but I'll knock and see if anyone opens up.'

'Maybe you'll manage to get Mr Kingsley's autograph after all.' Taylor's elbow contacted Connie's rib.

Maisie looked over her shoulder. 'I'd rather have my thimble back.' She gave a wistful sigh.

'But you do happen to have your autograph book with you?'

'I might.' She raised her clenched fist to the door and hammered. Nothing happened.

'Now what?'

'We wait.' Taylor folded her arms and propped herself against the wall. 'Listen.'

Gradually a faint background noise infiltrated Connie's thoughts. 'It's the applause. The play's finished.'

Maisie raised her fist and hammered on the door again. 'There's no point. I'll have to wait a bit longer. It's the last night; there'll be flowers and congratulations, probably champagne in the dressing rooms. Shame we're out here in this stinking alleyway.'

Taylor stood with her shoulders resting against the brick wall and one booted foot crossed over the other, a picture of studied calm and indifference. Nothing seemed to ruffle her. How Connie wished she was able to take Taylor into her confidence and tell her about the attic and the intruder. She could keep her promise to Maisie, not mention her name, and she'd certainly value Taylor's support.

The applause rose to a crescendo. The George Street end of the alleyway flooded with light and the hum of voices and laughter drifted in the air. An eternity passed and finally the rattle of chain and padlock heralded the opening of the stage door. Maisie toppled down the steps and came to stand between Taylor and Connie in the gloom against the wall. The door was flung wide and a tall gentleman in evening dress stood silhouetted at the top of the steps.

'It's Mr Kingsley.' Maisie's excited cry rang in the darkness.

Connie gave Maisie a prod in the back. 'Go on, ask for his autograph.'

Maisie simply stood, glued to the spot, mesmerised.

As Kingsley reached the bottom of the steps Connie stepped forward. Maisie wanted the man's autograph so much, it was the least she could do … 'Mr Kingsley, good evening. I wonder if you …'

He swept off his topper, gave a theatrical bow, and her mouth gaped.

A wound running from temple to sideburn glowed in the half-light and what looked remarkably like dried blood clumped in his hairline. He raised his hand to his head, grimaced, replaced his hat and strode off down the alleyway.

Connie gasped and covered her mouth with her hand.

'Oh, good grief.' The weight of Maisie's body threw her back against the wall. 'Did you see it? His head.'

'See what?' Taylor peered into the darkness.

'Kingsley's forehead, the wound on his temple.' She traced a line with her finger. Kingsley couldn't be the man she'd hit over the head with the candlestick, could he? She lifted her skirts and took off after him.

When she reached George Street she skidded to a halt, fruitlessly searching the crowd.

A heavy hand came down on her arm. She wrenched away.

'It's me, Taylor. Come on. He went that way, down Church Street.' Without waiting for a reply Taylor flew across the road, skirting waiting cabs and the milling crowd, and headed towards the river.

It wasn't until Connie crossed Lennox Bridge that she caught up with Taylor, bent double gasping for air. 'I've lost him,' Taylor wheezed.

'Maybe it wasn't him.' But it was. Connie had no doubt about it, and she had seen the livid red mark running down his forehead, exactly like the wound she'd inflicted last night.

'Don't be ridiculous; of course it was Mr Kingsley. What I don't understand is why we're chasing him?'

'The man I clobbered in the attic was tall, long and lanky and his hair flopped across his forehead; I remember brushing it aside when I checked to see if he was alive.' She closed her eyes, recalling the horrid moment.

'That sounds like Kingsley, but it doesn't explain what you were doing in the attic, why you clobbered him or why we're chasing him.' Taylor eyed her with a look of blatant curiosity, perhaps also with a slight hint of being impressed. 'Or why you wanted to catch him, come to that.'

Connie let the air whistle out between her lips while she tried to make up her mind how much to tell Taylor. Not about the yellow dress, not without Nell's permission, but what about the fact Maisie was with her? She narrowed her eyes and studied Taylor. Could she trust her? She had to. 'I saw someone prowling around a couple of nights ago; they went up into the attic. Maisie told me about the ghosts that haunt the guesthouse and I—'

'You can't believe that rubbish.' Taylor shook her head.

'No, I don't. Not really but it was the only thing that made sense. Maisie wanted to go ghost hunting. It was just a lark really but when we got up into the attic someone came up the stairs and tried to grab Maisie. I went for him and struck him with a candlestick. It was the first thing to come to hand,' she finished lamely.

'And you think it was Mr Kingsley?' Taylor chuckled.

'It's not funny; I thought I'd killed him. He crashed to the floor, blood all over his face. We had to get help. I didn't know what to do. So, I told Nell but when we went back up there to see if he truly was dead, he'd gone.'

'Gone?'

'Vanished into thin air. Well, not quite; there was blood on the floorboards. When Mr Kingsley tipped his hat, he had a wound on his forehead exactly where I brought the candlestick down.'

'So, we chased after him. Not that bright under the circumstances. And what does Maisie think about all this?'

'I promised her I'd keep her name out of it. She was worried she'd lose her place at the guesthouse and her job with Miss Pettigrew if I told Mrs Alexander.'

'Told Mrs Alexander? Are you out of your mind? Why would you do that?'

'Because the attic was full of trinkets and valuables, all the bits and pieces Mrs Alexander claims are missing, and I think the man—Mr Kingsley—is responsible.' Connie turned a full circle. 'More to the point, where is Maisie? I thought she was behind us.'

'I told her to go and see about her thimble.' Taylor pulled off her hat and wrangled her riotous curls back into some sort of order. 'We should go back. I thought the chase was all a bit of tomfoolery but obviously there's more to this than I imagined.'

By the time they reached the theatre the lights were once more dimmed, the front doors locked and chained. The alleyway seemed even darker and more dismal than it had earlier. Connie rubbed her hands over the goosebumps on her forearms.

'Come on.' Taylor strode up to the stage door and without a moment's hesitation, shouldered it open and barged inside. The smell of greasepaint, perfume and tobacco laced the thick air and caught in Connie's throat. Raised voices and laughter drifted from the stage—some sort of party to celebrate the last performance as Maisie had said. They stepped through the wings and into the crowd.

Maisie stood, centre stage, hands on her hips, haranguing a tall woman dressed as Connie imagined a trollop would look.

A sweeping open velvet robe revealed a flowing satin chemise. Long dark curls in wild disarray framing a face with painted red lips and the darkest eyes imaginable. Connie glanced at Taylor who nodded back at her and together they marched up to the pair and stood either side of Maisie.

'You took it.' Maisie poked the woman in the chest with her finger.

'I did no such thing. It was a gift.' The woman stepped back and unclasped her hand, Maisie's silver thimble nestled in her palm, then she scoffed and rammed the thimble on her forefinger before waving it under Maisie's nose. 'Mr Kingsley gave it to me, in appreciation of my work as wardrobe mistress.'

'If that's the case go and get him. Prove it.' Maisie snickered. 'Wardrobe mistress!'

'Easy said. Not so easy to do. He's left.' The woman spun on her heel and presented her ample rump.

'Is there anyone else who can back up your story? Or should we go down to the police station?' Taylor enquired.

The woman spun around. 'What, for the sake of a thimble?' She stamped her foot. 'It's only plate, not solid. Take it.' And with that she thrust the thimble into Maisie's hand and disappeared through the wings to the dressing rooms.

27

Nell had left the dining room before she said anymore, worried that Mrs Alexander would guess what she was thinking. She was so certain she was correct. The woman was selling off the trinkets and valuables and she'd put money on the fact that the man Connie had hit in the attic was in it with her. Where was Connie? She glanced at the clock. How much longer would the girls be?

She stuck her nose against the glass and peered down into the darkness. No sign of them on the carriageway. Not that they could take the dress back into the attic yet. It was far too early. She'd left the dining room pleading a headache rather than join Miss Pettigrew, Mr Ballantyne and Mrs Alexander in the drawing room for coffee. No doubt she'd be regaling them with more stories of the treasures of Government House. The gall of the woman. How did she think she'd get away with it?

She lowered herself down onto her hands and knees and pulled the calico bag from under the bed. One last look before it went back to the attic.

Her hands sank into the bag, the silk cool against her skin as she brought out the pieces one by one and laid them on the top of the bed, then studied the hem. No one would think it had been unpicked. Maisie had done an excellent job. How she'd love to keep the dress. Have it remade for Connie's wedding. The thought brought her back to earth with a thump. She was losing track of her original mission. She couldn't be associated with the dress. How would she explain the gold? No one would believe her and without it she wouldn't be able to deal with that despicable man. Far more important that the Montague name and reputation remained intact, that Connie's future was not tainted by scandal.

How to explain that all that she had loved in Montague— his devil-may-care attitude, his bravery and his bravado—had somehow become distorted in his son. From his very first step Fred had teetered on the brink of disaster, always demanding so much attention and admiration. And as he'd grown, his childish sense of self-importance had only increased, not diminished. She'd blamed herself, blamed Montague, for the way they'd pandered to his every whim, and in the end, she'd given up. Done the only thing that made any sense. Let him live the life he wanted and then once Connie grew demanded she take over responsibility for her upbringing, determined history wouldn't repeat itself.

The knock on the door brought her heart to her mouth. Was it Connie? What if it was Mrs Alexander? She scrabbled around trying to stuff the dress back in the bag but what had seemed such an easy task with Connie's help defeated her.

The knock came again. Connie would simply walk in. Maybe she wasn't alone; there was nothing to hide from Maisie, but Taylor …

Better be safe. She stuffed the dress under the eiderdown and pulled the bed curtains. Threw back her shoulders and opened the door. Maisie, Connie and Taylor … Taylor! Thank heavens she'd hidden the dress. The three of them stood looking somewhat dishevelled and unless she was very much mistaken, sheepish. 'Come in.' She ushered them through the door and closed it behind them.

'Nell, something has happened. Something you need to know about.' Connie's bright red face shone in the light, Taylor's hair was all over the place and Maisie appeared to have been crying, and all three of them looked as if they'd outrun the devil. 'Sit down.'

Maisie and Taylor took the two chairs and Connie backed towards the bed.

'No, not there. Sit here.' Nell patted the blanket box at the end of the bed. 'You could all do with a glass of water. There's only one glass I'm afraid. Connie, have you got one in your room?'

Taylor stood up and chose a spot by the window so Connie plonked down next to Maisie. 'I'll get a glass later. This won't wait. The strangest thing happened when we were waiting outside the theatre. Mr Kingsley came out of the stage door.'

'Mr Kingsley?'

'The actor who is playing the lead role in the play.'

Nell lifted her shoulders slightly. She really had no idea, or interest for that matter, in this actor. All she wanted was to return the dress to the attic and move on. She should never have let Connie talk her into seeking Maisie's help, though the girl had done a wonderful job. And now there was Taylor to contend with. She dreaded to think how much Connie had divulged to her.

'The point is …' Taylor pushed off the wall by the window '… Mr Kingsley raised his hat to us.'

'And he had a large bruise on his temple and a long wound running down into his sideburn, the shape and size of the candlestick.' Connie drew a line down the side of her face with her finger. 'He's exactly the same build as the prowler I saw, and the man I hit in the attic.'

Nell jerked back to the conversation. So much for Taylor not knowing about Connie and Maisie's escapade. 'Are you saying what I think you're saying?'

'Yes. I'm sure it was Mr Kingsley I hit in the attic. When he saw the look on my face, he must have realised what I'd seen and took off up Church Street and then across the bridge into the park.'

'Connie was so stunned she just stood there like a dummy in a shop window, but Taylor chased off after him, so she followed,' Maisie added.

Nell dropped her head into her hands; this was getting worse by the moment. 'And ...' she hardly dared ask.

'I'm afraid I lost him. He outran me.' Taylor grimaced.

'He probably took a turn down one of the lanes and you missed him.'

'He didn't. I'm certain. I didn't lose him until he crossed Lennox Bridge. He disappeared into the trees.'

'None of this is of any consequence. You can't very well accuse a man of breaking into the guesthouse just because he's hit his head and didn't want to speak to you.'

'But there's more, more proof.' Maisie stuck her hand into her pocket—what was it about these girls and their pockets? She pulled out a silver thimble and held it aloft. 'I got my thimble back. Mr Kingsley gave it to the woman who calls herself the stage manager and wardrobe mistress.' She gave a derogatory snort. 'He must have stolen it.'

'And if Kingsley is stealing from the guesthouse he should be brought to justice,' Taylor added with a ferocious stare.

'You could have lost your thimble at the theatre.' Nell waved her finger in the air. 'You're leaping to conclusions all over the place.' Surely Taylor had more sense. 'Taylor and Maisie, I think it is time you both went to your rooms. Connie, I want a word with you.' She most certainly was not going to discuss the return of the yellow dress in front of Taylor. The girl already knew too much by half, and she wasn't about to add to it. 'Off you go. Sleep on it and I'm sure you'll come up with a suitable explanation by the morning.' She gave her best impression of a regal wave and after Taylor and Maisie threw rather confused glances at Connie, they left.

The door clicked shut and Nell turned to Connie. 'Now I have some questions. First and foremost, what exactly have you said to Taylor?'

Connie at least had the good grace to look a tad contrite. 'Just that I'd seen a prowler and the next night Maisie and I went ghost hunting, that I hit the prowler on the head, and when we went back to see if he was truly dead, he'd vanished.'

'Nothing about the dress?'

'No, nothing. And neither did Maisie. We agreed we would keep quiet about it.' She paused. 'But I don't think Taylor thought that was the full story. She's not stupid.'

Her sense of relief was a little premature. Connie was quite right. Taylor was nobody's fool. 'In that case I think the best thing we can do is return the dress as we planned, and you can tell Mrs Alexander about the intruder and the cache of missing items in the morning. I'm sure there's a perfectly good explanation about this Kingsley fellow, and you've just let your imagination run away with you.' She reached out to pat Connie's hand, but she snatched it away and jumped to her feet.

'I'm not mistaken. But if you won't believe me then I shall have to find some other way to convince you.' She bent down and dragged the empty calico bag from under the bed. 'What have you done with it?'

Nell pulled back the eiderdown to reveal the dress. 'It's got some blood on the sleeve.'

Connie's face paled. 'How?'

'I can only presume it was when I dropped it on the attic floor.'

'Have you tried to get it off?' Connie scrabbled around on the bed until she found the sleeve. 'What are we going to do?'

'I've had some time to think it over. And I believe the best solution is simply to leave it as it is. It could have happened years ago.'

'But the blood on the floor?'

'Is probably nothing more than a stain now. And the prowler ...'

'Mr Kingsley ...'

'Your description would fit half of the men in Parramatta.'

Connie gave a disgruntled grumble, bundled the dress into the calico bag and hefted it over her shoulder. 'I'll take this back to the attic. It's past ten o'clock. I could do with a decent night's sleep.'

'There's no need to be petulant. I'll come with you.'

'I don't need you to come with me. I'm not a child.'

'No, you're not. So, stop behaving like one. Let me go downstairs and make sure everyone is in their room. If not, I can say I'm in search of a glass of milk to help me sleep. You wait at the top of the stairs. I'll let you know when I've got the key and the coast is clear. It's my responsibility too, and I don't want you coming to any harm.'

Never one to hold a grudge, Connie acknowledged her with a brief nod and a wry smile.

Nell wasn't overly worried about Maisie or Taylor lurking around, and since she'd heard Mrs Alexander say goodnight and Ballantyne take Miss Pettigrew to her room there was no problem there. Mrs Alexander rarely set foot outside her suite of rooms in the evening; the only difficulty would be passing Mr Ballantyne's and Mr Whitfield's rooms—if Mr Whitfield had returned. Connie and Taylor's story had piqued her curiosity.

It was unlike Connie to be mistaken. She had a sharp eye and was one of those people who always recognised and remembered everyone's name even if she'd only met them briefly. Maybe it was a characteristic of youth that diminished with age. These days she remembered names and faces, but on more occasions than she'd like to admit she had difficulty marrying the two.

The polished wood of the banister released the faint scent of beeswax and lavender as she drifted down the staircase. Darkness wrapped around her, a blessing rather than a hindrance. No light shone from Mrs Alexander's rooms, and dim shadows cloaked the dining and drawing rooms. Keeping her hand on the wall, she headed for the servants' quarters; not a sound, just the flickering of the dying embers of the kitchen fire visible through the door. She eased open the dresser drawer and her fingers closed over the brass tag attached to the attic key.

Once she'd unlocked the door she returned to the bottom of the staircase.

Connie stood waiting on the first landing and when Nell raised her hand, she glided down the stairs without a sound, the calico bundle cradled in her arms.

The attic door swung silently open. 'Wait here,' Connie whispered then slipped up the stairs and disappeared into the darkness. Only then did the foolishness of their plan hit Nell. The prowler could well have his own key to the attic. What if he was waiting up there and she'd sent Connie into his hands? Her heartbeat thundered in her ears blocking out any sounds which might give credence to her panic. Without another thought she lifted her skirts and hurried up the stairs into the blackness.

'Nell!' The hissed reprimand brought her up short. 'What are you doing? I told you to wait.'

She gasped as she reached the top step; she didn't want to admit to Connie her sudden fear.

'I think we should have a look around and see exactly what is hidden up here. If it is Mr Kingsley, we want to be able to make a case.'

Nell blinked owlishly in the gloom. 'Make a case? Why would we want to do that?'

'Because Mrs Alexander accused you of taking the jewellery box, and by implication all the bric-a-brac. Mr Kingsley shouldn't get away scot-free.'

Or Mrs Alexander, if, as Nell suspected, she was somehow involved. All she wanted to do was to leave Parramatta, exchange the gold and get back to Maitland and deal with Jack Edwards. And now this fly in the ointment. 'Let's just get the dress back in the trunk and then once you've spoken to Mrs Alexander we can go home.' Nell squeezed past Connie and made her way to the window, ran her hand over the engraved name on the front of the trunk then eased open the lid.

Together they pushed the calico bag back into the trunk, fastened it tight and made their way back down the stairs.

Nell locked the attic door and slipped the key back into the drawer. 'Now, let's go to my room; I need to speak to you.'

'We're both exhausted. I just want to crawl into bed.'

'We have to agree on our plan.' She tugged Connie back up the stairs and into her room.

'Sit down.' Nell gestured to the bed. 'Neither of us will sleep unless we decide on how we're going to progress. Our original plan was that as soon as the dress was returned, you should speak to Mrs Alexander and tell her what you found in the attic.'

Connie nodded. 'I'll speak to Mrs Alexander tomorrow, and leave Maisie out of it as we agreed, but first I'm going to ask Taylor what she thinks I should do about Kingsley.'

Nell bristled. 'Why does Taylor have to become involved?'

'Because she saw the wound on Mr Kingsley's head and because I'm just so confused. I'm certain that the man I hit in the attic was the one I'd seen the night before but was that Kingsley? It's possible he'd just walked into a door and it's all a coincidence.'

'Bringing Kingsley into it will just confuse the situation and put you at risk. I feel responsible. If you hadn't followed me here none of this would have happened. It would be far better if you left both Taylor and Kingsley out of it.'

'Nell, it is my responsibility. I won't mention the gold and I'm not sure whether I will admit to walloping a man on the head with a candlestick but I am going to tell her I went up into the attic and found her so-called missing items.' A hysterical laugh bubbled between Connie's lips.

'Why don't we both sleep on it and decide in the morning?' Nell wrapped her in a warm embrace then patted her cheek. 'Off you go. I'm sure after a good night's sleep everything will seem much clearer.' The last thing she wanted was for Connie to bring up Kingsley; it would simply prolong the agony and she'd never get back to Maitland in time to deal with Edwards.

28

Tuesday, 7 May, 1889

Connie awoke as the sun rose. Much to her surprise the moment
her head had touched the pillow she'd sunk into a deep and
dreamless sleep.

She had every intention of clearing Nell's name. It was her
sole responsibility. If the matter of the gold came to light Nell
would be behind bars before her feet touched the ground. She
couldn't stomach the thought of breakfast. The sooner she spoke
to Mrs Alexander the better.

Once she'd washed her face and hands and dealt with her hair
she made her way downstairs to Mrs Alexander's rooms.

'Mrs Alexander, may I speak to you for a moment?' Connie
doubted it would be a moment, more like an hour. She had her
story down pat. She would make no mention of the yellow dress.
She would admit to snooping, and seeing the strange figure,
to taking the keys from the dresser and then she'd offer to go
and retrieve all the bits and pieces, including the ivory box and

thus clear Nell's name. Quite what she was going to do about Mr Kingsley she wasn't sure. It was all a bit difficult.

'A moment, not a lot more. I have menus to prepare; today is shopping day for May and June.'

'I believe I have found the missing items, all of them.'

Mrs Alexander's head came up with a snap, her eyes narrowed. Suddenly Connie had her undivided attention. 'Have you indeed. Where?'

'In the attic, the old servants' quarters.'

Mrs Alexander blinked, patted her hair, and fussed with the cameo she wore pinned to the high collar of her blouse, then tipped her head to one side. 'And how did this come about?'

Not exactly the question Connie expected. She anticipated more of a reaction, questions about keys and outrage at her impertinence, entering areas that were not open to guests.

'Two nights ago, I was unable to sleep. I was standing at the window, and I saw a figure slip from behind the trees and run around the back of the house. I'd heard a story that the guesthouse was haunted, and I went to investigate.'

'Very bold for a young girl.'

Connie tried for a coy laugh. 'You know how we young flibbertigibbets can be. My curiosity was aroused. I crept downstairs and saw the figure slip up to the attic. I hid in the doorway of the drawing room until he reappeared. I intended to follow but he just vanished into thin air.'

'Are you trying to tell me you believe a ghost is responsible for the thefts?' Mrs Alexander scoffed.

'Of course not but my curiosity was aroused and the following night I went back up there, and I found the silver candelabrum from the dining room, a pair of candlesticks and other silverware, the Jane Austen books.' She gestured to the empty shelf. 'Some jewellery, Miss Pettigrew's oil portrait, a pair of miniatures.'

Connie ground her palms together. 'And other bits and pieces,' she finished lamely.

'The attic has been used for storage for many years and the door is kept locked. What makes you think this so-called intruder is responsible?'

This wasn't going as well as she'd hoped. She really did not want to admit to walloping the man.

'How did you gain access?' Mrs Alexander's hand went to her chatelaine, fingers compulsively running over each of the keys, no doubt checking for the one belonging to the attic.

'I took the key from the dresser outside the kitchen,' Connie murmured.

'Does your grandmother know what you were up to?'

Connie shook her head. 'Mrs Macquarie's jewellery box was also there. My grandmother couldn't have stolen it.'

Mrs Alexander gave a derisive sniff.

'Ah! Now I understand. Your loyalty is commendable, but ill-placed.' She moved to the door and opened it. 'I will continue to hold Mrs Montague responsible until the jewellery box and the other items are back where they belong. See to it. Now if you will excuse me, I have matters to attend to.' She turned back to her desk.

Connie stood for a moment as the older woman ran her finger down a long list—apparently the subject was closed. So be it. Once everything was returned, honour would be satisfied and she and Nell could leave.

A bright shaft of sunlight swept across the black and white chequered floor lighting the path to the front door. Some fresh air would clear her head before she hunted down Nell and told her what had happened with Mrs Alexander.

Connie released her hair from the knot she'd hastily wrangled it into earlier and rammed her hands into her pockets. More than anything else she wanted to rush up the stairs into the attic, rescue the missing treasures and thump them all down right under Mrs Alexander's nose and demand she apologise to Nell. Suddenly she longed for the peace and quiet of Maitland, the regular pattern of the days; days which she'd once found boring now beckoned with a soothing familiarity—there were too many unanswered questions batting around like moths trapped against a windowpane.

Connie stopped in her tracks. A windowpane ... she ducked around the corner of the building into the courtyard where June's washing billowed in the wind, and gazed up at the attic window, then back down again to the row of ground-floor windows. Miss Pettigrew's room, Mr Whitfield's, Mr Humbert's (now Mr Ballantyne's) next door, the large window over the staircase before Mrs Alexander's wing opened up, stretching to the east reflecting the kitchen wing opposite—a perfectly framed courtyard. She'd put it down to chance that she'd been at her window and seen the figure slip around the side of the house, but the full moon had woken her and then the following night when the intruder had surprised them in the attic she had presumed he'd entered the same way as he had the first night, but was it possible that he was already in the building?

As she retraced her steps, the rap of knuckles on glass caught her attention—Miss Pettigrew's smiling face, pressed against the window and her waving hand.

'Hello.' She waved back and Miss Pettigrew beckoned her. Bored by her solitude the poor woman had spotted her. It couldn't be midday yet; more than likely she wanted some company. She crossed to the window and attempted to lift the sash, but it was locked tight. Pointing to her chest, then making a circle with her finger, she indicated that she would come inside. She'd go and get her a quick cup of tea and then take one to Nell. She could do with one herself: she'd missed out on breakfast again and was parched.

She ducked under the washing line and slipped into the kitchen where Mrs Trotter sat in front of the stove, her feet stretched in front of her, shelling a bowl of peas. 'Good morning. I don't suppose I could make a cup of tea?'

'Kettle's hot and the pot just needs a bit more water. Help yourself. It's market day and for some reason Mrs Alexander has decided I am not capable of organising the weekly shop, so she has taken May and June into town. I need to get these peas done, and the spuds. We usually have fish on market day. Depends what Mrs Alexander decides.'

'More like three cups if you wouldn't mind. I was wandering around outside and saw Miss Pettigrew at the window. I thought I'd take her a cup, and then one for Mrs Montague and me.'

'Cups over there on the dresser, milk and sugar's here. Miss Pettigrew will miss you when you're gone.'

Connie stalled, teapot in hand. 'We're not leaving just yet.'

'Mrs Alexander mentioned you and Mrs Montague would be off in a day or two.'

'Well, yes in a day or two. It's up to Mrs Montague.' Connie added a little milk to Miss Pettigrew's tea then placed the three cups and saucers on the tray. 'I'll bring it back later and take Miss Pettigrew her lunch if that helps.'

'It would, dearie. It would.'

Miss Pettigrew's door swung open the moment she knocked. 'I've brought you a cup of tea.' Her eyes darted around the empty room. How very strange.

'Ah! There you are.'

Connie swung round to see Miss Pettigrew teetering through the door precariously balanced on a pair of sticks. 'Call of nature. So handy being right next door to the water closet.'

It hadn't crossed Connie's mind to wonder how Miss Pettigrew coped all day. She shrugged. No business of hers. 'I've brought you a cup of tea. I'm afraid I can't stay.' Connie gestured to the other cups on the tray. 'One for Mrs Montague, and another for me; I missed breakfast. I'll bring you your lunch when I come back down.'

Miss Pettigrew's mouth went down at the corners. 'That's a shame. I was hoping we could have a little chat.'

'Later on. Mrs Montague needs me.' Connie turned on her heel. As sorry as she felt for Miss Pettigrew, Nell came first.

29

Nell paced up and down her room. She'd sat in the dining room waiting for Connie to appear until May and June had barged in and almost bundled her out as they frantically cleared up, chattering all the while about shopping day—obviously the highlight of their week.

When she'd left the dining room after breakfast Mrs Alexander's door had been ajar, and she'd presumed Connie was still with her and hadn't wanted to interrupt. She interlaced her fingers and peered out of the window. No sign of anyone. A cascade of curiosity played havoc with her insides, and a quiver of fear that Connie might have accidentally mentioned the gold. The time was long overdue to tell Connie why she needed it, but that was a conversation she didn't want to have. She carried a burden of responsibility, knowing the appalling details surrounding Fred's death, but how to admit that to his daughter?

A bump on the door sent her heart into her mouth and she flew across the room.

'I've brought us a cup of tea.' Connie's dear, smiling face appeared.

Nell's shoulders dropped. 'I've been waiting and waiting. Where have you been?'

'I'm sorry. After I'd spoken to Mrs Alexander I went out for a quick walk, just to clear my head and then Miss Pettigrew—'

'Never mind, never mind. Come and sit down and tell me what happened.' She took the tray from Connie, placed it on the table and handed her a cup.

Nell smothered a prickle of irritation while Connie concentrated on her tea for an eternity.

'Well?' Nell asked when Connie eventually settled her empty cup back in the saucer.

'Not much really. I told Mrs Alexander what happened but left out Maisie, the fact that I'd hit the intruder and the yellow dress.'

'Did she believe you?'

'Not about the ghost, no.' Connie gave a laugh. 'But I got the distinct impression she was covering something up. But she said if the jewellery box and other bits and pieces were returned she'd let the matter drop.'

'She expects you to go back into the attic and retrieve them?'

'I can't see what else she means.'

Nell gritted her teeth. She didn't trust the woman, convinced she was in some way involved with the thefts but unable to summon one skerrick of evidence. 'Oh!' She clapped her hand over her mouth. What if Mrs Alexander had discovered the gold in the hem of the dress and was just waiting to accuse her or Connie of taking it? It would be like history coming back to haunt her and the repercussions could be so much worse. Connie could end up accused of theft—stealing far more than a gaudy, ivory-encrusted, Indian bauble.

'What is it?'

She had to tell Connie. Tell her the full story. What a foolish old woman she was. She'd kept quiet to protect Connie but in so doing had put her in greater danger. She cleared her throat. She had no idea where to begin. 'There's something I haven't told you.'

Connie sat up a little straighter, her blue-black gaze fixed on her face.

'Nell, please. I can't help if I don't know what's going on.'

Nell inhaled, licked her lips, and sent a silent prayer to Montague. 'I received a letter.' There—she'd started at the beginning; it could only get easier. 'Hand delivered.' The thought that Edwards had walked up the path, stood on the step, bent and slipped the letter under the door made her skin stipple—the odious man.

Connie narrowed her gaze. 'What did this letter say?'

Wasn't admitting the truth meant to lighten the burden? Nell pushed back to her feet. The enormity of her responsibility threatened to overwhelm her. Connie's world was about to come toppling down. She picked up her fountain pen and clasped it tight, Montague's last gift, a talisman to give her strength, then took her notebook from the dressing table and pulled out the folded piece of paper. Good quality paper—the audacity; a streak of anger flashed through her, gave her courage and she handed it to Connie.

'*In accordance with the partnership agreement drawn up between the Montagues and myself ...*' Connie started to read the words, then her gaze skipped to the bottom of the page, a frown creasing her brow. 'Who is Jack Edwards?'

'I would have thought that is obvious from the letter.' Her anger built; not anger at Connie—rage and frustration that she had known nothing of the arrangement. 'Edwards worked for us as a stable boy, then trainer. When he decided to go his own way he and your father formed a partnership. Edwards would take the young horses to the country races, build their track experience, and they would split the winnings.'

'Nell, this is a blackmail letter—extortion. Why didn't you take it to the police?'

'And have our private affairs bandied around the town? We have our reputation to consider—your reputation.'

'But is it true? Was this man … Jack …' she glanced down at the loathsome letter '… Edwards … Pa's partner? How can he claim all this money?'

Nell let out a long sigh. The truth had to come out but not all of it.

Connie's gaze returned to the letter. 'Five hundred pounds! *Or I will make public the Montagues' dubious activities on and around the racetrack.* Stop beating about the bush and tell me what's happening. I have a right to know.' Connie trembled.

'Jack Edwards is threatening to destroy everything your grandfather worked for, created; the property, the stud farm, our livelihood is in jeopardy. The Montague name and reputation would be destroyed.'

Connie pushed her hand away. 'And so, you came in search of Montague's gold, hoping to silence Jack Edwards, pay him off.'

'That's about the sum of it.'

'I wish you'd told me in the beginning. I'm not a child anymore. This isn't the solution, Nell. He'll just come back, in a few months, a year or so, and demand more. Then what?'

'Things haven't worked out the way I thought they would. I was so determined to find the yellow dress I pushed everything else aside and now I have just two days to get the money to him or he'll go public.'

'Public with what?'

A great wave of heat, or was it shame and despair, coursed through Nell and she shook her head slowly.

Connie screwed up her face, jumped out of the chair, made three rounds of the room, and came to a halt with her back to the window. 'Nell ... you don't suppose Mrs Alexander is hoping you'll lead her to the gold?'

A goose tiptoed over Nell's grave. The very same thought had crossed her mind more than once, but it couldn't be true. Surely she couldn't know about the gold. 'Don't be ridiculous. She would have found it years ago, be living a life of luxury, not running a guesthouse in Parramatta and attempting to feather her nest.'

'I think we should leave as soon as possible. Mrs Alexander has hinted—more than hinted—that she wants us gone. Mrs Trotter told me she'd said we'd be leaving in the next day or two, so she obviously expects it. The sooner we get the gold out of here and back to Maitland the better and then we can face this blackmailing business. I'm going to bring everything down from the attic and put it in Mrs Alexander's room while she's out shopping. You start packing ...'

'We could take the train to Sydney this afternoon, spend the night at the Berkeley, I'm sure Mr Sladdin will find us a room, go and visit Mr Golding and be back in Maitland in time for luncheon.'

'Mr Golding?'

'The man who cashed Montague's Californian gold over the years. He won't ask any questions.'

30

Connie had to agree with Nell—the thought of going home shone like the brightest of lights. Jack Edwards and his extortion threats could only be dealt with in Maitland but before she allowed Nell to do anything else she intended to go and speak to Messrs Brown; they'd handled all of the Montague finances since Grandfather passed.

There was no sign of Mrs Trotter or May and June in the kitchen, so she headed straight for the dresser to retrieve the attic key. Slipping her hand into the drawer, she felt for the large bronze tag. Nothing there.

She spun around and tried the handle; the door swung open without a sound. In daylight the narrow flight of stairs appeared far less intimidating, and with the door ajar a beam of light made the ascent so much easier. Once she reached the top of the stairs the full extent of the attic stretched to her right and left crammed full of furniture wrapped in dust sheets like skeletons in a graveyard. Her steps faltered. In the dark she hadn't appreciated how large the attic was. A quick glance at the floor at the top of the stairs revealed just the slightest dark stain from the blood.

The jewellery box sat in the same place, reflecting shimmering shafts of jagged light. Nothing had moved. The inlaid box, the miniatures, Miss Pettigrew's portrait, the calfskin-bound first editions, the silverware—all as she'd last seen them. She bundled everything up and popped as much as she could inside the jewellery box then pushed the bound cutlery into her pockets, knives and forks on the right, dessert and soup spoons on the left, tucked the portrait under her jacket, in the waistband of her skirt, hefted the box and began her careful descent.

'Stay right where you are and don't move.'

Connie froze and stared down the stairs where an intimidating silhouette filled the doorway.

'Take it slowly and bring everything down here.'

Whatever was happening? She shot a look over her shoulder to the right and the left. No one. Just the man at the foot of the stairs. Not a ghost. Most definitely not a ghost. Whoever he was, whatever he wanted, there was no escape, and she certainly didn't want him to come up the stairs and find herself trapped in the attic; besides, she was doing nothing wrong. Mrs Alexander had told her to come and retrieve all the bits and pieces.

Taking a moment to steady herself, she took a careful step, the weight of the box disrupting her balance. Then the next. Concentrating, keeping her mind on her descent and not on the figure at the bottom of the stairs.

Finally, with only three more steps to go, the figure spoke again. 'I think we have the culprit, Mrs Alexander.'

'Thank you, Constable.'

Connie snapped her mouth shut. What on earth was happening?

'I'll take those things, thank you, Miss.' The constable reached out, took the candelabrum and candlesticks from under her arms and the box from her hands and placed it on the dresser. Then reached for the cutlery poking out of her pockets.

She slapped his hands away. 'I'll do that.' She pulled out the bundle of knives and forks, resisted the temptation of throwing them at him, and followed smartly with the spoons and dumped them on the dresser. 'What is this all about?'

'Mrs Alexander has alerted me to a series of thefts. You are Miss Constance Montague, are you not? I'd like you to come down to the station with me.'

'The station?' Her heart drummed a ridiculous tattoo. She had played right into Mrs Alexander's hands. 'Whatever for?' A ridiculous quiver traced her words.

'I am arresting you on a charge of theft.' The preposterous man flapped his hand over his shoulder at the pile on top of the dresser.

'I haven't stolen anything!' Damn, she was well and truly rattled. 'Mrs Alexander asked me to retrieve the box, which she had accused Mrs Montague of stealing, and the other items.'

He turned to Mrs Alexander who stood, arms folded with the slightest of smirks tipping her lips. 'Is that correct?'

'No, it most certainly is not.'

Connie whipped around. Bob Ballantyne stepped from the doorway of Mr Humbert's room. 'I can vouch for Miss Montague.' His raised eyebrow made a wash of heat rush to her cheeks. 'I overheard Mrs Alexander asking her to retrieve the jewellery box this morning.'

Mrs Alexander took two steps towards him. 'The man is lying, blatantly lying. How could he possibly have overheard such a conversation?'

The constable groaned and ran his fingers through his thinning hair. 'And you are?'

'Robert Ballantyne. I am staying here.' He flicked a thumb over his shoulder, indicating Mr Humbert's room. 'As I was leaving the dining room this morning I passed Mrs Alexander's sitting room. Miss Montague stood on the threshold, and

I heard Mrs Alexander say, "I will continue to hold you and Mrs Montague responsible until the jewellery box and the other items are returned. See to it."'

'*Mrs* Montague?' The constable scratched his head. 'I was under the impression you were *Miss* Montague.'

Connie's shoulders dropped; she could throw her arms around Ballantyne's broad shoulders and plant a kiss on his cheek.

He stepped closer. 'I think you would agree, Constable, that there is some confusion about the series of events. I don't believe you can charge Miss Montague under the circumstances.'

The constable gave a loud sniff, raised his arm and thought better of wiping the end of his somewhat bulbous nose on his sleeve. 'Mrs Alexander, could you please confirm that these are the missing items you were referring to when you came to the station this morning?'

Mrs Alexander pursed her lips, then flounced past Connie, opened the box, and pulled out the selection of earbobs, beads and cameos. 'I shall have to consult my inventory. Everything must be accounted for.'

'In that case please ensure that you remain at the guesthouse, Miss Montague, until Mrs Alexander has accounted for all the necessary items and reported back to me. I could by rights arrest you and detain you at the station but if you are prepared to give me your word you will not leave we can let the matter rest there for the time being.'

Connie nodded and the constable turned on his heel and made his way to the front door, Mrs Alexander scurrying after him. Her knees wavered then wobbled and she sank down on the bottom step of the attic stairs. 'I can't thank you enough, Mr Ballantyne, I had no idea that you were …' the word *eavesdropping* hovered on her lips '… there. I cannot imagine the outcome if you hadn't spoken up for me.'

'It was my pleasure. If there's one thing I cannot stand it is misrepresentation. I have some experience of such matters.' He gave a wry smile. 'I see a lot of this kind of thing during my research. However, I do think it would be a good idea if you took some legal advice. I wouldn't put it past the woman to continue her crusade against you and Mrs Montague. Have you any idea what has caused it?'

'My grandmother knew Mrs Alexander many years ago …' Her words petered out. How to explain? She didn't want to go into too many details. 'That's why I was on the train. I was coming to meet her.'

His lips twitched and his chocolate brown eyes twinkled. 'Wrong Government House? If I remember correctly you were searching for Government House in Sydney last time we met. I wonder what Mrs Alexander is intending to do with all her missing items.' He gestured to the pile sitting on top of the dresser. 'We should take them to her room.'

'I don't ever want to touch them again.'

'That I can understand but better not leave any opportunity for confusion. Come on. You take the box, I'll carry the silverware.'

The door to Mrs Alexander's sitting room was open but there was no sign of her, so they deposited everything on the table just inside, and as they turned to leave, she appeared through a door from the other side of the room. A great wave of guilty heat coursed through every inch of Connie's body.

'We thought these would be better in here, safe and sound,' Mr Ballantyne said, offering his lovely wide smile. 'We'll see you at dinner, no doubt, Mrs Alexander.' He gave a nod of his head, extended an arm and ushered Connie from the room before any more could be said.

'Thank you for your help. I keep saying thank you but …' Connie stood at the bottom of the stairs with her hand on the newel post. 'I must go and see Mrs Montague. We're planning on leaving tomorrow.'

But then she remembered what the constable had said. 'It could take forever for Mrs Alexander to search her inventory. We have an appointment in Maitland the day after tomorrow.'

'Right. Then I think a little bit of advice wouldn't come amiss.'

'Advice?'

'Legal advice. I am certain the constable can't prevent you leaving. He hasn't pressed any charges, but it would be best to make sure. You don't want to make matters worse. My father had dealings with a firm of solicitors in Parramatta; he was thinking of buying some land.' He scratched his head. 'Ramsbottom & Son, if my memory serves me right. We could have a word with them.'

'Ramsbottom & Son? Taylor works for them.'

'I'm sorry? Taylor.'

'You met her last night at dinner. Taylor Fotherby.'

His eyes widened. 'Oh!' A pink flush stained the tips of his ears. 'Charming girl. She works for a solicitor? How very interesting.'

'Your idea is excellent. Let me run upstairs and grab my hat and tell Nell. She's waiting for me to …' Connie waved her hand in front of her face. Too complicated, far too complicated.

'Yes, she is waiting for you.' Nell appeared halfway down the stairs. 'What's all this about constables and solicitors?'

'I'll tell you when we get back. I just need my hat.'

'I'm not sitting for another hour twiddling my thumbs waiting for you. And if it's important enough to speak to a solicitor I'm coming.'

31

Nell made her way back up the stairs. She had no intention of letting Connie out of her sight nor allowing her to go gallivanting around unchaperoned with a young man who she had initially met unaccompanied on a public train. Never mind all this chatter about constables and solicitors.

'I presume you're going to tell me what happened.'

'Yes, but it will have to be on the way to see Taylor. We're leaving straight away. Nothing turned out quite the way I expected.'

If that wasn't an understatement nothing was. But Connie seemed in remarkably good spirits. 'What does this young man know?'

'That he's just saved me from a stint in gaol.' Connie rammed a pin into her hat, pulled down her jacket and grimaced.

'What is it now?'

She carefully unbuttoned her jacket and pulled a small oil painting from her waistband. 'It's Miss Pettigrew's missing portrait. I forgot I had it. I must put it in Mrs Alexander's room with the other bits and pieces.'

The air wavered and Nell drew in a fortifying breath. Would this matter never be concluded? 'You better take it back on our way out.'

Connie frowned, stopped and shook her head. 'I don't see why. It belongs to Miss Pettigrew. I'll take it back to her when we return. Come along; we haven't any time to waste.'

Nell secured her own hat and picked up her gloves. The matter would have to wait until they returned. 'I'm ready.'

Within moments they were as good as galloping down the carriageway towards the bridge. Thankfully neither Connie nor Mr Ballantyne gave her the opportunity to speak, which was probably just as well because the simple act of keeping up drained her energy. Connie's tale made her hair stand on end. Mrs Alexander's actions and her audacious accusation left her speechless. She glanced at Mr Ballantyne. She had been quite incorrect in her assumptions—he was a delightful young man; she would have to thank him properly for the way in which he had spoken up for Connie.

Connie pointed her finger down the road. 'It's just down here on the right in O'Connell Street.'

Nell glanced up at the sign. O'Connell Street indeed. The past seemed to be closing in on the present. Threatening to take over. 'Why is it we need to see the solicitors? Messrs Brown in Maitland have always seen to our needs.'

'I need someone to speak on my behalf otherwise I won't be able to come back to Maitland with you.'

'Here we are.' Mr Ballantyne pushed open the door, courtesy never came amiss, and then stood back to allow Nell and Connie to enter the rather drab timber-panelled outer room, very similar to that of Messrs Brown; obviously there was some sort of code the legal profession followed.

Once she'd crossed the threshold she ground to a halt. There the similarities ended. At a desk, front and centre, perched Miss Fotherby, nimble fingers flying across a set of keys. She glanced up for a second and continued a moment longer before pushing aside a lever, making a little bell tinkle, and giving them her full attention.

'Mrs Montague, Connie and Mr Ballantyne.' She leapt to her feet and came round in front of the desk. 'What can I do for you?'

'Some advice if one of the solicitors has a moment.' Mr Ballantyne gave her one of his wide smiles, almost as though he couldn't believe his eyes. 'So, you truly do work for a solicitor.'

'Were you in any doubt?'

A hint of colour touched his cheeks. 'No, no. It simply came as something of a shock to see you ...' The poor boy's words trailed.

'If you'd like to tell me what you require, I'll see how we can help.'

'The matter requires the advice of a solicitor.'

Taylor narrowed her eyes.

'I need some advice, Taylor,' Connie interrupted. 'Mrs Alexander brought the constable to the guesthouse and accused me of stealing the missing curios.'

'She did what?'

'She told me to go and fetch them from the attic. When I came down she and the constable were waiting. I'm certain she hoped I would be taken to the lock-up but fortunately Mr Ballantyne overheard her. The constable backed down but told me I shouldn't leave Parramatta. It's vitally important that we return to Maitland as soon as possible. I need someone to speak in my favour ...'

'I see. I'm sure it can be sorted out. It just sounds like a misunderstanding. Come with me.' She led the way to a door at the side of the room and knocked. 'Mrs Montague, if you'd like to take a seat; you too, Mr Ballantyne. Come, Connie.' And

with that she and Connie walked into another office and closed
the door.

'They shouldn't be in there alone ...'

An hour or so ago Nell might have agreed with Mr Ballantyne
but seeing Taylor exuding such an impressive degree of confidence
had calmed her erratic heartbeat and made her question her own
attitude. 'I have no doubt they are capable of dealing with the
situation.'

A smothered harrumph came from Mr Ballantyne as he threw
himself down in the chair next to her.

'Taylor's father was also a solicitor, he's retired, and she has
worked here since she finished her schooling. Not only does she
deal with correspondence and law briefs, she types contracts and
documents ...' Nell scoured her mind—what was it Taylor had
said she did? She'd intended to ask for a more comprehensive
explanation but hadn't wanted to sound like a fool. '... she also
helps with drafting and conveyancing.' She sat back with a smug
smile, thankful her memory hadn't let her down.

'A working woman.'

'As is Miss Milling.'

He waved a dismissive hand. 'She is a seamstress. That's
different. I've never heard of a girl working in a legal practice.'

'Times are changing, Mr Ballantyne. We cannot fight it.' Nell
covered her mouth with her gloved hand. It wouldn't do to let
him see her laughing at the look on his face.

Thankfully the conversation ended abruptly when the door
reopened and Connie and Taylor bounded out, faces wreathed
in smiles.

'Taylor is going to type up a quick note and we're to take it
to the police station. It seems that neither Mrs Alexander nor the
constable can demand that I stay in Parramatta unless they press
charges and all I need to do is provide our address in Maitland.'

What a relief. 'Very good, very good. I shall ask Mr Ballantyne to escort me back to the guesthouse and I'll inform Mrs Alexander that we will be leaving first thing in the morning.' A telegram for Faith would be a good idea. 'Connie ...' On second thoughts, no. Before she met with Jack Edwards again Nell wanted another word or four with Faith and it would be better if she didn't have time to prepare any answers. Pray god Faith hadn't learnt of Edwards's demands and attempted to take matters into her own hands. Though she couldn't see what Faith could do. The financial arrangements Montague had organised before his death were trussed up tighter than Mrs Orchard's Christmas turkey.

With an ear-splitting rip, Taylor pulled a sheet of paper from her machine. 'I'll get Mr Ramsbottom's signature and we'll go.'

'Mr Ballantyne, are you ready?'

His gaze was fixed on Taylor who had reappeared and was clamping her ridiculous little bowler hat onto her irrepressible curls. She suspected he didn't relish the thought of escorting her back to the guesthouse, would rather go with the girls to the police station.

'Mr Ballantyne?'

'Yes, yes. I'm quite ready. We shall be waiting with bated breath to hear how you get along.' He opened the door and with one last mournful gaze at Taylor and Connie ushered Nell out into the street.

Nell took her place at the dinner table—almost a full house tonight. Mr Ballantyne was grinning amiably, Miss Pettigrew livelier than ever before, but no sign of Mr Whitfield. Maisie and Taylor were both in attendance, as was Connie though she looked quite pale, not surprising after the shock she'd received this morning. When she'd arrived back after her trip to the police station, she had assured Nell that she was free to leave and had then taken herself off for a rest, most unusual, and when Nell had peeped into Connie's room, she'd been fast asleep.

Mrs Alexander swept in, the last to arrive, in a somewhat staged appearance. She hovered for a moment at the door and surveyed the assembled group, but it wasn't until she cleared her throat that Mr Ballantyne leapt to his feet and escorted her to her seat and she offered a supercilious smile. 'Good evening, ladies and gentleman. No Mr Whitfield, I see—that's a shame; I was hoping he would be here.'

Had Connie told Maisie of today's events? She certainly had more than a small stake in the matter, although as far as Nell knew Connie hadn't had the opportunity. They'd find out in due course.

June placed a large tureen in front of Mrs Alexander who doled out a ladle of soup into the bowls and June passed them to each guest. No mistaking the flavour, white onion; she'd put money on the fact there would be roast beef to follow, possibly even Yorkshire puddings. A ripple of appreciation flickered in her stomach; all the exercise today had stimulated her appetite, or simply relief that they would be leaving tomorrow.

It wasn't until Mrs Alexander signalled the start of the meal by settling her napkin on her lap and picking up her soup spoon that Nell noticed the unnatural silence. A few murmurs of approval after the first sip of soup but none of the usual conversation.

Finally, Mrs Alexander put down her spoon and dabbed at her mouth with her napkin, then cleared her throat as though about to make a pronouncement. 'Constance and I had a very interesting discussion this morning ...' Mrs Alexander's gaze swept the table and came to rest on Nell. The tiniest ripple of satisfaction traced Nell's skin—an apology, undoubtedly an apology for Mrs Alexander's outlandish behaviour summoning the constable.

'It seems we might have an unwanted nocturnal visitor.'

Spoons clattered as they were lowered. Nell frowned. Whatever was the woman up to?

'As you may or may not know there's an interesting story or two about Old Government House. It was one of the first substantial buildings in the colony. A young man is said to haunt the house searching for his long-lost love but there hasn't, until now, been a sighting in my time here.'

Maisie's eyes darted from side to side, but Connie kept her gaze firmly glued to her soup bowl and from the rigid set of her shoulders was as confused as she was. Nell wrinkled her nose. Where was the apology? This wasn't playing out the way she expected.

'However, Constance tells me she saw a figure enter the house from the kitchens, climb the stairs to the attic then descend and disappear. Until recently this story has been thought to be nothing more than a romantic tale, but it seems Constance has proved it to be true.'

Poor Connie—her face had turned the colour of a plum.

'Constance discovered a stash of the missing items, in the attic and had the foresight …'

Foresight!

'… to bring the matter to my notice.' Mrs Alexander rested back in the chair and gazed down the table. 'So, I can happily inform you all that everything has been recovered.'

No mention of the constable, no mention of the accusations. As though they had all vanished in the ether.

Nell couldn't remain silent a moment longer. 'Are you suggesting that the house is haunted, and a ghost is responsible for your "missing items"?' A hum of conversation greeted her words. Everyone, almost everyone at the table knew part if not all of the truth. How could the woman sit there and spout such nonsense?

'The house isn't haunted.'

Silence descended like a shroud and all eyes turned to Miss Pettigrew.

'Our nocturnal visitor is very much alive. I have seen him on several occasions. A tall, elegant chap, wearing dark trousers and riding boots, at least as tall as Mr Whitfield, though not as rotund, and his hair is longer; it flops over his forehead in a Byronesque manner. Quite a handsome man.'

Nell shot a look at Connie. Who else had she told about the man in the attic? Maisie sat, her mouth gaping open and her eyes fixed on Connie's pale face.

'We mustn't let imagination get the better of us, Miss Pettigrew. A Byronesque intruder?' Mrs Alexander gave what might have passed as an amused titter.

Quite the wrong thing to do.

Miss Pettigrew reared to her feet, hands pressed firmly on the table, arms shaking with the effort. 'I know what I have seen. The gentleman carries a Gladstone bag and enters through Mr Whitfield's window.'

Mrs Alexander bestowed a patronising smile on the old woman. 'All those novels you like to read. Surely a gentleman would use the front door like everyone else?'

'Highly unlikely that an intruder would use the front door, don't you think?' Miss Pettigrew's voice echoed with amazing clarity in the high-ceilinged dining room. 'I may be hard of hearing but there is nothing, absolutely nothing, wrong with my eyesight.' She subsided into her chair, nostrils flared, and indignation written all over her face.

'I can see this matter needs to be resolved.' Mrs Alexander rose, a resigned, possibly tedious tone to her voice. 'Unfortunately, Mr Whitfield isn't here to offer his opinion. June, go and fetch Mrs Trotter and your sister, immediately.'

32

'Is there a problem with dinner, Mrs Alexander?' Mrs Trotter stood in the doorway, arms akimbo, May and June hovering behind her, attempting to make themselves invisible.

'No, not at all. I wondered if you could give us the benefit of your insight. Miss Pettigrew believes she has seen an intruder climbing in Mr Whitfield's window from the servants' courtyard. We think he may be responsible for the stolen items Miss Constance unearthed in the attic.'

The gall of the woman. Unearthed. How Connie wished she'd told the truth, the whole unvarnished truth, but then her gaze met Maisie's pleading expression. She couldn't live with herself if she went back on her word and Maisie suffered.

'How would I know about an intruder, or what's been stolen? If you're suggesting me or one of my girls is responsible, then you better have proof.'

Well done, Mrs Trotter. She could learn a lesson or two from the woman. If she'd spoken more forcefully when the constable had appeared …

'Where's that inventory of yours? None of this nonsense started until you received notice that the leaseholders wanted an inspection.'

Mrs Trotter's words brought Connie back to the moment. An inventory. The list she'd seen in Mrs Alexander's room. The sudden accusation of missing items blamed first on Nell and then the finger had pointed at her. If Mrs Alexander had unexpectedly discovered there was to be some sort of accounting pending it would send her to the inventory. Had she known all along that there was more than old furniture stored in the attic? More to the point, was she responsible? No, that didn't make any sense. It didn't account for the ghost. No ghost! Mr Whitfield's visitor, the intruder. But that didn't make any sense either. Unless the stolen goods had to be returned to the house because of the unanticipated inspection of the premises.

Connie dragged herself back to the conversation.

'I have consulted my inventory, and all the missing items are accounted for.'

Except for Miss Pettigrew's portrait. Connie sneaked a glance across the table at Miss Pettigrew's alarmingly red face.

'Then what are we worrying about?' Mrs Trotter spread her arms and raised her palms to the heavens. 'Sounds like a storm in a teacup to me. May, June, clear the table. I've got better things to do than this.' Sticking her nose in the air she gave a loud sniff, turned on her heel and stomped off.

'I know what I saw and if none of you are going to take my words as truth then I better get that nice constable back here for a chat.' Miss Pettigrew slammed her hand down on the table, making the glasses jump. 'Maisie, I'm no longer hungry. I'd like to return to my room.'

While Maisie wheeled Miss Pettigrew out, May and June brought in the main course, plated up in the kitchen. Mrs Trotter was obviously not in any mood to pander to Mrs Alexander's pretensions.

Connie chewed her roast beef, a thousand thoughts flitting through her mind, largely dominated by the connection between Mr Whitfield and the intruder.

Once Mrs Alexander had consumed her dessert she cast a glance around, placed her napkin on the table and stood, the usual signal that dinner was over, and they should make their way to the drawing room; instead she offered a terse 'Good evening' and headed for her rooms.

Connie could barely contain herself. She pulled Nell aside while everyone trooped out of the dining room. 'Nell, I think I have an answer to our intruder.'

Once everyone was settled and June had served coffee, Connie rose from her seat next to Nell on the sofa and closed first the drawing room door and then the one opposite Miss Pettigrew's room.

'I've had a few thoughts about our intruder, and I'd like everyone's opinion before I take the matter any further.' She fidgeted with her cup and saucer. 'Mr Ballantyne, I'm not sure you wish to be involved. You may prefer to leave?' She raised an eyebrow in question.

'If you're happy for me to be here, I'll stay.'

'I would, however, ask for your discretion.'

He nodded. 'Never divulge my sources. Might even be able to offer some suggestions.'

'Is everyone else happy for Mr Ballantyne to remain?'

Taylor and Maisie nodded but Nell chewed on her lips, no doubt concerned Maisie might inadvertently mention the dress. After a moment's hesitation she inclined her head.

'A quick recap for Mr Ballantyne's benefit. I first saw the intruder on Saturday night slinking through the trees and around the back of the building. The following night I went up to the attic to see if he would reappear. He did. I panicked and hit him with a candlestick. I thought I'd killed him, but while I was getting help he disappeared.'

Mr Ballantyne's gaze drilled into Connie before she had time to continue. He shifted forward in his seat. 'Who did you go to for help?'

'I went directly to Nell. I didn't know what to do and she returned to the attic with me and that's when we discovered the intruder had disappeared.'

'I see.' Mr Ballantyne rubbed his fingers up and down his chin. 'And you didn't report the matter to anyone?'

'I told Mrs Alexander that I'd found the articles she'd believed stolen.'

'But not about the intruder?'

Perhaps allowing Mr Ballantyne to stay was not the best idea. He was far too astute. 'No. There was nothing I could do as he had vanished into thin air. When I told Mrs Alexander I had found the stolen items she called the constable and blamed me for the thefts. It seemed better to keep quiet about hitting the intruder.'

'Until Miss Pettigrew's revelation over dinner.'

'Well yes, and no.' Suddenly Connie felt as though she had really landed herself in the most dreadful mess. She sat down on the sofa and buried her face in her hands.

'Let me take up the story.' Taylor patted her shoulder and stood up. 'While we were waiting outside the stage door the other night Mr Kingsley, the lead man, doffed his hat to us. He had a wound on his forehead, remarkably like the one Connie had inflicted—'

'A tad coincidental,' Mr Ballantyne interrupted.

Taylor glared at him. 'The point is Miss Pettigrew's description of the man she's seen climbing in Mr Whitfield's window fits

Mr Kingsley, and Mr Whitfield hasn't been here at the guesthouse since the night Connie hit the intruder.'

Mr Ballantyne blinked a couple of times, scratched his head, and rocked back in his chair. 'Are you suggesting that Mr Kingsley and Mr Whitfield are one and the same person?'

Taylor put her hands on her hips. 'It fits. Whitfield never had dinner here on the nights of the play and hasn't appeared since we saw Kingsley sporting a great gash to his forehead.'

'It'd make a great story for the paper, but I doubt anyone would believe you. I certainly wouldn't describe Mr Whitfield as Byronesque.'

Maisie leapt to her feet. 'But he does spend a lot of time at the theatre. Taylor's right, he never eats dinner here when there is a performance, and I've seen him backstage; he was there on opening night. With a bit of stage makeup and a false moustache, it's easy to make a younger man look old. A bit of padding here and there changes the body, a different hairstyle, some pomade to hold it in place and Mr Kingsley's thick hair could become Mr Whitfield's greasy combed back style, a cane, and a limp ...' She threw her hands up in triumph. 'You can make yourself into anyone you want to be with a bit of artistry. Mr Whitfield arrived here at the guesthouse a few days before the play opened, at the same time as Mr Kingsley arrived in Parramatta for rehearsals. That's when things started disappearing. We've never had a problem before.'

Ballantyne narrowed his eyes and pursed his lips, deep in thought, then looked at Maisie. 'Where's this Kingsley fellow from? What do you know about him?'

Connie glanced at Taylor who lifted her shoulders then turned to Maisie.

'He's quite a well-known actor. He's played in Newcastle and Sydney. I don't know where else, but the Parramatta Players were thrilled when he offered his services. We're just an amateur dramatic society and he's an established actor ...' Maisie's face contorted, and a flush raced across her cheeks.

'Hmm! Still coincidental.'

'In that case we'll need proof.' Taylor rubbed her hands together as though the possibility filled her with a great deal of pleasure.

'Isn't the wound on his head proof?'

'I doubt it would stand up in court.'

'There is one thing you have forgotten in your excitement in playing amateur sleuths.' Nell's voice rose above the excited chatter and all faces turned to her. 'Mrs Alexander has accused several people, namely Connie and myself, paid little or no attention to Miss Pettigrew's account of an intruder, and then for no apparent reason chose to drop the matter, gloss over it even, and encourage Connie and I to leave. Do you think there is a possibility she may in some way be involved and is covering her tracks? As Mrs Trotter said, she has received notice of a lease inspection and all items on the itinerary must be accounted for.'

The air in the room crackled.

Connie practically dragged Nell up the stairs. She threw open Nell's bedroom door and fell in after her, closing the door with a bang and resting her back against the timber as if in some strange way she could ensure their safety.

'I don't think the intruder was taking anything. I think he was returning the pieces that had been stolen; that's what he had in the Gladstone bag when Miss Pettigrew saw him the other night. Mrs Alexander had discovered there was to be a review and she panicked. But what I don't understand is why Mrs Alexander would steal them in the first place.'

'When you reach a certain age, you start to think of the years you have left. She can't run the guesthouse for much longer. She's a good ten years older than me.'

'So, she was setting herself up for her old age? That makes sense but why did she draw attention to her actions by accusing us when she knew full well what was going on?' It seemed so strange to think that Mr Whitfield and Mr Kingsley could be the same person. They looked nothing like each other but as Maisie said, stage makeup and a bit of extra padding here and there could make all the difference. 'Mr Whitfield, Kingsley, I don't know what to call him. I suppose his real name must be Kingsley if he's a well-known actor.'

Nell nodded in agreement. 'And probably the reason he chose to disguise himself. It wouldn't do his reputation as an actor any good if he was caught. I suspect Mr Kingsley intended to sell the pieces for Mrs Alexander once the play was over and he left Parramatta. And in answer to your question, we're going to leave and finish the task I set out to accomplish.'

'But Mrs Alexander …'

'Wants us to leave as soon as possible so that's what we'll do. She's not going to draw attention to herself. I suspect Mr Kingsley will quietly disappear too. His stint at the theatre has finished and then sometime later Mr Whitfield will move on.'

'It seems all wrong that they should get away with it.' Connie sighed.

'They haven't broken any law as far as I can see. Mrs Alexander is quite within her rights to move items to different places in the house and employ whoever she likes to assist. We'll ask Taylor to keep an eye on matters and leave before any more questions are asked. Now, a good night's sleep and we'll catch the train to Sydney in the morning.'

The familiar scent of lily-of-the-valley enveloped Connie as Nell patted her cheek and dropped a kiss on her forehead. 'Goodnight.'

33

Wednesday, 8 May, 1889

Breakfast was a subdued affair. Miss Pettigrew chose to remain in her room, and unsurprisingly there was no sign of 'Mr Whitfield'. Maisie's long face stared at Connie across the table and Taylor didn't look much happier. There was so much Connie wanted to say to them both—thank them for their friendship and what had possibly been the most exciting few days of her life—but with Mr Ballantyne grinning amiably down the table the time didn't seem right.

Nell broke the silence and took matters into her own hands. 'Taylor, we must return to Maitland as I have an important business engagement. If there's anything we can do, please don't hesitate to get in touch. A telegram to Maitland Telegraph Office will find us. Now, Mr Ballantyne and I will leave you three girls alone to make your goodbyes.' Ballantyne rose and escorted Nell from the room.

The moment the dining room door closed Taylor leant across the table. 'I'm going to be late for work, but rest assured I'll keep an eye on things. I'm certain you have nothing to worry about.'

Connie reached for her hands. 'Thank you so much for all your help. Particularly at the police station, and as Nell said, please come and see us soon.' Just maybe not too soon because there was the sordid business with Jack Edwards to sort out. The less anyone knew of that the better, although she'd appreciate Taylor's level-headed advice. 'There is just one other thing. Do you know anything about partnerships?'

'Not a lot. I can ask a few questions. Why?'

Connie scrunched up her face. She was so thoroughly tired of keeping secrets. 'What happens if one of the partners dies?'

Taylor lifted her shoulders. 'I'm not sure. I'll ask some questions, see what I can find out. I'll see you this evening, Maisie. And Connie, try and stay out of trouble.' Taylor brought her fingers to her lips and blew a kiss before picking up her hat and heading for the front door.

'I better get going too.' Poor Maisie's face remained a picture of misery. She pulled a handkerchief from her sleeve and held it out in the palm of her hand. 'I think it would be better if you took this.'

Connie took the scrunched–up bundle and as her fingers closed around it, she stared deep into Maisie's eyes. 'But it is yours. We couldn't have managed without your skill … and your little seam ripper,' she added, hoping to bring a smile to Maisie's wan face. The gold nugget was Maisie's; she'd earned it fair and square.

'I wouldn't know what to do with it. Please take it. And then there is no proof that there was anything in the hem of the dress. I couldn't bear it if I unintentionally caused you and Mrs Montague any trouble.'

'Oh, Maisie.' Connie reached out and pulled her into a quick embrace. 'Remember, if there is anything you need, if anything happens, send a telegram to Maitland, or alternatively jump on a train. Mr Marsh, the stationmaster, knows where we live; just about everyone in town does. On the river at Horseshoe Bend, Carrington Street.' She held Maisie away and looked deep into her swimming eyes. 'Promise me.'

Maisie nodded, offered a frail smile then squared her shoulders. 'I'll be fine. It's just that you've become the closest thing to a sister I've ever had. I'm going to miss you.' She lifted her chin, raised her hand in farewell and closed the door quietly behind her.

Connie flopped down in the chair. It hadn't crossed her mind to imagine Maisie would be so upset. How lucky she was to have Nell, a family, a home. The sooner they got back to Maitland and sorted this nonsense out the sooner life could get back on an even keel and she'd suggest to Nell that Maisie might like to come and stay for a short holiday. They could take a trip down the river, picnic at Morpeth and see whatever was showing at the Victoria Theatre. She slapped her hand over her mouth, muffling a snort—hopefully Mr Kingsley wouldn't be appearing.

'Has everyone finished with breakfast?' June's head appeared around the door. 'Oh, it's just you. Mrs Trotter's in a fair state. She wants everything sorted quick as. Says she's got business in town and we're to look after the evening meal.'

'Mrs Montague and I will be leaving this morning. We're going home. So that'll be two less for dinner. I'm not sure about Mr Ballantyne but it might be worth asking.'

'That'll make things a bit easier though we'll be sorry to see you go, Miss. It's been nice meeting you.' She bobbed a bit of a curtsy then glanced up with a quizzical expression. 'You're not Mrs Montague's companion, are you?'

'No, June. I'm not. It was a bit of a ruse because we thought it might get me a bed when I turned up unexpectedly.'

'Me and May picked it right, we did. Thought you were a bit too fancy.' A flush tinted her cheeks as she offered her crooked smile. 'Real nice though.' She rushed to stack the plates, almost as if she thought she'd overstepped the mark. 'I hope you have a good trip home,' she added as she left the room, balancing the enormous tray with the skill of a circus performer.

As Connie left the dining room Nell appeared from Mrs Alexander's quarters, dusting her hands as though she'd completed a particularly unpleasant task. 'Is everything all right?'

Nell slashed her hand through the air. 'That's it. And our dues are paid. It's time to leave. Are you packed?'

Connie nodded. Packing had taken no time as she'd brought very few things with her in her haste to find Nell. 'I just need to get my bag. Where's yours?'

Nell gestured to the foot of the stairs. 'I'll wait for you outside. The sooner we reach Sydney the sooner we'll be back in Maitland. Do you think we can do it in one day like you did? I'd like to have my wits about me when we meet Mr ...' She brought her fingers to her lips. 'I'll see you outside.'

Connie ran up the stairs, collected her bag and tucked Miss Pettigrew's portrait in her waistband then took a quick look around Nell's room to make sure she hadn't forgotten anything. Mrs Macquarie's jewellery box once more held pride of place atop the tree of life cabinet. She bit back a smile. Mrs Alexander must have replaced it while they were at breakfast. It gave Connie a sense of satisfaction to know that it would remain in the room Mrs Macquarie once claimed as her own and all the other knick-knacks where they belonged. Mrs Alexander had inadvertently done herself a great disservice when she'd called the constable and tried to lay the blame on the Montagues.

With her lips twitching at the irony of the situation, she left the door wide open and set off. Miss Pettigrew hadn't appeared at breakfast, and she wanted to return the portrait, thank her for speaking up and say goodbye. Without her courage Mr Whitfield-Kingsley's ruse might never have come to light. She quelled a tremor as she passed his room. She did not want to have to face him in whatever guise he might assume.

She rapped loudly and opened the door a fraction. 'Miss Pettigrew?'

Much to her surprise the old woman was standing at the window, her fingers gripping the sill. She turned her head slowly.

Connie pulled the portrait from her waistband and held it out. 'I found it in the attic but since it belongs to you and won't be on Mrs Alexander's inventory I thought you should have it back immediately.'

Tears welled in Miss Pettigrew's eyes and her hand shook as she took the tiny painting, brought it to her lips and kissed it. 'I didn't think he'd come back to me. How can I thank you?'

'No thanks are needed. It's yours. It belongs to you.'

'I did do the right thing, didn't I?' Her voice wavered, her eyes fixed on the portrait.

'Absolutely. And I can't thank you enough. If you hadn't spoken up, we would never have known what Mr Whitfield was up to.'

'I don't believe Mrs Alexander is very happy.'

A huge understatement. Connie was certain she wouldn't be.

'There was something else I should have mentioned—the daguerreotype in Mrs Alexander's sitting room. It has pride of place on the mantle.'

Connie frowned, trying to remember if she'd seen any daguerreotype. The last time she'd been in Mrs Alexander's room she'd been too worried about explaining what she'd found in the attic. The only other time she'd been in there was the first morning after she'd sent the telegram to Faith and she certainly hadn't noticed much of anything then.

'A lovely silver frame. Mrs Alexander and a young man. I've been trying to remember who the intruder reminded me of. It was the hair, so thick for a man, flopping down over his forehead, almost hiding his eyes. I didn't speak up because I thought I'd said enough, that I would lose my place here. And Maisie will be staying too, so life can resume its normal pattern.' She lowered herself into her chair. 'Would you like to read me the next chapter of my book?'

'I'm afraid I can't, Miss Pettigrew. Mrs Montague is waiting for me. We must leave. I called in to say goodbye.'

'That's a shame. I shall miss all the excitement. I hope *you* found what you were looking for.' Her eyes twinkled.

Connie's stomach turned. What was the woman implying? Her gaze drifted to the two sticks propped against the table. If she could manage a trip to the water closet without her chair how much further could she go unassisted?

'Off you go, my dear. Safe travels. Drop me a line and let me know how Mrs Montague gets on.'

'I will, Miss Pettigrew. Goodbye.' Connie made for the door and closed it as fast as she could behind her before crossing the chequerboard floor and leaving the guesthouse.

34

Nell hoisted her bag and wriggled, trying to find a more comfortable position.

'Why don't you put your bag down? It won't come to any harm.'

She clutched the bag tighter and shook her head. 'I'm all right.'

'You can't be comfortable.' Connie reached across and tugged at the handles.

'No!' The word exploded out of her mouth and every face in the carriage turned—exactly what she didn't want to happen. It was as though she had a sign hanging around her neck, *This woman's bag is full of gold nuggets, and she can't prove ownership.*

'What is it, Nell? This isn't like you?'

'Ssssh!' She placed her finger over her lips. She couldn't believe her good fortune. The thought of speaking to Mrs Alexander again after that dreadful dinner last night kept her awake most of the night but there was no alternative. Apart from the fact she had to pay for their accommodation she had to ascertain whether the woman had any suspicions about the gold. She could argue the truth until she was blue in the face, but she couldn't prove that she'd put the gold there all those years ago, nor that Montague had given it to her. She gave a quiet groan.

Connie's cool fingers grasped her hand and squeezed gently. 'Did you speak to Mrs Alexander?' she murmured.

Nell nodded. 'She has three rooms, four if you count the room next door to mine, empty now.'

'I thought Mr Ballantyne was staying for a few more days.'

'He is.'

'Oh!' The word slipped between Connie's lips in a rush of air. 'The thespian is no longer in residence?'

'*Still Waters* has run its course.'

'That's very good news for the girls, and Miss Pettigrew.'

'Indeed it is.' Nell narrowed her eyes. The woman sitting opposite them appeared to be very interested in their conversation. 'Why don't we go and sit further down the carriage, where it's a little less crowded?' Before Connie had an opportunity to speak she stood up, bag clasped tightly to her chest and made her way to four empty seats closer to the door. Connie flopped down beside her. 'I don't see why we had to move; these seats aren't any better.'

'Much better. We don't have an audience. I want to tell you what happened when I spoke to Mrs Alexander.'

Connie's eyebrows shot up and she turned sideways in the seat. 'She apologised?'

'Not exactly, no. Mrs Alexander is never wrong—I learnt that a long time ago. She continued to bluster until I suggested she had perhaps reached a time when she needed to consider the future. She agreed and admitted she'd contacted Kingsley, knew that he'd been doing well for himself, and asked him to repay the money she'd lent him. To cut a long story short, he hadn't got the money and his career was on the wane so he offered his services to the Parramatta Players and together they hatched the plan, intending to make the non-existent Mr Whitfield the culprit should anything go awry. What they didn't anticipate was the leaseholder's inspection, and your nocturnal wanderings. For which I am very grateful.' Nell patted her carpet bag. 'She gave a fine performance herself, wringing her handkerchief, tears welling in her eyes. It seems she has known Mr Kingsley for quite some time, and that he too worked at Government House in Sydney.'

'You knew him?'

'No, no. Long after Montague and I left Sydney. He was an under footman, with a hankering for the stage. Mrs Alexander helped him to establish himself, lent him money on and off over the years.'

Connie slid her fingers under her hat and scratched her head. 'I need a moment to take that all in.'

'Let's leave it be for now. I think I'll rest my eyes until we arrive in Sydney. It's been a taxing few days.' Nell let her eyelids fall and her shoulders drop. She was exhausted but she couldn't unwind until she'd exchanged the nuggets. It had been years since Montague had needed Mr Golding's services, but she couldn't imagine he'd closed his business ... her eyes snapped open and she cast her mind back; she could picture him as though it was yesterday. His neatly trimmed beard, bird-like eyes, dressed in an immaculate Prince Albert coat no matter the temperature, presiding over the little shop in George Street. Maybe he had a son, or grandson. She squeezed Connie's fingers. 'Nearly there.'

Connie peered out of the window at the familiar outline of the city buildings. 'I miss our excursions to Sydney. Do you remember when we came down for the International Exhibition and we travelled on the steam tram? Almost ten years ago. It was the first time we stayed at the Berkeley and do you remember that clock under water in the goldfish bowl? It fascinated me.

I wonder if it still works. It was such a shame Garden Palace burnt down; I'll never forget standing under the dome and looking up at the sky ...'

'... and getting into trouble for trying to climb into Queen Victoria's lap.' Not really the queen's lap, just the statue, but it had become something of a joke as Connie was growing up, in the good old days before ... she would not get maudlin.

'Shall we go directly to the Berkeley and see if Mr Sladdin has a room for us?'

'No. I think we'll find a hansom cab and take a ride down George Street.' Then she wouldn't look so conspicuous walking with a carpet bag clutched to her chest. She couldn't shake the fear someone might be following them. 'There's always the chance our business can be rapidly concluded and there'll be no need to stay overnight.'

'I was quite looking forward to seeing Mr Sladdin again.'

'I'm quite looking forward to sleeping in my own bed. Come along; we've no time to waste.'

Nell hailed one of the hansom cabs outside the railway terminal. 'Do you know Mr Golding's shop in George Street?' The driver jumped down, opened the door with a flourish. 'That I do.' Nell ushered Connie inside; the sooner they were off the street and out of sight the better.

The door closed with a satisfying clunk. The trip down Pitt Street should have taken only a matter of minutes but with the endless stream of wagons, drays, carriages and carts the hansom cab managed nothing more than a slow plod. Nell sat gritting her teeth in frustration.

After an eternity they drew to a halt. Nell gazed through the open window at the bow-fronted shop. Just as she remembered. Handing the cab driver a collection of coins, she hurried inside and her steps faltered. No Mr Golding in his immaculate frockcoat;

instead a young man, very young, quite nicely presented in a dark jacket, white shirt, and tie. 'I would like to speak to Mr Golding.' She cleared her throat, hoping to mask the waver in her voice.

'Yes, Ma'am. How may I help you?'

'Mr Golding, please. My husband and I have conducted business with him over the years ...' She'd seen the name Golding painted over the top of the front window. Maybe she should ask Connie to go and check; she wasn't wearing her pince-nez ...

The cheeky young fellow murmured something indecipherable under his breath. 'I am Mr Golding. My grandfather passed away three years ago.'

A horrible wave of embarrassment flooded her face. 'I do beg your pardon.'

Connie stepped up to the counter. 'And you conduct the same business as your grandfather?'

'Indeed, we do.'

'We?'

'My father and I; he's just stepped out for a few moments. If—'

'I have some private business to transact,' Nell interrupted. 'Mr Golding ... senior ... attended to our business in the backroom.' She gestured to a heavy velvet curtain hanging behind the young man.

'Ah, yes.' He lifted a section of the counter. 'Please, follow me.'

The unnaturally loud rattle of the curtain rings brought Connie to a halt, and she threw a wide-eyed, questioning look. In response Nell prodded her back and they slipped through the low set doorway into a small, darkened room.

A table and chairs sat in the middle of the room empty but for a cedar box supporting a pair of brass scales, two pans each dangling from three chains—just as she remembered.

'Please take a seat.' Mr Golding lit an oil lamp, the fishy smell of whale oil tainting the close air then he gestured to the two chairs, before walking around the table and opening the little drawers in the base of the scales to remove two sets of weights. 'My father will be with you in a moment.'

Nell gave a relieved smile. If she couldn't have the original Mr Golding, then his son would have to be a better option than this whippersnapper barely dry behind the ears.

'Is this as you expected?' Connie whispered.

'Exactly. Sit tight. Everything will be fine.' Brave words. She unbuckled her bag and brought out the shawl holding the gold nuggets and hefted it in her hand. She could remember Montague talking of purity and market price per troy ounce, but she had no idea if the value had changed over the years. She didn't care as long as it was sufficient to close Jack Edwards's mouth once and for all.

The sound of a door opening drew her attention. She lifted her head and her heart stuttered. She shot to her feet. 'Mr Golding. How delightful to see you again.' She slapped her hand over her mouth. Young Mr Golding had already said his grandfather had passed.

A deep rumbling laugh filled the small room. 'A mistake many make, Mrs Montague, and one I tend to perpetuate. It's good for business. Please.' He gestured to her chair then flipped back the tails of his coat and sat opposite. 'And this is …'

'My granddaughter, Constance.'

'A pleasure. And Mr Montague is keeping well?'

'I'm afraid he passed away some years ago.'

'My apologies. I was unaware.'

Nell inclined her head, closed her eyes for a moment to bring herself back from the surreal situation to the task at hand. The man was a replica of his father, even down to the carefully tied cravat.

'Now how can I help you?'

She placed the shawl on the table and gently pushed it towards him. 'I have some nuggets I wish to sell.'

His nimble fingers untied the shawl and his prodigious eyebrows rose. Then he lifted a monocle to his right eye and squinted at one of the nuggets pinched between his finger and thumb. 'And these nuggets are from Mr Montague's Californian discoveries?'

Colour flooded Nell's cheeks. It hadn't occurred to her that the gold would in any way be different. How could he tell? Maybe it was just a guess. She inclined her head.

'Found without a doubt in a riverbed.'

'How can you tell?' The words popped out of her mouth. She really must be more circumspect.

'Alluvial gold is worn smooth.' He ran his thumb over one of the nuggets. 'The passage of water and the constant movement over small rocks and pebbles on the riverbed gradually erodes the surface. Mr Montague's Californian finds were primary gold.'

Beside her Connie fidgeted, her fingers drumming on her knee in that annoying habit she had.

Nell pulled a handkerchief from her sleeve and patted her brow. 'It's very warm. Could we trouble you for a glass of water and wait in the front of the shop?'

Mr Golding pushed back his chair. 'How thoughtless of me. The lack of windows is a security measure. Please …'

He led them back into the shop. 'Samuel, fetch a carafe of water and two glasses and look after the ladies while I complete the necessary business.'

Young Mr Golding led them to two conveniently placed chairs in the bay window overlooking the street. 'I will be back in a moment.'

'Nell, what are you doing? Shouldn't we wait inside? What happens if he diddles us … keeps some of the gold for himself?'

'He won't. He has his family's reputation to maintain, one that was hard won and is carefully guarded.' Wasn't family reputation what had led her here in the first place?

A glass of water and the breeze from the door which Samuel propped open restored Nell's equilibrium and before she knew it Mr Golding stood before her, an envelope in his hand. The relief of it took her breath away. 'Several drafts drawn on the Bank of New South Wales for the full amount. It's been a pleasure to do business with you again, Mrs Montague, Miss Montague.' He executed a neat bow and retreated through the curtain at the back of the shop.

'Aren't you going to check the amount?' Connie hissed.

'No need. Montague had absolute faith in the man, and so do I.'

'But he's not his father.'

'For goodness' sake, Connie. Finish your glass of water and we'll ask Samuel to call a hansom cab. I intend to go directly to the rail terminal and see if we can get back home today.'

Connie rolled her eyes. 'I hope you know what you're doing.'

35

After a remarkably good luncheon in the ladies' refreshment rooms opposite the rail terminal Connie and Nell settled into their seats on the train. 'This will be your first trip over the Hawkesbury Rail Bridge.'

'There's no need to show off.'

'Mr Ballantyne told me all about the construction on the way down to Sydney. He was writing an article for the newspaper. I wonder if it was published.'

'It was.' Nell continued to peer out of the window.

'How do you know?'

'I read it in the *Cumberland Mercury*. Mr Whitfield brought it to my attention.'

'Don't you mean Mr Kingsley?'

Nell made a noise, suspiciously close to a snort, which she quickly turned into a small cough. 'I never had the pleasure of meeting Mr Kingsley.'

'He was a lot more attractive than Mr Whitfield. As Maisie said, he must have worn some sort of padding under those lurid waistcoats of his. The stoop and walking stick completely changed his gait.'

'Now you sound as though you're talking about one of your father's horses.' Nell frowned and rubbed at her forehead. 'I'd almost forgotten what lies ahead. How could I have done that?'

'You can't worry about it all the time. You'll go mad.'

'No, that's not going to happen.' Nell's features firmed. 'I have every intention of ensuring Jack Edwards never sets foot in the Hunter again, or for that matter on any racecourse in the country.'

'Are you sure it wouldn't be better to speak to the police.'

'How can I? I can't explain where the money came from without taking Messrs Brown into my confidence.'

'What about Faith? She must know this Jack Edwards. Did you tell her about the letter before you left? Did you tell her about the gold?'

'I didn't tell her anything other than the fact I wanted her to stay away from the racecourse. I will explain everything after I have dealt with Edwards. And I want you to promise me you will not discuss the matter with her.'

Faith certainly hadn't stayed away from the track. Connie clearly remembered having to lend her sixpence to pay the hansom cab only the day before she left in search of Nell.

The rhythmic clickety-clack of the train on the tracks soothed Connie. She had no doubt Nell would explain everything to Faith once Edwards was paid off.

It was just past three in the afternoon; the bright clear autumn sun reflected flashes of silver, and in the shadows, pewter, on the surface of the river. Nell sat staring out of the window lost in thought as the train crossed the bridge and gathered speed.

Two hours later they pulled into Maitland Station. Connie opened the carriage door and stepped out onto the platform inhaling the scent of home that even the steam from the engine couldn't mask. Before she'd had a chance to pick up their bags Mr Marsh came dancing down the platform. 'Ladies, ladies, I am so very pleased to see you both. The whole town has been wondering when you would return to us. Young Mrs Montague had nothing to offer.'

'A very good thing too,' Nell murmured as Connie handed her down from the carriage onto the platform.

'Let me call you a cab; you'll want to get home as soon as possible and spare her agonising over your whereabouts.' Without waiting for a reply, Mr Marsh snatched up their bags and made for the station forecourt.

Connie offered Nell her arm, but she waved her aside, her fingers tight around her reticule, tight around the envelopes containing Mr Golding's drafts. Next stop home and no doubt a confrontation with Faith.

Nell clambered down from the cab. 'There were times in the last few days when I wondered if I'd ever set foot in my own house again.'

'All I want to do is sleep in my bed.' Connie rapped on the front door. It flew open before she'd had a chance to lower her hand.

Mrs Orchard stood on the threshold beaming. 'I was beginning to think I'd never see the day. In you come, in you come. I've got the kettle warm and some fruitcake ready.'

She couldn't have been standing waiting at the door the entire time they'd been away. 'How did you know we were home? We've come directly from the station.'

'Ah! I've had young Jonas meeting all the trains.'

'Jonas? The boy who sleeps at the station? How did you …'

'A decent meal is an excellent way to a boy's heart.' Mrs Orchard winked at them both.

Nell cleared her throat. 'May we come inside? Your tea would be very welcome. And ask young Mrs Montague to join us.'

'She's already in the sitting room.' Mrs Orchard finally stepped back from the door. 'I'll bring the tea. I can't wait to hear about your adventures.'

'Maybe not,' Nell murmured as she swept through the open door.

Faith stood by the mantelpiece, her fingers tapping out an irritated tattoo on the polished marble. 'Welcome home.' Her brow furrowed and she narrowed her eyes. It had never crossed Connie's mind to explore Nell and Faith's relationship in any great detail. To the best of her knowledge, they maintained a polite distance, but Faith looked positively irate.

Nell unpinned her hat, removed her gloves, and arranged herself in her favourite chair. 'Sit down, Connie.'

'I thought I might go upstairs and …'

'Sit down, I want you here. We'll just wait for Mrs Orchard to bring the tea.' She threw a glacial stare in Faith's direction. 'What have you been up to since we left?'

Colour tinted Faith's cheekbones. 'Very little. As per your instructions.' She flounced across the room and threw herself into a chair.

'No trips to Rutherford?'

'Not since Connie left. No.' She rolled her eyes. 'Did you have an enjoyable trip?'

The door opened and Mrs Orchard wheeled in the tray. 'Shall I pour?'

'No. That will be all.' The gimlet glance in Nell's eye sent Mrs Orchard scuttling out. Without asking what anyone would like, Nell poured three cups of tea and circled her index finger indicating that Connie should give Faith a cup. 'We had a very interesting few days, and I achieved what I set out to do.'

'And took in the sights no doubt, as Connie said in her telegram.' Faith raised her eyebrows, disbelief written plainly on her face.

Connie squirmed in her seat.

'You will not.' Nell finished her cup of tea and rose. 'Now if you will excuse me ...

'I have a business meeting tomorrow. Until I return, I would like you both to remain at home.'

A business meeting! Nell couldn't go alone to meet Edwards. What a ridiculous suggestion. 'I'll come with you.'

'You will not.' Nell finished her cup of tea and rose. 'Now if you will excuse me, I would like to rest. I'll leave Connie to fill you in on the delights of Parramatta. I will see you both at dinner.' And with that Eleanor Montague swept from the room.

36

Thursday, 9 May, 1889

Gentle tapping on the door roused Nell. She opened her eyes to the familiar mellow wash of morning light and the reflections of the river patterning the wall. In a little less than three hours it would all be over, and life could resume its familiar, comfortable pattern. 'Come in, Dora.'

'Your morning drink, Ma'am, just as you like it.' Dora placed her favourite rose-patterned cup on the nightstand. 'I hope you slept well. Shall I plump up your pillows?'

'Thank you.' She leant forward. She'd slept surprisingly well. 'Please tell Mrs Orchard I shall be down to breakfast at the normal time.'

'We're very pleased to see you home, Ma'am.' Dora bobbed a curtsy and closed the door quietly behind her.

A short walk around the garden first, just to make sure everything was as it should be, then after breakfast she'd ask Cracker to call her a cab. A twenty-minute, possibly half-hour ride, plenty of time to compose herself and clear her head. Not like last time when she turned up in such a state. Her hand shook as she placed her cup back on the nightstand. She'd organised each of the five drafts into individual envelopes and buried them at the bottom of her reticule and written a statement last night for Edwards to sign, guaranteeing it would be full and final payment and that he'd have no call on the Montague family again. She was rather proud of the way it sounded.

She smoothed down her high-collared white blouse and buttoned her navy skirt, thankfully no bustles to contend with any longer, then reached for her favourite dusty rose jacket, turned it this way and that, before discarding it in favour of a matching navy jacket. Nothing flippant or feminine today—this was business plain and simple. It seemed young Taylor might have the right idea. After a quick glance in the glass, she nodded and made her way down the stairs.

Connie stood in the hallway waiting. 'It's a beautiful morning. I thought I'd come with you for a walk.'

Not exactly what she had in mind but from the determined look on Connie's face and her sober attire, very similar to her own, she'd hazard a guess there'd be further discussions about her meeting with Edwards.

They hadn't even passed the scullery when Connie asked, 'What time are you leaving?' No preamble, no polite enquiry.

'After breakfast. I'll ask Cracker to call a cab. I don't have to be there until nine-thirty.'

'I am coming with you.'

'No, you most certainly are not. I told you last night.' Not that she'd be meeting Edwards at the new racecourse; that was a little bit of a white lie. The Spread Eagle Inn had once been the epicentre of Maitland racing but since the new track and grandstands had been completed the building had fallen into disrepair, a suitably disreputable setting for such a dishonourable transaction. The collapsing remains didn't instil confidence although the name seemed somehow appropriate—spread-eagled, vulnerable and exposed; she shook the thought away. 'The racetrack is no place for a young girl. The jockeys will be training. You never know what might happen.'

'Exactly my point. You shouldn't go alone.'

'I'll not hear another word on the matter.' So much for a nice stroll through the garden and some fresh air. 'It's time for breakfast.' Without giving Connie the opportunity to respond she made a sharp detour back up the path and entered the house through the kitchen, closing the door firmly behind her to prevent Connie following. 'Good morning, Mrs Orchard.'

'Mrs Montague. Breakfast is in the dining room.'

She found Faith sitting at the table picking at a piece of toast. Quite why Mrs Orchard bothered with such a lavish breakfast for the three of them she couldn't fathom; it put the guesthouse to shame … she must remember to talk to her about it. 'Good morning, Faith.'

'Good morning.' She dabbed at her mouth with her napkin. 'I thought I'd come with you to your meeting.'

That was the final straw. 'No! You will not.' She glared down the table. 'And neither will Connie.' Faith met her stare with a defiant toss of her head. 'I won't hear another word about it.' She toyed with a boiled egg and some toast and finally pushed back her chair, her appetite ruined. 'I expect to be home by eleven.'

Hat firmly anchored, she slipped out of the front door. The thought of anyone else deciding she needed to be accompanied made her scalp itch, so she simply waved a greeting to Cracker as she walked down the path. She'd easily find a cab outside the station and since her morning walk had been interrupted, she could do with the exercise.

At the end of Carrington Street she turned left and crossed the road outside the *Maitland Mercury* offices. The usual array of wagons, drays and gigs flooded High Street. Not bothering to acknowledge the greetings of the various shopkeepers along the way, she turned into Victoria Street and followed the railway track. So much for the clear blue sky first thing this morning; a definite band of clouds hovered over the Watagan mountains. Refusing to allow the prospect of rain to muddy her mission she headed for the station.

A lone hansom cab stood in the forecourt, the horse's nose buried in a bag of chaff and the cabbie leaning against the wheel, deep in discussion with a young woman wearing what looked remarkably like a man's bowler hat. She ground to a halt—unless she was very much mistaken it was Taylor, or her twin sister.

As she approached, the cabbie turned. 'There you go. No need for me to take you to Mrs Montague's residence. Here's the lady herself.'

'Taylor, whatever are you doing here?'

'Hello! Could we have a word? A private word.' She gestured to the seat against the station wall.

'I'm sorry to arrive so unexpectedly but Connie asked me a question before you left the guesthouse, and I discovered some information which I believe might be of use to you. Mr Ballantyne is with me. We spent the night in Newcastle and caught the early train …'

Not what she needed at this very moment. 'I'm on my way to a meeting and I don't have time. Connie is at home. I'm sure she'd be delighted to see you. Follow the railway tracks and take the second street on the left; you'll see Carrington Street on your right. It's the house with the roses. I hope you don't mind if I take the cab?'

The girl took absolutely no notice of her and planted herself in front of the steps. 'Mrs Montague, this is important. Connie asked me about partnerships. I discovered something after you left which I believe may be significant.'

Dear god, she was determined.

'A partnership is between two people.'

Yes, yes, she knew that and if Fred hadn't gone into partnership with that villainous Jack Edwards, she wouldn't be here with drafts worth five hundred pounds burning a hole in her reticule.

'I thought you should know in case it has any bearing on your … difficulties.'

Nell straightened her back. 'Explain,' she barked. 'On second thoughts explain to me in the cab; I can't be late. Come along. Mr Ballantyne can wait until we return.'

It wasn't until the cab was bowling along at a rapid pace that Nell's heartrate began to settle. Taylor's information might well give her the upper hand. Or would it? The problem was the same. If Edwards didn't get what he wanted the Montague reputation remained in jeopardy. And how much did she want to tell Taylor? 'I understand a partnership is between two people. I am on my way to deal with what could be best described as my son's failed partnership.'

'There's no such thing. A partnership ceases on the bankruptcy or death of either of the partners.'

Bankruptcy certainly wasn't an issue.

'If your son was in partnership with someone, that arrangement no longer exists because he's dead.'

The girl certainly didn't beat around the bush. Taylor leant forward, hands on her knees, in a frightfully masculine gesture. Nell shook the thought away. What difference did that make? Taylor seemed to be very certain of her facts. And then the image of the competent young woman in the solicitor's office in Parramatta who had attended to Connie's dilemma when Mrs Alexander attempted to have her accused of theft, sprang to mind.

'Mrs Montague, the partnership no longer exists. It died with your son. Unless new documents were drawn up there is no partnership.'

Nell blinked, not once but twice. The partnership didn't exist? Why then was she about to part with a large amount of money? It appeared she did need this young woman's assistance.

Taylor's eyes narrowed into a steely gaze. 'It might be helpful if I had a little background information.'

Before she could second-guess herself she blurted out, 'A man who used to work for us, Jack Edwards, is demanding payment, monies owed to him by the partnership. I wrote a statement last night for him to sign, guaranteeing it would be full and final payment. Connie says it is nothing more than extortion and I should report him to the police, but he has made accusations which could put the family name at risk.'

Taylor nodded, giving Nell the distinct impression she knew more than she had let on. 'Connie is quite correct. It is extortion—blackmail relies on the recipient being too scared to refuse—unless there is something you haven't told me.'

And that was the problem.

The remainder of the journey passed in a flash as Nell explained the story, starting with the arrival of Edwards's letter, their meeting, and his demands, but when Taylor leant forward again and pinned her with her shrewd gaze Nell couldn't prevent the colour flying to her cheeks.

'I fail to see how this Edwards fellow can threaten the family name. It's a simple business arrangement that no longer exists and he is in breach of law if he attempts to extort money from you under false pretences.'

Nell swallowed the lump in her throat. If she needed Taylor's help, which it appeared she did, then she was going to have to fill her in on the facts only she was aware of. She licked her lips; this was so very, very difficult. 'We have a family property outside Maitland, Coloma. We breed horses, have done since the 1850s not long after my husband and I first came to Maitland. Edwards and my son went into a partnership to provide the young horses with track experience.'

Taylor made a grunting sound and nodded in encouragement. 'As you have said. I don't see any problems there. Partnership laws would still apply.'

'Yes, but they reaped substantial profits through race manipulation—race fixing as it is more commonly known.'

Taylor slipped her fingers under her hat and scratched her head. 'I'm sorry I'm not sure I understand.'

This was impossible. The girl had no experience of the racetrack; how could she offer advice? Nell wasn't even sure she could explain the ins and outs of the obnoxious practice. 'A slow horse is entered in a race, and just before the start of the race the slow horse is swapped with a faster horse, who then goes on to win the race and the punters in the know reap the benefit of the high odds.'

'But the horse would be known, otherwise the odds wouldn't be calculated. Doesn't anyone realise that the horse had been swapped for another?'

'Not if the horse is of similar stature and colouring.'

'And since your son and Edwards were in partnership the Montague family's reputation will be threatened if this comes out. And that's why Edwards is demanding money—for his silence?'

Nell nodded. It all seemed rather foolish put like that. She was going to have to explain Faith's involvement. 'There is a little more which may be relevant. After my son's death, his wife, Faith, expanded her involvement at the racetrack. She takes wagers from the women in the ladies' stand; many of them like to place a bet. It is illegal.'

Taylor clapped her hands together. 'Oh excellent, how very, very enterprising.'

Nell made a little moue of disgust. Faith's activities couldn't be described as enterprising. They were totally inappropriate and none of this would have happened but for Faith's foolishness.

'Extortion without a doubt. The man hasn't got a leg to stand on. The police should be brought in. Edwards can't do anything without incriminating himself, drawing attention to his race fixing. You are not legally obliged to pay him out of a partnership that doesn't exist.'

Nell dropped her head into her hands. 'You don't understand. Should this get out everything my husband and I worked for would be ruined—the stud, the business, our reputation.'

'And you are prepared to pay this man's demands for the sake of the family name?'

'For Connie's sake. She will never be able to hold her head up in the district, never make a decent marriage. Her whole future lies in the balance.'

Taylor mumbled some sort of derogatory expletive. 'And what does Connie say about this?'

'Connie doesn't know the full story.'

Taylor didn't respond, simply stared out of the window as the cab drew to a halt outside the Spread Eagle Inn.

'We're here. I am to meet Edwards over by the old stables.' She reached across to open the door.

'Mrs Montague, will you allow me to speak on your behalf. The man's actions are nothing more than intimidation and entrapment. I do not believe you should pay him off, and certainly not ask him to sign any undertaking to keep silent because it immediately compromises your position.'

Nell brought her hand to her mouth, in an attempt to control a sudden wave of nausea. If Taylor was correct, she would have no need to use Mr Golding's drafts. Connie's future would be assured, and life could continue. It was certainly worth a try. 'Thank you, Taylor, I would appreciate your assistance.'

37

Arm in arm, Nell and Taylor picked their way across the rutted track. The twisted roof of the old stables corkscrewed drunkenly against a background of burgeoning thunderclouds, the loose iron sheets creaking and squealing with every wind squall.

'He was waiting just inside the tack room last time. He made me jump when he stepped out.'

'I can't believe you came alone. Did you give no thought to your own safety?'

'He wasn't going to harm me—not until he got what he wanted.' Nell's step faltered, belying her confident assertion. Her mouth dried and she nodded into the shadows.

Taylor's pressure on her arm increased as the bow-legged sparrow of a man stepped into the narrow rectangle of light cutting across the hard-packed dirt. When she'd met him the first time she'd been too apprehensive to notice how he'd gone to seed; his paunch hung low and fine veins traced his cheeks, testimony to years spent staring at the bottom of an empty bottle. A far cry from the wiry young strapper with fire in his eyes and an uncanny way with even the most ill-tempered stallion.

'About time.' Edwards ran an appraising gaze down the length of Taylor's body. 'Who's this?'

Taylor took a long stride towards him. 'Taylor Fotherby. Mrs Montague's representative.'

'And why would she be needing a representative? Deal's done. She knows the terms. I want what's owed me. She owes me. I want out of my partnership with the Montagues.'

'Unfortunately, Mr Edwards, you are labouring under a misapprehension. There is no partnership.'

'Don't give me that bull dust. What would you know?' He patted the breast pocket of his dusty jacket. 'I've got partnership papers, signed by Montague himself.'

Taylor's lips twitched; she appeared to be enjoying every moment. 'Papers which are no longer valid. According to partnership law the death of one of the partners terminates any such agreement.'

His mouth gaped, and he lurched forward in a cloud of fetid breath. Almost tripping, Nell staggered back but Taylor held her ground. 'The Montague family are in no way indebted to you. There will be no payment.'

'Don't be so feckin' ridiculous. I want what I'm owed.'

'Which is precisely nothing.'

He wrinkled his pock-marked nose in a snarl. 'You hand the money over or I'll tell the world what the Montagues are up to. There's people that'd pay for a story like that.'

Nell's knees wavered, and her vision blurred. Her fingers groped in her reticule. It was too much; no matter what the law might say she wanted it over. The Montague name would not be splashed across the newspapers. She pulled out several of Golding's drafts. 'Taylor, we'll ...'

'... see this man in court.' Taylor's hand wrapped around Nell's wrist, her grip tight, preventing Nell from handing over any of the envelopes.

Edwards dropped his head, his shoulders hunched, bloodshot eyes narrowed, a bull ready to charge.

'Hold it right there.'

His head came up, his eyes widened, and he froze.

Nell whipped around.

Legs braced, Faith held a pistol aimed at Edwards's head. Another body stepped into the shaft of light.

Connie!

'You heard what she said. Now bugger off.' Faith hitched the pistol with startling familiarity and trained the small dark circle of the muzzle on Edwards's forehead.

Nell cringed. Wherever had she learnt to use a gun? Never mind such language.

Edwards backed towards the darkness of the stables. 'Not that way. Out the front,' Faith growled in a tone Nell had never heard before, and pulled the trigger. The bullet hit the ground a few feet in front of Edwards, raising a puff of dust from the hard-packed dirt. Edwards leapt in the air as though bitten by a redback and hobbled out into the light before spinning around. 'You haven't got a hope in hell, and you haven't heard the end of this.' Ducking his head, he scurried towards the crumbling remains of the inn.

Faith lowered the pistol, fiddled with the hammer before tucking it into her waistband and dusting off her hands. 'Connie, take Nell home. I will make sure Edwards has gone then follow in the other cab.'

'What about Taylor?'

Faith's languid gaze raked Taylor. 'And you are?'

'Taylor Fotherby.'

'My legal representative,' Nell added. 'I asked her to accompany me.'

Faith gave a derisive sniff. 'She can travel back with me and tell me about her qualifications.'

'It would be my pleasure.' Taylor's eyes glinted.

'Game on,' Nell murmured.

Connie laughed. 'Come along.' She reached for Nell's arm and led her across the rutted ground, outside, into the damp clean air.

Nell lifted her face to the drizzle, the beginnings of the threatened storm, and inhaled the earthy scent of rain. 'I told you to stay at home.'

'Just as well we didn't.' Connie twisted her head and looked back at Taylor and Faith standing shoulder to shoulder, arms crossed, gazes fixed on the fleeing figure.

Foolish girls. 'What if he'd got a gun?'

'He hadn't; he would have brandished it long before. He wasn't expecting any arguments from you, just the money.'

All well and good because the thought of a shootout was more than she could bear. Where had Faith got the thing in the first place? 'Whose pistol is Faith waving about?'

'Her own apparently. Security when she's at the racetrack. I was a bit surprised too. It seems my mother is not what I believed.'

Nell had known from the first moment she'd set eyes on Faith that there was more behind her pretty face, but somehow over the years her determination and courage had slipped her mind.

'Up you get. Faith and Taylor will follow us once they're certain Edwards has gone.'

Nell stalled and turned to face Connie. 'You had this all planned from the outset, didn't you?'

A hint of colour flushed Connie's cheeks. 'Not from the outset, no, but I couldn't let you go alone. I was worried sick about you, so I told Faith about the letter.'

Nell's stomach turned turtle. 'You did what?'

'Promises don't count when a life is in the balance.' Connie stopped in her tracks and folded her arms. 'I told Faith about Edwards's demands and that you were going to pay him off. She knows the area around the racecourse far better than either of us and I thought that if anything happened ...'

Nell swayed and then stumbled. What else had Connie told Faith?

'Jump in; the rain's getting heavier.' Connie steadied her. 'I didn't know Taylor would turn up. Surely you didn't imagine I was going to let you manage this alone, did you?'

Nell slumped against the back of the seat and stretched out her legs. 'What about the gold? Did you tell Faith?'

'I didn't mention it.'

A small mercy. Two weeks ago, she was determined to manage the situation alone and now she couldn't be more thankful Connie, and Faith, had stepped up—Taylor too.

Faith and her pistol may have solved the immediate problem, but she couldn't imagine it would be the end of it and Taylor's bravado might well bring the circumstances surrounding Fred's death into the limelight once more—exactly what she hoped to avoid.

By the time they turned into Carrington Street the cab carrying Taylor and Faith had caught up with them. Nell rummaged in her reticule for some money to pay the driver but her hand came away empty. Not a coin to be had, only a bundle of drafts she had no intention of producing.

The door flew open. 'Rain's stopped just in time.' The cabbie grinned. 'Payment can wait—I know where to find you. Nice work, ladies.' He threw an exaggerated wink, leaving Nell in no doubt that their encounter would be all over town before nightfall. The cabbies at the racecourse had to have a fair idea that something odd had been going on, even seen Edwards run from the old stables, or heaven forbid, Faith brandishing her pistol.

'Thank you, Mr Rusty. Just send an account, and for the second cab too, please.'

Taylor and Faith tumbled along the path ahead of her, arms linked, hooting with laughter. Connie grabbed Taylor's other arm. 'I can't thank you enough. When did you get here?'

'I was at the station asking directions when your grandmother arrived. After you left Parramatta, I did a bit of research into partnership law, thought it might be useful after what you'd said.' Taylor's face broke into a wide grin. 'It wasn't hard to put two and two together. I asked Maisie what she thought and when Mr Ramsbottom said he needed some documents delivered to Newcastle I offered. I'm due a few days' holiday. I met Mr Ballantyne at the station.'

'Mr Ballantyne? Where is he?'

'I'm not sure. Last I saw of him he was chatting to the stationmaster. When I discovered Mrs Montague was going alone to the meeting, I insisted on going with her. I didn't know you and Faith had plans.'

'I'm so glad you did. Come inside. I'm sure Mrs Orchard has luncheon ready and then we'll see if we can find Mr Ballantyne.'

'Would that be the elusive Mr Ballantyne?' Faith waved her finger at two figures ambling up from the river.

'It is. Seems Cracker found him. Taylor, do you know why he's here?'

She lifted her shoulders. 'Something about following up leads. I'm not sure. We didn't talk much on the train. I was reading.' She patted the inside of her jacket. 'Partnership law is quite interesting.'

Cracker took off around the back of the house, no doubt to stash his fishing rod, and Ballantyne loped up the bank. 'Ladies!'

'May I introduce my mother, Faith Montague. Mother, this is Robert Ballantyne. I met him on the train to Sydney.'

He gave an expansive bow. 'It's my pleasure.'

'Will you join us for some luncheon, Mr Ballantyne?' Faith

batted her eyelashes. 'You can tell me all about my daughter's adventures.' She led the way into the dining room.

Mrs Orchard had pulled out all the stops and somehow managed to extend the table and rearrange the seating to accommodate Taylor and Mr Ballantyne. Nell presided over a steaming chicken pie and bowls of garden beans and mashed potatoes. It was the guesthouse all over again, but without the odious Mrs Alexander.

'And how was your morning, ladies?' Mr Ballantyne took the plate offered and helped himself to the vegetables.

Nell couldn't imagine Taylor hadn't given him some indication of the reason for her visit but it didn't appear so. 'We had a business matter to attend to which we have successfully concluded. I think you could say we had an excellent morning.'

Murmured approvals filtered around the table, a few meaningful glances and a silent decision made not to discuss the matter in front of him. He'd no doubt hear about their exploits if he spent any time in town because of the cabbies. 'Taylor says you have business in the Hunter.'

Ballantyne swallowed his mouthful and put down his knife and fork. 'A story that I have been pursuing for some time. I've taken a room at the George and Dragon. Miss Fotherby, I took the liberty of booking another in your name if that's suitable ...'

'Taylor will be staying here.' Nell's voice brooked no argument.

'Thank you, Mrs Montague.' Taylor gave an uncharacteristic, sweet smile. 'I don't have to be back at work until Tuesday, if that's convenient.'

'For as long as you like, my dear. It's the least we can do.'

And so, the desultory conversation continued although in many ways the normality provided a welcome relief except Nell couldn't control her gaze. It kept drifting to Faith. So much she didn't know or understand about the woman, a situation she intended to rectify at the first opportunity.

'There's tea and biscuits in the drawing room for those that have a mind,' Mrs Orchard announced from the door as the last mouthfuls of apple pie and custard disappeared.

'Could we have it in here, please?' Faith asked in a determined tone.

Nell pushed back her chair with a sigh. 'I'll leave you young things to chatter. I have some matters to attend to.'

Ballantyne shot to his feet. 'Thank you for the delicious meal, Mrs Montague. If you will all excuse me, I have a meeting organised for this afternoon. I hope we can catch up again before I leave.' Mr Ballantyne eased Nell's chair away from the table.

'I'll show you to the door.' Nell offered a tired smile; the morning had taken its toll.

38

Saturday, 11 May, 1889

Nell held her hands out towards the crackling fire. It was a little early in the season but after the rain the weather had taken a turn and besides, she liked the homely comfort of a fire in the evening.

Two days had passed since the meeting with Edwards and every hour brought a greater sense of security. Taylor had said, time and time again, that there was nothing Edwards could do without making his extortion threat known. He didn't appear to have done that and even when she'd ventured to a meeting of the Benevolent Society no one had thrown sideways glances or chattered behind their hands.

Faith had taken Connie and Taylor to a race meeting yesterday and they'd all come back flushed with excitement, though she suspected that Faith's bloom was more one of personal triumph. She'd always harboured the presumption Nell had taken Connie from her in spite. It wasn't what she'd intended; she simply wanted the best for the child—not a child any longer, a young woman with a mind of her own, it would seem.

Nell kicked off her shoes, stretched out her legs and wiggled her toes in front of the fire. Although she relished the peace, she was a tad lonely after all the excitement. Mrs Orchard had gone to visit her sister and taken Dora with her. Connie and Taylor were attending a performance at the Victoria Theatre and Faith … well she wasn't quite sure what Faith was up to; she'd disappeared to her room saying she had paperwork to deal with.

The creak of the gate caught her attention, then footsteps up the path followed by a determined rap of the knocker. Would Faith answer the door? The knocker sounded again, more insistent this time. With a grunt of displeasure, she slipped her shoes back on.

A ridiculous flutter worked its way to her throat as she donned her pince-nez, lifted the curtain and peered out, replaced by immediate relief when Mr Ballantyne's smiling face slipped into focus. She raised her hand in greeting, dropped the curtain and made for the front door.

'Good evening, I hope I'm not disturbing you, but I wondered if you could spare me a moment.' Ballantyne looked over her shoulder into the hallway. 'Are you alone?'

'Faith is upstairs. Please come in.' She held the door wide then led him into the drawing room. 'May I get you a drink?'

'I won't trouble you. I must admit that I was hoping to find you alone. Miss Fotherby mentioned something about Miss Constance and amateur dramatics, and it seemed like the perfect opportunity to have a private word.'

His dry laugh did little to alleviate her growing anxiety and the shiver of trepidation worked its way up her spine. 'Would you like to sit down?'

He flopped down into the other chair in front of the fire, a tangle of arms and legs and tousled hair then straightened up and fixed his gaze upon her. 'I haven't been entirely honest with you …'

Not the best start. She ran a hand across the back of her neck.

'Pray continue.' Her icy voice chilled the room and goosebumps rippled her skin.

'As you know, I write articles for various publications.'

She inclined her head.

'Many of these articles require a great deal of research.' He gave a self-effacing grimace. 'Research that involves talking to people, frequently not mentioning my occupation or intentions until the facts are gathered and the story written.' He raked back his hair. 'I've been following a series of leads for some time revolving around the racing industry.'

A large stone replaced the shiver she'd previously felt, rock hard in the pit of her stomach.

'Are you familiar with the practice of race fixing?'

She licked her lips and shook her head. More to stall for time than anything else. Of course she was familiar with it. Although she wasn't until the doctor had given her Fred's personal possessions after he'd signed the death certificate. Maybe Edwards had followed through with his threats and had contacted Ballantyne. Why hadn't she handed over the money as she'd intended instead of listening to Taylor and her legalese?

Ballantyne steepled his fingers. 'It's the practice of substituting a faster horse for a slower one at the very last moment, after the odds are set. Those in the know reap large financial rewards when the substitute horse comes home.'

She swallowed down the bile in her throat. 'And what does this have to do with me? The Montagues have bred and raced many horses in our time and have never been accused of any malpractice.'

'I spoke to a man named Jack Edwards ...'

... and here it was. A great wave of despair racked her body.

'Are you familiar with the name?'

Familiar with the name? It would haunt her evermore.

'He was somewhat the worse for wear when I spoke to him—in his cups is a polite way of putting it.'

'There is no need to beat around the bush, Mr Ballantyne, I am aware of the effects of alcohol.'

'He accused your son of race fixing.'

Nell shot upright in the chair. All the effort she had gone to, to suppress the truth and now it was going to come out. 'My son is dead, Mr Ballantyne.'

He nodded his head, a look of pain flitted across his face, and he ran his hand over his chin. 'There's no easy way to say this, Mrs Montague, forgive me please. Edwards claimed that your son's death wasn't an accident.'

A strange wailing sound filled Nell's ears. Rough fingers chaffed her hands, the smell of ink and soap enveloped her.

'Mrs Montague, Mrs Montague. Please.'

Gradually the room came back into focus and the ghastly moaning sound ceased.

'Is there someone I can fetch? Your daughter-in-law, your housekeeper?'

She shook her head.

'The girls should be home soon.'

Heaven forfend! She straightened her spine. 'No.' She had to bear this alone. The price she must pay for keeping the truth from everyone. 'What did Edwards say?'

'Are you sure you wish me to continue?'

'I am.' She clamped her lips tight but couldn't prevent her hands from creeping towards her face.

'Edwards appears to have a grudge against the Montague family. He said your son deserved to die, that he'd threatened to ruin his livelihood. He also made mention of your daughter-in-law's activities on the racetrack which he claimed were illegal.'

'I think I am best placed to deal with these accusations.'

Nell peeled her hands away from her face. Faith stood, hand on the doorknob and an imperious expression on her face.

Ballantyne leapt to his feet. 'Would you like to sit down?'

Faith didn't reply, instead walked slowly across the room, and came to rest, one hand on the mantelpiece. 'Pray continue.'

Ballantyne's questioning gaze swept Nell's face. His discretion impressed her—not a trait one would expect to find in a newspaper hound but what did she know? The man was obviously well versed in whittling out the truth. More than that, the repercussions would place an indelible stain on Connie— everything she'd hoped to prevent.

'There's little more to tell. Edwards is making wild accusations, said the family refused to pay monies owed to him and gave me the distinct impression that he intended to make public matters relating to Mr Montague's activities and his subsequent demise which would bring your family into disrepute.'

'And did you believe him, Mr Ballantyne?' Faith raised one eyebrow.

'I don't honestly know what to believe but felt you should know.'

Nell chewed the inside of her mouth. She was lost. Had no idea how to deal with this man, what to say.

Faith cleared her throat and caught her attention, suddenly reminding Nell of the way she had brandished her pistol. She threw back her shoulders. 'Where did you meet Edwards?'

A slight flush tinged the tops of Ballantyne's ears. 'I was at Rutherford racecourse following up on a lead.'

'There were no races today.' The corner of Faith's mouth curled as she revelled in his discomfort.

'No. I was there two days ago, after you were kind enough to offer me lunch. I wanted to have a look around the place. Rumour has it there is a group operating in the Hunter, substituting horses.'

'Ah! Race fixing.' Faith smirked at Ballantyne's discomfort. 'Pray tell.'

Nell's mind cleared. That was not what Ballantyne claimed when he arrived at Parramatta. 'More to the point, what brought you to the guesthouse at Parramatta? A story about the various government houses I believe you said.'

He fidgeted in his seat, then combed his fingers through his hair. 'I met Miss Constance on the train down to Sydney by coincidence. It wasn't until she was leaving, she gave me her name.'

'Montague!' Faith crowed. 'And you, after your poking around in the Hunter chasing scandals, thought you had hit the jackpot.'

Nell's hackles rose. The effrontery. 'I think it would be a good idea if you left, Mr Ballantyne.'

Faith held up a long, slender hand. 'Oh no, not yet. I want to hear what Mr Edwards had to say, word for word, with nothing, I repeat nothing, omitted.' She drifted across to the sideboard, held up the brandy decanter. 'Nell?'

Nell nodded and waited while Faith poured two tumblers, handed one to her and then stood in front of Ballantyne cradling the glass. 'You might have to earn yours, Mr Ballantyne.' With her trademark, cat-like elegance, she returned to her spot by the fire. 'I'd like to hear exactly what Edwards had to say about my husband's death.'

Ballantyne leant forward and rested his elbows on his knees, staring deep into the fire. 'I don't want to upset anyone. Mrs Montague?'

'Simply an initial shock.' Not that Fred's death wasn't an accident. She'd pondered the possibility over the last two years, ever since it had happened, simply had no proof.

'As I said, Edwards had been drinking. He just started talking and couldn't stop. What he said about you—the Montagues— wasn't particularly pleasant ...'

'… but your curiosity was aroused.' Nell couldn't control the hint of asperity in her tone.

'He claimed that you refused to pay monies owed to him, that you thought yourselves above the law and the true facts behind Mr Montague's death were suppressed, because there were papers in your son's jacket pocket outlining the substitution racket he'd been operating.' He lifted his head and pinned Faith with an enquiring gaze. 'He also intimated you operated an illegal betting scheme.'

Faith slammed the glass down on the mantelpiece. 'What a load of poppycock! There were no papers. Edwards was responsible for the substitutions; Fred found out and told him to stop. He continued after Fred's death, and I caught him out when he got too big for his boots and tried to substitute one of our horses at Rutherford.'

Nell blinked once, twice, and widened her eyes. Had she heard Faith correctly? *Edwards was responsible for the substitutions*; *Fred found out and told him to stop.* She raised her index finger. She had to get her thoughts in order. 'Fred found out Edwards was responsible for the substitutions and Edwards continued running the racket after Fred's death and knew about the papers?' The records she had locked tight in the safe in Montague's study. It took a few seconds before Nell grasped the significance of Faith's and Ballantyne's words and recovered from the shock that she had misjudged her own son. She clapped her hands together, a short sharp sound a little like a pistol shot. Now, how to proceed?

Nell leant forward and held out her hand. 'I take it Edwards showed you said papers, Mr Ballantyne. May I see them?'

'Well, no, not exactly. He seemed to have a detailed knowledge of the contents.'

'Despite the fact he was in his cups, as you delicately put it.'

A red flush tinted Ballantyne's cheeks.

Faith rolled her eyes. 'Mr Ballantyne, as soon as you can produce evidence of the Montagues' dubious activities on and around the racetrack, we would be happy to discuss the matter further.'

Nell gritted her teeth; it couldn't continue to be dragged out any longer. 'We shall expect you tomorrow morning at nine, and until then I suggest you leave any mention of race fixing or the Montague family out of your scandal sheets.'

39

Connie pushed open the gate. 'The lights are on. Faith and Nell must be having a chinwag; that's unusual.'

'Chinwag? Not an expression I'd associate with your grandmother,' Taylor chuckled. 'However, you come from a line of formidable women. I was wondering if Faith would teach me to use a pistol. I rather like the idea of being armed, should the need arise.'

Connie pushed open the front door. 'You better ask her.' She ground to a halt and raised her finger to her lips. 'It sounds as though we have company. Is that Ballantyne's voice? I thought he said he was going back to Newcastle.'

'Hello, everyone. We're back.' The atmosphere of the room held a curious weight, the intense conversation they'd overheard suddenly cut short by their arrival.

Nell sat to one side of the fire cradling a glass of brandy— she never drank brandy—and Faith hovered at the mantelpiece eyeing Ballantyne with a look that could only be described as suspicious. 'I'm sorry, are we interrupting?'

'No, not at all. Mr Ballantyne is just leaving.' Faith's raised
eyebrow and her ominous tone filled Connie with a sense of
foreboding.

Ballantyne nodded, raked back his hair, then stood. 'Good
evening, ladies.'

Faith escorted him from the room. No other words were
spoken. The front door closed, and she returned. 'Taylor, I
wonder if you could give us some legal advice.'

'Legal advice?' Taylor frowned. 'I can try but I am not in any
way qualified. The matter of the partnership was simply a case
of looking up the relevant information and confirming it with
Mr Ramsbottom.'

'Mr Ballantyne has stumbled across some information
regarding my husband's death. It seems it might not have been
the accident we believed. How would you suggest we approach
the situation?'

Connie clamped her hand over her mouth. Pa's accident; it had
always been referred to as an accident. What could Ballantyne
have possibly discovered?

'The problem is if he brings the situation to light we run the
risk of the Montague name being brought into disrepute.' Nell
spoke for the first time.

The Montague name … disrepute? Nell sounded like some
eighteenth-century matriarch.

Taylor shook her head from side to side. 'I am afraid that is
far beyond my capabilities. There must be solicitors in town who
manage your affairs.'

'There are—Messrs Brown—but would you be prepared to
attend our meeting with them?' Nell asked. 'I'm not sure they
will understand the situation. And you are across the events of
the past few days. We would welcome your advice.'

Taylor wiped her hand around the back of her neck. 'I'm happy to assist in any way I can but this is first and foremost a family matter.'

'I have no intention of having this conversation rehashed in the morning. I would like you to stay. Connie, pour me another brandy.' Nell held out her glass.

Connie leapt to her feet, pleased to have something to do. It had never crossed her mind to question the facts she'd been presented with when Pa had died. She handed Nell her glass.

'Thank you, Connie.' Nell raised the glass a fraction in a silent toast. 'Mr Ballantyne spoke with Edwards. He claimed there were papers in your father's jacket pocket when he died that proved he was race fixing.'

Surely not? Pa was all about the sport. He valued his reputation, the quality of the animals. 'Was he?' Connie turned to Faith.

'No.' Faith strolled across the room and topped up her glass. The sharp fruity smell of the brandy blended with the wood smoke from the fire creating a relaxing atmosphere so far removed from the topic under discussion it was laughable. 'When your father discovered what Edwards was doing he threatened to expose him unless it stopped immediately. Edwards refused, and your father died.'

'But that doesn't prove Edwards was responsible for Pa's accident.'

'No, it doesn't.' Nell leapt to her feet, a glint of determination in her eyes. 'It is the information he let slip to Ballantyne that proves he was involved. He referred to the records of the race fixing that were found amongst your father's possessions.'

'And where are those records?' Taylor's voice cut like a knife through the ominous silence.

Connie had almost forgotten she was in the room.

'Locked in the safe where they have been since your father's body was found.' Nell's voice echoed. 'Only I knew of their existence.'

Taylor nodded furiously. 'I see. It seems Mr Edwards has signed his own arrest warrant. Although it does leave you in a rather dubious position, Mrs Montague. I fail to see how this can be kept quiet. I suggest we all sleep on the matter and that you take advice from Messrs Brown in the morning.'

'Sound counsel as always, Taylor, thank you. Goodnight.' Nell's voice sounded slightly slurred. 'Time for bed.' She swayed a little as she pushed out of the chair.

Connie glanced at Nell's empty glass. Had her grandmother overindulged? 'Why don't we go up together?' She linked her arm through Nell's and guided her through the door and down the hallway.

It wasn't until they reached the bedrooms Nell hissed, 'I need to talk to you.' She dragged Connie into her bedroom and closed the door, her back resting against the timber, eyes flashing, no sign a single drop of brandy had passed her lips. 'What I have to say is for your ears only.'

Good heavens! Connie sat down on the bed, hands clasped in her lap.

'There are several things amiss. There is only one person who knows about the papers found in Fred's pocket.'

Connie nodded; Nell had already said that.

'Yet Faith denied there were any papers. She said Edwards was responsible for the race fixing and after Fred's death she caught him out. Ballantyne also said Edwards accused Faith of running an illegal betting scheme. Faith denied that too.'

'Faith?' Connie's mouth gaped. Surely Faith's trips to the racecourse were purely social—she and the ladies in the stand especially built to accommodate them, away from the rough and tumble of the male-dominated racetrack. Connie's heartbeat raced. 'Are you suggesting Faith and Edwards are somehow involved?'

'She seems to know an awful lot about the goings-on at the racetrack.'

'Naturally, she's there almost every day.'

Nell simply raised an eyebrow and reached for Connie's hand. 'You were only young when Montague died. He was not a conventional man and when his will was read, he hadn't left his fortune to his son and heir as one would expect, but in trust.'

Connie nodded. The trust was no secret. Messrs Brown administered it. Nell was one of the trustees. Connie and Faith both received a monthly allowance, as did Nell. That was why Nell had rushed off searching for the yellow dress because she had no other way of meeting Edwards's demands without alerting Messrs Brown.

'Fred had no problems with the trust. He hadn't a head for money; he was only interested in the horses, famous breeding, prime conformation, and speed. His memory for bloodlines was prodigious; whenever he bought a new horse, he insisted on full breeding records. He'd lived his life never having to think about money or where it came from—something both Montague and I came to regret. Faith was another matter. She expected Fred to inherit the Montague fortune; she'd set her heart on a life of privilege and luxury the moment she clapped eyes on him. When she discovered Edwards continued with his race fixing after Fred died she saw it as a way of reclaiming what she believed was rightfully hers. I suspect she put Edwards up to the extortion demands. That they are in cahoots, as they say.'

Bile rose to Connie's throat. Her mother attempted to blackmail her own family. Surely she wouldn't. 'What makes you so sure?'

'It was when Faith told Ballantyne he should return when he could produce evidence of the Montagues' dubious activities on and around the racetrack. I knew the words sounded familiar.

They are the same as those in the blackmail letter. It hadn't occurred to me before to wonder why a strapper, a jockey, had such an excellent command of the English language. I don't think Edwards wrote that blackmail letter. I believe Faith did.'

'What are we going to do?'

Nell rubbed her hands together. 'We're going to call her bluff but first we must get the papers from the safe. And then we will ask Mr Ballantyne if he can match the names and dates to the race meetings where there have been accusations of race fixing, because we need proof Edwards was at those race meetings and not Fred. I also want to confirm my suspicions about the blackmail letter. It is in the safe along with the papers.' Nell moved swiftly across the room to the small desk in front of the window, and picked up her fountain pen and wrote *ELEANOR* in her notebook. 'The combination for the safe. Just one moment.'

Using Nell's name was far too simple and besides, weren't combinations meant to be numbers?

Before Connie had a chance to speak, Nell inscribed a series of numbers underneath the letters: 5,12,5,1,14,15,18. 'Their place in the alphabet but we combine the two-digit numbers so the combination is 5351569.'

'Wouldn't it be easier to simply remember the number?'

'It would but I was always concerned I might forget, and Montague devised this scheme. Come along. Hopefully everyone is abed.'

Nell stuck her head out of the door and grunted in satisfaction at the darkness. 'So much easier to find your way in your own house,' she murmured then slipped out of the door.

Connie followed her down the hallway, moving in unison from one side to the other to avoid the squeaky treads. Hands against the wall, they made their way to the front of the house. The last vestiges of the fire in the drawing room afforded a little light and Nell turned the handle of the door opposite, ushered Connie inside.

'Over here.' She knelt in front of the bookcase and ran her two hands along the plinth at the base and then gave a sharp press. The panel popped open, like a drawer. But there the similarity ended. A metal box filled the cavity. Nell turned the lock, the tumbler mechanism clicked. 'And now the combination.' Nell held up the piece of paper and tilted it this way and that. 'I can't read it,' she sighed and rocked back on her heels. 'My pince-nez ...'

'Five, three, five, one, five, six, nine,' Connie parroted. 'I can't read it either in this light, but I can remember it.'

Nell's cheeks filled with air and she blew out a series of puffs. 'Slowly. One number at a time.'

'Five... three ... five ... one ... five ... six ... last one ... nine.'

Nell gave the tumbler a final turn and with a satisfying clunk the top of the box sprang open. 'There!' She raised the lid. Bent forward, she peered inside, ran her hand around the space and pulled out a leather-bound folder. 'The trust documents.' She pushed it aside and rummaged a little more and groaned. 'The papers have gone.'

'What do you mean gone?'

'The papers the doctor gave me, from Fred's pocket with the list of the races where substitutes were run.'

'What about the blackmail letter?' Connie dropped to her knees and ran the flat of her hand over the empty space. Her stomach performed a ragged cartwheel.

'It's not here.'

'Are you sure? Is there anything else missing?' Please, not the drafts from Mr Golding.

'A bundle of five-pound notes secured by a piece of string, my emergency fund. Fortunately Mr Golding's drafts are still in my reticule.'

Their gazes met.

Nell closed the lid of the safe, spun the tumbler and pushed the plinth back in place. 'You don't think …'

'I do.' Connie scrambled to her feet and charged upstairs, Nell dogging her heels, giving no thought to the amount of noise they made, and threw open the door to Faith's bedroom.

40

A willy-willy might have hit the room. The window wrenched open, curtains billowing in the chill air, the dank, night-time smell of the river permeating the entire space, the doors to the clothes press swinging in the breeze, hats and dresses scattered across the bed.

And no sign of Faith.

'Do you think the room was broken into? Maybe she's still downstairs?' The quaver in Connie's voice turned Nell's stomach.

Nell placed a hand on Connie's shoulder. 'No, sweetheart. She's gone. Come along. We'll go down to the kitchen and make a nice cup of tea. Neither of us are going to sleep for a while.'

Nell led the way down the stairs, Connie trailing behind her. Of course the poor child would be upset, although she couldn't have more than a few recollections of Faith as a mother. From the moment they had moved from Coloma into the town house Faith became an infrequent visitor. She'd only taken up residence in town at Nell's insistence after Fred's death. Nell bent to the range, stoked the remnants of the fire, and added more wood from the basket Cracker kept filled next to the hearth. 'Faith must have realised she couldn't bluff it out any longer. That since she and Edwards had failed in the blackmail attempt he would let slip her involvement. By taking the papers and the letter, any accusations were simply hearsay.' Nell put the kettle onto the hob.

Connie slumped down next to the fire and dropped her head into her hands, a picture of abject misery.

'Try not to let Faith upset you.' Nell stroked Connie's tumbled curls. 'I know it's difficult and I understand. Faith was always going to have to accept that she wouldn't get what she wanted, what she believed she was entitled to and deserved. She knew the terms of Montague's will and knew I wouldn't bend—that you would inherit the Montague fortune when you came of age.' An heir, someone to remain behind, to take her place, testimony that she and Montague had not lived their lives in vain and now so very feasible after the passing of the Married Women's Act. 'Faith's ridiculous scheme with Edwards was a last-ditch stand.'

'But if I had …'

'Sweetheart, the die was cast long before you were born. Faith married Fred with an eye on the prize. Somewhat ironically, Edwards, her partner in crime, has brought about her downfall.'

'How so?'

'The only way Edwards could have known about the papers in Fred's pocket was if, as Faith said, Fred had discovered Edward's race fixing scheme. Edwards had too much to lose. He planted the papers on Fred hoping they would be found and Fred accused, albeit posthumously, for orchestrating the race fixing scheme. Ballantyne said … Edwards claimed Fred's death wasn't an accident.'

'He murdered Pa? That can't be true.' Silence hung, dark and heavy. Connie clutched the table for support, disbelief and bewilderment etched on her features as she came to accept the awful truth.

Then she opened her eyes, wiped away the tears and squared her shoulders. 'How? I thought ...'

'Oh, Connie, I'm so sorry. I shouldn't have told you.'

'You've kept enough secrets to last a lifetime.'

Connie's flash of unexpected anger was no more than Nell deserved; it came as a relief.

'Tell me how Pa died!'

Nell swallowed. 'Fred had travelled hundreds of times in the loose box with the horses to tracks all over the country. He wouldn't have used a frayed rope to tether a racehorse; neither would he have put himself in danger.' She shook her head from side to side. 'I hoped to shield you from the gruesome details. His injuries were such that it was impossible to know how the blow to his head, which the doctor believed killed him, was inflicted. Man, or beast?' She rubbed her hands over her face. 'Nothing anyone can prove; I doubt we will ever know.'

'There must be something we can do.' Connie dumped an obscene amount of sugar into her teacup and stirred slowly, probably hoping to sweeten the filthy taste of the truth.

Nell didn't trust herself to speak. If only she'd taken more notice of Montague's reasons for moving into town and setting up the family trust. For a while she'd taken it personally, as an indication that Montague didn't think she could manage, and upset on Fred's behalf, that his father had as good as disinherited him, but now it was abundantly clear, and Montague, as always, was right. He'd set up the trust to ensure that Faith had no opportunity to fritter away Connie's inheritance. 'After Montague died Fred went into partnership with Edwards. He couldn't commit the family money; the partnership only covered the winnings on the track and Edwards was perfectly placed—links to all the Hunter studs, and further afield. But what no one knew, not even Fred, was that Edwards was substituting horses at the country races and benefiting from the odds.' Nell gave a jaw-cracking yawn, fatigue seeping through her bones. It had been just over two weeks, fifteen days since she'd found the pernicious letter on the doormat.

'I don't understand why Faith …' Connie's voice caught.

The poor child … she must stop calling her a child; if anything, the past days had dragged her from the cocoon Nell had encased her in and thrown her into a world she never imagined existed. With a pang Nell accepted her responsibility. Her sole intention had been to make Connie's life perfect—she'd failed miserably. It was time to rip out the festering splinter and cleanse the wound. Only the full unvarnished truth would suffice.

Nell reached across the table and took Connie's hands in hers. 'I didn't voice my objections to Fred's choice of bride although both Montague and I saw her for what she was—a gold-digger with her sights set on the future. I can only blame myself.' Nell dropped Connie's hands and rubbed at her eyes. Connie didn't need to know her birthdate was a mere seven and a half months after Fred and Faith's marriage. 'Your arrival thrilled everyone.' Poor Connie, this was going to hurt but she needed to understand. 'But Faith had little interest in you as a baby and within a week or so was back out with the horses doing what she loved best. I ensured you lacked for nothing and when Montague's health began to fail, we moved to The Bend and you came with us. It wasn't until Montague died and the details of the trust became known that Faith's disappointment, more displeasure, revealed her true intentions. She expected to be queen of Coloma and the racetrack; instead, she and Fred ended up with a monthly allowance and the right to run the property, but they were accountable to the trust. Faith was aware of Fred's partnership with Edwards but no one knew what Edwards was up to behind the scenes until Fred caught him out.'

A strangled sob caught in Connie's throat.

Nell didn't dare stop. If she did, she might never reach the end. 'I don't believe Faith had any knowledge of Edwards's plan to do away with Fred. I am certain she believed, as we all did, that it was a horrible accident.' She hadn't pieced it together, no one had; it was only when Ballantyne said that Edwards had spoken about the papers in Fred's pocket, she realised the implications.

Connie rubbed at the frown creasing her forehead. 'Wait. If that's the case, then why has Faith taken the papers? Why has she left? Has Edwards kidnapped her? Maybe he is going to hold her for ransom, get the money that way.' Her eyes pleaded with Nell, begging her to say something that would exonerate Faith. No one wanted to believe their sole surviving parent, their mother, vengeful and vindictive.

'I am convinced Faith was behind the blackmail attempt. She got wind of Ballantyne's investigations into the race fixing and saw it as an opportunity to gain the money she believed she was entitled to.' What a foolish woman she was. What was it Taylor had said? Blackmail relies on the recipient being too scared to refuse. Faith knew any threat to the Montague name would send her into a flat spin, that she'd pay up, but she hadn't known about the yellow dress. She'd expected Nell to go to Messrs Brown, exercise her right to have the trust amended. 'When she turned up at the Spread Eagle Inn brandishing her pistol Edwards thought she'd double-crossed him. I'm certain that was the reason he told Ballantyne everything. If he couldn't get the money, he'd bring the Montagues down, just as the blackmail letter threatened.'

41

Sunday, 12 May, 1889

'Ow! Lemme go! I ain't done nothing wrong.'

'We'll see about that. You come along with me and tell Mrs Montague what you just said.'

Nell lifted her head from the newspaper and raised an eyebrow.

'Sounds like someone has got Mrs Orchard's goat.' Connie took a mouthful of scrambled eggs.

'That's a particularly common expression. Can you come up with something a little more refined?'

Connie didn't respond. It seemed totally appropriate after all the talk of the racecourse. It was one of the few memories she had of the Coloma stables. The dear little goats placed in the stall with highly strung thoroughbreds to keep them calm—no such luck. Faith's activities at the racetrack hadn't surprised her as much as she expected. In many ways, they made sense of so many things. First and foremost, the fact that Faith either had money—far more than her allowance from the trust would cover, now she thought about it—or none. In a strange way she rather admired her, possibly for the first time ever, breaking down the monopoly men had at the racecourse with their exclusive betting rings.

The door flew open, scattering her thoughts. A red-faced, heaving and puffing Mrs Orchard as good as threw Jonas onto the floor. He crouched, hands over his ears, whimpering. A definite need to restore calm.

'Whatever is going on?' Nell peered over the newspaper. 'Who is this?'

Ah! Connie had forgotten that Nell hadn't met Jonas nor knew of the role he had played in her search for her or the fact he was taking most of his meals at The Bend. 'This is Jonas. He's been giving Cracker a hand. Is there a problem, Mrs Orchard?'

'Yes, there is. This young scoundrel ...' she prodded Jonas with the well-polished toe of her boot '... has been sticking his nose in where it doesn't belong. Go on, you tell Miss Montague what you just told me.'

Jonas uncovered his head and straightened up. 'Same as last time, only different. Thought you'd want to know ...'

'Last time?' Nell pushed the newspaper aside, her attention riveted on the boy.

'When youse went missing. I thought Miss Montague might want to know.'

'Go on.' Mrs Orchard's boot shot out again, but Jonas slithered out of reach.

'Young Mrs Montague, she turned up at the station in the middle of the night. Sat in the waiting room until the first train came.'

Connie and Nell exchanged glances.

'I thought I told you I didn't want to hear any more of your lies. Tell the truth, boy.' Mrs Orchard took a step closer.

Obviously, she wasn't aware that Faith had left last night.

'That will be all, thank you. Connie and I will see to young Jonas. Come and sit down here.' Nell pointed to the chair opposite, Faith's usual spot. 'So, you saw young Mrs Montague get onto the morning train. Is that right?'

Jonas nodded his head.

'And what were you doing at the station? Why weren't you home in bed?'

A look of sheer terror crossed poor Jonas's face. Connie reached out her hand to him. 'It's all right, Jonas. You haven't done anything wrong. I'll explain to Mrs Montague. Why don't you take a plate and help yourself to a couple of those sausages over there?' Before she'd had a chance to point to the sideboard Jonas was on his feet lifting the cloche from the chaffing plates and making his selection. 'Mr Marsh allows Jonas to sleep in the waiting room at the station on the condition he leaves before the first train and Mrs Orchard occasionally gives him a meal in exchange for a bit of work around here. Go on, Jonas.'

He swallowed his mouthful. 'She slept in the waiting room. I had to make do with the floor, under the seats, case she saw me. That's how I knew she got on the train. I couldn't leave the waiting room 'til she did, could I? Had a huge suitcase with her, too. Mr Marsh had to help her get it on the train. He told her she'd have to change trains if she wanted to pick up the Melbourne express.'

Nell cleared her throat, the corner of her mouth twitching in a grin. 'Well, thank you very much, young man, for your information. Now why don't you take your plate out to the kitchen and finish your breakfast there? Tell Mrs Orchard I sent you.'

Jonas threw Connie a wink and took off down the hallway.

'Well, that answers that question. It sounds like Faith has decided to go home.' Nell dusted her hands together. 'I can't say

I'm disappointed. Now, I think you better tell me the rest of the story about Jonas before Taylor comes down for breakfast—'

A great hammering silenced Nell.

'Is that the front door? Oh dear, it's going to be one of those mornings. Will you see to it, Connie, please?'

The thumping increased in volume as Connie made her way into the hallway. She threw open the door and Cracker collapsed onto the doormat. 'Whatever is it?'

'Oh, Miss!' He bent double and gave a rasping cough. 'Mr Ballantyne said I had to come and get you and take you down to tell Sergeant Black.'

'Tell Sergeant Black what? Cracker, come in for a minute. We'll get you a glass of water; you look all done in.'

'No, Miss. We got to go now. I caught a body.'

'A body?'

'With my fishing line. Mr Ballantyne thinks you should come with me, 'case they think I'm joshing. He said he'd stand guard. Come on.' He grabbed her hand and pulled her through the door.

'Let me go and tell Mrs Montague where I'm going.'

The grip on her hand tightened. 'No, Miss. Mr Ballantyne 'specially said don't tell Mrs Montague. It ain't a sight for an old lady.' His whole body shuddered. 'All bloated he was, kinda red and yellow and waxy and his tongue hanging out like one of those ox tongues in Mr Boneham's shop window.' Cracker stuck out his tongue, curled it, then made a disgusting vomiting sound. 'He's pretty sure it's Mr Edwards.'

'Nell,' she called. 'Cracker's got a bit of a problem. I'll be back before long.' Without waiting for a response Connie slammed the front door behind her and charged after Cracker.

By the time they reached the police station, puffing and wheezing, Connie regretted her instinct to blindly follow Cracker. She'd probably end up having to explain to Sergeant Black how she'd found Nell and get a sanctimonious lecture about jumping to conclusions before Cracker even got a word in.

She shouldered open the door and found Constables Button and Bonnet grinning amiably at her from behind the desk. 'Morning, Miss Montague. What can we do for you?'

'We have a bit of a problem. Young Cracker, here ...' she rested a hand on his shoulder ... 'was fishing at The Bend this morning and he's hooked what looks remarkably like a body. We're not quite sure what to do next.' She wiped her other hand across her forehead, increased her grip on Cracker's shoulder and staggered a little.

Bonnet shot around the desk. 'Let me help you, Miss. Here, sit down.' As he eased her into a chair, she caught Cracker's nod of approval. 'Sergeant Black's not in yet. Got some business at the courthouse. Why don't you sit here for a while and get your breath?'

No! That would not do at all. She drew in a lungful of air. 'Thank you for the thought, Constable, but really, I would like your assistance. If my grandmother ...' She let her words taper off and gave a hiccupping sob.

'I understand. Not something for an old lady, any lady, to see. We'll leave a note for Sergeant Black, lock up and get straight down there.' He glared at Cracker. 'You take Miss Montague home. Leave this in our hands.' He rubbed his palms together as though he relished the prospect.

Cracker played his part to a tee. Eased her to her feet and led her towards the door. 'Get the lady a cab, boy,' Bonnet called after them.

'Do you want a cab, Miss?'

'Might be a good idea. We'll get back before them then. Are you sure it was Edwards?'

Cracker lifted his shoulders. 'Mr Ballantyne seemed certain. Someone had a hand in it. He had a lump the size of a volcano on his head. Must have been knocked senseless. Wouldn't have had a hope in hell, poor bugger.' He clapped his hand over his mouth. 'Beg pardon, Miss.' He stuck two fingers in his mouth and produced an ear-splitting whistle.

Connie flinched. She'd orchestrated her behaviour in the station for effect, but truth be told she did feel a little fragile.

A cab drew to a halt. 'Montagues', Horseshoe Bend.' Cracker opened the door and helped her inside and went to climb in after her.

'Oi! What d'you think you're doing, boy?' the cabbie scowled.

'Can't you see? She ain't well. I'm 'scorting her home. Hurry up, man.' And with that Cracker slammed the door and sat down opposite her, then thumped on the roof of the cab.

'Nicely done, Cracker.'

'Thanks, Miss. What're we going to do next?' He scratched his head. 'They're going to want to ask me questions.'

'They are. Was Mr Ballantyne with you, fishing?'

'Nah! I'd chucked my line in, same as usual, and it snagged. I was heaving and pulling when Mr Ballantyne came along. Said he was on his way to have a word with Mrs Montague, and he gave me a hand. We both near shat ourselves ...' He clapped his hand over his mouth again and shook his head. 'It was quite a shock I can tell you.'

'I bet it was. You've been a great help. I'll go and break the news to Mrs Montague.' Without the lurid descriptions of volcanos and lolling tongues. Mrs Orchard was going to have to take ox tongue off the menu. A surge of bile filled her mouth, and she swallowed it down.

'You all right, Miss? You've gone all white again. We're there now.'

The cab drew up to the house and Cracker tumbled out and took off back to the river.

Connie eased her way down. Held her hand to her forehead.

'I'll put that on the account, shall I, Miss Montague?' the cabbie asked.

She nodded and weaved her way up the path to the front door wondering how she would break the news to Nell.

42

Nell dropped the curtain. Connie looked as though she'd had the most dreadful time, white as Dora's washing and weaving up the path like a drunkard. She rushed to the front door, but Taylor had beaten her to it. 'Sweetheart, what's happened?' She elbowed Taylor aside and wrapped her arm around Connie. 'Come and sit down.'

'I'm fine. Cracker hooked a body.'

The air wavered and for a ghastly moment in her mind's eye Nell imagined Faith floating face down, her skirts ballooning around her and her hat bobbing in the current. 'Was it ...' A strangled cry passed her lips. No matter how difficult Faith had been over the years and the trouble she'd caused she wouldn't wish that kind of a death on anyone.

'Ballantyne thinks it is Edwards.'

Her great woosh of relief blew the escaped strands of hair from her forehead. Of course, it couldn't be Faith; that Jonas boy had said he saw her getting on the train. She wiped her hand over her face. She really did feel a little discombobulated.

'I'd kill for a cup of tea. I'll go and ask Mrs Orchard. Anyone else?'

'You and Nell sit down. I'll sort out the tea. But no explanations until I get back.' Taylor dashed down the hallway to the kitchen.

Connie pushed open the dining room door. 'I thought Taylor was going home today.'

'So did I, but when I said you'd rushed off with Cracker without a word she decided to get a later train and keep me company. She's got to see some solicitor in Newcastle; that's how she managed to wangle a few days here. Are you sure you're all right? Your colour's a little better.'

'Honestly, I'm fine. I had to play the pathetic female. I did too good a job!'

'Right. Now tell me what's happened.'

Taylor plonked a tray down on the table. 'I asked you to wait for me.' She put the teapot and cups and saucers onto the table and a plate of milk arrowroot biscuits. 'Start at the beginning, please.'

'Cracker was down at the river fishing. He hooked a body. Mr Ballantyne happened to be passing on his way to talk to you, I think, Nell.'

'Yes, we agreed to meet this morning at nine.' She looked at the carriage clock on the mantelpiece. 'He's late.'

'I expect he'll be a whole lot later. He and Cracker will have to give statements. And that's about all I know really.'

'Ballantyne thinks it's Edwards?'

Connie nodded. She really didn't want to go into details. 'Yes, and Cracker said he looked as though he'd hit his head.'

Taylor's eyes widened. 'An accident?'

'I really don't know but I suspect it might not have been.'

'There'll have to be a coroner's report to confirm what happened. We won't know for days.' Taylor picked up the teapot, poured three cups and slid them across the table. 'If it's all right with you I think I'd like to stay and see this through. I feel a certain responsibility since I told you about the partnership law. I'll send a telegram to Mr Ramsbottom later, explain what is happening.'

Nell's heart sank. She couldn't have that. All the trouble she'd gone to keep the Montague name in the clear and now this; add Mr Ballantyne's snooping and it was a recipe for disaster. She picked up an arrowroot biscuit and dunked it in her tea. 'I told Taylor about Faith's departure.' She hadn't had much option; Taylor had rather caught her off-guard just as Connie had taken off with Cracker.

The time ticked slowly by. Taylor fetched another pot of tea, and Nell ate more arrowroot biscuits than she should, while Connie and Taylor discussed all sorts of theories about Edwards's demise. There was little point in conjecture; they would simply have to wait for Mr Ballantyne.

After a couple of hours Mrs Orchard appeared with a plate of sandwiches, thankfully not curried egg, though she hadn't space for sandwiches of any variety after the biscuits, and a large jug of lemonade. Finally there was a knock on the door.

'I'll get it.' Taylor was in the hallway opening the door before Nell had even managed to stand and there stood a rather dishevelled and damp-looking Ballantyne.

'My apologies for keeping you waiting, Mrs Montague ...' He flopped down in the chair next to Connie and reached for a sandwich. 'I'm sorry. I'm starving. No breakfast.' Connie pushed the plate closer.

'Take your time.' Nell spoke through gritted teeth. Not the best but really, she didn't think she could wait much longer.

Six of Mrs Orchard's finger sandwiches later, Ballantyne pushed back his chair and gave a half-hearted smile. 'It's been quite a morning.'

'Just start at the beginning.' Nell interlaced her fingers and stared into his face. The poor man did look as though he'd been through the wringer.

'Edwards was pulled out of the river by Cracker this morning. I'd say he'd been in the water for twenty-four, maybe thirty-six hours. The constables agreed with me. Apparently, they've had a fair bit of experience with all the floods around here. I identified him as Jack Edwards—no doubt in my mind. He was wearing the same clothes as he was when I met him the other day at the racetrack.'

'An accident?' Taylor interrupted.

'No chance. His face was a mess: he had a rather nasty contusion on his head. He wouldn't have had a chance, particularly if he'd been drinking. However, that's for the coroner to sort out.'

'But who did it? Why?' Nell's voice quavered. Who else knew about the blackmail demands? The four of them sitting around the table, and Faith, but she couldn't imagine Faith overpowering Edwards. He was small like all jockeys but strong and wiry despite his paunch, unless she'd … 'Had he been shot?'

'Not as far as I know. The coroner will confirm that. Why do you ask?'

Oh, the nuisance man; he did have a mind like a steel trap. She licked her lips, framing her answer.

'You think Faith might be responsible?' Ballantyne's eyebrows rose. 'He said she'd waved a pistol in his face.'

Before Nell could reply Connie butted in. 'My mother left Maitland on the early train this morning, with a large suitcase and the papers found on my father's body which she took from the safe.'

'Along with his blackmail letter and a deal of cash, my emergency funds.' The words were out of Nell's mouth before she thought.

He narrowed his eyes and pinned her with a knowing look. 'I see—that does put a rather different spin on my theory.'

Nell's cheeks heated. 'Your theory?'

'Yes. Which is what I wanted to discuss this morning, Mrs Montague.'

Nell's heart stuttered. She clamped her hands tight between her knees. All she really wanted to do was cover her ears, not listen. How she wished Connie hadn't given her name to a good-looking stranger on the train.

'What I failed to mention when we spoke last night ...' he cleared his throat '... I've done a bit more ... investigation, might be the best word. It seems Edwards has been making quite a nuisance of himself, not only his blackmail demand. From what I can ascertain his racket has been extremely successful. There seems to be no evidence that your son was in any way involved; it was not part of their partnership arrangement.'

'But the papers ...' Nell groaned. Good heavens; when would she learn to keep her mouth closed?

'The evidence supports the fact your son discovered Edwards's sideline, shall we call it, and demanded that it stop. Everyone I spoke to was emphatic about young Mr Montague's honesty.'

Two years of anxiety leached from Nell's bones. She hadn't appreciated how close she had been to the truth when she'd thought Fred a fool but not a criminal. She owed him an apology; one she would never be able to offer.

'Edwards had no intention of giving away what was a very lucrative business. He had to silence Fred. He returned the papers used to accuse him to Fred's pocket, hoping to incriminate him, but through some twist of fate they didn't come to light.'

That twist of fate being the doctor who'd removed Fred's personal possessions from his body when he'd determined the cause of death, and in her own mind she'd incriminated her son. It would take a long time to forgive herself for that.

'Edwards, in his drunken stupor, told me the papers were not a list of Fred's activities but the notes he had drawn up to call Edwards to question.'

'Mr Ballantyne?' Taylor leant forward, a frown of concentration on her face. 'I'm not doubting the veracity of your research, but this all happened over two years ago. How could it have led to Edwards's blackmail demands?'

'Mother.' Connie dropped the word like a stone in a pond and the ripples encompassed them all. 'Nell and I both believe she was behind the blackmail attempt.'

'According to the bookies' gossip around the racetrack, she took up with Edwards, demanded that the partnership should continue and that she should receive a percentage of the earnings from the substitution racket.'

'There was no partnership,' Taylor threw in.

'No, legally there wasn't. You are correct. I am simply using the expression to describe the informal arrangement Faith and Edwards had. Edwards didn't like being under her thumb and when I started poking around and asking questions, they decided the time had come to walk away. I was getting too close to unearthing their profitable little sideline.'

'This is all conjecture.' Taylor pushed back her chair and stood. 'You have no evidence to back it up.'

'And nor will I ever have unless I break the confidence of the bookies that spoke to me, and confirm my suspicions regarding Edwards's death, and in so doing I'd be signing my own death warrant. They don't like their livelihood being threatened.'

'Another drowning?'

Ballantyne nodded his head and suddenly Nell caught up with the implications. 'Which means, Mr Ballantyne, you are not in a position to write a story about your findings.' She could barely control her whoop of excitement. The Montague name would not be tarnished, Connie's future was assured, and she had achieved her goal—and, as luck would have it, regained Montague's gold.

Epilogue

It had been a long time since Nell had last attended the Picnic Races, in the distant days before the new stands, the railway siding and the immaculate track. Back then there was nothing more than a flattened piece of dirt behind the Spread Eagle Inn, but it had seen the beginning of the Jockey Club, a vibrant and bustling centre for horseracing and social gatherings, and had spawned the Montague reputation for breeding the best horses in the Hunter.

The racecourse Montague championed had become a vital hub for the local community, offered entertainment, social events, and, of course, horseracing—a sport as deeply embedded in the Australian culture as in the Montague blood. The well-defined tracks, marked by neatly trimmed grass, where horses thundered down in heated competitions, drew crowds from near and far. Spectators gathered along the sidelines, in the grandstands and pavilions, eagerly cheering on their favourite riders and horses. The atmosphere crackled with excitement and anticipation as the horses raced down the tracks, vying for victory, the men and women sporting their best attire, adding more than a touch of elegance and style.

The day sparkled, not only the blue of the sky and the light spring breeze but also myriad facets of brilliant colour: the ruby, garnet, sapphire and topaz of the jockeys' silks and of the wonderful hats and costumes worn by the ladies as everyone flooded into the course.

'Good morning, Mrs Montague. It's so lovely to see you.'

'Mrs Pinkerton, what a delightful hat.'

'Isn't it just. We have a new milliner in town. Madame Milling. She has simply been run off her feet since she opened her shop. Not only her hats but also her costumes and gentlemen's clothing too. Her waistcoats are a delight.'

Nell curbed a smile. Taylor had written to say that Mrs Alexander's lease on the guesthouse would not be renewed, due to some discrepancies with the inventory, missing silverware, the dilapidated state of the building. Old Government House would no longer run as a guesthouse, not under Mrs Alexander's hand or anyone else's.

While she couldn't bring herself to feel very much sympathy for Mrs Alexander, she was mortified to discover that Miss Pettigrew, Maisie and Taylor would have nowhere to live and then in a stroke of serendipitous good fortune the Wilmingtons who owned one of the other houses along Carrington Street had decided to relocate to Sydney.

Thanks to Mr Golding's drafts she had been able to secure the property with an outlandish offer well above market price. Taylor had handled the conveyancing with a deal of skill, and very little assistance from Messrs Brown, and Nell had offered Taylor, Maisie and Miss Pettigrew a home. And once Maisie and the girls had settled their differences, May and June accompanied them, determined, after Mrs Trotter's retirement to her sister's in Parramatta, to take on not only the housework but also the cooking and kitchen garden now they were in receipt of Mrs Trotter's parting gift, her recipe book. They were making excellent strides.

The room at the front of the house, with its large windows overlooking the street, was turned into a showroom and Madame Milling's Milliner and Costumier came into being. It was intended that the rooms on the upper floors would become a large sitting and dining room with bedrooms at the back and one of those new-fangled lifts fitted to enable Miss Pettigrew a deal of independence but, in the meantime, Nell had offered Miss Pettigrew the guest bedroom at home. The arrangement suited everyone.

'Cor blimey! This is a treat and a 'alf. Thanks, Mrs Montague.' Cracker and Jonas skidded to a halt in front of her, faces glowing after the scrubbing they'd received from Mrs Orchard and looking quite the part in their new tweed suits and matching cloth caps. Another excellent job on Maisie's behalf. Their ever-present group of acolytes hovered behind them, sadly not as well scoured and definitely in need of Mrs Orchard's ministrations.

'Don't you boys get yourselves into trouble, and stay away from the betting ring.'

Jonas snatched at his cap, reefing it from his head to reveal a bunch of burnished locks most girls would die for. 'Ow! Why? Miss Constance said she'd take a bet for us.'

A sudden palpitation caught Nell off-guard. 'She can't. Ladies aren't allowed to place wagers.' Connie's interest in Coloma and the racetrack had blossomed since Faith's departure and she spent more and more time overseeing the management of the stud— her father's daughter after all.

Cracker's foot ground Jonas's toe into the turf. 'You weren't supposed to say nothing.'

Jonas clapped his hand over his mouth. 'No, no. She's in the ladies' stand.' He pointed to the tiered seats crammed full of brightly dressed women, their clothing rivalling the jockeys' silks. 'It's all right and proper, like.'

'You go and tell her from me that I have no intention of reliving the past.'

'What's past?' Jonas scratched his head.

'Never mind, never mind. Off you go and enjoy yourself.' Nell shooed them away and strode across to the stand. Ever since Taylor had accepted Messrs Browns' offer of a position, she and Connie had become virtually inseparable, their Saturdays and Sundays spent gallivanting around the area picnicking and of all things bicycle-riding. They had also managed to inveigle their way into the amateur dramatic society. Connie had discovered a flair for stage sets while Maisie continued to find time despite her blossoming business to play wardrobe mistress. Who would have thought little over a year ago life had seemed insurmountable?

There was still the unsolved mystery of Edwards's death. Sergeant Black and his two constables had questioned just about every bookie in the Hunter but no one was talking.

'Mrs Montague.'

Nell clamped her hand on top of her ridiculously extravagant hat and spun around. It seemed her thoughts were capable of conjuring characters from the ether.

'Mr Ballantyne, how lovely to see you. It's been months. Are you well?'

'Very well, thank you. Pleased to be back in the Hunter.'

'You've been travelling?'

'I decided I'd like to experience the pleasures of the Great Northern Line in its entirety. So I've been all the way to Brisbane and back, then after a brief stop in Melbourne, across to Adelaide.'

Nell gazed into his chocolate brown eyes, her fingers blindly fumbling for her pince-nez, certain there was more behind his words than his expression indicated.

'I have something for you.' He held a pristine envelope, nothing to indicate the intended recipient. 'Some papers that came into my possession while I was in Melbourne.'

Her fingers closed around her pince-nez and she wrangled them onto her nose before taking the envelope and sliding her finger under the flap. She pressed her lips tight as she recognised Fred's flamboyant handwriting. 'Melbourne you said. Flemington racetrack, I presume.'

Ballantyne nodded. 'You can consider the matter of the Montague involvement into race fixing closed.'

It wasn't often Nell found herself lost for words but on this occasion, she could do nothing but smile with relief.

'I'm looking for Connie and Taylor. Have you any idea where I might find them?'

'In the ladies' stand I hope; I was on my way over there myself. The *ladies'* stand,' she reiterated.

'Maybe you could ask them to come and have a word? Truth be told, I've missed their company.'

Nell narrowed her eyes and peered into his guileless face searching for a greater meaning to his words. She shook the thought away. She intended to enjoy the day, and the days to follow, not become embroiled in matters she couldn't control.

And besides, with the breeze caressing her face and the sun on her back she could sense Montague's smile of approval—that all-encompassing beam of warmth keeping him alive in her heart and her memory forever.

Historical Note

In the 1970s, a yellow silk damask dress was found in a calico bag in the attic of Old Government House, Parramatta. It was in pieces and appeared to have been restyled several times. How the dress came to be in Australia is not known, never mind how it got to the attic of Old Government House. It was donated to the National Trust and in a joint effort with a team from the National Institute of Dramatic Art (NIDA) in 2022, the dress was recreated and it has been on display at various National Trust venues since then. Further details and a short video are available online: www.nationaltrust.org.au/news/students-piece-together-the-mystery-of-a-280-year-old-yellow-dress/

I received an invitation from the National Trust to view the dress at Grossman House in Maitland. From the moment I saw it I knew there was a story begging to be told, and when Jasmin Gray, one of the NIDA team who reconstructed the dress, mentioned they'd found spots of blood on one of the sleeves, I was captivated!

And so we have *The Golden Thread*, a fictionalised account of how a dress created in the mid-eighteenth century in Spitalfields,

London, came to be in the attic at Old Government House and why it stayed hidden away for so long.

There are a few other bits and pieces of history that snuck into the story.

From the mid-1850s until after the turn of the century, Old Government House at Parramatta was leased. Very few details of the occupants are known, but between 1865 and 1877 it was tenanted by Andrew Blake. From 1878 a Mrs Abrahams ran the 'Government House Boarding Establishment' and from 1885 to 1895 DJ Bishop was proprietor. Mrs Abrahams again leased the property after that until, in 1897, she was given a week's notice to quit.

Maitland racecourse began life in the grounds of the Spread Eagle Inn, around the middle of the nineteenth century. The 'new' racecourse, with its railway siding, opened in the 1880s and operated until the outbreak of the Second World War, when the land was sold for a munitions factory and then a textile mill.

The Hawkesbury Rail Bridge (also known as The Hawkesbury River Railway Bridge, The Hawkesbury Viaduct and The Hawkesbury Bridge), did open on 1 May 1889 and Nell's descriptions of the events are taken from accounts of the day. Ballantyne's descriptions of the building of the bridge are factual. I may, however, have tinkered somewhat with the train timetable for the sake of the fictional story!

Gold was first discovered by European settlers in 1823 in the Fish River, east of Bathurst, but the possibility of serious exploration wasn't entertained until the late 1840s. The Reverend William Branwhite Clarke, geologist, secretary and curator of the Australian Museum and principal of Kings School, discovered particles of gold near Hartley. In 1844 he informed Governor Gipps. He was promptly told, 'Put it away, Mr Clarke, or we shall have our throats cut.' In my mind, Montague was aware of

Clarke's discoveries and I have merged the factual and fictional stories!

The play *Still Waters Run Deep* written by Tom Taylor was first staged in 1855. A British silent film based on the play was made in 1916. A transcript is available online. To the best of my knowledge, it was never performed in Parramatta.

Horseshoe Bend exists in Maitland and is known locally as The Bend. Several houses from that era still stand, including the Barracks built in the 1840s and workers' cottages dating back to the 1850s.

Seam rippers such as the one Maisie uses were invented sometime in the late 1800s, and I like to think a travelling salesman such as Mr Humbert might well have carried them when they first became available.

Faith's activities at the racecourse are inspired by an Englishwoman Helen Vernet who, having inherited some money following the death of her father, developed a taste for gambling and a fondness for the racetrack. The rough and tumble of the betting ring was very much a male preserve and socially out of bounds to females. Helen noticed that many women wanted to bet. The problem was that those women only wanted to place a small wager, their pin money, and the bookmakers refused to accept stakes of less than a pound. She began collecting small bets from women, friends and acquaintances in the members' enclosure at race meetings. Unfortunately, her activities came to the attention of the bookies and the authorities, and she was forced to quit. I was pleased to note that she was later employed by Ladbrokes, and in 1928 she became a director of the company!

The rest of the story is the musing and meandering of a fertile imagination!

Acknowledgements

Much of this story is set on Burramatta Dharug Country in Parramatta, and I would like to pay my respects to the Elders past and present, also to the Darkinjung, Awabakal and Wonnarua nations and extend that respect to other Indigenous people within the Wollombi Valley community where this story was written.

First and foremost I would like to thank the National Trust of New South Wales and the team from NIDA, particularly Jasmine Gray and Lucy Francis, who remade the yellow dress and unravelled its provenance, and Grossman House Maitland for extending the initial invitation to view the yellow dress— without you there would be no story!

Yet again, my trusty support team has come up trumps. Chief Researcher and plot wrangler Charles, and Denis Brown, Chief Engineer, who will be so sadly missed, for his information about steam trains and the delightful story about breakfast cooked on the coal shovel. Fellow writers Sarah Barrie and Paula Beavan for their patience and advice, and Renee Dahlia for introducing me to Helen Vernet and Bob Charley's book *Pioneers and Racecourses*, and also the welcoming volunteers at Old Government House,

Parramatta, who answered all my questions and guided me through the lovely old building.

As always, I am indebted to the team at HQ/HarperCollins. My long-suffering publisher Jo Mackay, whose enthusiasm and support knows no bounds. The wonderful Alex Craig, the best structural editor in the business who somehow manages to unravel the complexities of my stories and make sense of my ramblings no matter how 'shonky'. Annabel Blay, managing editor and superb organiser who keeps me on the straight and narrow. Darren Holt of HarperCollins Design Studio, who has yet again produced the most perfect cover for my story, and Jo Munroe, Stuart Henshall and the HarperCollins sales team for taking my books out into the world. Without these very special people, my stories would, like the yellow dress, remain hidden, mouldering away in some cobwebbed attic.

And finally to you, my loyal readers whose support and enthusiasm makes writing such a rewarding pleasure—thank you and enjoy!

Book Club Discussion Questions

- How well does *The Golden Thread* capture the essence of Australia in the 1890s? Did you learn anything new about this period?
- In what ways do the various settings influence the characters and the story? Could the story have taken place anywhere else?
- How are the various social, political and economic issues of the time portrayed in *The Golden Thread*? Do they affect the characters' decisions and lives?
- Which character undergoes the most significant transformation throughout the story? What events or experiences contribute to this change?
- Were there any aspects of the story that you found historically inaccurate or unrealistic? How did that affect your reading experience?

- What are the central themes of the novel? How are they developed through the characters and plot?
- Are there any symbols in the novel that stand out to you? How do they enhance the story or its themes?
- How are family relationships portrayed in the story? Are there any particular family dynamics that are central to the plot?
- How are women's roles and experiences depicted in the novel? Do they align with or challenge the historical context of the era in Australia?
- What moral dilemmas do the characters face, and how do they resolve them? Do their choices reflect the values and beliefs of the time?
- Have you read the historical note. Did the facts improve your understanding of the story?
- If you could ask the author anything, what would it be?
- Are there lingering questions from the book you're still thinking about?

talk about it

Let's talk about books.

Join the conversation:

f @harlequinaustralia

♪ @hqanz

◯ @harlequinaus

harpercollins.com.au/hq

If you love reading and want to know about our
authors and titles, then let's talk about it.